For Such a Time as This

Rai
Lindsay-Wallace

BLESSED PRESS

First Blessed Press print edition published in 2017.

Book cover designed by Elena Kosharac

Book Edited by Joanie Chevalier

Photo Credit: Kent Wallace

ISBN: 978-0-692-85278-1

Printed in the United States of America

Special Dedication

*To Dr. James A. Taylor and Mr. Nathan White
- Principals used by God to make major
transformations in the lives of their students, staff
and the community. Forever, you will hold a special
place in my heart.*

*To Officer Markilo Anderson and Officer William
Hilton – your expertise kept the students, staff and
parents safe and secure. Without you, education
wouldn't be possible.*

*Lastly, to Mr. Eugene Koon, an amazing Athletic
Director, who went above and beyond the call of
duty to help the students, on and off the field/court.
Forever my friend!*

Contents

Acknowledgements

All glory and honor goes to my Abba Father, Jesus Christ and the Holy Spirit. Without You, there is no me; but with You, I can do all things.

To my amazing, awesome family: Kent, Maurice, Karlton, Grace, Ashley, Kalya, Briana, Lauren, Mariah, Lamad, Alisa, Ralph, Robert, Tammy, Mary and Willie Watts, and Norris and Grace Wallace.

To God's House of Healing – My church family. I love you all dearly!

To all my family, friends and fans, I dedicate this book to you. You have supported my dream of writing without fail. I appreciate all of you and love you even more.

"If you [Esther] keep quiet at a time like this, deliverance for the Jews will arise from some other place, but you and your relatives will die. What's more, who can say but that you have been elevated to the palace for just such a time as this?"

(Esther 4:14)

CHAPTER 1

The Terminator

"Sit up!" the firm command oozed out of Ashley Finley's clenched teeth to her brother, who was slouching in the chair. Thomas was in trouble yet again. However, this time Thomas' fate to return to school was solely in the hands of the principal at Brookland High School.

He didn't budge.

"Thomas!"

Grudgingly, he complied. "You're not my mother!"

"No, I am not," she quickly agreed, "but I am responsible for making sure you get back into school."

"Whatever!" he rolled his eyes. "They have to let me back in. That's what the hearing board letter says."

"They don't have to do anything, Thomas. The world doesn't owe you anything. You have to earn what you want. Stop taking and start giving. If you didn't steal that teacher's iPad, you wouldn't be in trouble and I wouldn't be here, which is making me late for work."

"Not another sermon." Thomas shifted restlessly in his seat.

"You need to grow up Thomas and stop being so angry at the world. You need to stop blaming everybody else and take a good look in the mirror," she let out a long sigh. "Thomas, every time you get into trouble, you're just digging a bigger hole for yourself."

"Don't worry about me, Sis. I can take care of myself."

"Sure you can," she frowned. "You're doing a good job of it now. Stealing. Lying. Hanging out with the wrong crowds. Flunking almost every class." Ashley was frustrated, tired of cleaning up after Thomas' mess. His rebellious behavior was draining the life out of her. "Don't you want to be somebody, Thomas? You are so smart. Why do you keep messing up?"

Thomas just shrugged his shoulders and turned the other way.

Ashley folded her hands and silently prayed for her brother. The joyful times she and Thomas had once shared seemed like eons ago. Thomas used to idolize his sister, tagging behind her and always mimicking Ashely's every move. Back then, he was such a sweet, mannerly, bright boy, always sensitive to the needs of others. Then everything changed two years ago. Their entire world came crumbling down from the explosive aftermath of their father's fatality. Life as they knew it would never be the same.

The blasting sound of the fire alarm halted Ashley's trip down memory lane. Suddenly, a man came flying out of his office, assumingly the principal.

"Tell Mr. Weaver to hurry to the second floor," he ordered his secretary.

"Faculty and students, disregard the fire alarm. It's a false alarm." The tall man flatly stated over the intercom and then repeated the announcement.

"That's the Terminator," Thomas leaned over and whispered in his sister's ear.

"You shouldn't call him that."

"You'll see," he smirked.

"One to seven," Dr. Jefferson thundered on his walkie-talkie. "Come in seven."

"Go ahead for seven."

"Meet me on the second floor," he rushed toward the door, still barking orders via walkie-talkie. Reaching for the doorknob, the principal's eyes glimpsed Ashley. Their eyes locked. Though she appeared worried, something about the woman commanded his attention. Those crystalline eyes arrested him to a temporary halt. Then like hot flashing lightning, the principal bolted out of the office.

Ashley felt off-kilter by his presence, which left her flustered. *Lord, please surround me with Your favor like a shield with Dr. Jefferson.*

Shortly afterwards the principal returned with two boys and Officer Anderson, the school's resource officer. Like soldiers, they all marched back to the principal's office and closed the door.

"That's it for them," Thomas mumbled.

"You think they pulled the fire alarm?" Ashley asked.

"Yeah and the Terminator saw it on his computer monitor. There are cameras everywhere in the school."

"Is that how he knew you stole the iPad?"

"Duh," he scoffed. "He loves catching people doing wrong."

"Well, if you didn't do wrong, he wouldn't have to catch you, would he?" Ashley turned the tables. "Stealing! Dad is probably rolling over in his grave."

"Who cares if he rolls over in his grave or not!"

"Thomas Finley, don't you go disrespecting the dead,

especially not our dad."

"He was *no* saint, Ash."

"Hush up!"

"You don't know anything, Ash." He looked at her earnestly. "Dad was a..."

The principal's door abruptly opened. "Escort these troublemakers off my campus!" he demanded of the officer. "And have Ms. Myers to call their parents."

"Okay, Dr. Jefferson," Officer Anderson replied. "Come on guys."

"He's not taking them to jail, is he?" Ashley fretted.

"Yes. The Terminator likes to lock kids up."

"Stop calling him that."

"You'll see."

"Send in my appointment." The principal ordered his secretary and then returned to his office.

"Well, my word," Ashley mumbled under breath.

"Miss Finley, please follow me," she escorted Ashley and Thomas to the back office.

"Please have a seat," Dr. Jefferson summoned, looking over the file he had in his hand. Quietness filled the room for some time before he spoke again.

"Thomas, why do you think I should allow you back into my school?" Dr. Jefferson put down the file and intensely eyed the student, who had been in his office several times already this year.

"Because the director of the hearing office said I could return."

"I know what the director said," Dr. Jefferson stiffly responded. "It was my recommendation that you be sent to an alternative school. However, the system had pity on you.

4

Understand this…I have no pity for anyone who keeps messing up. You stole from a teacher, who used her hard-earned money to purchase that iPad. She worked for it and then you just came along and stole it. Why should I have pity on you? You didn't have pity on Ms. Perry."

Ashley was speechless. He surely acted like the Terminator. The principal's demeanor was very brusque and caddish. Though her brother deserved it, she knew the real reason Thomas had stolen the iPad.

Thomas sat dumbfounded. He didn't know what to say to the man who offered no mercy and no pardon. The Terminator had caught him red-handed with the iPad in his book bag. Now the Terminator was ready to terminate his time at Brookland High School for good.

"Answer me. Why should I allow you to return to this school?"

"I don't know," he shrugged indifferently.

"You don't know!" Dr. Jefferson repeated, his voice harsher, swiftly climbing the ladder of vexation. "Well, if you don't know, then you can just go home."

"Dr. Jefferson," Ashley stood up. "The letter states that Thomas can return to Brookland."

"I know what the letter states, Miss…" he looked down at the folder, "Miss Finley." He found himself distracted for a split second. Her crystalline eyes were mesmerizing. Although her dress attire was homely and her hair tightly pulled back in a bun, which gave the appearance of a spinster, Miss Finley was effortlessly attractive. "Nevertheless," Dr. Jefferson cleared his throat, endeavoring to regain his composure, "this is MY school and I will not allow students who continuously disrupt MY school to stay here."

"You don't have a choice," Ashley refuted. "The letter states that he can return and if you don't comply with this letter, then I will go to your superior."

"Go right ahead, Miss Finley," he called her bluff. "Would you like the number to call?"

"No. I already have it," Ashely asserted, not batting an eye. "Thomas made a mistake."

"Thomas has made too many mistakes, it seems," the principal amended. "However, it was no mistake that he stole the iPad. He purposely took what did not belong to him. That's not a mistake. That's a crime. If he weren't sixteen, he'd be locked up right now." *He is only sixteen in the twelfth grade.* It just hit the principal like a rock to his forehead. *He should be at least seventeen.* He jotted a note to himself to check Thomas' file. *It has to be a mistake. Maybe he is old enough to be charge with a crime.*

"And that would make you happy, huh?" Ashley lashed out, her feelings riled up.

"Listen, Miss Finley, it is my responsibility for the safety and education of the students and faculty here at Brookland. In order for the environment here to be conducive for learning, there has to be safety and security. Without it, a good education is not possible. Therefore, those students who cannot obey the rules, respect others right to an education, and continue to disrupt the school setting, are not welcome here. My feelings aren't the issue; but the welfare, of the students and staff, is most definitely the issue!"

"Thomas deserves an education!"

"Thomas deserves discipline!" he nearly shouted, momentarily, losing self-control. This woman was getting under his skin. Dr. Jefferson was not used to this sort of thing happening. Whether dealing with a disgruntled parent, irate student or upset employee, the principal always remained cool, calm and collected. Ashley Finley ruffled his shipshape feathers without even trying.

"He has been disciplined," her cheeks flamed with indignation.

"Something is lacking in the home. Perhaps his mother should be here instead of you. Maybe I should be talking to her about disciplining Thomas."

"My mother is sick!" Ashley snapped back. "I'm here for my brother. Trust me...Thomas behaves properly in our home."

"He doesn't behave properly here and that's the problem."

Taking a deep breath, Ashley replied, "Listen, Thomas has been disciplined from home and by you already. You suspended him for ten days."

"He only served five days due to the recommendation of the Hearing Office," corrected the principal.

"Five is plenty."

"He will spend the next five days in In-School Suspension." The principal stood up and went to Thomas. "I will be watching you," he warned. "And if you mess up one more time, you're out of here for good. Do I make myself clear?"

"Perfectly." Thomas looked up at him.

"Base to 5." Dr. Jefferson called on the walkie-talkie to the ISS room. "Thomas Finley is on his way down. He will be there for the rest of the week. If he's not there in three minutes, radio me."

"10-4."

"Go!" he ordered Thomas.

"See you later, Sis," Thomas felt bad.

7

"We'll talk at home," Ashley hugged him. "Please do right," she whispered in his ear. "You've been given another chance."

For a moment, Thomas stared at Ashley. His heart spasm, fully aware that he was the root of the outward pain displaying on his sister's face. Of all people, she did not deserve it. If it weren't for Ashley, their family would be hopeless, helpless and ultimately homeless.

"You're going to be late, Thomas." The touching scene did not move the principal the slightest bit.

Watching her brother leave, Ashley pivoted around, squared her shoulders, ready for a fight, if need be. "My brother is a good boy. He is going through a lot right now and…"

"There's no excuse for stealing, Miss Finley," he gave her an assessing look. *First mistake!* Overlooking her spinsterhood dress attire, Dr. Jefferson found himself strangely attracted to the woman. She was picturesque. Her skin flawless, with no makeup at all. Her lips were full, perfectly shaped and naturally pink. She had high-cheek bones. Her petite frame, probably 5'7 in stature, gave her the natural look of a model. However, her crystalline eyes were intoxicating. He could drown in those eyes. *Second mistake!* Immediately, he shook the thought right out of his mind. *Get a grip!*

"You're right. I don't condone it, for any reason," Ashley lowered her head. Inwardly, she struggled to find the right words to say hoping to convince the principal to have a little compassion for her brother. "Thomas only took the iPad because we needed the money at home. It has been tough on him. We…we…." Ashley's pride got the best of her, so she briskly changed the subject. "He will not do it again," she straightened her shoulders and lifted her head. Ashley was a

Finley and *Finleys* cowered to no man…at least that's what her dad had drilled into her head growing up.

"He better not," Dr. Jefferson held his stance. "Are you aware that he's failing three classes?"

"Yes, I am." Ashley planted her hands on her hips, a sure sign she was upset. "And are you aware that he was on the Principal's List his entire 9th and 10th grade years?"

"No. I was not the principal then."

"It's in his records. He has always been an honor roll student. He skipped second grade because he was so smart. They wanted to skip him in the sixth grade, but my mother wouldn't let them," she said proudly. "Everything changed two years ago…after our father died."

Hmm, that is why he is only sixteen! "My condolence for your family's loss," Dr. Jefferson cleared his throat, at last feeling a hint of compassion. "Bad things happened to good people every day. However, that doesn't give anyone the right to behave badly." Swiftly, compassion went right out of the window, like a bird flying out of an open cage.

"Thomas is right," Ashley closed her purse and headed for the door. "You are the Terminator. Look at Thomas' records." Ashley stormed out of the room, madder than a bull at a matador. *Unsympathetic jerk!*

Dr. Jefferson stood there a moment, bothered by Miss Finley's clincher exit. She might as well have slapped him in the face when she called him the Terminator. He felt its sting, which was odd. Words did not affect him. Dr. Jefferson was not easily moved by name-calling or crude remarks. He would simply brush them off like lint and keep it moving.

Miss Finley's spunk stimulated him. She was a woman of dignity. Even more evident, she cared for her brother, selflessly.

Why was she here and not the mother? Oh, she mentioned that her mother was sick.

Returning to his desk, Dr. Jefferson reviewed Thomas' file once again. *Hmm, Ashley Finley is listed under guardianship. She is so young but seemingly wise beyond her years.* He closed the file and turned to his computer. Pulling up Thomas' transcript, he was surprised. Not only was Thomas on the Principal's List in high school, throughout his middle school years he maintained all A's. *No discipline problems, whatsoever...until the last two years.*

Did his father's death affect him that much? Or was it something else? She said something about him taking the iPad because they needed money. Gregg searched for Thomas' address. They lived in Bryson Complex, public housing, in one of the poorest areas in town.

"Still no excuse. Most of the students here are poor," Gregg mumbled to himself.

"Terminator!" he said indignantly. "So that's what the students call me. Perhaps that's a good thing." He got up with his walkie-talkie in hand and exited through his side door. He walked the halls making sure everyone was where they were supposed to be. Luckily, the halls were quiet. He was not in the mood for any more foolishness.

Purposely, Dr. Jefferson walked toward the ISS room. Peeping through the window, he observed Thomas, slouched in his chair, doing nothing.

"Mr. Adger," the principal called to him at the door.

Speedily, Mr. Adger came to the door.

"Why is Thomas idly sitting there? Have you contacted his teachers for class work?"

"Um...yes, Sir," timidly, he replied. The principal had a

way of making everybody nervous around him. "Ms. Neal, his guidance counselor, is gathering work right now."

"Don't you have something else for him to do, until work arrives?" No excuse was good enough. Dr. Jefferson expected everyone in ISS to doing classwork or homework without exception.

"Yes, Sir, I do."

"Then give it to him." Dr. Jefferson demanded before exiting the room the same way entered—like a thief in the night.

CHAPTER 2

Hanging On by a thread

Such an egotistical, pompous man! Ashley brooded while riding the bus. *He should not be a principal. Maybe a judge or Warden at a prison would suit him better. The nerve of him insinuating that my mother is not a good parent. He did not even care that our father died two-years ago. He is a stiff-necked, conceited, heartless man!*

Intensely upset, Ashley replayed the conversation in her head. *Sure, Thomas was wrong. On the other hand, he only took the iPad so he could sell it to pay the electric bill. Three days with no electricity pushed Thomas over the edge. Tommy was such a good boy. It's not his fault that his life has been turned upside down. He is only acting out because everything he once loved has been taken from him...including basketball.*

Thomas played a vital role his ninth and tenth grade years as a shooting guard on the varsity team. His clear-cut 3-pointer shots kept the fans on their toes. Things changed on that dreadful night of their father's tragic accident. Tom Finley's death also marked the death of Thomas and Ashley's dreams. Thomas had to stop playing basketball, which took the wind completely out of his sails, leaving Thomas drifting into trouble. Young Thomas became the babysitter and paternal figure, walking in the shoes of manhood, whether he wanted to or not.

Their mother, Sandra Finley, suffered from an acute form of Rheumatoid Arthritis, known as RA, and depression. She was always in physical pain and emotionally depressed. Sandra hardly ever got out of the bed. The wellbeing of the family rested on the shoulders of Ashley and Thomas. Sandra's world was Tom and when he died, a great part of Sandra died, as well. Although Tom had his share of problems, in his own way Tom loved his family and provided for their daily needs. However, Tom had an overpowering weakness—women. Tom's infidelity throughout their marriage had caused such sadness in Sandra's life. She quietly endured the other women, the late night outs and her husband not coming home for days at a time. Humbly, Sandra played second fiddle to his extra-curricular activities because she depended totally on him. She felt unworthy of anything or anyone else better.

Ashley knew exactly what her brother was talking about when he mentioned that their father was no saint. On the night of his accident, his mistress was also in the car. Though no one spoke of it, Ashley vividly remembered the scene of her mother and the other woman at the hospital.

Upon arriving in the emergency room, Ashley and her mother literally collided with Tom's mistress. She was a tall, slender, beautiful, blond model—literally. She escaped the accident without a scratch on her body, which infuriated Sandra. Instantly, the green-eyed monster, called jealousy, arose within the crevices of Sandra's heart. This woman was with her husband when he breathed his last breath. All the mistress could say was, "I'm sorry."

With tears falling freely, Sandra replied, "Yes, you are."

The mistress lowered her head and walked away. The model nor the affair was never mentioned again.

After the funeral, her mother stayed in bed, which probably activated her Rheumatoid Arthritis again. Sandra moaned, cried, wept, grieved and stayed buried under the covers. Since there was no life insurance, the *Finleys* could no longer afford to stay in their suburban home and were forced to move to Bryson Complex, one of the most impoverished housing projects in the South.

From sunrise to sunset, Ashley Finley cared for the needs of her family, working two jobs, library by day, and waitress at The Palace, by night. She cooked, cleaned, did homework with the twins, Donny and Danny, and toddler Lacy, nursed her mother and did whatever needed to keep the family afloat.

Before the tragic accident, Ashely's life was so much simpler. She was in her senior year in college, majoring in English education and minoring in journalism. Ashley enjoyed writing. Nothing satisfied her more than making words come alive on paper. Life back then was joyous. Ashley's faith was strong and her family contentedly happy. Like Thomas, things changed for her. She too had put her life and dreams on hold. Ashely dropped out of college and became the caretaker, fulfilling a motherly role.

Back to reality…

Still waiting on the bus, Ashley began journaling about her meeting with Dr. Jefferson, the Terminator. Usually, journaling calmed her. Hopefully, today journaling would not fail her. Initially, angry words were scripted on paper, pumping her adrenaline. As always, optimism overrode negativity. There was always some good in the midst of bad. It just took a caring heart to see it.

I wonder, behind the principal's gruff exterior, if there is a hurting soul. Perhaps, he gives no mercy, because no mercy has been extended to him. Though he has an unkind demeanor, and even after his harsh remarks, I did detect warmth in his eyes, as well as sadness. I shall pray for him, for I feel he needs it, just as Thomas needs it. Perhaps, their paths have united by One who has a bigger plan and a bigger purpose. Perhaps, they need each other for such a time as this...

Closing her journal, Ashley closed her eyes and allowed her thoughts to drift back to the principal. Her memory envisioned every detail of the man who charged her inward battery.

He has an athletic physique, not easily hidden in his expensive tailor-fitted navy suit. He is probably in his early thirties. He is a good-looking man, no doubt about it—tall, dark and handsome. Though he did not smile, Dr. Jefferson had perfect white teeth, to match his perfect chocolate skin tone and neatly trimmed haircut. He's definitely easy on the eyes and...

Stop it! He's a bully! Ashley warred with her mind. *He takes his anger out on the students. Yet, he had warm eyes. Mom says warm eyes means a warm heart.*

I wonder how the staff feels about him.

Okay, he had a right to be stern with Thomas. He needed it. He's been getting away with way too much. It is just so hard to discipline Thomas when I see his heart bleeding for love and basketball. I just wish...wish mom would try to get better.

Straightaway, Ashley felt guilty for her thoughts. Her mother was sick, which was not her fault. It just seemed that after the death of husband, Sandra Finley lost her will to fight the disease and depression. She just gave up on her family, leaving the load of everything upon Ashley's shoulders. Oftentimes, Ashley felt like she was being pulled in every direction at the same time. Like a rope, she would eventually

16

be stretched too thin, causing her to either pop or completely unravel. Ashley's faith in God kept her holding on—hanging by a thread most of the time.

Forgive me Lord. I know I should not judge momma, but I am so tired. Ashley got off at the next bus stop, in front of the library.

"Hi, Ashley!" Harvey greeted as soon as she entered the library. "You look nice today."

"Thanks, Harvey." Ashley kept walking toward the backroom to clock in.

"I brought us grilled chicken sandwiches today and potato salad for lunch." He was always bringing lunch for Ashley. It was his subtle way of making sure she shared her lunch break with him, seeing how Ashley rejected every invitation to date after working hours.

"Thanks, Harvey. You shouldn't have," she said for the zillionth time. "Actually, I was thinking of working through my break. I have so many books to check in today."

"You still have to take a break. You know how Mrs. Washburn feels about us taking our lunch breaks."

Ashley sighed. She was grateful for Harvey's friendship, but sometimes he was just too clingy. Today, she just wanted some quiet time to herself. Time to come up with a plan to earn extra money to get the twins much-needed shoes. Plus, Lacy needed a new coat before the winter season.

"I have two tickets to the Panthers' game on Sunday." Harvey accompanied her to the front counter.

"Oh, really!" Ashley was a Panthers fan, just like her brother Thomas. Before her dad's death, the family had season tickets to the Panthers' games. Tom's extra social life afforded them with such lavished perks. "How in the world did you get tickets? I thought the game was sold out."

17

"My uncle's friend gave them to him." Harvey's uncle was a big-shot attorney for the rich and famous. "I was hoping you would go with me."

"Harvey that's so sweet of you, but you know I can't leave momma," Ashley declined as usual.

"Thomas can watch her. It's only for a few hours."

"Why don't you take Thomas? He really needs this. He has been going through so much. Maybe this will cheer him up."

"I was hoping we could spend some time together."

"I'm sorry, Harvey, but I can't."

"Will you at least think about it?" Harvey did not easily throw in the towel when it came to Ashley. He had been trying to turn their friendship into something more for over a year with no success—yet.

"I'm not going to change my mind." Ashley keyed in the surplus of returned books on the computer. "I really must work now, Harvey."

"I guess I can take Thomas," his desire to please Ashley superseded his disappointment.

"Good!" Ashley flashed a chucky-cheesy smile. "He'll be so happy. When Thomas returns from the game, he will tell me everything. And you know the way Thomas dramatizes everything…it will be like being at the game, firsthand."

Not really! "See you at lunch. Do you want to go the park across the street?"

"Yes."

"Okay." Harvey shoved his hands in his pockets, feeling somewhat better. At least he would spend lunchtime with the girl of his dreams.

18

"Hey Momma," Ashley sat on the side of her mother's bed. "How was your day?"

"Painful," Sandra answered. "I need my medicine."

"I'll go get you some water and your pills. Be right back." Ashley rushed to the kitchen. It was the same answer every day. Nevertheless, Ashley fervently prayed anyway. Her longtime doctor, Dr. Phelps was doing all he could do for Sandra, but the rest was up to her. *You could lead a horse to the water, but you cannot make it drink.*

"Here you go, mother," Ashley handed her the glass. "I'm going to go fix dinner. Do you think you can eat with us tonight? The children miss suppertime with you."

"I'm in too much pain," Sandra replied, always the same.

"Momma," Ashley hesitated. "Thomas needs his mother. The principal allowed him to return to school today, but Thomas is on thin ice. Perhaps if you come to dinner and talk with him…"

"I'll see. Let me just take a nap." Sandra raised the covers upward and closed her eyes. That was the end of the story. Ashley knew her mother would not be sharing supper with them.

What can't be cured must be endured. Ashley reflected on her mother's truism. While preparing the family meal, Thomas entered the kitchen.

"Hi, Thomas," Ashley quickly observed the scowling look upon his face. "How did it go?"

"How do you think it went?" he slammed his books down on the table.

"Stop that, Thomas! You're going to wake momma up."

He shrugged his shoulders as if he didn't care. *So what! She's always sleeping.*

Thomas walked over to the stove and took the lid off one of the pots. "Beans and rice again," he grunted. "I'm sick and tired of beans and rice with no meat."

"We'll have meat on Sunday like we always do," Ashley stated firmly. "You know meat is too expensive right now. You should be thankful for a meal to eat and a roof over your head. So many people…"

"I don't care about what other people don't have!" Thomas rudely interrupted another one of his sister's *'being thankful'* speeches. "We used to have meat every day of the week, not just on Sundays, before dad…" Thomas left the sentence unfinished.

Ashley looked at him with concern. She knew her brother was still struggling with his dad's tragic death. It had hit them all hard, especially the cruelness of the way he died with his mistress. The root of bitterness ate away at Thomas even more now, than back then.

The sound of the telephone ringing broke the awkward moment. Thomas and Ashley both ran to the phone. "I'm sorry," Ashley beat her brother to it, "but Thomas cannot take phone calls until Sunday."

"What!" Thomas shouted.

"Be quiet," Ashley warned. "He'll talk to you later. Bye." Ashley placed the phone back on the hook.

"You can't do that!" his temper flared. "You're not my mother!"

"No. But, I am in charge until mother gets better."

"Yeah right! Like that will ever happen." Thomas attempted to walk away, but Ashley grabbed his arm.

"That's uncalled for."

"Whatever!"

"Thomas, why is Marty calling you?" Ashley recognized his voice over the phone.

Thomas didn't answer.

"Marty is in a gang. He sells drugs to kids. You are playing Russian Roulette with your life, hanging around those kinds of guys."

Still he said not a word.

"Thomas, you know better," Ashley's voice softened. "You have been brought up in the church with Christian values. Mom and dad taught you right from wrong."

"Dad didn't teach me anything but how to be a cheater!"

"Dad wasn't all bad, Thomas. Just because he did wrong doesn't give you a pass to do wrong. Please stop messing up. Please let go of your anger and replace it with something more productive. Do your work in school. Stop hanging with those guys. Don't you want a better life than this?"

"It doesn't matter what I want." Thomas turned and faced her. "I didn't want to stop playing basketball, but it didn't matter. I had to stay home and babysit. And I didn't want to move from my nice home and leave all my friends to come live in this dump, but here I am!" Thomas threw up his hands.

"It's not a dump, Thomas. It's our home…for now." Ashley understood his anger. It was hard leaving everything behind— their middle-class home, schools, relatives, and friends—to move into such an unsafe, underprivileged, poverty-stricken community.

"You will get the chance to play basketball again."

"In my dreams," Thomas doubted. "I'm a senior. If I don't play now, then my chance of ever playing in college or anywhere else is zero."

"Thomas, we just have to trust God and believe that no

matter what…all things are working out for our good. We may not always get what we want, but God will always give us what we need. We just…

"Save it!" Thomas cut her off. "And I sure don't WANT beans and rice again…but look," he picked up the pot, "beans and rice…AGAIN!"

"At least we have food."

"If you say so," Thomas grunted. "I'm going to get the *kids* from school." Thomas headed for the door.

"By the way, Thomas," Ashley called after him, "Harvey has two tickets to the Panthers game on Sunday. I told him you could go. But, if you're still mad at me…"

"Oh, Ash!" Thomas rushed to her side, lifting his sister off her feet in a bear hug. "You know I'm not mad at you."

"You know I love you, Thomas," Ashley's eyes moistened. "It's tough being hard on you because I understand your pain. We must stick together. We have to do what is right. We are *Finleys* and *Finleys* are good Christian people. Do you understand what I'm saying, Thomas?"

He nodded. "I'm sorry."

"I forgive you."

"Can I have my phone privileges back?"

"Nope!" Ashley stood her ground, "But you can go to the game Sunday since you'll be off punishment."

"Okay." Thomas accepted his sister's form of correction even though he didn't like it one bit.

In the meantime, Sandra overheard the siblings' conversation. With tears in her eyes, she slowly ebbed herself upward in a sitting position. It was painful. She was worked up with anguish, replaying her son's frustrating words in her head. Ashley had not revealed to her mother just how angry Thomas had been. Her daughter was trying to spare her the unpleasant things going on in the household, while she was sleeping her life away. Sandra felt like such a failure. Her body was in so much pain that Sandra reclined slowly back down and snuggled under the blanket. Guilt consumed her. She knew she had to find the willpower to fight this disease again, but somehow pain and depression got the best of her. Realizing that the weight of the family was resting upon Ashley's young shoulders crushed her spirit but not enough for Sandra to get up. In a matter of seconds, Sandra slept.

CHAPTER 3

The Palace

"**H**ey, who's the new cook?" Ashley whispered to her friend Pam, also a waitress at The Palace.

"That's Andrew. He replaced Michael."

"What happened to Michael?"

"He just up and quit last night," Pam blabbed. "He and Ms. Melrose got into a huge argument. You know Michael. He *ain't gonna* let nobody disrespect him in public. So, he walked out. She was yelling at him, telling him he had better come back or she would fire him. He yelled back, 'You can't because I quit,' and Ms. Melrose went berserk! It was funny watching her bark like a Chihuahua. You know how she sounds when she gets loud—squeaky and out-of-tune. She acted like a fool."

Ashley snickered. Pam always had a way of making her laugh, especially in these pressure-cooker days—slow, but long. Pam was good for her. She kept Ashley upbeat and sane, making the very dark days, less gloomy. Particularly, when most days all Ashley wanted to do was crawl under her covers and stay there. Yet, her mother had already claimed that position.

"I am going to miss Michael," Ashley sighed. "He was more than a great chef; he was a good friend."

"This guy seems to be good, too," Pam replied. "He doesn't say much, but he can cook, that's for sure."

"He is gawking at me," Ashley frowned.

"He's old enough to be your daddy," Pam laughed. "Then again, perhaps he *likes 'em* young. He's not bad looking either. If you don't want him, then maybe I'll throw myself at him."

"You're crazy, girl!"

"Ladies," Ms. Melrose interrupted, "we have customers. We don't want to keep them waiting, now do we?"

"No, Ma'am," Ashley quickly answered. "I was just getting my customers' drinks."

"We're doing our jobs," Pam snapped back.

"Good," Ms. Melrose walked away. "Perhaps you can do it without all the babbling."

"I'll babble her!" Pam mumbled under her breath. "She gets on my last nerve."

"Calm down," Ashley advised. "We both need this job. We cannot afford to rattle her feathers."

"Her feathers are already rattled," Pam retorted. "Look at that ghastly red hair of hers, feathers flying everywhere."

"You're *gonna* get us in trouble," Ashley giggled. "I'll talk with you later."

It had been a long night for Ashley. *The Palace* was constantly busy because it was such a classy place. Typically, the crème de la crème dawned The Palace's doors. The amazing delicacies offered on the menu, along with the serene ambiance only brought in the affluent clientele. On Friday and Saturday nights, well-known singers and musicians were booked to perform live performances. Celebrities, professional athletes, well-off entrepreneurs, etc., were regulars.

Preparing to call it a night, Ashley and Pam counted their tips. They had developed this peaceful rivalry some time ago. Usually, Pam came out the victor.

"Must have been the frugal crowd tonight," Pam pouted. "My tips are lower than the gutter?"

"Mine too," Angela agreed. "At least I have enough to pay the water bill."

"Girl, all you do is pay bills. Why don't you go buy yourself some new shoes? Those shoes you are wearing look like they have been run over by a train."

Ashley peered down at her scruffy, weatherworn black shoes. If only she could buy herself something. What a treasure that would be. Foremost, she needed to buy the twins shoes, and Lacy a coat. Thomas needed shoes and jeans. *The jeans he had on today were definitely high-water.* There was never enough money to take care of all of the family needs.

"We better hurry out of here or we will miss the bus?" Ashley promptly changed the subject.

"Randall is picking me up tonight. You want a ride?"

"No thanks. Who is Randall? You have never mentioned him before."

"I know," Pam giggled. "I met him last night."

"What?" Ashley's anxious antennas launched. "Where did you meet him?"

"Here, of course," Pam put on fresh lipstick. "He's loaded, that's for sure. He is picking me up in his convertible BMW. Isn't that grand? I think he's the one, Ashley. My horoscope *said* I was going to meet my Prince Charming."

"That's crazy, Pam. You don't know anything about the guy. He could be a psychotic murderer or some perverted sex offender. Who knows what!"

"You watch too much Law and Order," Pam showed her a picture of him on her cell phone. "He's gorgeous!" she slipped her phone back into her purse. "I'll tell you all about it tomorrow. Oh, but you don't work tomorrow. Well, I'll call you."

Hope the phone is still on tomorrow. "No, call me tonight. I don't care how late it is."

"But I'll wake everyone up."

"I don't care. Just call me the minute you get home."

"Alright," Pam agreed. "After dinner, we're going to ride around and talk. He's a great talker. He's a great looker, too. He gave me a forty-dollar tip last night."

"Be careful, Pam. I don't have a good feeling about this."

"You worry too much. You worry about your mother, your siblings, the bills, and now you are worrying about me. Scratch me off your list. I've been taking care of myself since I was sixteen."

"Here," Ashley handed her a small can of mace. "You may need it."

"Got my own!" Pam pulled out her matching can. "A lady never knows when she's going to need it."

They both laughed.

"See!" Pam peered out the window at the black BMW convertible with the top down. "I feel like royalty," she turned to her friend. "Things are finally looking up for me. See you later. Get home safe."

"You too," Ashley waved, deeply disturbed by her friend's late night rendezvous with a stranger.

"Are you walking to the bus stop?"

Startled, Ashley turned and faced the new chef. "Umm… yes."

"It's dangerous out there uh…uh." Andrew could not remember her name, although her face was unforgettable. She reminded him of someone.

"Ashley," she replied hesitantly.

"Well, Ashley, I can take you home."

"No, thanks." Ashely didn't trust him. "The bus is fine."

"I don't mind," he insisted.

"But I do." She turned and sauntered out the door. *Who is he? Why is he constantly staring at me? Creep!*

"I'm sorry if I offended you." Andrew caught up with her. "I would never hurt you. I am a nice guy. I am not trying to pick you up," he chuckled. "I'm old enough to be your father."

"And…" *as if that matters! Guys your age are always hitting on younger women. My dad sure preferred the young ones!*

"And, I was only trying to offer you a ride. Where do you live?"

Ashley pivoted to face him and gave him a *'You must be out of your mind'* look. "That's none of your business!" Ashley felt vulnerable. Impulsively, she opened her purse, ready to use her mace if need be. Though *The Palace* usually hired very reputable chefs, Ashley still felt uneasy with this man.

"Never mind," Andrew walked away, slightly baffled. Here he was trying to do a good thing when the lady had unjustly tagged him to be some degenerate. "Get home safe."

Ashley watched him walk away. *Maybe he was just being nice.* Swiftly, Ashley ran to catch the approaching bus.

Though her body was exhausted, sleeping was out of the question for Ashley. She wouldn't close her eyes until she knew her friend was okay. It was after two o'clock and she still hadn't heard from Pam. She had left several messages on her voice mail. Ashely was worried.

"Call me the minute you get in," Ashley left another message. "I don't care if it wakes the whole house up. Call me!" Something did not feel right. *Lord, put a hedge of protection around Pam. Bring her home safe.*

Around five o'clock, finally, Pam answered.

"Thank God, you're home." Ashley heaved a sigh of relief. "I called you all night, but I kept getting your answering machine. Are you okay?"

Pam blubbered through the phone, crying hysterically.

"What happened?"

Pam rambled incoherent statements.

"I don't understand. What are you saying?"

"H-e...tr-i-e-d—to-ra-pe me!" Pam howled loudly in anguish.

The five words sent chills down Ashley's spine. "Oh, my word!" Ashley shuddered. "Are you alright?" *Stupid question!*

"He...did—n't go all the...way. I...*maced* him," Pam muttered her way through the explanation.

"Did you call the police?"

"No, and I'm not going to!"

"You have to go to the police," Ashley urged. "He's probably done this before."

"He'll just buy his way out of it, while I'm humiliated. He warned me not to say anything. He reminded me that I voluntarily came to his home and led him on. Who would believe me? Who goes to a man's house after knowing him for only a day?" Pam discredited her own judgment. "It was as much as my fault as it was his. I should not have been there in the first place."

30

"What you did was a simple mistake in judgment. What he did to you was a crime. There is no comparison. He's the jerk, not you!"

"Go ahead and say it," Pam bitterly wept.

"Say what?"

"I told you so."

"I wouldn't say that. That's not me, and you know it."

"I'm sorry. It is just that I am a wreck right now. I bathed myself repeatedly in the hottest bath I could take and I still feel so dirty...even though nothing happened. He ripped my blouse." Like a child, Pam sat on the floor, rocking in a fetal position.

"It's not your fault, Pam. It is that...uh, Randall's fault. *If that's his real name.* He's a sick, twisted perpetrator! He picked you out, knowing full-well he had dishonorable intentions."

"He picked me out because I was easy," Pam acknowledged. "He would have never been able to do this to you."

"Stop beating yourself up."

"I don't have to," she blurted, "he did that, too."

"I'm so sorry, Pam. What can I do to help you?"

"Nothing," she sniffed. "There's nothing anyone can do for me. I just want to go to bed."

"Okay. I'll be praying for you."

Pam didn't reply. The thought of Ashley praying for her gave no comfort to Pam's hurting soul. Her heart was hardened as a rock. Pam would let no one in–including Ashley's God.

"I've got to get ready and get the children up. I will call you as soon as I get to the library. Are you going in tonight?"

"No. I was sort of hoping you would cover for me?"

"No problem. You know I need the money."

"Thanks for everything."

"I still think you need to call the police and go to the doctor, as well."

"I'll think about it." Pam pacified, with no intentions of ever calling the police or going to a doctor.

"If it's okay with you, I would like to stop by before I go to *The Palace*."

"No. I don't feel like company."

"I understand," Ashley paused. "I love you, Pam."

"Love you, too. Bye."

Ashley replaced the receiver, dropped to her knees and burst into tears. Her spirit grieved. *No matter what you go through in life, truly there is always someone worse off than you.*

"Father God, help my friend!"

CHAPTER 4

The Proposal

Putting on a happy face for the patrons in the library deemed exhausting for Ashley. Concealing her melancholy was nearly impossible. Weighing heavily on her mind was Pam's pain and her family's financial strain, which left Ashley drained.

If God brings you to it, He will bring you through it. Another one of her mother's familiar clichés resonated in the depths of her soul.

My trust is in You, God.

I am with you. I will never leave you or forsake you*.*

I surrender Lord, all to You.

"Today I have fried chicken and pasta salad for us." Harvey chattered while Ashley was placing the new shipment of books on the shelves.

"No thanks," Ashley replied. "I am not eating today." She felt too guilty about eating meat when her siblings could not enjoy such delicacy during the week.

"You have to eat."

"I don't have to do anything Harvey!" Ashley snapped, letting out her frustration on the one person who would do anything and everything to eliminate Ashley's burdens. Convicted, she turned and faced a hurt Harvey. "I apologize,

Harvey." Ashley gently touched his shoulder. "I have a lot on my mind right now and food isn't one of them."

"Let me help you, Ashley." Harvey's gaze held hers, briefly. He desired nothing more than to be Ashley's Rock of Gibraltar. It was no secret to Harvey she was struggling both financially and mentally to take care of her family of six. Ashley had given so much of herself to her family and seemingly, it was never enough. Never allowing herself to wallow in sadness for long, the only time Ashley let her guard down were the times she confided in Harvey. During their lunch breaks, sometimes Ashley would expose her frail side to Harvey, allowing him to see her imperfections and insecurities. It was easy to talk to Harvey because he didn't judge or question her faith.

"That's sweet of you," she smiled warmly, "but you can't help me."

"Oh, but I can." Harvey reached for her hand.

Ashley felt awkward standing in the middle of bookshelves with Harvey holding her hand. *What if a patron comes over? This scene is a little too cozy. They might get the wrong idea. Harvey might get the wrong idea.*

"Financially, I can take care of you, Ashley. I can provide a home for you, your mother and siblings. As you know, I inherited my parents' five-bedroom home. It has three and a half bathrooms, a den, dining room, large kitchen and an office, which we can turn into something else…even a smaller bedroom. It is more than enough for all of us and it is in a good neighborhood. If I am not mistaken, I think it is in the same school zone as Thomas's previous school, so he will meet up with his old friends. It'll be good for him and for you." Harvey knew that Thomas was Ashley's soft spot. She would do anything for her brother—and family. "Emotionally, I can be there for you, as well. Someone to lean on and to support you. You can go back to school, perhaps night school, because I'll be there to help take care of the family." Harvey shuddered, witnessing the look of terror shadowing Ashley's face.

Ashley's countenance was pale as white sheets. Bittersweet pang stabbed her chest. She couldn't speak. She could barely breathe. Did her ears deceive her? Was Harvey really proposing to her?

"You know how I feel about you?"

"No, I don't," Ashley shook her head, imitating her need to shake off his proposal. Ashley adored Harvey's friendship. It sustained her. It gave her strength when she was at her weakest point. Yet, now he would mess it all up. Harvey was crossing boundaries that Ashley didn't want to be crossed.

"I love you, Ashley. I have loved you from the first time you walked in our Sunday school class. I was just a kid then, and it was more like puppy love, but my love for you has grown. Every time I see you, you take my breath away. I want nothing more than to take care of you and spend the rest of my life with you. I want to marry you."

Marry me? "I…I…uh…" Ashley fumbled for a response, but there was none. Confusion took over. *How could his be happening?*

"Don't say anything, yet." Harvey put his finger to her lips. "Just think about. Pray about it. I know you will say yes. I have prayed for a godly wife and I know God has answered my prayers." His expression was sincere and heartfelt. "He brought you to me, a long time ago."

"Excuse me," a lady patron interrupted them. "I'm looking for the book, *Sunset/Sunrise*."

"Umm yes, Ma'am," Ashley cleared her throat. "Let me

show you where it is." Ashley was thankful for the brief escape.

Watching Ashley walk away, Harvey petitioned the throne room for His divine favor.

Throughout her workday, Ashley's felt flustered and confused. She couldn't stay focus on her job duties. The proposal pushed her to the edge of insanity.

Harvey was an exceptionally caring man, with good Christian values. Ashley grew up with Harvey, attending the same church since they were toddlers. His parents were the sweetest people she had ever met. When they both died in a car accident, everyone in the church felt the pangs of death and sorrow. It shook the church up and it numbed Harvey's faith, at first. It was Ashley who brought him out of the pit of despair. She stayed by Harvey's side, visited him and brought him food, forcing him to eat when he didn't want to. Many times, hush engulfed them, neither saying much of anything, but the companionship of the other made the difference. Slowly, but surely, Harvey pulled through his battles with depression, anger, and fear with the help of his true friend. Ashley's friendship was a sure anchor during his turbulent season of grief.

Harvey had worked at the county library since his sophomore year in high school. Then after graduating from college, he returned taking on the role of an Assistant Librarian. Though he had several other lucrative job offers, Harvey loved his hometown and did not desire to live anywhere else. It wasn't about making a lot of money because money wasn't an issue for Harvey. His parents had left him well off.

When hard times hit the *Finleys* and Ashley had to drop out of college Harvey put in a good word for Ashley at the library to be hired for the vacant clerk position. She was forever grateful for that.

Early on, Ashley perceived that Harvey had feelings for her, but she never encouraged it. Though he had always hovered over Ashley, she never breached the unwritten rules of their friendship. She only saw Harvey as a dear friend, more like a brother. Then when they separated for college, Ashley figured Harvey would move on. However, regularly she received cards and very personal letters from him. It was nice receiving mail on a routine basis, since most of her collegians didn't. Faithfully, Ashley replied, enjoying journaling with her friend. They shared everything through their letters, private thoughts, secrets, rough times regarding classes, etc. Ashley even wrote to him about a Keith, a junior she dated. Harvey never broached the subject of her newfound boyfriend in his letters. It was as if she never wrote it. That should have been an indicator back then that Harvey had never moved on. Ashely was too absorbed in her own life to notice.

But now…marriage? With Harvey? Sure, it would make my life a whole lot easier. Imagine five bedrooms, instead of two small bedrooms. Thomas could have his own room, and Danny and Donny could share a room. Mom and Lacey would have their own rooms. And that leaves me with a room…with Harvey.

During her break, Ashley closed her Bible and opened her journal. Scribbling the pros and cons of marrying Harvey on paper made the truths tangible.

MARRYING HARVEY

PROS	CONS
• Home for Family	• I am not in love with Harvey

- Christian husband
- No more working 2 jobs
- Finish my college degree
- Siblings better school
- Support
- No worries about food, electricity, water bill, etc.
- Thomas will be in a better environment
- Thomas can play basketball

I just cannot marry Harvey. I love him like a brother, not a husband-to-be. I do not want to lose his friendship. It will hurt him deeply if I say no. I need Your help with this, Lord.

Ashley avoided Harvey the rest of the day. She could feel his eyes watching her every move, but she ignored him. When she was about to leave, Harvey offered Ashley a ride, as usual.

"I worry about you, Ashley. It's so unsafe where you live."

"I'll be fine, Harvey," she gave him a hearty smile. "I have angels all around me."

"That you do," he smiled back. "But, I'd feel better if you let me take you home."

"You need to stay here. Besides, I am used to it. The ride on the bus clears my mind. It's the only time I have quiet time for myself." *Although sometimes the riders can be boisterous.*

"See, if you marry me, you'll have all the free-time you want and need." Harvey couldn't help himself.

"Please don't," she discouraged his pushiness.

"I know." Harvey put both his hands on her shoulders. "I promise not to pressure you. Just know that I will wait for you, forever."

"You don't...."

Once again, Harvey silenced her by putting his finger on her lips. Then impulsively, Harvey leaned over and brushed a soft kiss upon her mouth. It was over before it even started.

When he pulled back, Ashley stood dumbfounded. It wasn't a mushy kiss, but it definitely broke the rules of their friendship.

Friends don't kiss on the lips! What in the world has gotten into Harvey? Ashley was in a daze as she walked to the bus stop.

She touched her lips, still feeling the warmth of the brief kiss. It didn't stir her insides like the kiss she had with Keith, her former boyfriend. It was missing something.

Passion! There is no passion. It was like kissing my brother. Oh, God, how can I marry a man when there is no passion? Maybe I should get my head out of the clouds and take a real look at my life. Fairytale love is nice to read about in a book, but that kind of love doesn't pay the bills.

As soon as Ashley got home, she looked in on her sleeping mother, then began cooking dinner for the family.

Shortly, Thomas came barging in the door, obviously in a sour mood.

"How was your day?" Ashley asked as usual.

"You look awful," he replied instead of answering her mundane question. "I guess it is hard getting a good night sleep on the couch." Ashley slept on the couch, the twins, Lacy and Thomas all slept in double bunk beds in one room, while Sandra occupied the other bedroom.

"I do fine," Ashley countered. "You didn't answer my question."

"Because it's a stupid question," Thomas mocked. "School is stupid! ISS is stupid! And the Terminator is stupid!"

"Enough Thomas Finley!" Ashley was at a breaking point. "You should be thankful for an education. Our people fought hard for us to have an education for you just to throw it all away and call it stupid. What's stupid is not taking full advantage of your education and being receptive with those who are working in the educational system without complaining all the time. I have to give momma her medicine, please wash your hands and put the rice on for me."

"Beans and rice again," Thomas mumbled under his breath. "That's stupid!"

"I heard you," Ashley shouted back. "You should be thankful for…"

"Food to eat," Thomas completed the familiar phrase. "I know, I know."

Ashley took a deep breath, put on her happy face and entered her mother's room. Ashley felt drained. Really, she had nothing else to give. She needed replenishment both, spiritually and physically.

"You look worn-out," Sandra could not overlook her daughter's haggard look. The noticeable bags under Ashley's eyes, premature worry lines etched on her forehead, made Ashley appear older than her young twenty-three years.

"I'm fine, Momma," Ashley fibbed. "Didn't sleep well last night."

"Thank God you don't have to work tonight."

"I do." Ashley hated to add any more stress to her mother. "Pam isn't feeling well. She needed me to cover for her."

"Oh, my sweet Ashley, you're going to fall flat on your face if you don't get some rest. Did you even comb your hair this morning? You don't look like yourself." Her mother felt guilty for putting so much of the family's burdens on her daughter.

"You have dark circles under your eyes. You are losing weight. Oh, it's my fault!" Sandra Finley burst into tears.

"No, it's not, Momma," Ashley embraced her frail mother. "I'm fine. I promise I'll get some rest and take better care of myself." The teardrops fell freely from Ashley's eyes. She was too weary to hold back her innermost suffering. "You just promise me that you'll keep the faith and get better."

"Oh, sweet child of mine, I promise."

CHAPTER 5

Wearing Several Hats

Returning from a mandatory principals' meeting with the Superintendent Dr. Epson, Dr. Gregg Jefferson entered the helter-skelter main office. Instantly, his anger arose. He couldn't leave the school for one moment without it turning into a zoo. Leaving his assistant principals in charge didn't help matters. Ms. Myers, in charge of curriculum and instruction, was too one-dimensional, never wanting to step outside of her curriculum duties. Mr. Weaver was too timid, a pushover with the students, staff, and parents.

"I want to see the principal now!" an irate parent shouted. "How dare he lock my son up and take him away in handcuffs in front of the entire school!"

"Ma'am, you're going to have to quiet down," Mr. Weaver spoke too softly for Dr. Jefferson's liking.

"She *don't* have to quiet down!" A man put his finger in Mr. Weaver's face.

Gregg looked around at the chaotic office setting, his anger boiling like a pressure cooker about to blow its lid. Six students, who should have been in class, were in the office being nosey. A man and woman were ganging up on Mr. Weaver, screaming at the top of their lungs. Apparently, also with them was the mother of the other boy who had set the fire alarm. Missing in action were the school's resource officer and the monitors. At least they should have been around, making sure that the students got to their assigned classes. And of course, the other Assistant Principal, Ms. Myers, was nowhere around.

Dr. Jefferson bypassed the commotion and walked over to the secretary, who was nearly shouting through the phone, due to the noisy environment. Taking her walkie-talkie Dr. Jefferson bellowed out, "Officer Anderson, Ms. Myers, all monitors report to the main office ASAP!"

Suddenly, a hush filled the main office. Everyone turned and stared at the principal as if he was crazy.

"Mr. Weaver, escort these parents into my office," he ordered showing no emotion.

"Yes, Sir," his voice quivered. Mr. Weaver reckoned that he would be reprimanded later for the disruption in the main office.

In rushed everyone else.

"Officer Anderson, I may need you to assist with the parents in my office. Mr. Weaver is with them now. Let him know that he can go through the side door and walk the halls, making sure all students are where they need to be." Officer Anderson marched to the principal's office.

"I need for you monitors to escort each of these students to their classes now and write their names down so I can investigate why they were here in the main office and not in their classes."

"Yes, Sir," they echoed.

Waiting for everyone to leave, Dr. Jefferson turned to Ms. Myers. "Where were you? Didn't you hear the loud commotion in the main office? I heard it outside. Surely, you heard it from your office, which is directly across from my office."

"I was talking with a teacher," she stammered.

"And talking to a teacher is more important than keeping order and safety in our school?"

"No, but..."

"There are not *buts*, Ms. Myers," authoritatively his voice roared like a lion. "We've had this discussion too many times. Either you are on board or you are not. I suggest you figure which side you are on immediately because I will not stand for such insubordination. Let me know your decision by Friday and I'll let you know mine." And just like that, Dr. Jefferson walked away leaving Ms. Myers nearly in tears.

"Insufferable!" Ms. Myers murmured, supposing the principal was not in proximity to hear her.

"Insufferable is right!" The principal turned and fixed his eyes on her before closing his office door.

Her knees knocked together. She couldn't move. Dr. Jefferson intimated her. Ms. Irene Myers had never felt so humiliated and sheepish than when she was in the principal's presence. Never a good word, but always a sharp scolding, as if she was a child or one of his students.

I am in charge of curriculum, not discipline! That is Mr. Weaver's job, the monitors, resource officer, and the Principal. In her mind, Ms. Myers was not paid enough to risk her life by getting involved with violent parents, who would fight for their kids even if they were in the wrong. A student had already assaulted her and that same student returned to the school within a month.

On board! I am not on board to get shipwrecked or overthrown! Who does he think he is? He cannot fire me. I have tenure. Only the board can fire me. The students are right.

He is the Terminator!

In the interim, Dr. Jefferson sat in his chair and calmly addressed everyone in the room. "This is not a zoo where animals can just run wild. This is a school where the environment should be conducive for the students to receive a good education and a place where the students should feel safe and secure. I expect everyone who enters Brookland to behave properly, without disrupting the school setting. Disruption of any kind will not be tolerated at Brookland High. That includes disruption from the community and from parents."

"Wait a minute," the man stood up. "Are you calling us animals?"

"No, Sir, I am not. What I said is that this is not a zoo where animals can run wild, neither can people behave indecently, offensively or disruptively here."

"Sounds like you're calling us animals," the man insisted.

"Sir, let's address the matter at hand," the principal cleared his throat. "I assume you are here because," he looked at his file, "Shane and Kareem were arrested."

"Treated like criminals," the angry mother interjected.

"Is Shane your son?"

"No, Kareem!" she yelled. "How is pulling a fire alarm worthy of being arrested?"

"It's a federal crime, Ma'am," Dr. Jefferson answered. "However, it wasn't just for the alarm. Kareem and Shane…" he briefly observed the other mother who sat quietly. She looked as if she had been through a lot with her son. "Both boys assaulted my monitors."

"They were trying to run away," the man defended. "Who wouldn't?"

"Are you Kareem's father?" The antsy man was getting on

Dr. Jefferson's nerve.

"I'm her boyfriend," he pointed to Kareem's mother. "I'm Tyron Gates."

"Mr. Gates, it seems to me that if they were trying to run away as you put it, they would have ran in the opposite direction. However, that is not the case. They charged at the monitors and physically assaulted them. That's a crime and it will not be tolerated here at Brookland High."

"You didn't have to handcuff them and humiliate them in front of everyone," Kareem's mother replied.

"They were combative." Officer Anderson interceded. "We couldn't risk them endangering themselves or others, so I had to handcuff them."

"My boy is only sixteen-years-old," she argued.

"Age is not the issue." Dr. Jefferson refuted as he stood up and walked in front of his desk to speak with no barrier between them. "The criminal behavior, of both Kareem and Shane, is the issue. The crime warranted the punishment. I empathize with your distress right now. Nonetheless, perhaps the boys will learn from this, which hopefully will prevent anymore wrongdoings."

"You're heartless!" Kareem's mother stood up and faced him without fear.

Dr. Jefferson eyed her, saying nothing in his defense. *Perhaps I am.* He never went toe-to-toe with a parent. They had a right to express themselves…just as he had a right to discipline any student at his school, who disobeyed the rules.

"You don't have any kids, do you?"

"No, Ma'am, I do not."

"Figures," she scuffed.

"If there isn't anything else…" Dr. Jefferson was ready to

end this impromptu meeting. Obviously, the meeting would not resolve anything to Kareem's mother satisfaction. Instead, she was becoming more irritated and so was her boyfriend.

"Go to *hell!*" The man shouted.

"I'm going to the district and tell them how rude you were to us." Kareem's mother pointed her finger at him.

Officer Anderson immediately stood by the principal. "Ma'am please step back."

"You think you're better than us," she continued, not budging her stance. "But you're nobody! The kids hate you! The teachers hate you and your own assistant principal told us that you were a bully! The District people need to come down here and see how cruel you are to everybody. I'm going to get some parents together and we're going to make your life miserable, just like you do to the kids!"

"Are you threatening me?" Dr. Jefferson stood eyeball to eyeball with the woman."

"Ma'am," Officer Anderson intervened, "I think its best you leave before…"

"I'm leaving!" she rolled her eyes. "But remember, I'm your worst nightmare. You *messed* with the wrong parent this time," she warned and stumped out the door.

"I'll follow them to make sure they exit the campus quietly," Officer Anderson replied.

"Good." Dr. Jefferson wasn't worried. Since being assigned to Brookland High, disgruntled parents often threatened him by going to his superiors at the district office or rallying together to attack him. He was up for the fight because he followed the rules and guidelines set by the board. Not only did he know them, but also Dr. Jefferson helped outline most of the discipline codes and ethics in the school's handbook set by the

48

board and the school district.

Quietly, Shane's mom got up and stood in front of Dr. Jefferson.

"Thank you," she spoke softly. "I have been praying for the Lord to reach my Shane and to do whatever it takes to bring him back home. I believe God sent the answer through you."

Expecting another irate parent's verbal assault, Gregg was speechless by the kindness of the woman's voice and approving words. He didn't know how to respond to such a declaration, especially one that involved God. He wasn't on good terms with God. He hadn't been for a long time.

"God bless you," she touched his hand. "You have a difficult job working under difficult circumstances, dealing with difficult students and parents…but, you are the man for the job, chosen by God for such a time as this. I will be praying for you."

Flabbergasted, Gregg still said nothing as he watched the woman leave his office. It was hard to shake him up, but surely, this soft-spoken woman shook his world—temporarily.

Amazing how different the mothers were. One wanted to blame and the other wanted to bless. One agitated while the other mother remained calm. Shane's mom words were soft-spoken and simple, yet profoundly impacting.

His phone beeping interrupted his thoughts.

"Dr. Epson is on the phone," his secretary replied.

"Put him through."

"Hi Roy," Gregg relaxed. He and Dr. Epson, the superintendent for the school district, had been friends for years. Being his right-hand man for six years generated a professional and personal bond.

"I know I'm putting a lot on you by asking you to hold dual

roles, but I promised in the end you'll thank me."

"I hope so," Gregg wondered how in the world he would execute the superintendent's expectations of him. "It's hard running a school like Brookland High and still performing my Ombudsman duties, as well."

"I sympathize with you. It is not easy wearing several hats. You do not have to come to the Board meeting tomorrow if it is too much. I know that you have a home football game."

Gregg didn't respond. Attending a football game was the furthest thing from Gregg's mind. In fact, Gregg hadn't attended one football game this season. Besides, his athletic director was there and kept him abreast of the team. In any case, Gregg had better things to do, but watching a losing team was not one of them.

"A good principal always supports his athletic department," Dr. Epson added.

Gregg got the not so subtle hint. "I'll be at the game."

"I knew you would. How about you join Carla and me for dinner tonight? You haven't been over for some time now. And I need to get that report from you for the Board meeting."

"I can't tonight. I'm meeting with my administrative team around five and I'll probably be deadbeat after that."

"We'll have to meet tomorrow…" he paused, looking over his calendar. "I have back-to-back meetings tomorrow, but I have to stop at the library on Main Street to pick up some Christian movie for Carla. Can you meet me there…around eleven-thirty?"

Checking his calendar, Gregg responded, "Yes, that will work."

"I wish I had time to grab lunch, but my day is packed tighter than a can of sardines," Roy laughed.

50

"I know what you mean."

"So what's the administrative meeting about?"

"Being a Team-Player."

"Sounds interesting. Someone playing solo?"

"Yes. I wanted to talk to you about it," Gregg took the bait. "Ms. Myers, she's a good C&I administrator, but she's lousy at everything else. The building could be on fire and she would only think of saving herself, leaving her peers and students to burn."

"That's kind of harsh," the superintendent broke in.

"Maybe, but, she's self-centered. She wants to sit back and not get involved in anything else. Roy, we are too understaffed for that and you know it. She talks about me behind my back, which personally, I could care less. However, it is causing friction between me and the other staff. A parent told me today that my assistant principal called me a bully. She is having a negative impact on the school. She's been here for nine years and she doesn't want to change."

"Sounds like trouble," the superintendent understood Gregg's plight. "What do you want to do?"

"I told her she is either on board or she's not; and that if she couldn't support the vision, I would transfer her out of here."

"Whoa," the superintendent sat straight up in his chair. "Things don't work like that Gregg. You cannot just transfer her so easily. She's got tenure on her side."

"I want her out of here," Gregg did not bite his tongue. "She's hazardous to Brookland. You sent me here to do a job. To transform the school's image and reputation, to start out with. I can't transform the image on the outside until the inside is cleaned up."

"Let me look into it. I think J.T. Moore High School needs

an Assistant Principal for C&I. I will call the principal and hopefully get back with you before your meeting."

That's fast! Gregg Jefferson was used to getting his way. "Thanks, Roy. I truly appreciate it."

"Don't thank me, yet."

"Oh, I know it's a done-deal," Gregg felt confident. "You're Dr. Roy Epson, the best superintendent ever! You make things happen for the good of the students."

"Okay, stop kissing up," Dr. Epson stated. "I'll call you back as soon as I can. See you tomorrow."

Gregg felt good. Yes, Ms. Myers knew her craft, but she could not or would do nothing else to better the school. Her negative attitude and influence upon other staff members were a poisonous combination. Plus, her blackballing bewitched the parents. Ms. Myers stayed in her own little world, refusing to think or step outside of the box. He could not work with someone like that. Someone with a closed mind for change and progress toward success.

Gregg was physically tired. Handling two jobs was overwhelming, especially since both equally involved great responsibilities. Although Gregg had more parental, faculty, and student contact, he was more comfortable in the role of an Ombudsman. He was savvy with the educational system and astutely knowledgeable with the politics, rules and regulations set by the school district.

His weakness—humanity. Dr. Jefferson was not a people-person. Gregg purposely barricaded his heart from any emotional ties. It was hard for him to see behind the tears of the students, or to show compassion to the disrespectful student, or the teacher having a bad day, and wasn't giving his/her all in teaching rigor instruction in the classroom. All Gregg saw was wrongdoing and that was that. Personal issues were just that personal and shouldn't impact the educational setting on way or the other.

Gregg hadn't always been so hard and callous. Before his mother's death, he was a gentle boy with a compassionate heart for others, just like his mother. After his mother's death and experiencing such rejection from his father, Gregg resolved never to be vulnerable to humankind again. He became cold and unfeeling. Consequently, Gregg had turned into the man he resented—his father.

CHAPTER 6

Teamwork

"There is no "I" in Team," Gregg opened up his administrative meeting. "Turning this school around is not a solo assignment. It is going to take one-hundred-percent team effort. There is too much work to do at Brookland for all of us not to come together as one and make the necessary changes around here." Right away, Gregg made direct eye contact with everyone sitting at the table, making sure he had everyone's undivided attention.

To his right sat Ernest Weaver, AP of Building Operation for the past two years. Gregg believed that Mr. Weaver was on board. He just needed to be more assertive, not so wimpy with students, parents, and staff. Sitting next to Mr. Weaver was Jesse Koon, Athletic Director, and this year's interim basketball coach. Coach Koon had a true love for sports and a stronger bond with his players. He was concerned about their wellbeing on and off the court. Definitely, he was on board.

Jean Neal, the guidance director was also on board. She had been at the school for over twenty years. Though considered a veteran, she was supportive of the new administration. She had a heart for the children, which secretly impressed Gregg.

To the principal's left sat Irene Myers, the thorn in his

flesh. With her squared-black-rim glasses slightly on the edge of her long-pointed nose, Ms. Myers kept her focus on her black notebook. She was unquestionably not on board. Daniel West sat next to her. He was the principal assistant, working close with Mr. Weaver regarding security. He had worked at Brookland for ten years. Daniel was a big guy in stature. Having a strong military police background, Daniel could handle his own with the students, parents and staff. He knew the students and he knew the law. Gregg considered him the more trustworthy of all.

"I'm not here to make friends or build a family," Gregg stated to his administrative staff. "Contrary to belief, I already have friends and I come from a good family." *Okay, I am fabricating, but they get my point.* "I am here with one purpose and one purpose only and that is to transform the image and status of Brookland High. We will do that by bridging the academic gap, increasing our test scores and improving safety. For years, people have called this an alternative school. Parents, who can afford it, take their children anywhere but here. It has been called a zoo, a hoodlum school, a prison, a detention center for rejects, a house for gangs, drug addicts, and alcoholics, you name it. Many students are afraid to come to school, fearful of violent fights, shootouts, etc. The faculty and staff fear retaliation from the students and parents.

"However, there is a bright side to all this gloom and doom. We are slowly making strides to change all that. By removing the repeat offenders, tightening up our security, and not allowing former students or gang bangers onto our campus during school hours, we have curtailed the violence at Brookland. I commend you for your support in this effort, but we still have more to do.

"As I have said before and I will say again, disruption of any kind will not be allowed or tolerated at Brookland. Once we put a lid totally on our security and safety issues, we will see a change in our test scores, which I will get to in a minute. There can be no learning in a chaotic environment.

"Mr. West, I commend you in your handling of the guys who painted graffiti on the eastside of the school. Maybe we should do more of that. You do the crime, you pay the time by cleaning up our school."

"Thank you, Sir," Mr. West knew compliments did not come easy by the principal, so he felt honored.

"Now about the test scores," Gregg broached the subject. "We need to do something to motivate the students for the District Standardized Test (DST). I think we need to start out by making sure the students have a healthy breakfast since many of them come to school hungry. Does anyone have any suggestions?"

"For the next two weeks, the teachers will be going over the DST, giving quizzes and homework assignments geared toward improving test scores," Ms. Myers answered precisely. "This should help elevate our test scores."

"But it doesn't motivate our students," Gregg countered. "First of all, we have to make the students a part of the whole scheme of things. The students have to buy-in to their success. They have to want to take pride in their scores and their school. We have to get them on board, as well, making it more than about the scores, but about them."

"I think we should have a Test Pep Rally," Jean Neal spoke up. "Have a motivational speaker to encourage them about the DST. Perhaps even some famous person to rap or sing. Each week we could give incentive rewards to the students who bring in homework assignments geared toward DST and those who do well on their class assignments."

"I like the suggestions," Gregg flashed his unusual smile. "Can you and the guidance counselors come up with a plan regarding incentives and have it on my desk next Monday?"

"Yes, Sir," Ms. Neal heaved a sigh of relief.

"Now we have to work on getting a motivational speaker and…"

"Pep Rallies are dangerous and the students go crazy whenever we have someone speak at our school," pessimism flowed from Ms. Myers's lips. "It's embarrassing the way they act in front of the guests."

Gregg did everything possible not to make his response personal. Professionally, he respected her knowledge of curriculum and instruction; however, personally, he disliked Ms. Myers. Her negativity was stifling. Clearing, his throat Gregg looked Ms. Myers directly in the eyes and said, "I can only take your word for the students' abrupt behavior since I haven't participated in a pep rally. Nevertheless, I assure you that things will be different. The students will behave properly and the speaker will feel welcomed."

Ms. Myers made a funny noise, scoffing the very idea of the students behaving properly.

"Since Ms. Myers doesn't believe it is possible, I am asking that the rest of the team come up with a motivational speaker and perhaps Mr. Koon could ask Sterling Johnson, the former professional basketball player of the Carolina Bulldogs to speak to our students." Gregg knew that Jesse Koon had graduated with Sterling and remained in contact with him.

"I'll call Sterling after our meeting," Coach Koon replied.

"As a matter of fact, perhaps we can talk to him about

mentoring a few of our students and getting some of his colleagues involved, as well," Gregg injected.

"I'm sure Sterling would be on board," Coach Koon nodded.

"Dr. Price is an awesome motivational speaker. He came from poverty and now is a millionaire." Mr. West spoke up. "I know him personally. I am sure he will do it pro bono, since he graduated from Brookland. I can also check with him about helping us with breakfast. I am sure he will support us financially in this endeavor. He has in the past," Mr. West informed.

"See what we can accomplish as a team," Gregg commented with pride.

Ms. Myers's cheeks flushed red with anger, as she nervously tapped her pen on the table.

After going over this month's calendar Gregg dismissed everyone.

"Oh, and let's support Coach Jackson and the football team tomorrow for the rivalry game against Richview," Gregg stood up. "I know it's a Tuesday's game, but let's try to show some school pride and support the team. I know Coach Koon will be there, but we can demonstrate a more unified team by all of us showing up."

Everyone gave him a bewildered look. With a record of five straight loses, the principal had attended none of the games.

Coach Koon patted Dr. Jefferson on the back and gave him a hearty smile before exiting the room. That simple gesture touched Gregg. For the first time since he became principal at Brookland, he felt like he was on the right track in leading the school to a positive turnaround. *I will have to thank Roy later.*

Ms. Myers waited for everyone else to leave, before

approaching the principal. "I'm on task with the DST preparations," she opened up the conversation. "I still don't think any motivational speaker is going to make a difference."

"We'll see," he baited, "won't we?"

"You're just trying to make me look small in front of the administration team and I don't appreciate it," Ms. Myers boldly accused. "I have been here for…"

"Nine years," Gregg finished her sentence. "And that's noteworthy, but things haven't changed Ms. Myers. We have been unsatisfactory for ten years. We have the highest dropout rate, highest gang population and we are at the bottom of the pole when it comes to test scores. We have to change in order for test scores and our students to change."

"I'm an Assistant Principal, in charge of curriculum and instruction. I'm doing the job I was hired to do, more than satisfactory I might add."

"Ms. Myers, you are a good C&I administrator," he agreed freely, "but we all have to wear many hats here. We are understaffed as it is, so we have to adjust and do whatever it takes to work as a team. Your job requires you to wear more than one hat, Ms. Myers. We all do. However, if you cannot get onboard and work as a team player instead of playing solo, then I will transfer you out of here, tomorrow. The ball is in your court. Let me know what you decide."

"No disrespect, Dr. Jefferson," her voice cracked, "but you're a bully."

"So I have heard from Kareem's mother," he said in proud insolence, letting it be known that he knew what she had said to the parent. "A bully is one that intimidates another, who is either weak or unsure of him or herself? Am I intimidating you, Ms. Myers?"

She stood shaken and shattered, saying nothing.

"Good day, Ms. Myers." Dr. Jefferson walked away.

The following day.

"Where is Harvey?" Ashley asked Ms. Washburn, the librarian.

"He went to pick up some displays from the Northeast Branch. He should be back within an hour," she answered.

"Can you check in those books for me?" Ms. Washburn pointed to the cart, stacked with returned books. "I didn't get a chance to do it yesterday. Also, Dr. Epson may be picking up the movies in the tray. Just have him sign for them."

"No problem."

"I'm going in the back for a minute. Let me know if you need my help."

Ashley nodded. Instantly, she began logging in the books, enjoying the quietness of the library. There were only two patrons in the library and both were on the computers.

Hearing the door chime, Ashley looked up and straightway, her heartbeat amplified. Surely, everyone could hear the thumping sound. Something about that man did strange things to her insides.

"Excuse me," Gregg Jefferson stood before her – all handsome, in his tailored fitting black suit, crisp white shirt, and yellow printed tie. From head-to-toe, the principal painted a picture of a model on the cover of GQ Magazine.

"Yes, can I help you?" Somehow, Ashley kept her professional mannerism. *He is way too handsome!*

"Good morning, Miss…Ashley Finley," he greeted.

He remembered my name!

"What a...surprise." Gregg smiled, he too feeling off-balance. *Those eyes! They are lethal!*

"Good morning Dr. Jefferson. How can I help you?"

He ran his fingers through his hair, suddenly experiencing amnesia of some sort. "Umm... I'm...someone..."

"Huh?"

"I'm meeting someone here," he swiftly snapped out of it, feeling like a complete nincompoop. "Dr. Epson, he's the superintendent of the school district, have you seen him?"

"No, I haven't."

Nervously, he looked around. *Get a grip! You are making a fool of yourself.* "So, I guess I'll wait by the door," Gregg walked away.

"Dr. Jefferson," Ashley called. "How is my brother? Is he doing alright in ISS?"

"He seems to be," he turned to her. "I reviewed your brother's file. I was impressed with his academics. He was an all A student. His teachers thought he was sure to be a success in whatever career path he chose. I apologize for my prejudgment. You were right."

"Thank you, Dr. Jefferson." Ashley's heart softened. "Thomas was a good boy; he still is. He is just going through a rough spell right now. Please be patient with him."

This petite, ordinary, yet extraordinary woman had touched Gregg's soul in places that had not been touched in a long, long time. Though she dressed plain and took no thought about her outward appearance, Ashley Finley was irrefutably beautiful. "I want the best for Thomas and all of my students."

"Gregg!" Roy rushed in. "I'm sorry I'm late, but my meeting went over. Do you have the file?"

"Yes and..." Gregg looked at his watch. "Good afternoon

to you, too."

"Sorry, Gregg. Good afternoon," the superintendent noticed the woman behind the counter. "Hope I'm not interrupting anything," his eyes held a hint of merriment.

"Oh, no," Gregg turned to Ashley. "This is Miss Ashley Finley. Her brother goes to Brookland."

"Nice to meet you," Dr. Epson cordially shook her hand.

"You as well. Here are the movies you requested," she handed them to him. "If you will just sign here."

"Sure. Thank you," he replied. "Well, I've got to go. I'll call you later…about Ms. Myers."

"I'll be waiting on that call."

"I bet you will." Dr. Epson hurried out the door.

"Well, I've got to get back to Brookland. It's was nice seeing you, Ashley Finley."

"And you, as well."

"Have a good day." Peculiarly, Gregg didn't want to leave.

"You too," Ashley wished he could stay a little longer.

Getting in his car, Gregg momentarily sat there, envisioning the woman with the crystalline eyes. She was the exact opposite of the women who usually attracted him. Nothing about her exemplified a good time or shouted easy-street. Gregg liked no-commitment females, a one-night stand and such. Ashley Finley was the wife-type—Forbidden! Purposely, Gregg steered away from women like her. Anytime any woman got too close, Gregg would conveniently disappear–vanish without a trace.

But…Ashley Finley is one special lady.

Clear your head! She is not for you! But she sure is beautiful.

Tuesday night, Gregg stood on the field, next to Mr. Koon. He hadn't attended a football game since his college days. Those were the good old days when he and his frat brothers would hang out all the time. Gregg even played football his freshmen and sophomore year, until a knee injury. It was refreshing to be on the field again…as the principal.

Watching the football team charge through the banner, and running onto the field sparked something within with excitement. Then suddenly a cloud of sadness shrouded him. Gregg realized at that moment, he didn't know a single football player's name. He couldn't identify with his students, only the troublemakers. Undeniably, Gregg had the academic and the discipline piece down pat. However, the interpersonal piece of knowing the student body, individually and collectively, he found himself inept.

Several times he leaned over and asked Mr. Koon the name of the player tackling, or the player attempting a touchdown, or the player throwing the ball, and so forth. He hated being so clueless. However, Gregg was determined to change all that for future games. He would get to know his players. Perhaps even share their game-time pre-meal and observe some of their practices.

To no one's surprise, Brookland lost 28-3.

"We're going to have to do something about this losing streak," Gregg consulted his athletic director. "What is the problem?"

"Coach says the boys aren't consistent. They don't come to practice regularly. Most of them work after school so they can help take care of their families. Since many of them don't have a father in the home, the boys have to man-up early with fatherly responsibilities."

"Can't we get more players? I notice that we don't have a lot of players."

"The guys, who can play, aren't eligible to play because of their grades. And those who want to play can't because of their working schedules."

"What about tutoring after school?" Gregg wanted an instant solution to the problem.

"They don't show up," Mr. Koon responded, "for the same reason…they have jobs."

"Something has to be done." Gregg walked with the athletic director to the end of the field where the boys were kneeling, listening to Coach Jackson's pep talk.

The coach looked up, surprised to see the principal. "Hey, Dr. Jefferson. Glad you could make it to the game."

"It was my pleasure," he eyed the boys. "Tomorrow morning, I want to meet with each of the team members, individually. Mr. Koon will give the team's roster to my secretary, and she will be calling you down so that I can speak with you, individually for no more than ten minutes. Good game fellows. Next time we'll win!" Gregg shouted energetically. "Do you believe that?"

The team stared at him as if he was bonkers.

"I said," Gregg repeated loudly, "Tigers, do you believe that you will win the next game?"

"Yes," they responded timidly.

"Come on, what kind of yes is that?" Gregg pumped the team by his own enthusiasm. "You're tigers, aren't you? Tigers pounce on their opponents. You have to believe it here first," he pointed to his chest, "and then the results will show up on the field. Aren't you tired of losing?"

"Yes!" Some of the guys answered.

"Well then, let's change that. It is going to take teamwork, but I know we can do it. I will ask you again, Tigers, do you believe that you will win the next game?"

"Yes!" This time, they roared in unison.

"Tigers, do you really believe it?" he shouted louder.

"Yes!"

"Okay, then!" Gregg had accomplished his goal of making them have some gusto. "See you tomorrow!"

The coach, athletic director, and the team watched in awe as Principal Jefferson strode away with his swaggered walk. They had all witnessed something different in him tonight.

Passion!

CHAPTER 7

Weariness

Very few things in Ashley's life were constant, but she could always rely on her church. Even though her family moved from their suburban community to the inner city, the *Finleys* gladly took the long bus ride every Sunday morning to attend their home church. Fellowshipping with her church family afforded Ashley an escape from reality. It renewed Ashley's faith and restored her joy, in times when life virtually pushed her to the edge of despair. Sunday was her only day off from both jobs. Ashley could ride away and hide away from all of her responsibilities.

Also constant was Harvey. Come rain or shine, good or bad, sick or well, Harvey did not change. He remained a loyal friend through thick and thin. No matter what, Harvey was always there, not just for Ashley, but also for the entire Finley clan.

Still, it was rather awkward for Ashley being around Harvey now. There was a silent elephant in the room that they pretended did not exist. Their relationship had transcended friendship boundaries for good. Thankfully, Harvey didn't bring up the marriage proposal again. Although Ashley felt that Harvey would be a great husband for someone else, she foresaw a loveless, passionless marriage if she were his bride. She wanted more.

Witnessing the passionless marriage of her parents, especially on the part of her dad, Ashley vowed never to settle for less than God's best in a helpmate. Her dad was always gone while her mother made up excuses for him. There was never any real joy and laughter between them. Just two roommates sharing a home and children. Though her mother would never leave him, the cost Sandra paid by staying seemed too steep of a price to pay. Ashely would rather struggle and be alone than to follow her mother's example.

"You look sick," Harvey met Ashley in the back of the library as she clocked in.

"I'm fine," she smiled up at him. Taking a moment just to really see Harvey, Ashley admired Harvey's facial features. His naturally curly jet-black hair suited his chocolate brown skin tone. His large eyes and full lips caught her attention for the first time. Harvey was nice-looking, for sure. He was tall but lanky. Though the thing that made Harvey special wasn't anything physical. Harvest greatest asset was that he was a compassionate man. He cared about others, more than he cared about himself.

"Forgive me for saying this, but you don't look fine. You are overdoing it, Ashley. You're taking care of everybody else, but not yourself."

"I'm fine," she repeated firmly. "But I won't be if I don't get to work. Talk to you later, Harvey." Ashley brushed passed him.

Working non-stop, re-shelving the books, stamping and coding new books, assisting patrons and reading a book to the Thursday weekly toddlers' class, by the time it was time for her to go home, Ashley was dog-tired. It would take supernatural strength for her to make it through the rest of the day. Mentally and physically, she felt beaten down.

After rushing home, taking care of her mother, and sharing a simple family meal together, she cannonballed out the house to catch her bus to *The Palace*. Ashley hated leaving her mother this Thursday. Sandra had a low-grade fever all night and this morning it had elevated slightly.

Between her mother's ailments; the rent being overdue; Thomas' aloof attitude; the pressure of two jobs; and now being highly sensitive to Harvey, Ashley felt as if she was being torn in too many directions. She was sorely pressed and did not know what to do about it. The weight of the world rested upon her frail shoulders.

Needing to release on paper her jumbled feelings while riding the bus, Ashley searched her purse, but couldn't find her journal. *I wonder where I left it.*

The last time I remember having it was when I put my purse down on the kitchen counter and poured a glass of milk for momma. It was in there because I remember pushing it further down so that I could properly close my purse.

Arriving at work on time, Ashley conversed briefly with Pam and then they dispersed to wait on the customers. As always, *The Palace* was crowded. People did not mind paying for a relaxing evening of charm, sophistication, and soothing music.

Instead of being her usual flirtatious self, Pam was quite the contrary. She was quiet with her customers and rather subdued. As Ashley observed her taking the customers' orders, two tables down, she noticed how Pam avoided eye contact with the four businessmen. It was evident that the men found Pam to be rather charming and beautiful. Her aloofness probably enticed them even more. Fear was shadowing in Pam's footsteps as she walked away.

Ashley offered up a silent prayer.

"Hey, you alright?" Ashley came from behind and handed her order to one of the cooks.

"Of course," Pam tossed her head. "Why do you ask?"

"You don't seem yourself tonight." *Truly, she has a right not to.* "Maybe you came back to work too soon."

"I'm fine," Pam turned to her. "Remember your promise. We will not speak on the matter again. Everything is fine."

"I don't believe you." Ashley reached over and hugged her friend. For a split second, Pam trembled in her arms, and then abruptly pulled away.

"Let's get back to work before the *wicked witch of the west* comes and casts a spell on us." Pam feigned laughter.

Ashley scowled.

"Lighten up, scrooge."

"I got your scrooge," Ashley playfully shoved her. "We're catching the bus together, right?"

"I was sort of hoping you would ride home with me tonight."

"Ride?" Ashley's forehead creased with wrinkles. *Not another stranger.* "You don't have a car."

"No, but Andrew the chef does, and he offered us a ride home."

"He's creepy," Ashley frowned. "The way he stares and me. Something is not right with that."

"He's a nice guy," Pam defended.

"You thought that about…"

Pam's face turned pale.

"I'm so sorry," Ashley grabbed her fiend's hand. "Please forgive me. It is just that I do not trust any man right now. We can't afford to."

"I don't feel comfortable catching the bus, and then walking home in our dangerous neighborhoods, alone," Pam confessed water-eyed. "Not right now."

Ashley understood. Even though she felt apprehensive about Andrew, she would not allow Pam to ride with him alone. "Alright, I'll ride with you."

"Thanks!" she gave her a quick hug. "You're a real friend, Ash. We'll talk later."

Ashley turned, catching Andrew staring at her. She glared back at him. *What is his problem?*

After a long night at The Palace, Pam and Ashley sat close to each other in the backseat of Andrew's car. Neither had the courage to sit up front.

"Andrew," Pam addressed him, "are you from South Carolina?"

"Yes, I am."

"Have you lived here all your life?"

"No. I returned to the south about two months ago."

"Where did you last live?"

Ashley looked over at her friend as if she was crazy. Suddenly, Pam was all chatty.

"New York."

"Wow! That is a long way from here. Why did you come back?"

"My mother's funeral."

"Sorry to hear that."

"Me too," Ashley mumbled, still feeling edgy about riding in his car.

"She's in a better place," Andrew smiled. "She was ready to go home and be with my father."

"That's a good way to look at it." Pam replied indifferently, not a believer of heaven or spiritual things.

"It's the only way to look at it." Andrew glanced over his shoulder at Pam. "You're either going one of two places when you die, heaven or hell. Both my parents are in heaven now with the Master."

Pam shrugged her shoulders, not wanting to discuss the matter anymore.

"Do you believe in a heaven and a hell, Ashley?" Andrew inquired.

"I sure do," she said proudly. "More important, I believe that the only way to get to heaven is by accepting Jesus Christ as your Lord and Savior."

"So do I," Andrew's smile broaden. "Good to know I'm working with a Believer. I guess that makes us kindred."

"I guess so," Ashley still felt unsettled. If he really was a Believer like the one he professed to be, then why did he gawk at her all the time?

"Here's my cottage," Pam made light of her rundown apartment complex. "Are you sure you feel safe to travel around the corner by yourself? Or do you want to get off at my stop and I'll walk you halfway."

"That's ridiculous," Ashley whispered back. "I'll be fine. He says he's a Believer."

"And…" Pam scoffed. "He's still a man."

"I have angels all around me."

"Call me the minute you walk in the house."

"I will."

The girls embraced.

Pam looked back several times, worrying about the safety of her one and only friend. Her one-night stand had put a fear in her like nothing else she ever experienced. Paranoid, Pam looked around to see if anyone was around. Even after closing her apartment door, she feared the possibility of danger lurking on the inside. Darkness terrified Pam, but so did the light.

"Don't worry," Andrew interrupted Ashley's silent prayer. "I won't harm you. I fear God and love Him all the same."

Still cautious, Ashley relaxed and rattled off the directions to her home. God was with her and He would not allow harm to come nigh her dwelling.

"We'll have to pray for your friend, Pam, to know the Lord for herself. She seems to be a troubled soul." Andrew stated with concern in his voice. "She lacks peace."

If only you knew?

"Please forgive me for prying into your life, but I couldn't help but notice that you look a little peaked tonight. Are you feeling well?"

"Just tired."

"Are you a college student by day?"

"I used to be," her voice was laced with regrets. "I work at the library in the daytime."

"No wonder you're tired," he was sympathetic. "I know a lot about working two jobs. Shoot, sometimes I had to work three jobs to make ends meet, before getting my break as a respected chef. Now I can pretty much pick where I work. That's because of God's favor upon my life."

Ashley liked the way he talked of God as if he had a personal connection to Him. She used to feel that way before life got so hard. Now, her relationship with God seemed so disconnected and distanced.

"You need to get yourself some rest."

"I'll try. Thanks for the ride," she said as the car came to a complete stop in front of her duplex.

"Anytime," he smiled. "It's not safe for two lovely ladies to be out in this neighborhood at night."

"I have angels all around me," she quoted for the third time that day.

"God gives us wisdom," Andrew countered.

"Goodnight," she said and closed the door. As soon as she entered her home, Ashley went to the counter to see if her journal was there. Disappointed, she searched the kitchen, but to no avail. Her journal was gone.

Peeping in on her mother, who was sound asleep, Ashley then peeked in her siblings' room. With two bunk beds in the small room, all four were sleeping.

Ashley went back into the living room and pulled out the sleeper couch. Ashley was too tired to take a shower. Too tired to change into her nightgown or brush her hair. She was even too tired to read her Bible. Pulling the covers to her chin, Ashley prayed …but she was too tired to finish the prayer.

CHAPTER 8

Brookland Tigers

"Thomas," Ashley whispered to him at the breakfast table, "have you seen my journal? I thought I left it on the counter."

"No," he kept eating.

"I've looked everywhere for it. It's not here."

"Maybe it's at the library."

"It's not there," her heart languished. Though the book cost little, the secret treasures it held inside, were Ashley's most prized possession. Ashley feared that someone would read the secret treasures of her heart. For in the journal Ashley wrote her deepest fears, greatest hopes, desires, and her private struggles that only she and God knew about.

"*Gotta* go!" Thomas leaped out of the chair. "We are going to be late for school."

Seven-thirty sharp Gregg stood outside the main entrance door, which was propped opened for him to greet his staff and students. This was so out of character for Dr. Jefferson. In order to see change, you have to change —and do something different! Gregg was practicing what he had been *preaching* to his administration.

"Good morning," the principal greeted each student. They were surprised not only by him standing at the front door but also by him acknowledging them, personally. Usually, the students only made contact with the principal when they were in *big* trouble.

"Good game." Gregg recognized one of the football players. "Talk to you later."

"Okay," the boy stuttered.

Just as the tardy bell sounded, Thomas ran down the pavement. Gregg had noticed him talking with two other boys, who were known gang bangers.

"Good morning, Thomas," Gregg greeted. "You're late."

Thomas didn't say a word. He just brushed by him.

"Thomas," he called after him. "When someone speaks to you, the polite thing to do is speak back."

Thomas frowned and walked away.

"Thomas!" again Gregg shouted after him.

"What!"

"In my office!" Gregg pointed to the main office. "Now!"

"You mean I'm in trouble because I didn't speak to you?" Thomas looked at him in disbelief. "That's crazy!"

"In my office!" The principal gave him a stern look and walked ahead of him, trusting that Thomas would follow.

And he did.

Closing his office door, Gregg sat down in his chair and waited for Thomas to do likewise.

"Judging from your sister, I know your mother taught you manners."

Thomas remained silent.

"That angry chip you are carrying on your shoulders is a destructive force with destructive consequences. Why are you so angry?"

76

"Like you care!" Thomas lashed out.

"If I didn't care, Thomas, I wouldn't have called you in here." He waited for Thomas to say something, but he said not a word.

"Again, I'll ask you the same question. Why are you so angry?"

"I don't know." Thomas kept his eyes on the floor.

"Let me try this again." Gregg stood up, walked around to the front of his desk and sat on the edge. "Who are you angry at, Thomas?"

Thomas bit his lip. He didn't like the principal and he didn't want him all up in his business.

"I looked over your file. You were an "A" student up until a few years ago. Last year not only did your grades suffer, but you got into all kinds of trouble. What happened? What changed you?"

"Life!" Thomas barked out an answer wanting to get this man off his back.

"Life happens, Thomas. As the old cliché goes, *when life hands you lemons—make lemonade*. Sometimes life deals us some bad cards, but we have to make the best out of the hand we are dealt."

"How would you know?" Thomas sucked his teeth, scrutinizing the principal, covertly estimating the cost of his suit to be more than his entire wardrobe. "Have you ever loss a parent?"

"I have...my mother," Gregg answered calmly. However, the pain of her death was still an open wound.

"Oh..."

"I also understand that you were a good basketball player your junior year and that you quit the team in mid-season."

Gregg acknowledged, revealing just how much he had checked into Thomas' school records. "Not only do you have the height but I've heard that you were really fast and could shoot a nice three-pointer."

The principal's unexpected praise warranted Thomas to look up at him. "I was alright," humbly he replied.

"I hear the team could surely use you for this basketball season."

"I'm not playing."

"Why? Do you have a job after school?"

"Yes and no," he shrugged. "I don't get paid for it."

"I'm confused."

"It doesn't matter. I'm not playing basketball," he reiterated.

"If you work hard on pulling up your grades, I know Coach Koon would be glad to have you back on the team."

"Coach Koon," Thomas was perplexed. "He's the athletic director."

"He will be filling in for Coach Javis until he recuperates from his surgery."

"Doesn't matter anyway. I'm not playing."

"Don't you know that you can possibly get a scholarship to college with your basketball skills?" Gregg wanted to reach this young man. Something about Thomas affected him. Possibly, it was his sister with the crystalline eyes. Perhaps by helping him, Gregg could help the young lady who seemed weary and tired. "You're talented, but if you don't rid yourself of all that anger, you'll never be successful at anything because that anger will handicap you."

"Am I in trouble?" Thomas eyed him indifferently.

"No, son, you are not." Gregg felt defeated. "This is your last day in ISS for the week; let's try and make it for the year."

Thomas stood up.

"Oh, by the way," Gregg spoke again. "Those guys I saw you talking with this morning, you should stay away from them. They are dangerous."

"Life is dangerous," Thomas flouted. "Every day we wake up, danger lurks outside."

"True," Gregg admitted, "but we shouldn't run to danger, we should run from it. Stay away from those guys. You're not only hurting yourself, but you're hurting your family." *Especially your sister.* The mentation flustered Gregg. Why couldn't he get her out of his head?

Thomas looked at him, long and hard. Though the principal was surely at least 6"2' and could certainly crush any opponent, Dr. Jefferson didn't fit the *shoes* of the Terminator today. He was much nicer. He displayed signs of a caring heart.

Nah! Thomas left.

Following, Gregg pushed the button on his phone to get his secretary.

"Yes, Dr. Jefferson," she answered promptly.

"Did Coach Koon give you the roster for the football team?"

"Yes."

"Okay in about fifteen minutes, send in two players. When they leave, which should only take about ten minutes, send in the next two and we will go like that until lunch. I want to see all the players today."

"Yes Sir," she responded. "I'll get on it right away."

"Thanks." Once again, his thoughts drifted toward the petite young woman who appeared poor, but proud. Gregg could not clear the unseen cobwebs of Ashley Finley from his subconscious.

Stop it! Gregg reprimanded himself. *She is not my type.*

Before his thoughts zoomed into another atmosphere, Gregg's secretary beeped in on his phone.

"I have a call for you. It's your father," his secretary informed. She didn't even know the principal's father was alive since Dr. Jefferson never talked about him or anyone else. She just assumed that he was all alone.

My father! Gregg was stunned. His dad never called him at work, or at home. He didn't call at all. "Put him through."

"Hi Gregg," his father spoke. "How are you?"

"Fine," he stammered, still shocked by the caller. "And you?" he formally returned the gesture.

"That's what I want to talk to you about."

Immediately, Gregg sensed that something was wrong. It had to be for his father to call him. "Go on."

"Not on the phone," Gregory Jefferson, countered. "I made a reservation for two at *The Palace*, tomorrow at six o'clock."

Just like him! Gregg's chest tightened, which was typical when talking with his father. *He makes a reservation without even asking me if I already have plans or not.*

"You know tomorrow is my birthday," his father went on. "I'll be 58."

"Oh, yeah," Gregg ran his fingers through his hair. He had forgotten all about his dad's birthday. "I…uh…I'll pick you up."

"No need," Mr. Jefferson was always in control. "I will just meet you there. Please be on time."

"I will," Gregg replied, a little miffed. His father was the one always late. Gregg was always the punctual one. He hated tardiness of any kind.

"See you tomorrow," Mr. Jefferson said and hung up.

Just like him! If that just don't beat all! Gregg slammed

the phone done. *Always have to have the last word!* He leaped out of his chair and paced the room back and forth. *What in the world does he want to talk about? Hope it is not a woman he wants to introduce me to without notice! Out of the blue, he calls me. He could care less about me. He either wants me to do something for him or to meet some well-to-do snob!*

His phone beeped again.

"Yes…" Gregg answered.

"The first two boys are here," she stated. "Rashaud and Maurice."

"Okay. After you send them in, can you find Shane…" he looked at his notes, "Shane Coffey. Send him after I have talked with all the football players."

"Of course," his secretary hung up, sending up a prayer. She was so thankful for the less tensed boss she had encountered today. Something was changing in him.

Gregg couldn't forget the sweet mother of Shane. Her kindness had touched him. If he could perhaps help Shane, the mother's life would be easier.

"For such a time as this," he remembered her familiar words. The same words his mother use to sing to him. For the first part of the day, Gregg spoke with half of the football team. Personally, he wanted to know about them. Why they were playing football? About their family life. What were their aspirations and goals after high school, etc.?

By the time lunchtime came around, the principal felt stressed, feeling the weight of what many of the football players were going through. Most of them came from a single parent home with several mouths that needed to be fed. Therefore, the boys had to pull their load by working. They were young boys leading men lives.

But the most touching story of all was Shane Coffey. The

sweet woman that had touched his heart wasn't even Shane's mother; she was his aunt. After Shane's mother had died of a drug overdose, when he was only five years of age, the aunt stepped in, even though she was a widower with four children of her own, two with special needs. Gregg was more determined to help Shane than ever before. He was a smart young man, who needed a male role model in his life.

Shane had bottled up so much of his pain and disappointment throughout his young life. He found comfort in likeminded males, who had no fathers but offered him camaraderie. Shane desired to do right, but the temptations of his so-called friends were hard to resist. Before leaving, Shane promised Gregg he would take the straight-and-narrow way after Dr. Jefferson promised that he would help him get a job and find him a tutor to help Shane with his Algebra II class so that he could play on the basketball team.

Needing to release some of his pent-up emotions, Gregg stretched his legs by walking the halls of Brookland. When he came to the ISS room, Gregg peeped inside observing Thomas. The lad was immersed in reading a book.

Entering the room, Gregg came from behind, looking closely at the book. It was not an ordinary book. First, the color of the book was deep purple with pink flowers, which seemed odd to him. Looking more closely, Gregg noticed on the cover, written in bold letters, '*Ashley Finely Private Journey.*'

What is he doing with his sister's journal?

Gregg cleared his throat, making his presence known to Thomas.

Thomas looked up with guilt plastered on his face. He had just been caught with his hand in the cookie jar. Thomas closed the book and slipped it into his book bag.

"Is everything all right, Thomas?"

"Yes." Thomas felt shamefaced, hoping and praying that the principal had not discovered his wrongdoing.

"Hmm," Gregg eyed him, not moving an inch.

Thomas took out some paper and began working on a report that was due next week.

Tardily, Gregg walked away and exited the ISS room. *I wonder if Miss Finley knows that her brother has her journal.*

The last one to leave the school, Gregg was ready to stop for the day. He had made small strides with the football team and felt more connected to them than before. He had to find a solution for them not practicing because of their other responsibilities. The athletic department would suffer during basketball season as well because the student population consisted mostly of poverty-stricken students from single-parent homes. Most important, Gregg wanted to help the young men and women to enjoy their teenage years.

Driven with a strong tenacity, Gregg wouldn't stop until he helped every one of the young people he spoke with today. Academics were important, still extra-curricular activities also permitted young people to discover their inner selves, making them well-rounded and happy.

He hated losing, and the football's losing record didn't sit well with him. After talking with Mr. Koon, it confirmed his theory that the upcoming basketball team might not be so good either. They needed more committed players and players with a passion for the game—like Thomas.

Somehow, I have to get Thomas back on the team. His mind is too idle. Obviously, he has not learned his lesson about stealing, because I am sure he stole his sister's journal.

Maybe, I will call her. Gregg thought about it on the way home.

Not a good idea. I cannot become too personal with the students or their family members.

While riding home, Gregg's cell phone chimed.

"Hello," Gregg answered.

"Ms. Myers can be transferred to J.T. Moore High School in two weeks," Dr. Epson began. "The assistant principal there is relocating due to her husband's military assignment."

"Wonderful!" What a great note to end the workweek on.

"Talk to her Monday and let me know," Dr. Epson suggested. "Did you go to the game?"

"Yeah," Gregg chuckled. "The team struggled. We need more players."

"I know you, Gregg. You will turn the team around with the help of the coach and athletic director. If not this year, then next."

"Next?" Gregg nearly slammed on his breaks in the middle of the road. "I thought this was going to be a year assignment, only."

"Like I said," Dr. Epson explained, "I know you. You hate to leave anything unfinished. It'll take more than a year to turnaround Brookland."

"I know that. I was sent to get the ball rolling and that is it. I'll train someone else to carryon when I return fulltime as ombudsmen."

"Hey, your job is waiting on you. The ball is in your court. You can come back Monday if you want to."

"I promised a year."

"Okay, a year it is."

CHAPTER 9

The Missing Journal

Ashley searched all over for her journal at the library on Friday. Frustrated, she was near tears when Harvey found her.

"I didn't see you when you…" he halted, noticing her pink eyes. "What's wrong?"

"Nothing," she fibbed.

"Something is wrong." Harvey put his arm around her shoulder, drawing Ashley closer to him. "You can talk to me about anything, Ashley. We have always been friends. I know something is troubling you."

She leaned into his embrace, needing to be comforted. "I can't find my journal."

"The purple one with the pink flowers?" Harvey had seen it so many times before. She wrote in it every time she got a break.

"Yes."

"And you think it's here?"

"It's not a home," she shrugged. "I have to find it."

"I'll look around for it." Always the one to come to her rescue, Harvey reached up and tenderly with his thumbs, wiped Ashley's tears away. "Why don't you go into the bathroom and freshen up." Her hair was like peach-fuzz. Harvey could tell when things were not right with Ashley because on those days she would rarely take the time to do anything with her naturally wavy hair.

Self-consciously, Ashley patted down her hair, knowing she looked a horrible mess. "Thank you." Ashley smiled and then walked away.

Harvey checked every inch of the library for the missing journal, but to no avail could he find it. He had hoped and prayed that he could give Ashley the one thing that mattered a great deal to her. So, he did the next best thing to ease Ashley's mind.

During their noon lunch break, Harvey and Ashley met at the park. Harvey placed a wrapped box on the picnic table.

"Harvey," Ashley reluctantly opened the box exposing a new journal, "you shouldn't have."

"I wanted to." Harvey reached for her hand and held it snuggly. "I know it will not replace the one you have lost. But for now, you can use it until you find the other one."

"Thanks."

"You are very welcome." Harvey's gaze lingered, which made Ashley obviously uncomfortable. Pulling her hand away, Ashley took a sip of ice-tea.

"A chicken salad sandwich for you," he handed it to her, "and one for me."

"I'm really not hungry." The thought of food made Ashley's stomach churn.

"You have to eat, Ashley," Harvey encouraged. "You're losing too much weight."

"I'll take it with me," she looked at him. "I'll eat it later."

"You promise?"

"I promise."

"So, is Thomas looking forward to the game Sunday?"

"He can't talk about anything else. I think this is going to be so good for him. He needs something positive in his life. I feel like he is missing out on so many things. No longer able to play basketball has produced a dormant anger. Consequently, he's acting out and getting into trouble."

"Could be," Harvey nodded. "I'll have to start doing more things with him on the weekends."

"That's so sweet of you." Harvey was such a thoughtful person. If only she could think of Harvey romantically. *He would be good for Thomas, for sure.*

"Can I take you home today?" Harvey asked, no strings attached. "I worry about you. You look so tired, Ashley."

"Okay." She did not have the strength to argue.

Her response nearly knocked him off the bench. "Good." *Maybe she will say yes after all.*

Later, the ride home was rather pleasant. Harvey put in a jazz CD, which was relaxing. "Just sit back and close your eyes," he suggested. "Allow yourself time to unwind before going home to cook."

She looked over at him, appreciating his kindness. "Thanks."

"Anytime," he winked.

Quickly, Ashley had fallen asleep. Once he pulled up at her door, Harvey hated to wake her up. Turning his car off, impulsively, he fumbled through Ashley's purse for her house-keys. Quietly, he got out of the car and opened the passenger's door. Carefully, Harvey picked Ashley up, eased her out of the car, and then carried her into her house.

"Ashley!" Harvey heard the frail voice calling out her name.

Hurriedly, he walked to the mother's bedroom and put his finger over his lips, to silence the mother from calling Ashley's name again. Worry was etched all over the mother's face as she witnessed her lifeless daughter in Harvey's arms.

Next, Harvey laid Ashley on the bottom of one of the bunk beds. Looking down at her, Harvey felt attached to Ashley. She meant the world to him. He wanted to take care of her. Truthfully, she was the closest person he had in his life. Being an only child, and his parents both deceased, Harvey longed for a family of his own.

"What's wrong with my Ashley?" the mother asked the instant Harvey entered her room.

"I think she's just tired," Harvey answered. "She fell asleep in the car and I didn't want to wake her. I figured I could just cook something if you don't mind."

"I couldn't let you do that," Sandra felt helpless. "Just help me up."

"No, Ma'am," he shook his head. "I know you don't feel up to it. I can cook. Really I can."

"I'm feeling better today," Sandra fibbed. "I just need you to help me up."

Hesitating, Harvey assisted Ms. Finley upward. She grunted and moaned several times, as he pushed the wheelchair near the bed. It took a while, but finally, he had her comfortably in the wheelchair.

Harvey pushed her into the kitchen and followed her orders. "There should be some noodles in that cabinet," she ordered. Before the children came home, Harvey and Ms. Finley had prepared meatless spaghetti and green beans from a can.

"Smells good in here!" Donald and Danny trotted in first with Lacey following closely behind them.

"Momma!" They all shouted, shocked to see her in the kitchen.

With tears, she hugged them all.

"You're healed, Mommy," Lacey held onto her. "I prayed really hard for you last night."

"I know you did, Sweetie." Sandra missed their warm hugs. Even though she was in much pain, witnessing her children's happiness made the pain worth it.

The buzzing commotion stirred Ashley. Groggily, she looked around, confused to why she was lying in Lacey's bed. Swiftly, she leaped up. Something was wrong. She had things to do. She had to cook and get the children ready to do homework before going to *The Palace*.

Running out of the room, "What in the world…" Ashley stopped moving and talking. Her eyes had to be deceiving her. Her mother was in the wheelchair, the one that sat on the side of her room, never used.

"Mother! What are you doing up? Do you feel alright?"

"I'm fine." Sandra gently stroked her daughter's unkempt hair. "Harvey helped me cook dinner."

Once again, tears freely flowed as Ashley looked up at the young man who had been her guardian angel for so many years.

"Thank you," she mouthed.

"You are welcome," he mouthed back. "I better be going."

"Oh, no, you don't," Sandra intervened. "You're having supper with us tonight."

"I don't want to intrude."

'You are not intruding," Sandra, stated firmly. "You are practically family, anyway."

Harvey felt thrilled by her statement, while his gaze rested on Ashley. Suddenly, Ashley felt as if she were suffocating. Why couldn't her mind wrap around the idea of committing to Harvey? He was her best friend. And his actions today surely made him go up a notch or two in her book. But was that enough for her to reconsider his marriage proposal?

People should marry their best friends, shouldn't they?

Looking around, Ashley panicked. "Where is Thomas?"

"He was talking to some guy and told us to go on home. He'll be here shortly," Donny answered.

"He yelled at us," Danny added.

"Yeah, he was mean," Lacy finalized.

Ashley fretted.

Timely, Thomas sauntered in, stopping at the sight of his mother. "Mom!"

"Hey, Thomas, you're late," gently Sandra chastised.

"Sorry," he wrapped his arms around her.

Everyone sat down for dinner. Thomas was bowled over to see his mother. Glancing at her often during the meal, Thomas noticed her squint a few times, obviously in pain. Yet, Sandra endured the pain, staying with her children, until Angela wisely insisted she returned to her bedroom for rest.

Harvey stayed until it was time to take Ashley to work, though she protested often.

"And I can't believe I fell asleep, like that," she said on the way to *The Palace.*

"Your body expired because you're pushing it too hard."

"I can't believe mother was up today. She hasn't been up in weeks." Ashley chattered freely. "Thanks for helping her today. I think you made her feel useful again."

"She is useful," Harvey acknowledged. "I think she needs to get up more. That will not only help you, but it will help her."

"I try to get her up, but she refuses."

"Today when she saw me carrying you, her face turned pale as a ghost. I think it frightened her to get up."

"Perhaps. I just want her to get better. After my father died, a part of her died with him."

"That happens when couples are so close."

"The thing is, I don't think they were that close," Ashley openly expressed. "You know how my dad was gone all the time. I mean, he took care of our family, financially; but he stayed away more than he was home. Somehow, back then, momma would not allow the disease to get the best of her. She would fight back. I mean she was bedridden sometimes, but not for long periods. She took care of us. When I went away for college, she ran the household."

"I know," Harvey stated. "She was active in the church back then, too."

"Yes, she was," Ashley sighed. "I miss her. It was so good to see a little bit of that tonight."

"It was." Harvey pulled in front of The Palace. "Can I pick you up tonight?"

"No thanks," she hopped out. "Pam and I ride together. Thanks again." Ashley trotted away, feeling rested and refreshed.

"Well, don't you look better," Pam was the first to notice. "You've actually combed your hair."

"I always comb my hair. It's just that sometimes I don't put oil or lotion on it to keep the curls from frizzing up."

"You're so lucky to have such good hair," Pam playfully pouted. "My hair doesn't frizz; it's just kinky, nappy hair.... you know like most black people. You got hair like white people."

"You're crazy!"

"That I am," Pam chuckled. "Crazy as a bat. Speaking of bats, have you noticed the outfit Ms. Melrose has on tonight. She's glittering more than the lights."

Ashley chuckled.

"Shoot," Pam went on, "we can turn out all the lights, put Ms. Melrose in the middle of the stage, and she'll light up the stage all by herself."

"Ladies," Ms. Melrose interrupted.

"Ms. Melrose," Pam nearly choked, "you look so lovely tonight."

"Well, thank you, Pam." Ms. Melrose delighted in the compliment. "My husband bought me this. It cost a pretty-penny, I tell you."

"I bet it did," Pam stifled her humor.

Ashley bit her lip, trying hard not to laugh aloud.

"Well ladies, we do have customers."

"Yes, Ma'am," Pam saluted. "We were just about to wait on them."

"That was close," Ashley mumbled as they walked outside the kitchen.

"Whatever!" Pam spoke nonchalantly. "Riding with Andrew tonight, aren't we?"

"I guess, if it's not any trouble."

"He likes taking us home," Pam stated. "It makes him feel like he's doing his *Christianly* duty or something. Doesn't matter to me why, I just don't want to ride the bus."

"Okay."

CHAPTER 10

Thomas' Crossroad

Ashley arose from her slumber feeling invigorated. Truly, God had blessed her with a peaceful, restful night of sleep. For that, she was thankful. Today would be a great day. It was Saturday and she only had to work one job, *The Palace*, which also meant that she had the good fortune of sleeping longer.

Out of habit, Ashley reached for her purse to get her journal. Heaving a low-pitched moan, she opened the new journal, while missing the old. Accustomed to writing out her thoughts before preparing breakfast for the family, soothed Ashley.

Last night Pam was not herself. Her fake smiles, bogus laughter, and chipper attitude did not fool me. Behind the mask, I can hear the cries of her wounded soul. Like a frighten child, trusting no man, Pam avoided eye contact with her male customers. She is walking in fear and understandably, after what she has endured. She needs the Lord. In the midst of darkness, may my light shine so that she can see Jesus, through me.

Dropping to her knees, Ashley bowed her head and prayed. Nothing would keep her from her daily moments with God.

"I'm hungry," Lacey trotted in the family room. "Can you cook blueberry pancakes?"

"What about grits and toast with jelly?" Ashley sat up, offering her sister a compromise since they were out of pancake mix. Gently, Ashley positioned her sister on her knee.

"Scramble eggs, too?"

"Not today, Lacey," Ashley answered. "I'll make the grits with extra love and the toast with extra sweetness so that you will not want anything else."

"Okay, Sis." The seven-year-old was satisfied. Lacey loved her big sister so much that it did not matter what Ashley cooked or what she did, Lacey knew it would turn out good.

"Alright, since you're the first up, I'll prepare your bath and get your clothes out. By the time you finish up, breakfast will be waiting."

"I hope so," Lacey pouted. "I'm really hungry. We didn't eat much last night," she trotted after her sister. It was true. After eating spaghetti, which stretched to seven people, the kids didn't get a snack or anything afterwards. "I just took a bath. I don't need another one."

"You need a bath every day to stay soft and clean," Ashley bent over and caressed Lacey's chubby cheeks.

"Like you?"

One couldn't help but adore Lacey. She was so innocent and loving. "Like me," Ashley playfully pinched her nose, then scooped the little one up and carried her into the bathroom.

Checking on her mother before going into the kitchen, Ashley let loose a loud sigh as she felt her mother's forehead. "Mother, you're burning up."

Sandra forced her eyelids opened. "I don't feel good. My body is aching all over and my legs…."

Ashley pulled the covers back to find both of her mother's legs swollen. "You overdid it yesterday."

"I'd do it again to make things easier on you," Sandra's eyes watered.

"I'm fine, mother." Ashley rushed away and got her mother's medicine. Swiftly returning Ashley handed her mother a glass of water and her medication. "Your knees and ankles are swollen badly. The deformity in your right knee is more noticeable, as well. I think you are going to need a shot. I'll call Dr. Phelps."

"I think you're right," her voice was weak.

"He said the last time you needed to exercise your joints. They have flared up again."

"I can't exercise," the mother rebuffed. "I am in too much pain. Dr. Phelps doesn't understand."

Ashley wanted to refute her mother's claim about Dr. Phelps but knew it would only upset her more.

"If you want to function without a wheelchair and constant pain, maybe you should consider the knee replacement surgery Dr. Phelps mentioned to you."

"I'm not having surgery!" Sandra shook her head back and forth in denial. "What can't be cured must be endured."

Perhaps, you should believe God for a cure, instead of enduring! Ashley pushed back the loose strands of hair from her mother's wet face. Sandra used to have such thick, long hair, but now it was thinning due to the medication. "I'm going to fix breakfast. You rest and I'll check up on you after I speak with the doctor."

"Call him first." Sandra was in an extreme amount of pain. She couldn't endure much more.

"I will." Ashley went to the kitchen and dialed the familiar number. She was so grateful that Dr. Phelps still did house calls. There was no way she could get her mother out of the house. A lack of exercise and movement resulted in Sandra's debilitation. Every time she exerted herself, like sharing a simple meal with the family, the next few days she would be so ill and even more dependent on Ashley and Thomas.

♥ ♥ ♥

The family was just finishing breakfast when Dr. Phelps finally arrived. The moaning and groaning sounds, from their mother's bedroom were upsetting the children, especially Lacey.

"Go tidy up your room quietly," Ashley spoke to the children, "and make sure there is nothing on the floor, under the beds, or on the dressers that shouldn't be there."

Donny, Danny, and Lacey heeded their sister's orders. Thomas remained by her side. He was the *man* of the house. "I want to hear what the doctor has to say. It seems that mother is worse."

Both Thomas and Ashley followed Dr. Phelps into their mother's bedroom, talking briefly before going in.

"Thanks for coming Dr. Phelps," Ashley said again.

"No problem at all," he replied, dressed down wearing blue jeans and a green polo shirt. "Did your mother have any medication at all this morning?"

"Yes, her normal medicine, but it's not working," Ashley answered. "She used her wheelchair yesterday. She even helped prepare dinner and ate with us. I think she overdid it."

"Actually, she needs to do more of it." Dr. Phelps admonished again. "She's not active enough. That's why her joints are so stiff and continue to inflame. I don't want her to overexert herself, but she needs to start living again."

Amen to that! Ashley kept quiet.

"But how can she when she's hurting so badly?" Thomas asked.

"Some days are worse than others," Dr. Phelps spoke to Thomas like a man, not sugarcoating anything. "Your mother has severe Rheumatoid Arthritis and she needs two knee replacements, one at a time, of course. She can live a rather normal life if she would—would—do more."

Thomas glanced at his sister. He was confused. If it were up to his mother, then why did she not fight? Why did she just lie there and just give up?

"We'll talk later," Ashley perceived his puzzlement.

After checking Sandra's vital signs and her legs again, Dr. Phelps left about thirty minutes later. He gave Sandra a corticosteroid shot, which would make her sleep for a while and hopefully, reduce some of the inflammation.

"What's all this mumbo jumbo about momma needing to do more?" Thomas asked after the doctor left. "How can she? Isn't she too ill to do anything?"

"Mother is depressed," Ashley answered, walking toward the kitchen to clean up the dishes. "After father died, she didn't have the willpower to fight the disease anymore."

"You mean she just gave up!" Thomas lifted his hands upward in disgust. "How could she? She has those children to think about. Look at what you have given up for her! Your scholarship. Your future career. Now you are overworking yourself, probably to an early grave. And I cannot play basketball! What right does she have just to quit?"

"Hush Thomas," Ashley cautioned. "She can't help it. She is sick, physically and emotionally. We just have to keep praying for her."

"I'm tired of praying!" Thomas was bitter. "Nothing changes! We are still poor. You are still working two jobs. We are still eating beans and rice every day. Oh…but we did have meatless spaghetti with water-down sauce, yesterday. Prayer does not work!"

"Nonsense!" Ashley dried her hands on the dishtowel. "God always answers. It may not be the way we want Him to sometimes, but rest assured He answers. God does what is in our best interest because He sees the entire picture. We only see a piece of the puzzle at a time."

"Whatever!" That was his word for everything. Thomas stormed out the door and plopped himself on the steps outside. His *temper* flared, thinking about how drastically his life had changed.

"Thomas," Ashley followed him and sat next to him. "I know things are rough for us, but we have each other. Mother loves us and she needs us to be strong for her. We can't give up or else…she'll lose the fight."

Thomas looked at Ashley with fear in his eyes. "She'll die?"

"I'm not saying that at all," Ashley tried to alter her words. "I'm just saying that we have to help her, that's all."

"Is that enough, Ash?"

"With God, all things are possible." She quoted the verse that gave her hope in hopelessness.

"Hey Tommy Boy," a guy yelled Thomas' boyhood nickname. "Why don't you come shoot some ball with me and the guys?"

Thomas looked to his sister, his eyes pleaded for her to say yes. "I'm off punishment. You said I didn't have to wait until tomorrow since I've been doing good."

Ashley looked at the guy. He looked like trouble. She didn't know him, nor did she trust him. "We have to clean up."

"I'll clean up later, while you're at work," he whispered. "Please, I really want to play ball."

Ashley felt sorry for him. "It's not playing ball that I am worried about. Who is that guy?"

"He goes to Brookland," Thomas answered. "He's alright."

"He looks like he is in a gang."

"You think everybody looks like a gang banger around here. I live here and I'm not in a gang."

"You better not be!"

"Come on, Sis! I've been in ISS all week and stuck in the house. I need to play ball."

"Go ahead, but be back before by 4:30." She yelled as Thomas sprinted away.

Shaking her head, Ashley went inside. Her heart was at the point of breaking beneath the manifold of tests and trials. *Help, Lord!*

I could see the boy's blue underwear. His pants were sagging so far down! Lord, protect Thomas. The guy is not good for him. I wish we could move back to our old neighborhood. Thomas had good, Christian friends there.

Ashley suddenly felt a wave of melancholy. She yearned for their former life. Everything was doubly hard now.

Living in a two-bedroom duplex with six people was stifling and oppressing. No matter how hard she tried to concentrate on the positive, living under such conditions dampened her spirit. The pressure of holding it altogether overwhelmed her. Sucking up the tears, Ashley wiped her eyes, refusing to shed another tear. Now was not the time. She had a family to take care of. There was no time to wallow in pity. No time at all.

"What's that smell?" Ashley asked her brother as Thomas entered the kitchen.

"What smell?" Thomas scrunched up his nose, feigning ignorance. "I don't smell anything."

"Of course you don't." Ashley came closer to him and took in a whiff of her brother. "You've been smoking!"

"No, I haven't!" Thomas stepped back, chickenhearted. He knew his sister would not let up.

"Yes, you have!" Ashley tried to keep her voice down, though she was steaming mad. "Do you think I'm stupid or something? I know what marijuana smells like. How dare you come into this house reeking of drugs!"

"I only had a puff or two."

"A puff or two!" She repeated in disgust. "You know you have to look after the children. How in the world are you going to do that when you're high as a kite?"

"I'm not high!" Thomas attempted to walk away, but Ashley jerked him around to face her.

"This is too much, Thomas!" Ashley's eyes welled up with fresh tears. "I can't take anymore! Now, you are doing drugs. What's next?"

"Just chill. I'm not doing drugs." Deep down Thomas hated stressing his sister out. "Drake offered it to me. Everybody was watching to see if I would *punk out*. I just figure if I take a sniff of it, then they would stop calling me soft. You don't understand what it's like here. It is nothing like where we came from. It's tough here. If you don't fit in, then they rag you for life. I'm not going down like that."

"You are going down," Ashley refuted. "Down to the gutter just like them. How do you think God feels about what you're doing?"

Thomas shrugged his shoulders.

"He's disappointed," she answered for him. "Just like I am.

Now I have to go to work, worried that you might fall asleep or behave crazy or something. I don't know what kind of side effects the drugs may have on you."

"I only puffed a little. Not enough to make me high."

"I don't care how much you had. One puff is too much!" Ashley stopped talking when Danny entered the room.

"Can we go ahead and eat, Sis?" Danny asked.

"Yes. Just fix yourself a hotdog and potato salad. Make sure you only put mustard on Lacey's hotdog."

"You all right, Ash?" Danny noticed her red eyes.

"I'm fine. Don't worry about me." Ashley went to him and hugged him. "I better finish getting ready for work." Ashley exited the room just in time before the water dam broke. Once more, Thomas broke her heart.

"You always make Ash cry," Danny rolled his eyes.

"Shut up!" Thomas barked.

Following, Ashley joined them at the table, eating only potato salad. She was saving the hotdogs for everyone else. They had eight franks, so her siblings could each have two hotdogs, which was a rare treat for them.

"Thanks for the hotdogs," Thomas mumbled at the table, so glad not to have beans and rice again.

"Harvey brought them by earlier."

After dinner, she rushed outside, afraid she would miss her bus. Thomas followed her outside.

"Ash, I'm sorry." He really meant it. Being a teenager in this neighborhood was hard. If only his sister could understand.

"You have to stop messing up, Thomas," she looked at him with sincerity and love. "Instead of turning to the world for acceptance, you need to turn the Lord for His approval. Let Him give you your identity and not the world.

"Be the young man He created you to be. Remember what Pastor Smallwood says all the time. *If you don't know who you are, anybody can label you. If you don't know where you are going, anybody can lead you anywhere. And if you don't know Who you belong to, anybody can control you.* Who is controlling you, Thomas?"

He didn't answer. "I have to go. Take care of the children."

Despondent, Thomas watched his sister running, flagging down the bus. Thankfully, it stopped for her. Thomas' restless spirit moved like troubled waters in a thunderstorm. He was definitely at a crossroad in his life—leading to either hopelessness or happiness.

CHAPTER 11

Jefferson & Jefferson

"**Y**ou look a mess," Pam made a face. "What's up with the hair?"

Ashley fumbled with her bun, securing it with a few more hairpins. As usual, she wore her only black dress, the one she wore every Saturday since Ms. Melrose required them to dress in all black on Saturdays. The simple dress fitted her small frame, making Ashley look her young age. It was so unlike the long, granny black skirt and the old-fashioned white ruffled shirt, buttoning up to her neckline, which Ashley wore most days.

"Thanks a lot," Ashley poured water in the fancy goblets for her customers at table one. "It's been one of those days."

"Should have been nice, since you didn't have to work at the library. You were either crying or didn't get sleep last night because your eyes are rather puffy." Pam turned to her. "Which is it?"

"Neither," she fibbed.

"Liar," Pam retaliated. "What happened? Is it your mother?"

"She had a rough morning. I had to call Dr. Phelps to come over and give her a shot."

"Poor thing," Pam sympathized. "I don't know how you do it. You're a mother to your siblings, caretaker for your mother, provider for your family and you're only twenty-three-years-old. You should win some kind of humanitarian award for being such a good person."

"It's my family." Ashley picked up the tray with the goblets on it. "What else am I to do?"

"I'd put my mother in a nursing home, put the kids in foster care and live my life."

"You wouldn't. Your heart is bigger than mine—you just hide it so others can't see it."

"Yeah, but after dealing with all those struggles, I'd need a heart transplant."

"Some days I feel like I need one," Ashley admitted sorrowfully. "Then most days I wouldn't trade it for anything. I love my family very much."

"All that love is dragging you down, Ash." Pam chewed on her gum, which went against Ms. Melrose long list of rules.

"I'm fine."

"Sure you are," sarcastically Pam retorted. "That's why your eyes are red, your hair a mess, and your shoes don't match."

Ashley inhaled deeply, realizing she had on the same shoes, but different colors–black and dark brown. "Oh, my goodness, what am I going to do?"

"Nobody will notice," Pam grinned. "Just walk around like you don't know and no one else will."

"I was rushing out," she tried to explain. "Thomas…"

"What has he done this time?"

"Nothing I care to talk about right now. I better take these drinks to table one. Talk to you later." Ashley walked away and then hurried back to her friend. "What's wrong with my hair?"

"Why don't you just take this bun out? It's not right." Pam started unpinning her hair without asking. "You need to wear it down sometimes. Act your age. You dress too *old-fashioned.*"

"You mean, show more skin like you," Ashley chuckled. "That's not me."

"See!" Pam removed Ashley's hair barrette and used her fingers to comb through her hair. "Ash, you look great. It's amazing how just allowing your hair to hang loosely accentuates your natural beauty. You have the most beautiful, natural, wavy, black hair I have ever seen. You should wear it down more often." Pam pinched Ashley's cheeks, making them turn a soft shade pink. Then, against Ashley's wishes, Pam retrieved her lip-gloss from her pocket and put a small amount on her friend's full lips.

"Oh, I don't know about this," she puckered her lips. Ashley felt weird. She hardly ever let her hair down. In college, she wore it free when she was dating Keith because he insisted she do so. She hated having to comb through it after wearing it down for a long period of time because it tangled so easily.

"Wait!" Pam took her mascara out of the small pouch. "Close your eyes."

"No."

"Close your eyes!" Pam repeated firmly. Ashley succumbed. Pam brushed on the mascara on Ashley's long lashes, making them appear thicker and longer. "Open up."

Ashley obeyed.

"Wow! Your crystal eyes pop now!"

"You are crazy!"

"And you are stunning," Pam stood in awe. "Now, go!" Pam pushed her forward. "Your customers are waiting and I see the witch coming."

"Hush!"

The Palace was filled to capacity. Not a single seat was empty. The live entertainment for tonight was Gabrielle Lane, a renowned jazz singer/actress. Reservations were booked months in advance. Ashley and her co-workers worked nonstop, as usual. No one complained because the tips tonight were sure to be substantial.

Several times upon picking up orders, Ashley noticed how Andrew was gawking at her. It unnerved her greatly. Finally, she had to say something.

"Stop staring at me. You're no Christian. You're a pervert!" Ashley stumped away.

"What's wrong?" Pam caught up to her.

"I'm not riding with that pervert ever again! He's got a sick mind and I don't trust him." Ashley judged him harshly.

Pam had never seen her friend so mad. "Did he say something?"

"Nope, but his *beady* eyes sure did. He was undressing me with his eyes. Hope he got an eyeful because that is the last time. Next time, I am going to Ms. Melrose and report him."

"Hold up," Pam cautioned. "He's a good chef. From what I have heard, he is one of the best. You can't go ruining his name because he's staring at you. Who wouldn't? Have you seen yourself tonight? Go to the ladies' room and take a good look at yourself. Letting your hair down makes a difference, not to mention you have the prettiest eyes in the world, and the mascara even makes them stand out more. You're gorgeous Ash, with a figure to die for."

"Please! It's still not right." Ashley was still mad. "He says he's a Christian, but he's always looking me up and down with one thing on his mind."

"They all do," Pam chuckled. "The only true Christian I know is you."

Ashley took in a deep breath, trying to calm her nerves. "Okay, I won't tell this time, but if he keeps it up, I'm going to have a talk with Ms. Melrose."

"Okay. I will back you up."

"I have new customers. See you in few." Ashley walked away disheartened by it all.

"Good evening. My name is Ashley," she began, taking out her pad. "What would like for.....d-r-i-n-k-s?"

"I'd like brandy," the older man spoke.

"Raspberry tea for me," Gregg Jefferson spoke, happily amazed to see Thomas' sister again. His eyes fastened upon her with a look she could not explain. Yet, it made her shiver inside. "What a pleasant surprise seeing you here."

"I uh, work here," Ashley stuttered. "I'll be back with your drinks." Ridiculously, she was ready to run for cover. Something about Dr. Jefferson made her feel skittishly scatterbrained.

"Miss!" called out the older man. "You can go ahead and bring us some garlic bread with the special house cheese sauce."

"Yes, Sir," Ashley smiled at the man.

"You know her?" his father asked. "She's a looker."

Yes, she is! Wow! She looks so different tonight. She should wear her hair down more often. And those eyes... Gregg cleared his throat. "She's a sister of one of the students at Brookland."

"So you know the *sisters* of your students?" with satire Mr. Jefferson spoke. "Must be a small school."

He couldn't wait even ten minutes before he found some way to belittle his son's accomplishments. "I oversee approximately 160 plus employees and over 900 students. It's a good size school," Gregg replied defensively.

"All the more why it doesn't make sense that you would know the sister of a student. I mean, I don't know the relatives of my employees."

"You own Jefferson Realty, not a school. There is no comparison. Besides, her brother, Thomas, got into trouble and I had a meeting with her before letting him return to school."

"Why didn't the mother come?"

"I think she was sick."

"She is a young, pretty lady for sure. I wonder if she is educated. She's working at *The Palace*. No education is required here."

"What difference does that make?" Gregg's voice was edgy. He loathed when his dad presumptuously judged people according to their occupations, clothes, cars, neighborhoods, or family's name.

"None I guess, unless you're seeing her," his father poked fun, behaving his true-persnickety-self. "Then that would be another story. Can't be dating common, low-class people. Remember, you're of royal blood. Your grandfather came from a genealogy of noblemen and women."

"Excuse me," Gregg had had enough. "I need to…uh… make a phone call."

"Now!" Mr. Jefferson was perturbed. "Sit down. Your phone call can surely wait."

"It cannot." Gregg firmly stated and walked away. *I can't take it! He'll never change!*

"Are you okay?" Ashley saw him barging off and followed him to the side entrance door.

"Uh…yes." Gregg ran his fingers through his hair. "My

father is too much. He knows how to push my buttons, that's for sure."

"When you allow someone else's words or actions to upset you, you're allowing them to control you. You give them power over you. In order to maintain your power, you have to overlook their offense."

Her words were true. Every time he was in his father's presence, he became unglued just by the things his father would say. He gave his father power over him.

"You're a wise woman," his eyes held hers for a moment.

Ashley smiled, her cheeks slightly inflamed. Her stomach was doing some strange things…churning, flip-flopping and fluttering all at once. Gregg had this effect on her.

The two seemed to be in a trance, neither moving nor neither saying anything.

"Ash," Pam approached them.

"I better go."

"Sure." Gregg watched her walk away and then returned to his table.

"Happy Birthday," Gregg returned, pretending to be in a cheerful mood. "This is for you." Gregg handed him a small gift-wrapped box, he retrieved from his coat jacket.

"Oh, you actually bought me a gift." Mr. Jefferson jabbed again with his mouth. "A timepiece," his comment was expressionless. "I don't think I have one of these. Thanks, Son."

"You're welcome." Gregg let out a repressed breath. He could never please his father, not even with presents.

"Although, I don't know what I am going to do with it. I have this Rolex already," Mr. Jefferson thrust out his arm, exposing the expensive watch.

Shove it wear the sun don't shine! Gregg thought as Ashley returned with their drinks and garlic bread just in the nick of time. Gregg smiled up at her, recalling her words not to give his father power. *It's going to be a long night!*

"Today, our house specials are..." Ashley rattled them off from memory, while Gregg rudely stared at her.

She's gorgeous. She doesn't look so spinsterhood tonight. Gregg was so absorbed in watching her that he only heard the first house special. The other specials were a little hazy.

"Are you ready to order?" Ashley politely asked the older gentleman.

"Yes." Mr. Jefferson answered and then ordered for them both.

"I think I'll have something else." Gregg stiffly intervened. "I'll have the first house special."

"That will be the fettuccine pasta sautéed with smoked chicken and green peas with mascarpone cheese." Ashley smiled as if she knew a secret. "That's one of my favorites."

"Good." Gregg handed Ashley the menu. His eyes lingered on her.

"Will there be anything else?" Once again, her cheeks flushed, appearing as if she had on rouge, which enhanced her beauty even more to Gregg.

She's blushing!

"I don't see why you didn't get lobster, as usual," his father's overtone was surly, for sure. "You always have to be contrary." Mr. Jefferson handed Ashley the menu, intentionally not looking up at her.

Gregg stared at his father, taking a few deep breaths before responding. "I don't like lobster," his tone was tense.

"You used to love it."

"No," Gregg spoke through gritted teeth. "I only ate it to please you."

Mr. Jefferson looked to his son, receiving the news as a shocker indeed. "That is juvenile behavior. A real man speaks the truth instead of pretending he likes something when obviously, he doesn't."

Ashley felt uncomfortable standing between the two squabbling grown men. If she didn't know better, she would think they were complete strangers.

Gregg looked at Ashley and felt somewhat remorseful. Looking down, avoiding Ashley's hypnotic crystalline eyes, he glimpsed her mixed-matched shoes. His forehead instantly creased. "Umm…that will be all."

"Yes…of course." Ashley's eyes met his for a fleeting second before she turned tail, making a dash for the kitchen. She wanted to crawl under a rock and stay there for the rest of the night. *Now he must think I'm loco for sure wearing mixed-matched shoes!*

"What's the matter?" asked Andrew, noticing her pallid face, when she pushed opened the kitchen door.

"Nothing!" She turned from him.

"Hey, I'm sorry if I am making you uncomfortable," he said, "but I don't mean too."

"Then stop staring at me!" She faced him with a look of wrath. "Every time I look up, you're watching me like a hawk."

"You remind me of someone," he reasoned. "And…"

"What's going on in here?" Ms. Melrose walked in.

"Nothing," Ashley answered, handing Andrew her customers' orders.

"It doesn't seem like nothing to me," she read fear in Ashley's transparent eyes. "Andrew is everything all right in here?"

"Yes, Ma'am," he busied himself with preparing the order. "All is well."

"I better go check on my customers." Ashley eased herself out of the kitchen.

In the meantime, father and son were finding it difficult to share a meal together.

"You embarrassed me in front of the waitress on purpose."

"I did not," Gregg scoffed. "All I said was that I didn't like lobster."

"It was what you didn't say that made the waitress turn white as snow," the father sipped his brandy. "Why do you have to be so obstinate? If I say the grass is green, you say it is brown. If I say it's raining, you say it is sunny."

"No, father," Gregg raised his voice slightly. "I have always agreed with whatever you said. However, that was when I was a boy, now I am a man. I can think for myself. I do not have to eat lobster to please you, not that it did anyway. Nothing I ever did pleased you."

"You went into education, making measly money when you could have been vice-president of Jefferson Realty, rolling in the money."

"That's it, isn't dad?" Gregg twisted uncomfortably in his chair. "You're still mad because I didn't follow in your footsteps. I did not want to do real estate. I love working in education. It's an honorable job and I make a pretty decent salary."

"It's alright for the average Joe, but you're not average. You don't come from an average family."

"Why did you call me here?" Gregg was annoyed and wanted this miserable dinner to be over.

"I thought my son would like to celebrate my birthday with me over dinner."

"If I recall, for your last birthday you were in Hawaii. The birthday before that you were in Jamaica. No, that was my birthday. You were in Tahiti."

"So what! I like to travel," Mr. Jefferson assented. "There is nothing wrong with seeing the world. Perhaps, you would travel more if you could afford it."

"I can afford it!" Gregg lashed back. "I just prefer being stable."

"That's what you call it."

The father and son's conversation came to a halt as Ashley served their meals.

Gregg kept looking at her, anything to calm his nerves. Being in her presence aroused something within his barren soul.

"Will there be anything else?" Ashley inquired.

"No!" Mr. Jefferson answered sharply. "That will be all."

Like father, like son! She quickly disappeared.

"I need for you to move back home." Mr. Jefferson uttered as if he was at some business meeting, barking orders to his employees.

Gregg nearly choked on his bread. "What? You can't be serious." *He must be out of his mind if he thinks I would ever move back into that mausoleum! It'll be a cold day in Hades before that happens!*

"I'm very serious." Mr. Jefferson took another sip of his brandy, feeling unsteady. "As a matter of fact, I need for you to move home immediately."

"No!" Gregg put down his fork. "I have my own home. It doesn't make sense. It's absurd, actually. Besides, when I was a child, you couldn't wait to get rid of me." Resentment toward his past plummeted forth as he spoke.

"Nonsense!"

"After mom died, you put me in a boarding school. Remember?" Gregg wanted to jog his memory. "I spent every birthday at a boarding school since the age of ten. Then during the summer, you signed me up for some camp, anyplace to keep me away from home."

"I was providing you with a good education," the father excused. "You had the best of everything."

"Except a father!" Gregg exploded. "You were never there for me and now you expect me just to move into your MANSION on a whim. That's nonsense, father! We can't even stay in the same room for ten minutes without disagreeing over something."

"It's not a whim." Mr. Jefferson's tone soften as he fixated his eyes on Gregg and awkwardly kept them there. "I'm having a heart bypass surgery on Friday."

Gregg sat speechlessly. A lump had lodged itself in his throat. He couldn't believe what he was hearing. It couldn't be. His father was never sick.

"It seems that I have multiple coronary artery blockages," he cleared his throat and continued. "Therefore a bypass is crucial for my survival. Without it, I would…die." The realization of such truth caused Mr. Jefferson to catch his breath before proceeding. "I need you to come home and help take care of me after the surgery. I could hire a nurse or some other outsider, but I figured…well…with you being my son that you would want to." Mr. Jefferson never had to ask anybody for anything. He could buy his way out of almost anything. The only thing he could not buy was his wife's health…and now his.

As a businessman, Gregory Jefferson was invincible, climbing the corporate latter of success without thought of others. He started at the bottom of the realty business, learning everything there was about selling, purchasing and investing in homes. He bought his first small Jefferson Realty Company when he was just twenty-four. Reared from a wealthy family, Mr. Jefferson never had to work a day in his life. However, he wanted to make his own mark. To this day, Mr. Jefferson had real estate offices in several states, all very lucrative offices.

Though Gregory Jefferson had always been a proud, hard man, his heart softened during his twelve-year marriage with his belated Sophia. Throughout their marriage, Sophia doted over her family. She established upfront that they were her priority. Gregory was a different man with Sophia. She made him happy. As his best friend and wife, Sophia could unveil the sensitive, caring side of him. After her sudden death, Gregory regressed back to his old ways. He reverted to being haughty, proud, and callous with everyone, especially his son. Gregg reminded him too much of Sophia. When he looked at his son, he saw Sophia, which was like adding salt to an open wound— constantly. He couldn't bear it. So he went on hiatus, the father keeping his distance from his own son. Weeks turned into months; months into years and years into the present condition of their relationship–dysfunctional–estranged–broken.

Gregg had his mother's hazelnut, slanted eyes. Also, like his mother, his hands were small, hair sandy brown, light complexion and he was tall, the exact opposite of his father. Mr. Jefferson was shorter and stocky, due to a lack of exercise and over-eating. He was dark-skinned in complexion, had narrow dark brown eyes and very thin lips.

"Senorita Rivas can help, but I refuse to impose on her like that," the father pled his case. "She was your mother's friend, and she's stayed, never complaining, even when...I didn't treat her kindly. I just couldn't ask that of her. The butler and my chauffer are still employed, but I can't ask hired help to take care of me."

Though the father and son sat in close proximity there was an iron curtain between them. Gregg did not know if he wanted to eradicate the wall. It kept him from being vulnerable to his father's ostracism again. It was Gregg's shield of protection.

I cannot do this!

For such a time as this! The words of his mother, Sophia, came to mind.

But…

For such a time as this… Were those his mother's words or…

CHAPTER 12

Not the Terminator after all

Timidly, Ashley approached the Jefferson's table. "Would you like more brandy, Sir?"

"No. Just some more water."

"More tea?" she faced the principal.

"Yes, please," he was glad for the distraction. She was definitely a distraction. *A person could get lost in her crystalline eyes. They are so large and magnetic, drawing the innocent bystander into its web unknowingly.*

Stop it!

"I'll be back." Ashley smiled and turned on her heels. The principal was rattling her feathers. He made her nervous and she could not understand it. After all, he was on her turf now. They were not at the school where he was running things and behaving like the Terminator.

"Well," Mr. Jefferson looked to his son, "are you going to move back home or not?"

"I…uh…yes…" he answered. Gregg's throat became dry and his palms were sweaty. *I sure could use a strong drink.*

"Good. I knew you wouldn't let me down."

"Just for a little while," Gregg amended, "until you get better. I still have to run a school, which is about an hour drive from your place."

"Can't you take a leave of absence or something?"

"No, I can't." Gregg became irritated again. This man practically pushed him out of his life and now expected him to just drop everything, for him. "I'll take off a few days, but that's about all. It is a busy time at school. Testing and…"

"I could die," Mr. Jefferson interrupted. "This is no light operation. I have a heart problem, among other health issues. Do you not understand how serious this is?"

"Yes." Gregg shifted nervously in his seat, grateful that Ashley was approaching their table again. "I will be with you through it all." He took a breather while she replenished their drinks.

God, help me! Gregg grimaced. *Where did that come from?* He hadn't talked to God in a long time.

"Will there be anything else?" Ashley asked.

"Just the check," Mr. Jefferson answered.

"Sure." Ashley left their table.

"Thanks for fitting me into your busy schedule," cynicism dripped from Mr. Jefferson's thin lips. The father felt helpless and at the mercy of his son, which left him in a vulnerable state. Mr. Jefferson hated being vulnerable to anyone. That chapter was closed in his life, since Sophia's death. Now, he had to reopen it again and it scared the father immensely.

"It's not like that father," Gregg never called him dad. It was too personal and signified they had a close-knit relationship. "I will be there for you. However, you must realize that this is awkward for me. We barely speak to each other. Now we are going to be staying under the same roof due to your illness, which I knew nothing about until tonight. Please give me a break. I need time for all of this soak in."

"Fine!"

"Fine!" Gregg wanted to scream.

"Gabrielle Lane will be performing in ten minutes," Ashley commented as she placed the check on the table.

"She's amazing," star-struck by the performer's talent, Gregg responded. "I'm looking forward to hearing her again.

"I'm not staying." Mr. Jefferson appeared to be pouting.

"Why not?" Gregg could not believe his father was pouting like a little spoiled boy, sore because he wasn't the center of attention anymore.

"I'm tired."

"Oh," Gregg felt guilty. "Should I see you home?"

"Don't be silly!" the father dismissed his son's thoughtfulness. "I'm not dying—yet." He stood up and handed Ashley money to cover the meal, plus a hundred-dollar bill for a tip.

The large bill both pleased Ashley and startled her. Never had she been tipped a hundred dollars. She stood there goggle-eyed. "Thank you, Sir," she stuttered.

"He's not dying," Gregg whispered, sounding not so convincing. "Excuse me," he stood up. "I'll be right back."

Ashley nodded.

"Father!" Gregg caught up to him outside the restaurant.

"Yes." Mr. Jefferson turned to his son.

"Happy Birthday!" Gregg awkwardly embraced him. The two never showed outwardly affection for one another.

His father held onto him a little longer and tighter. "Thanks, Son."

"I'll be there for you, Friday and I'll bring my clothes over on Thursday night."

"I appreciate it," Mr. Jefferson swallowed. It wasn't easy for him depending on anyone, especially since the father knew he had practically abandoned his son a long time ago. It hurt too much to love him or anyone else. Grief had occupied his heart for so long that there was no room in his heart to give or to receive love from his son—or anyone.

Gregg stood watching his father drive away. His shoulders slumped, his body tensed up at the thought that he was moving back home—even for a short-term.

How in the world can I go back to that gloomy place? There were no happy-home memories after his mother's death. When Gregg came home for a visit from boarding school or even college, he mostly spent it in isolation. His father was never home. If it weren't for the staff hired to maintain and keep up the mansion, Gregg would have had no one to talk to.

The housekeeper, Naomi Rivas, filled the parental gap as much as possible for the young Gregg whenever he was home. She would read to him, play games with him and even teach him how to cook simple meals. Gregg loved Ms. Rivas. She had a way of making him feel special and important. She never snubbed him or said she was too busy for him, like his father.

Realizing it was time for Gabrielle Lane to sing, Gregg shook off the memories and went back to his seat to enjoy the performance of a lifetime. The live entertainment would take his mind off moving back to the *mausoleum*.

"Is everything all right?" Ashley observed him returning. He did not look as self-assured as before.

"Umm…yes," he stammered out a response. "Can I please have your triple fudge cake with ice-cream?"

"Sure." Ashley was about to walk away, but he touched her

arm. The simple touch electrified her entire being. She pivoted to face him.

"I wanted to talk to you about Thomas."

What now? "Is he in trouble?"

"No." Gregg quickly answered, observing her worried look. "Perhaps, you can take a break."

"I have already had my fifteen-minute break," Ashley answered, noticing Ms. Melrose watching her. "I can't talk now."

Gregg looked around and saw the woman looking over in their direction. "What time do you get off?"

"Midnight."

"You don't turn into a pumpkin when the clock strikes twelve, do you?" Surprisingly Gregg had a sense of humor.

"Nope!" She played along. "I turn into a frog."

"I'd like to see that," his pearly white teeth sparkled.

Uncomfortably, she giggled. "You won't have to wait long. It'll be midnight before you know it."

"Can I take you home?" he asked without thinking.

"I...don't think..."

"So we can talk about Thomas." Gregg felt it his duty to tell her about the journal. "It's important."

"Sure, if you want to wait around until we close, which is about another two hours," she looked at her watch.

"I'll wait. Besides, I want to see your magic trick of turning into a frog."

"Maybe tonight I will just stay myself," her eyes twinkled like the stars.

His heart thundered. *That's even better!*

Ashley stood a moment, wondering about this principal everyone called the Terminator. Sure, he was brusque and rough on the outside, but his rugged mannerism was also charming. "See you later, out front," she stated and walked away.

Later, she spoke with Pam about riding home with her after work.

"Who is this guy?" Pam was surprised by tight-ship Ashley, who never gave a guy a second look. However, tonight when her friend spoke about the anonymous guy, her disposition rebooted, as if charged by this man.

"He's Thomas' principal. He wants to talk with me about Thomas."

"That boy is going to send you to an early grave," Pam spoke her mind. "What has he done now?"

"I don't know," she sighed. "Please, ride home with me."

"No, thanks. I'll just ride with Andrew. He doesn't give me the gaga look."

"Something is not right about him, Pam. I'd rather you ride with me."

"Are you scared?"

"Of course not. He may scare the students, but he doesn't scare me. The students call him the Terminator."

"Maybe you should be scared," Pam frowned.

"I'm not, but I am concerned about you riding with Andrew—alone. After what happened to you...."

"Don't go there," Pam held up her hand. "Andrew is different. He's no Randall. Besides, you promised not to talk about it."

"I'm sorry." Ashley was torn.

"Anyhow, you call me when you get home," Pam bounced back.

"I will. Let's go peep in on Gabrielle Lane."

"You go ahead," Pam snubbed. "All that jazz stuff depresses me."

"You're crazy. She is awesome. The lyrics of her songs are beautiful."

"Not my style."

"You need to broaden your music forte," Ashley winked.

"Hey, I like rap, hip-hop, and R&B…that's broadened enough for me!"

Gregg watched Ashley as she gracefully greeted her customers and devoted her attention to each one, making them feel inclusively important. Her smile was sweet and alluring. She carried the trays with ease, still managing to walk with grace. While waiting on her customers, Ashley appeared to be happy. However, when she was idle, looking around, there was an aura of sadness about her. Peculiarly, Gregg felt drawn to her. Everything about her was appealing. With her hair flowing freely down her shoulders, she appeared younger than when she was in his office or at the library. Standing still, motionless, watching Gabrielle Lane performance, Ashley appeared not to be standing alone. She was carrying a burden on her petite shoulders. *Thomas!* Then he thought about the journal that he had caught Thomas reading in ISS.

Why in the world would he have his sister's private journal?

While tending to her customers, Ashley felt Gregg's eyes boring upon her. She knew he was watching her, which made her skittish. A few times, she caught him in the act, and still he did not look away. Instead, his gaze intensified.

What is his problem? He is acting like Andrew. What is it with men? Yet, strangely, I'm not afraid of him.

Just before the restaurant closed, Gregg had Gabrielle Lane sign the CD he purchased in the foyer. Not only did she sign it, she boldly wrote her number on the CD cover.

123

"I'll be in town a few days," she flashed her long, fake eyelashes at him. "Would you like to show me around?"

"I'd love to." Gregg grinned like a school kid. "What about tomorrow?"

"Lovely," Gabrielle purred. "Call me around noon and we'll plan out our day." She then leaned over and kissed him on the cheek.

Ashley strolled out at that precise moment. Gregg was left standing with red lipstick on his cheek.

"You might want to wipe that off," Ashley walked ahead of him with jealousy right on her heels.

Gregg felt like an idiot. He was foolishly smitten by the songstress. *Who wouldn't be? She is Gabrielle Lane. Beautiful. Young. Talented. Famous.*

Wiping off the lipstick with his embroidered monogram handkerchief, Gregg strolled alongside Ashely and escorted her to his car.

"Let me get that for you," Gregg rushed to open the door for her.

Driving off, he buckled up, looked over at Ashley, and smiled. He had a look of enchantment in his eyes, and she, a look of complete terror.

"I promise I won't bite." Gregg's smile widened, once again revealing his straight-pearly whites.

Ashley's lips curb somewhat as she endeavored to make herself relax, which seemed impossible.

The Terminator is flirting with me. So what? A few moments ago, he was flirting with Gabrielle Lane. I can't hold a candle to her—and wouldn't want to.

No matter where he went, Gregg attracted women like a magnet. They flocked to him as if he were some famous movie star or rich athlete. Sure, he had the body, the good looks, and the charisma. And it didn't hurt that he was from a well-to-do family. He lived in a three-story home in an affluent neighborhood. His professional life of being an ombudsman and a principal was impressive to women. His bachelor's black book was filled with prospective dates, for Gregg dated often on the weekends because he hated being alone. Therefore, the bachelor crammed his free weekends with carefree dates, with no strings attached. Although Gregg would not be tied down by any woman, he refused to be alone for long.

"What about my brother?" Ashley addressed the reason she had agreed to ride with him in the first place.

"Are you missing something?"

"Huh?"

"Thomas was reading your journal in ISS."

"No!" she stammered. The revelation had kicked her in the gut and left her breathless. "He couldn't have."

"Is your journal purple with pink flowers and has Ashley Finley's Private Journey on the front?"

"Oh, my!" she gasped, her entire body shaking in disbelief. "I asked him, but he said he hadn't seen it."

"I thought you should know."

"Why would he take my journal and then lie about it?"

"Perhaps, he wants to know more about his big sister," Gregg surmised. "When my mother died, I read her diaries from beginning to end, all of them. I wanted to know what made her, her. She was such an extraordinary woman, but she was private. If she was hurting, you'd never know it. Anyhow, I missed her so much…." Abruptly, Gregg speech came to a sudden halt. He didn't know why he was ranting on and on about his private life. He never talked about his personal life to anyone—especially, not to females.

Ashley gazed over at him, sensing that the discussion of his personal life was over. Getting back to the matter at hand, she said, "Thomas had no right to take my journal. It was private and he knew it."

"You're right about that," Gregg agreed. "So now what?"

"I don't know," she shrugged. "He's my brother, but I am so tired of him."

Gregg figured there was more to her statement than she was saying. "He's a teenager."

"Did you smoke pot at his age?"

"No." Gregg turned to her. "Why? Is Thomas smoking?"

"When he came home today, he smelled like marijuana. He said he only had a puff or two."

"That's not good," Gregg stated, strangely disturbed by the news. "Your brother is a bright boy. Coach Koon says he has raw talent in basketball. He said it's been a long time since he came across an athlete so naturally talented like Thomas."

"He was good," Ashley smiled. "Those were the good days. Thomas loved basketball and he was good on and off the court. He had good grades, good friends and he never got into any trouble."

"Perhaps, basketball is the key."

"He can't play anymore," Ashley's tone flattened. "He has to help out at home."

"If Thomas could put his energy into basketball again, I think it will keep him from being idle and getting into trouble. Also, it will motivate him to keep up his grades," Gregg suggested, not really hearing Ashley's statement. "Coach Koon says if he pulls his grades up and stays out of trouble, he would gladly welcome Thomas back on the team."

"Did you hear me?" Ashley nearly shouted. "Thomas is needed at home to watch the children and momma."

Unable to say anything, Gregg pondered the predicament. So many of the young boys were like Thomas—Boys wearing men shoes. "Thomas needs basketball like you need your journal."

"Turn right here," she stated, thinking about Gregg's declaration. She was lost without putting her thoughts down on paper. She had to write. It was in her soul like bone to marrow, she needed it. It was her outlet. Her passion. Her purpose.

"That's my place," she pointed. "The yellow duplex," Ashley felt embarrassed. Her home was pitiful. The paint was chipping, the wood rotted and the place looked like a dump—just like all the other duplexes. The neighborhood was poverty-stricken and everybody knew it.

Parking his car in front of the duplex, Gregg turned off the engine and then turned to Ashley. "I know things are difficult right now, but I really want to help Thomas. He seems like a good student. He just needs to do what he likes and that is to play basketball. At one time, it helped him stay focus. I know he's needed at home, but possibly we can come up with some kind of arrangement."

"There's no arrangement to be made. There is no other family to help out." Ashley sounded so final. "Don't you think I want Thomas to play basketball? I hate robbing him of his childhood, of his dreams, but…but…" she could not hold back the tears. Covering her eyes with her hands, Ashley wept like a baby.

Feeling out of his league, Gregg leaned over and put his arm around her shoulder, drawing her into his embrace. "Just let it all out," he said. "Just go ahead and cry."

Unable to debate with him, Ashley released her inner turmoil through her tears. In his arms, her body quivered. He held her tight as possible with the inconvenience of the middle console between them. This was so unlike Gregg. He never allowed his guard to be down for then he would be susceptible to rejection or pain. Neither were acceptable to him.

Like father, like son.

Where did that come from?

Suddenly, feeling mortified, Ashley pulled away. "You must think I'm a wimpy, weak woman coming unglued with a stranger."

"Actually, we're not strangers." Gregg looked in her hypnotizing eyes, entranced by them. "And by far I could never think of you as a weak woman. You work at night, while Thomas takes care of the family. You are the family's sole provider. Thomas says you quit college your senior year to return home and take care of your sick mother and siblings.

"You work two jobs, having little or no time to yourself. In my book, I would say you are a woman of strength, character, and integrity. You are the epitome of a strong, black woman. I have only seen such unusual strength in one woman," he paused, "my mother."

With tenderness, Ashley looked over at him. The comparison to his mother touched her deeply. Words couldn't portray the value of such appraisal coming from Gregg the man, not Dr. Jefferson, the principal. At last, Ashley beheld his kind heart, hidden by his gruff exterior. He wasn't the Terminator after all.

"So, can Thomas stay after school to practice if the children were looked after?"

"That would be part of the solution," she nodded.

"What if Thomas could get the children after their school lets out and then bring them back to school with him. They can sit in the teachers' lounge and do homework until Thomas finishes practice. Coach Koon can bring them all home afterwards." Gregg was thinking aloud, working out the details as he went on. "You'd still come home and take care of your mother and prepare dinner or whatever you do."

"Sounds easy, but isn't that against some school policy?"

"I will be responsible for the children."

Ashley looked at him in awe. Yes, the Terminator had a heart after all. He was not as coldhearted as he seemed before.

"It can work. It'll take some effort on everyone's part, including the younger children. We can at least try it for Thomas' sake."

We! She didn't miss the pronoun linking them as a team. "How will Lacey, Donny and Danny get a snack? They're usually starving when they get home from school."

"Coach Koon always has something for the team. He'll see to it that they have something to eat."

"Okay," Ashley's eyes glistened. A burden had been lifted from her shoulders. A mixture of happy and frustrated tears spilled over in an abundance—again she was a bucket of tears.

"It's difficult, but not impossible." Gregg took out his handkerchief, reached over and wiped her tears away. If only life was that easy. "It will all work out. This is my purpose, to help young people obtain their education, maximize their skills, offer support and help them in becoming successful citizens," he uttered mechanically.

You were born for such a time as this!

Again, the whispering in his heart amazed Gregg. Suddenly, Ashley's countenance shone in the darkness.

Gregg felt thrilled to see her smile light up the darken car. She was so beautiful. All he could do was drank in her beauty like a cold drink on a hot day. So satisfying and so refreshing.

"Thanks, for everything," Ashley replied as she opened the door.

"Are you going to confront Thomas?"

"I have to."

"Don't be too hard on him. I think he just wants to know what makes his little sister tick." *I would sure like to know!* The thought shocked Gregg, as he looked away. "Well, you have a goodnight. We'll talk soon."

"Goodnight, Dr. Jefferson."

"Gregg," he corrected.

"Only if you call me Ashley," she offered a compromise.

"Goodnight Ashley," her name sounded like soft bells rolling off his lips.

"Goodnight Gregg," she waved and closed the door.

"By the way Ashley," he spoke through the opened window, "are you fashioning a new style with your shoes?" He smiled, showing no hint of sarcasm or pity.

Her cheeks flushed, looking down as if hoping her shoes had magically changed. "I was rushing out of the house."

"Just making sure. The students have all kinds of fashion statements. Wanted to be in the loop if this was a new one."

"Trust me. I'm never up-to-date with fashion. Thomas tells me all the time I dress from the old school and need to modernize my wardrobe."

"I guess we're two peas in a pod. I like old school."

"Me too."

Their eyes locked momentarily.

"Sleep well," he added.

"You too." Hesitantly, Ashley walked away. If only her time with Gregg could last a little longer. He made her feel hopeful. She hadn't felt that way in a long time.

All the way home Gregg could not understand how the humble woman had captured his attention. Every inch of her face, he traced through memory. She was gorgeous, but it was more to it than that. He had dated models. Yet, her beauty was fresh. Real. Pure. Authentic, nothing fake. No fake hair. No fake eyelashes. No fake body parts. Ashely was the real-deal, just like his mother. He hadn't met someone genuine and virtuous in a long time. *Ashley Finley is a rare gem! Mother would have liked her.*

CHAPTER 13

New shoes!

As customary, Sunday morning the Finley clan headed for the bus stop so they could attend the church they grew up in. This was their only link to their past life. Ashley allowed Danny, Donny, and Lacey to walk ahead, while she talked with Thomas.

"Is there anything you would like to tell me, Thomas?" Ashley began the conversation.

"Not really." Instantly, he felt convicted. "Other than I'm sorry about smoking."

"You should be and you better not do it again!" she said firmly keeping her eyes on her other siblings.

"I'm sorry for stressing you out."

"What else?"

He thought for some time before speaking again. "I don't know. Just tell me what you want me to say. I hate playing these stupid games with you."

"Do you have something that does not belong to you?"

Oh no! She knows! But how? I left the journal at school. She acts like a prophet. Always knowing my business with nobody saying a word.

Thomas halted and looked at her, "I'm sorry."

"For what?" Ashley would make him say it.

"For taking your journal."

"Why Thomas?" Ashley's tone elevated a notch or two. "Why would you take something so precious to me?"

"You left it on the table and…"

"That's no excuse! First, you steal from your teacher. Now, you're stealing from me."

Ouch! Low blow!

"I wanted to know something about you," Thomas stated simply. "You keep everything so bottled up. I just figured you'd be honest with the journal, but not with me."

Bewildered, Ashley pondered her brother's confession. Instantly, Gregg's words came to mind about how he read all of his mother's journals so he could find out what made her, her.

"My words are private," she finally spoke.

"Your life is private," Thomas retorted. "You try to be strong for all of us, but inside, you're dying. You're hiding. You're scared just like the rest of us."

"You don't know what you're talking about."

"You wrote that you were at a breaking point. You didn't know how much more you could take. You wrote that you felt guilty because momma was becoming a burden to you and you hated thinking that way."

"Hush up!" she scolded. "You had no right reading my personal journal. No right, Thomas Finley! And if you dare say another word about my journal to anyone I will never forgive you!"

"I just want my sister back." Thomas' voice cracked with emotion, mute tears held at bay. "I want my life back!"

Ashley stood still. Thomas was wounded, inside. She

observed his pain—and understood it. It sounded like her own silent war-cry. Her anger faded. She couldn't stay mad at her brother. They were both struggling, just handling things differently. Impulsively, Ashley wrapped her arms securely around Thomas, smothering him with her love. "If you want to know about me, just ask me."

"But that just it." Thomas looked down at her with moist eyes. "All you say is that you're fine and that God will take care of everything."

"He will."

"But look at us, Sis. We're living in the gutter. Mom is sick and refuses to fight for her life and for us. You're overworked and underpaid. We have little food. The lights were going to be cut off so that's why I took the iPad."

"I know," Ashley brushed his curly locks out of his face.

"Everything alright?" Danny and the others yelled back.

"Yes. We're coming." Ashley dried her eyes. "Let's go to church. We'll talk later."

"Can I still go to the game with Harvey?" Thomas just knew she would punish him. He deserved it.

"You can still go," she grabbed his hand, "but things have to change, Thomas. I want to trust you, but..."

"You can."

"You have to earn my trust, Thomas."

"I will." Thomas wanted nothing more. "Your journal is in my locker at school." He stopped walking. "How did you know?"

"God never has me ignorant," she had quoted for the zillionth time. "The Holy Spirit will always show me things to come. He tells me what I need to know."

"The Terminator told you," Thomas remembered him

looking at the book. "Didn't he?"

"Yes. God used him to tell me the truth."

"That dirty-rotten-snake!" Thomas bellowed. "He can't even mind his own business!"

"He was trying to help," Ashely whispered, moving forward. "He has a plan for you to play basketball again."

"What?" Thomas was flabbergasted, his heart halfheartedly lifted with hope.

"We'll talk later. Let's catch up with the children before they think something is wrong."

After church service, Harvey offered to take Ashley and the children home, as he always did. Once again, Ashley declined. It was hard for Harvey to understand that Ashley wanted to be independent, not dependent on a man like her mother. Anyway, today Ashley had other plans. She wanted to treat the children with the big tip she received from Mr. Jefferson. She would buy them some much needed shoes. All of her siblings needed shoes. So instead of going straight home from church or stopping by at the nearby park, the children rode the bus to the mall.

"We're not going to the park," Lacey made a sad face. "I wanted some ice-cream."

"Me too," Donny and Danny echoed.

Whenever Ashley had a few extra dollars, she would treat the children to ice-cream cones. They would walk to the park and just enjoy each other before going home for supper. It was her way of spending quality time together, allowing the kids the freedom just to be kids.

"It's a surprise," Ashley answered.

"I like surprises," Lacey sniggered.

"I'm hungry," Danny pouted.

"Me too," Donny copied.

"Hey Ash," Thomas leaned over her seat on the bus. "What's up? I have two dollars. I can pay for the ice-cream."

"The children can wait on ice-cream. I have a better surprise for them...and you," she said with a sheepish grin upon her face.

"For me?" he was puzzled. "I don't need anything. We can't afford anything, Ash."

"Stop worrying," Ashley shushed him. "I got this."

"How?"

"Someone blessed me last night; so I'm going to bless my family. Now, sit back before you ruin the surprise."

"You're crazy, Ash."

"I am," she whispered back. "I'm crazy about my family."

An hour later, Lacey, Danny, Donny and Thomas acted as if they had been given the greatest gift in the world. Trying on new shoes was a real treat for the siblings. They were all filled with unspeakable, indescribable joy. It had been a long time since they had something new. Most of their clothes and shoes came from thrift stores or were hand-me-downs from complete strangers or church folks. With wet eyes, Ashley felt overwhelmed witnessing their delight. Truly, they were all grateful.

"Thanks, Sis!" the twins squeezed her tightly in a loving embrace.

"You're the *bestest* sister in the whole-wide world," Lacey hugged her leg.

"Thanks, Ash." Thomas echoed.

"You are all welcome." her cup *runneth* over. *Lord, bless Mr. Jefferson a hundredfold in return! Heal, touch and deliver him in the area he needs it the most.*

"Can I wear my shoes now? My feet hurt!" Lacy entreated with puppy-dog eyes. "My old shoes are too tight."

"Me too!" Danny shouted.

"Mine hurt really bad," Donny added. "See, how small they are." He put the old shoe up to the new shoe to show the big difference. The old shoe was significantly smaller.

Ashley's heart dropped, struggling to keep her hurtful tears at bay. Her siblings had suffered, wearing their crammed tight shoes and none of them complained.

Father God, please let this be the last time they have to wear small shoes.

"God provided the money through one of His human angels on earth. I want you all to keep Mr. Jefferson in your prayers. He blessed us, so we're going to pray for him to be blessed. Okay?"

"Okay!" They all shouted.

"Harvey is here," Thomas let him in. He came early to take Thomas out to eat before the game.

Ashley, the twins, and Lacey were sitting on the couch, watching a movie. While her siblings remained glued to the television, Ashley got up to greet her friend.

"Hi Harvey. You look spiffy in jeans." She had never seen him in jeans before. He was more the khaki and oxford shirt kind of guy.

"Thanks." Harvey smiled, pleased that he had pleased Ashley.

"You two have a good time, tonight. Thomas, please be on your best behavior."

"I'm not a kid!"

"No, you are not."

"Well, us MEN," Harvey emphasized for Thomas's sake, "better be going." He bent over and pecked Ashley on the cheek. His spontaneous gesture caused her cheeks to flame.

Thomas chuckled. "I think I should be the one telling you to be on your best behavior."

"Go!" she shoved her brother.

"Don't wait up!" Thomas winked before closing the door.

That boy! He thinks he is grown!

Going back to the children, Ashley could not concentrate on the movie. Her mind drifted back and forth to Harvey.

Harvey sure has changed. I cannot believe he just kissed me on my cheek in front of Thomas. Now Thomas will think that we are an item, which we are absolutely not!

Ashley touched her cheek. Nothing. No sensation. No pleasant feeling. She just felt blah!

How can I just turn him down? Harvey has been so good to me. He is spending the day with Thomas, who needs a man in his life.

What am I going to do?

He who finds a wife, finds a good thing!

Horror nearly suffocated Ashley as the common verse arrested her heart.

He may have found me, but I am not the one!

"Momma," Ashley talked as she brushed her mother's long black curly hair. "Thomas needs our help."

"What's wrong with my baby?" Sandra's voice was husky with fright.

"Thomas has been getting into trouble and…"

"Not my Thomas," she cried.

"Don't cry, Momma, not now. I need for you to listen to me." Ashley would not allow her mother's tears to stop her from saying what needed to be said.

"You are mad at me," Sandra whimpered like a child. Truly, the mother-daughter roles were reversed.

"I'm not mad, Momma…but, this is not about you or me. It's about Thomas."

She nodded.

"Like I said, Thomas has been getting into trouble. He was suspended for stealing a teacher's iPad…"

"Stealing!" the mother gasped. Trying to protect her mother, Ashley had revealed none of Thomas' rebellious deeds to her mother. Now things were changing. They had to if Ashley wanted to keep her other siblings from falling through the cracks of this poverty life they were forced to live in.

"Yes, he stole it to help pay the electric bill, which was going to be turned off."

Things were worse than the mother had imagined. "Oh my! We're dirt poor and it's all my fault."

"We're not dirt poor," Ashley corrected. "Anyhow, Saturday Thomas reeked of marijuana. He says he only took a puff or two."

"My son is on drugs!"

"He's not yet; but, we have to help him."

"How?"

"He needs to play basketball. It is his life, Momma. He loves it."

The mother nodded

"So that means you are going to have to fight to get better. We need you to help us, Momma. Thomas will have to stay after school. Dr. Jefferson…"

"Who is that?"

"He's the principal at Thomas' school. He says that Thomas can bring the children over after school so he can stay at practice. However, he will have games on Tuesday and Fridays. The kids can't stay with him on most games days because of school." Ashley paused, giving her mother time to take in what she saying. "Do you think you can help out, especially on Tuesday and Fridays?"

Sandra wept. She had let all of them down. She had become a burden to the family instead of a caretaker. "I'll try."

"Momma, you're going to have to do more than try," Ashley had heard this promise so many times before. "You're going to have to just do it—by faith. Dr. Phelps says the more you get up and move about the better you will feel. Of course, you will have days when it is too hard, but they will become less. Thomas needs you." *I need you!*

"You don't understand my disease," Sandra reasoned. "The pain is unbearable."

"I know, Momma. I think you are more depressed than anything else. If you'd only take the medicine the doctor prescribed for your depression, you might feel better."

"I'm not taking that medicine. I am not depressed. I'm sick."

"Your heart is sick," Ashley's tears now matched her mother's.

"I loved my husband," Sandra's voice was hoarse with emotion, "and he died in another woman's arms." That was the first time Sandra spoke aloud the secret that everyone else knew. "He humiliated me over and over again, and I still loved him. I treated him with respect, though he gave me none. Still, he provided for us. We had a nice home and a good life."

"We had a house," Ashley interposed, "but it wasn't a home. We were all unhappy, walking on eggshells in his presence. One minute he was upbeat and then the next he was yelling and ranting about nothing. Truthfully, we were glad when he didn't come home. At least there would be peace in the house."

Sandra wheezed at her daughter's heart-wrenching admission. She did not know how miserable her children were then and how miserable they were now. "Tom provided for us." Sandra defended him still. "When I was sick, he took care of me."

"Financially, he did his part. We did not starve. We had a roof over our head. However, emotionally he was not there for us—not even for you, most times. You just pretended everything was all right." Ashley had wanted to speak these nuggets of truth for so long. "You say you loved him, but was it love mother, or dependency? Maybe you thought you couldn't do any better because of the disease. You fought the disease because of Tom," she hesitated, "but now you have surrendered to it."

Sandra closed her eyes as the teardrops continued to collide down her frail cheeks. She permitted her daughter's assumptions to sink in. Only the words were more than assumptions. They were the truth. Did she really love Tom even after he treated her so badly? Did she think she deserved it because he married her to cover up her secret? Sandra felt she had owed Tom a debt she could never make good. Sandra mourned the loss of a life of happiness and freedom. For truly, she carried a guilty stain, which marred her from experiencing goodness. Sandra opened her eyes for a moment and gazed up at her daughter. Ashley was beautiful and wise beyond her

142

years. She had gone from depending on Tom to depending on Ashley. The truth hurt. She had failed them all, including her faith—including her God.

Lord help me! I have fallen so low and I don't know how to get back up! My children need me!

I need you!

CHAPTER 14

A little piece of heaven on earth

Bolting straight up in his bed, sweat pouring down his face, Gregg had awakened from a nightmare. It had been a long time since he had dreamed about his mother's death—the car accident that took her life. Gregg felt the pangs of that day as if it just happened.

He was just ten then. His mother was taking him to his soccer game. They were late because they were waiting on his father, who was working late. A drunk driver crossed the medium and hit their car head on. Sitting in the backseat, he watched his mother's body sling forward as her seatbelt came loose. It wasn't fastened properly, he found out later. He watched her sitting so lifelessly, blood everywhere.

Gregg could still visualize the blood tangled in her sandy brown hair. He remembered screaming, "Momma," over and over again. Somehow, she turned and looked over at him, her face a bloody mess. She mouthed the song she used to sing to him, "For such a time as this…" Then she whispered, "Remember, I love you." And just like that, she was gone.

Getting out of bed, Gregg tiptoed across the room, where

a portrait of his mother holding him hung on the wall. He was just a year old. Under the picture were the words of the song she sang to him every night before going to bed. Sophia wrote it while carrying Gregg in her womb.

When you entered this world
It was as if the sun, the moon & stars had kissed
You were born to bring joy into our home
For such a time as this
Your life has a purpose
And only God knows what it is
You were created to help others find their way
For such a time as this

His mother was a beautiful woman, inside/out. Sophia taught Gregg how to pray and how to live right in his primary years. She doted over him as if he was the most important part of her life. She made everyone feel that way. There was sweet laughter in his childhood home whenever she was around. Never did she raise her voice or argue. Gratefully, Gregg was an obedient child. He never wanted to disappoint his mother, so he typically did the right thing.

While living, his mother would have guest over all the time. She loved entertaining people from the church, family, and friends. The house was always ready and prepared for visitors. Only, no one was a visitor for long, because the moment you entered their home you became a part of the family.

Everything changed after Sophia's death. The happy home Gregg once knew and loved became a habitation of misery and melancholy. It was nothing more than a *mausoleum* for the dead, not the living. Now Gregg was expected to return to such a place to care for the same father who had abandoned him when he needed him the most.

Why now after all these years? I do not need my father's approval or acceptance. But he needs me! Huh! Funny trick, Lord! It was bizarre for him to have any dialogue with the Lord. Now thirty-three, Gregg was still mad at God for taking both of his parents from him. Though his father was very much alive, as far as Gregg was concerned he died the same night his mother died.

For such a time as this!

He looked around. It was as if his mother's words had come to life.

You were created to help others find their way.

Gregg felt perplexed. What was happening to him? He looked at his mother's portrait again. He missed her dearly. With melancholy, he slipped on his running gear and jogged out the door. Three to four times a week, Gregg jogged to the lake, approximately three miles roundtrip. He would mentally outline the day's schedule by the time he had finished running.

However, today his mind was cloudy. He dreaded moving back home. Somberness ran with him as Gregg contemplated living with his difficult father. The two had nothing in common. Yet, it was his obligation to take care of his sick parent. His mother would have expected nothing less of him.

Returning home, drenched from perspiration and frustration, Gregg went to his home office and jotted down a few notes for Monday's morning conference with Coach Koon. Shortly afterwards he ate a small breakfast while reading the Sunday paper.

Around noon, he called the infamous Gabrielle Lane. Following their short phone conversation, Gregg showered and readied himself for his big date with a superstar.

Gregg drove to Gabrielle Lane's private rented beach

house about an hour drive away from his home, not far from his family's home. After getting clearance through the gate, Gregg drove down the long driveway and parked next to Miss Lane's limousine.

"Miss Lane says for you to make yourself comfortable on the patio," her female assistant greeted him at the door. "Please follow me."

Gregg admired the elaborate beach house. *Spectacular!* The beautiful scenery captivated Gregg. The ocean waves were rippling as the water glistened with sunlit sparkles. The sky was bright. The air was refreshing with a gentle breeze. It reminded him of his family home. On the inside, the house was a *mausoleum,* but outback, it was heavenly. His mother described it as having *a little piece of heaven on earth.*

"Hello darling," Gabrielle greeted him with kisses on the cheeks, welcoming him as if they had been friends for a long time.

"Hello," Gregg stammered, sighting her skimpy halter top and fitted blue jeans. From head-to-toe, Gabrielle flaunted the role of a famous singer. Her face was freshly made up, every strand of her short haircut was in place, and her abs were flat as a board, not a pinch of fat anywhere. Gabrielle Lane was a beautiful woman, for sure. She fit the profile of his female companions—the model-type with a figure to match. She had a superficial look like a Barbie doll. Most of all, she was a woman with no strings attached—a one-night-stand.

"My assistant will bring us out something to drink in a little while." Gabrielle sat on the plush lounge chairs. "I have some imported red wine. Will that do?"

"Just water for me." Gregg didn't drink. It was a promise he made to his mother, which kept him from indulging in the social ritual of his father and peers.

"What?" she sat up. "You don't drink?"

"No," he said without regret. It was the one thing he was most proud of. His mother asked little of him, but when she gave him the talk about avoiding drinking and smoking of any kind, he promised never to do either. His mother smiled then and somehow, every time he said no to drinking or smoking, Gregg imagined that she was smiling from heaven.

"I've never met a man who didn't drink. Are you some kind of saint or something?"

"I assure you I'm no saint." Gregg laughed, looking at her with devilment.

"I didn't think so!" she batted her fake eyelashes. "I knew you'd show me a good time today."

"I aim to please."

"I bet you do."

"I have a few places I'd like to show you," he began.

"I was thinking we would spend the day here," her eyes held his. "I spend so much time in the public eye, I just want to relax and enjoy this delightful day with you. My assistant will make sure that we have a wonderful dinner, later. But for now, let's just sit and talk. I hate being alone."

Something they both had in common.

For several hours, they both relaxed on the patio, soaking up the sun and enjoying the frisky conversation. They were both very flirtatious and goading the other to see how far either would go.

"Do you pick up a man in every place you perform?"

"I told you I hate being alone," Gabrielle answered honestly.

"There has to be a special man in your life," Gregg deduced because of her high profile celebrity status, not to mention her outward beauty.

"Not anymore. I am too busy with my career to get serious with any one man. It just doesn't work out."

"Inviting strangers over could be rather dangerous, don't you think?"

"I usually *pick'em* right," she smiled. "Besides, my bodyguard is always nearby."

"Your assistant?" Gregg scoffed, figuring the little woman could protect nobody.

"No," she laughed. "My bodyguard is in the house. The moment you drove up, he saw you. I asked him to stay in the background. But if you were to try anything I did not want you to try, Brute will be all on you in a split second."

"Brute," Gregg repeated, "sounds scary."

"He is."

Later, after sharing a delicious meal in the dining room, Gabrielle escorted Gregg into her bedroom chambers.

"Sing to me." Gregg propositioned as she sat on his lap.

"I don't want to sing. I have something else in mind." Gabrielle leaned over and kissed him passionately.

Gregg kissed her back, slowly allowing his body to descend upon the bed.

"You're a great kisser."

"I bet you tell all the guys that," Gregg said without thinking. Beholding her eyes, he saw something familiar—shallowness. It was like looking at his own reflection through her eyes. It saddened him, causing Gregg to feel empty.

"I'm not a slut," she sat upward. "You and I are a lot alike. I knew it the first time I laid eyes on you. We just want to have a good time." Gabrielle began unbuttoning his shirt.

Unexpectedly, Ashley's virtuous face invaded his space.

He could literally see Ashley's crystalline eyes. They were not shallow but filled with warmth and tenderness. Suddenly, Gregg felt unwell. He felt hollow and he felt dirty.

"Don't!" Gregg's voice was thick. This had never happened to him before.

"What?" Gabrielle continued unbuttoning his shirt.

"Don't!" Gregg's tone was louder as he got up, positioning himself on the side of the bed. "I'm sorry. I just can't go through with this." Swiftly, Gregg buttoned his shirt, his fingers trembling. Gregg felt awkwardly on edge. *What's wrong with me?*

"You've got to be kidding!" Gabrielle mocked. "I know you're not turning me down. No one turns down Gabrielle Lane."

Gregg turned and looked at her. He stood face to face with someone like himself, and for the first time it bothered him. Gregg saw Gabrielle for what she was—superficial, just like himself. Her music was entertaining and she had an awesome voice, but she was not real. Her music was real, but she wasn't. As she batted her fake, long lashes…Gregg felt deflated.

"You're right." Gregg finally spoke. "We are a lot alike. We both recycle people to satisfy that empty hole in the depths of our souls. Deep down, you and I are two miserable, lonely people. Well, I do not want to be like that anymore. I know it seems crazy…but…you helped me to see that."

"What a waste!" Gabrielle went to the door and opened it. "You can see yourself out!"

"I'm sorry about…"

"You're right," angrily Gabrielle shouted at him, "you are sorry!" Gabrielle slammed the door. Immediately, Brute appeared in the doorway.

He is scary! "I was just leaving." Gregg stuttered, observing the huge man standing before him.

Driving home, Gregg could not understand the sudden sense of loneliness that overshadowed him. His heart ached for something more. For something tangible. For something real. He had dated countless women, never wanting or desiring anything more from them than companionship for a day or two.

To be committed to one person was out of the question. His persona was to date them, have fun, and then walk away. To his credit, Gregg was always up front with the ladies, letting them know that he wasn't interested in a committed relationship. Nevertheless, the females would call him repeatedly, but Gregg purposely would not return their calls. A one nightstand was all he wanted or needed. Once he had captured their hearts, he had no use for them anymore. He had conquered his quest. The thrill was gone. Gregg did not want to risk loving and losing. The thought was too painful. He had loved and lost his mother and that was enough. To this day, still, her death was a freshly opened wound, which needed healing and closure.

Since Gregg was not far from his family home, he decided to stop by. Something he would not have done before his previous conversation with his father. Senorita Naomi Rivas, the cook and housekeeper on the surface, warmly greeted him. Naomi Rivas was more than an employee. She was practically a member of the family. His mother loved her dearly and so did Gregg.

"Mi Nino has returned home!" she kissed him.

"I'm not moving back until Thursday," he embraced her.

"No es bueno (*no good*)," she sucked her lips. "Your Papa needs you."

"Is he home?"

"Papa on the terrace."

"I think I'll join him," he said. "Do you have any of that delicious lemonade of yours?"

"Si," her smile widened. "I'll bring it to you."

"Gracias."

With feet of steel, Gregg marched onward to face his father. Stepping out on the terrace, he watched his father, who appeared to be sleeping. There was an oxygen tank beside him.

When did he start using an oxygen tank?

Although the weather was quite warm, his father had a blanket on him. He looked as if he had aged overnight. Watching, Gregg remembered the days of old when the family would come out on the terrace for a picnic lunch. Their home was surrounded by a beautiful lake. Back then, his mother had insisted that his father come home for lunch on Wednesdays and Fridays. It would be their quiet family time. Before returning to work, they would walk on the sand, enjoying the fresh air. Then Gregg would enjoy a piggyback ride by his father.

A little piece of heaven on earth! He could hear his mother say.

Gregg sighed at the delightful memory.

"Hi, Son," Mr. Jefferson awakened from his nap. "Surprise to see you."

"I was visiting someone in the neighborhood, so I decided to stop by."

"Here's your lemonade, Gregg," Senorita Rivas handed him the crystal glass. "Anything else?"

"Well," he coyly smiled.

"Would you like some fresh baked chocolate chip cookies with walnuts?" She slid the tray from behind her back.

"You know me too well," Gregg brushed a kiss on her

cheek. "Gracias."

"De Nada," she beamed. "Anything for you, Mr. Jefferson?"

"No, thank you." The older Jefferson focused on Naomi longer than need be, which caused her cheeks to flush before she exited.

Biting into a cookie, Gregg sat next to his father. "When did you start using an oxygen tank?"

"About a month ago," he answered. "I don't need it often. Today, it has been difficult breathing. I am feeling better now."

An awkward silence followed. Gregg racked his brain trying to come up with small talk. The wall of separation was too high to go over and too thick to get through.

"Senorita Rivas fixed up your old room. You can move in at any time." Mr. Jefferson was eager for his son's companionship.

"I'll move in Thursday."

"Fine," the father sat up. "The weather is good today, isn't it?"

"Sure is."

"Nothing like fresh air to cleanse the soul," he repeated the familiar sentiment.

"Mom used to say that all the time." Gregg was surprised his father even remembered. He had shut the door on the past a long time ago, never wanting to talk about his mother. He said it was too painful.

"Sophia loved this time of the year," the father's eyes glimmered at the memory. "And those picnics on every Wednesday and Friday she lived for them. She'd have Naomi Rivas prepare a special lunch each time. Of course, she had to add your favorite chocolate chip cookies with walnuts," Mr. Jefferson winked at his son.

The gesture shocked Gregg. "I was just thinking about

that. She'd say…"

"A little piece of heaven on earth!" they both cited.

"Those were the good ole' days," Mr. Jefferson's voice was flat. "I sure miss them."

"Me too." Gregg was stunned at how emotional he felt. He was on the verge of tears, but Gregg held his emotions in tack. He did not want his father to see him cry.

Mr. Jefferson reclined back on the chair and closed his eyes. Gregg astutely observed the single teardrop trickling down his father's worn cheek. They both were hurting. The father and son were lonely. The joy that the mother had once bestowed in their home, each longed to feel again.

A little piece of heaven on earth!

CHAPTER 15

Possibilities....

Monday morning was hectic in the Finley's home. Sandra had endured a night of excruciating pain and sleeplessness, which meant Ashley didn't sleep. Ashley stayed by Sandra's bedside all night, offering words of comfort and constant prayer. By the time the children got up for school, Ashley was *deadbeat* tired.

Walking with her siblings to school, so she could retrieve her journal from Thomas, Ashley's felt as if her shoes were filled with cement, making it difficult to put one foot in front of the other.

"So, Thomas, did you learn anything about me from reading my journal?" Ashley was curious.

"I learned that you're just as unhappy as I am. Only, you don't act out like me. You just keep it all bottled up inside, or in your journal. Your faith in God keeps you afloat. However, at times you feel as if you're sinking deeper and deeper under the circumstances of life. You believe, like I do, that mom can get better; but, it's up to her and right now she has lost her willpower."

Silence followed as Ashley considered her brother's accurate statements.

"Also, I learned that you are overworked and underappreciated. Albeit, your faith has wavered at times, you still believe that things are going to work out for our good. I admire your faith. Even when you wanted to give up, you knew that God's Word would prevail and that He would make a way out of no way. If He brings us to it..."

"He'll bring us through it," Ashley finished.

Thomas chuckled. "And I understand that you miss your college friends and our old home. You want a relationship with a man, but you don't have the time...nor do you feel pretty anymore, but old," he paused. "You're pretty, Ash. You're beautiful, actually."

"Thanks, Thomas," she smiled shyly.

"You gave up everything to return home and take care of us," Thomas articulated his earnest feelings as they neared his school. "Sis, you sacrificed your life of happiness for us. You gave up your journalism dream and I gave up basketball, neither by choice. Circumstances required it. Giving up our dreams quenched our spirits. It changed us. I became bitter and angry. You became withdrawn and lifeless."

Ashley looked up at her tall brother, wise beyond his years and said, "We are a lot alike."

"It's an honor to be like you."

"We're both learning each other and understanding each other...better."

"I'm sorry for all the pain I have caused you," Thomas held Ashley's hand. "I promise I am going to do right by you."

"Do right by God, Thomas, and everything will work out."

"I promise," he kissed her hand.

Upon entering the school, Ashley was surprised to see Gregg standing at the door, greeting his students.

"Good morning, Thomas," Gregg greeted first. "Good morning to you, Miss Finley," his smile was warm and inviting.

"Good morning, Dr. Jefferson," she walked passed him. *Why do I get all scatterbrained around him?*

"Miss Finley, can I please speak with you and Thomas in my office."

"Am I in trouble?" Thomas fretted.

"No, Thomas," Gregg answered. "I just need to speak with you concerning basketball."

Immediately Thomas' eyes lit up like fireworks.

Once in his office, Gregg closed the door and sat behind the desk, still trying to remain professional. However, he felt a strong connection to Thomas and Ashley.

"Has your sister spoken with you about my proposal of the children staying here while you practice?"

"Yes, Sir. Thank you so much for helping us out. This means a lot to me."

"Coach Koon says you are the best. He believes you can help lead the team to the state championship."

"I'll do my best."

"More important, you must stay focused." Gregg eyed him keenly. "You have to keep up your grades, change your attitude and live up to the expectations of your sister, Mr. Koon, and myself. We expect you to excel academically. You were an honor roll student before, and we expect no less from you now. Playing basketball is secondary. Although, I'm sure it means more to you than your grades, right now; but your grades are a priority. Do you understand?"

"Yes."

"Also, I expect there to be no discipline problems from you. Any trouble from you and the deal is off with us going out of our way to make it possible for you to participate in basketball. Do I make myself clear?" He sounded like the Terminator, but Thomas and Ashley knew that he was only concerned about Thomas' overall wellbeing.

"Yes, Sir. I won't let you down." He turned to his sister and said, "And I won't let you down, Ash."

Ashley smiled at him.

"So, starting next week, when the last bell rings for the day, you go get your siblings from school and upon returning take them to Coach Koon's office. You can at least start training and conditioning with the prospective basketball team. Miss Finley, you will probably need to complete some paperwork at their school so they can be released into Thomas' care. With some effort from all of us, we can make this happen."

"I don't know how to thank you for helping us work this out," Ashley spoke as the first bell rang.

"Thomas, you better hurry to class." Gregg turned his attention to Thomas, fleetingly. "You have a lot of work to catch up on if you want to pull up those grades."

"Yes Sir," Thomas leaped out of his chair. "You want me to walk you out?" he turned to his sister.

"No. You hurry along. See you later." Ashley felt so much lighter. To see the light back in her brother's eyes was like the beholding the sunrise in all its glory.

"Oh, your diary," Thomas remembered why she came to school with him.

"You are going to be late for class," Ashley sighed.

"Go get the journal and I'll give you a pass to class." Gregg solved the problem.

While waiting on Thomas to return, Ashley sat quietly, feeling slightly uncomfortable. She knew Gregg was looking at her but she kept her eyes fixed on her hands.

Boldly eyeing her, Gregg surmised that Ashley purposely dressed in a way not to draw attention to herself. She was a beautiful woman, no doubt about it. However, she hid her beauty behind a mask of antiquated fashion. At her age, Ashley shouldn't be dressing like an old maid. Guessing she was in her early twenties, Gregg wondered why she wore her hair in that tight bun, instead of letting it hang free like she did at work. Ashley was a perplexed woman, which intrigued him greatly.

There was no comparison to Ashley and Gabrielle Lane. Gabrielle had fame and outer beauty, but nothing on the inside. She was shallow and hollow. Ashley had something more precious—integrity. Her outer beauty matched her inner soul. There was more to her than the natural eye could see. She was strong, caring and loving. Yes, Ashley definitely reminded Gregg of his mother. Putting her family needs above her own was so like his mother. Though Ashley looked frail, he knew there was an inner strength in her that would defeat a lion if it came near her cubs.

"How is your father?" she shattered the stillness.

"He's fine. He has to have a heart bypass on Friday."

"Oh," she felt floored, remembering his statement about dying. "I will definitely keep him in my prayers."

"Thanks," he smiled, not taking his eyes off her.

Ashley lowered her eyes, not trusting herself to gaze back at him.

"Thomas appears happier."

"Oh, he is. He went to the Panthers' game last night and they won. Then today he realizes it's not a pipedream that he has a chance of playing ball again. I think Thomas is probably walking on cloud one-hundred right about now."

"I bet so. The Panthers game was sold out. How did he get so lucky?"

"My friend Harvey has season tickets."

Harvey? Is he more than a friend? "Will you be attending some of our school games?"

"Tuesday home games, hopefully. I have to work on Fridays."

"Too bad." Gregg got up and sat in the chair previously occupied by Thomas. "Friday games are usually the best, I'm told."

"You don't attend the games?" she turned to him, surprised by his remark.

"Well, the football season is winding down and I have attended two games," he answered truthfully. "But I plan on making all the basketball games this year. Thomas isn't the only one who has to make some changes in his life."

"Change is good." Lastly, their eyes met.

"You have the most amazing..." *Eyes!*

"I'm back!" Thomas abruptly cut Gregg off.

"That you are." Gregg wrote out a pass for Thomas. "Quickly, get to class."

"Sorry, Sis." Thomas kissed Ashley on the cheek and handed her the journal. "I will earn your trust again. I promise I will."

"Have a good day, Thomas." Ashley stood to her feet and hugged him.

Watching her brother leave, Ashley put her journal in her purse and turned to Gregg. "Thanks again for everything. I better go or I'll be late for work."

"Do you ride the city bus?"

"Yes."

"If you wait a few, I can take you," Gregg blurted without thought. He did not want to part company with her.

"That won't be necessary," she said. "I enjoy riding the bus. It gives me a chance to write."

"So, you like writing?" *Duh!* Gregg wanted to keep the conversation going.

"I love writing. Writing is my passion. I was majoring in English Education and minoring in journalism before returning home at the beginning of my senior year in college."

"Do you plan on going back?"

"I pray so," she was uncertain. "Things are just so tight. Financially, it's impossible to even think about college right now. We do all we can to just survive." Ashley didn't know what came over her. She couldn't believe she had voiced her hardship to him.

"Well, things worked out for Thomas. I believe things will work out for you, as well." Deep down Gregg wanted to help her just as much as he wanted to help Thomas—even more.

"I better go or I will miss my bus."

"Have a good day, Miss Finley." The way the principal looked at her made her skin tingle all over.

"You too, Dr. Jefferson," she opened the door. "Oh, and can you keep me posted on your father's health?"

How sweet. She doesn't even know him and she is concerned about him. "If it's okay, I will call you after the operation?"

"That will be fine."

"You're an extraordinary woman," Gregg praised, his eyes dancing with truth.

"Thank you." His compliment surprised her and moved her at once. Ashley had never met a man like Gregg. Being around him did strange things to her heart.

She is blushing! I haven't seen a woman blush—since my mother!

CHAPTER 16

Lord, Help!

Thank you, God! I have my journal back! As the bus pulled away, straightaway, Ashley began writing.

Never judge a book by its cover. The inside could be packed with marvelous mysteries of possibilities. Hmmm. Who would have ever imagined it? The Terminator is not so bad after all. Gregg is not a mean, brutal, heartless man. He is going out of his way to assist Thomas in getting back on the basketball team. My heart feels lighter. One burden lifted makes a huge difference.

I wonder what he was going to say before Thomas interrupted. "You have the most amazing..." Amazing what? Why does my heart skip several beats in his presence? Why do I feel all tingly inside? He makes me blush. The way he stares at me—it's different from the way Andrew does it. Andrew makes me feel like he seeing through me, but Gregg makes me feel like...like I'm beautiful. How crazy is that? Me, beautiful? If Pam knew I had my hair in a bun today, she'd fuss at me... If only I could feel this way about Harvey!

Later, working in the library, Ashley felt so carefree and lighthearted, as if she could float on air. Things were finally looking up. Though Ashley hated having to speak to her mother so harshly about the families' problems, she knew she did the right thing. She would not allow Thomas to go down to the gutter without trying to save his life. Ashley had to throw him a lifeline and that lifeline was basketball.

"Hey, you sure do look happy today." Harvey joined her at the book counter.

"I am."

"I enjoyed my time with Thomas yesterday. He's a fine young man with a good head on his shoulders."

"Harvey," she laughed, "only you would say such a thing."

"Well, it's true. I think I'll start spending more time with him."

"Thomas might not have much time to spend with you. He's going to be playing basketball again."

"How?"

"I had a talk with the principal and he has arranged for the children to stay after school with Thomas while he practices. Coach Koon will bring them home when practice is over."

"What about your mother?"

"She'll be alright," Ashley spoke through faith. "We had a heart-to-heart talk and I think she's going to try to do more for herself."

"But can she?" Harvey wondered. "I mean the last time she got up you had to call Dr. Phelps."

"Harvey, my mother is a fighter. She will fight for her children. I told her all about Thomas' rebellion and it scared her witless. I think it scared her enough to get up and out of the bed, and on her knees."

"Wow!" It was not in Ashley's nature to confront things or people. Usually, she would stifle her feelings or just write them in her journal. Standing up to her mother took *guts*.

"Close your mouth Harvey." Ashley headed to the bookshelves.

"Lunch in the park?" he called after her.

"See you there."

She likes me! Now if only she could love me and say yes to my proposal!

As normal, Ashley arrived home just in time for Sandra to take her medication.

"Hello, M-o-t-h..." Ashely found her mother's room empty. Darting out the room, she ran through the small house finding her mother on the bathroom floor.

"Oh, my goodness!" Ashely dropped to her knees. *Lord, help!* "Momma, are you okay?"

She was unconscious.

Quickly, Ashley ran to the phone. There was no dial tone. *Doggone it! I was going to pay the bill Friday when I got paid. Oh, Lord, what now?*

Swiftly, she ran to the neighboring duplex. She knocked several times before someone finally came to the door.

"Ma'am," Ashely didn't even know her neighbor's name, "can I please use your phone? My mother fell and she unconscious."

"I don't have a phone," the woman replied.

"Oh, no," Ashley fretted. "Well, thank..."

"Mother, who is at the door?" A young lady came from behind.

"She lives next door," the mother answered. "She needs a phone. Her mother is unconscious."

"You can use my cell phone." The younger version of her mother dashed out of the room to retrieve it. "Here," she was back in a flash.

"Thank you," Ashley called 911 to get an ambulance to her residence immediately. Then she called her mother's doctor. "I can't thank you enough."

"Would you like for me to wait with you?" the daughter asked.

"No, thank you." Ashley's eyes swelled up with tears. "But if you can pray for my mother, Sandra Finley, I will be most grateful."

"We will," the mother and daughter replied.

Lord, please let the ambulance come before the children get home. I do not want them to see momma being carried out in an ambulance. Lacey had nightmares for the longest the last time.

It is all my fault. I shouldn't have pushed her so. She cannot help she is sick.

Do not fear. I am with you. Have faith in God.

Ashley's prayer had been answered. The ambulance arrived before the children came home from school. However, her mother was still unconscious.

"Where's Momma?" Thomas was the first to arrive. He would have to leave in a few to get his siblings from school.

"At County Memorial Hospital."

"What happened?"

"It's all my fault, Thomas." Ashley collapsed in her brother's arm. "I pushed her. I told her she had to do her part to help because we needed her."

"Shhhhh," Thomas patted her back gently. "It's not your fault. Things have to change around here…and change starts with momma. She's got to want to do better and it starts with getting out of the bed."

"But she fell and hit her head," Ashley pulled away. "She's unconscious."

"She'll be all right, Ash. God is with her. We *gotta* have faith," he said confidently. "Right?"

She felt her spirit sailplane at Thomas' strength. He may have strayed away, but his spiritual upbringing was prevalent. "Right. Do you mind praying, Thomas," Ashley suggested as they held hands.

"God…You know everything and right now You know that our mom isn't doing so good. She needs Your healing touch. We will not fear, but we walk in faith. We believe Your Word that says, by Jesus' stripes we were healed…already. Our mother is healed already in Jesus' Christ name we pray, believe and receive, amen."

"Amen," Ashley agreed. "Well, I better fix the children something and then I'm going to rush to the hospital."

"What about work?"

"Oh!" she hadn't even thought about it. "Maybe I can call at the hospital," she looked at her brother. "Our phone is dead. I pray I don't lose my job."

"Just go to the hospital first and then go to work."

"I can't just leave momma. She'll be by herself."

"God is with her," Thomas reminded.

Ashley smiled. Thomas was his mother's son, for sure. "You're right. He knows what to do and how to do it."

On the way to the hospital, riding on the bus, once again Ashley found solace in her ballpoint pen.

My mother is unconscious. I feel guilty. I pushed her to get up and be there for us. She suffers physically from RA, but the disease that is killing her slowly is a broken heart. I want to be strong, but I'm so weak. Every time things start looking up, something bad happens. The Calm before the storm. Yet, I know God is with us. Lord, I believe, but, help my unbelief...

Arriving at the hospital, Ashley discovered that her mother was in emergency surgery. Anxiously, she waited in the lobby to hear the status of her mother.

"Hi Ashley," Dr. Phelps sat down next to her, later.

"Why did they do surgery on Mother?"

"She was hemorrhaging. She took a pretty bad fall," he began. "She'll probably be in surgery a little while longer."

"Be upfront with me, Dr. Phelps," Ashley earnestly looked at him. "Is she going to pull through this time? I know she's weak already."

"She's in good hands. She has one of the best surgeons operating on her. Dr. Mack is an awesome brain surgeon and he just happened to be here checking on a patient. Tell me God doesn't work miracles every day. More importantly, she is in God's hands."

Ashley was so thankful that her mother had a Christian doctor. Medically speaking, Dr. Phelps was great in his profession; but his greatest attribute was that he knew God.

Following, Ashley called *The Palace* to inform them she wouldn't be at work tonight. After explaining her mother's condition, Ms. Melrose told her if she needed the next day off to just call and let her know. Still, Ashley agonized about not working. Her family needed the money. No work, no pay.

Several hours later, the surgeon, Dr. Mack, came out to

speak with Ashley about the operation.

"The surgery went well," he began. "Your mother is not out of the woods yet, but we were able to stop the bleeding. She will be taken to ICU shortly. You can see her briefly, but she needs her rest. Visiting hours in ICU are every two hours."

"Thanks, doctor," Ashley shook his hand.

"Someone will come get you in a moment to take you to see your mother."

Later, when Ashley finally visited her mother, she was not prepared for what her eyes beheld. Her mother had been in and out of the hospital numerous times, but not like this. Sandra's head was bandaged. She was on a breathing machine. Tubes were everywhere. However, the thing that frightened her the most was her mother looked as if she was at death's doors, waiting to enter in.

Ashley's face marred with tears as she held her mother's cold hand. "Oh Mother, I'm sorry. Please fight for your life. We need you. I need you...I need you, so much!"

Lord, help!

Cast your burdens on the Lord and He will sustain you.

Lord, I surrender all.

CHAPTER 17

The Day Off

Ashley went throughout the week in a daze. Between going back and forth to the hospital, working two jobs endeavoring to make every dollar count, caring for the children, riding the bus from one place to the next, Ashley didn't know if she was coming or going. Everything was a blur. Life's responsibilities were overstretching Ashley like an accordion. Surely, if something didn't give soon, she would pop like a rubber band.

Sandra Finley was still in a coma, unresponsive to anything. The longer she was in the coma the doctors feared whether or not she would fully recover.

"You look horrible," Pam mentioned at work. "When was the last time you slept?"

"I don't know," Ashley sighed heavily. "I'm tired, Pam. My body aches. I need a toothpick to prop my eyes open. Danny and Donny both were sick yesterday with fever and vomiting. They seem a little better today."

"You need a vacation." Pam felt sorry for her friend. "Why don't you take tomorrow off?"

"I can't. I need every dollar to make ends meet. I've already missed one day and that's going to set me back."

"You're going to end up in the hospital right next to your

mother if you don't get some rest."

"I'll be all right." Ashley feigned a grin. "Got tables to wait on…see you later."

"She looks sick." Andrew came and stood by Pam.

"She sure does," Pam sighed. "That girl has too much on her plate. She's taking care of her entire family. Her mother is sick and in the hospital. Her brother stays in trouble. The twins are sick. She is working two jobs and it *ain't* enough to pay all the bills."

"No wonder she looks ill. How about you give her this." Andrew reached into his pocket and gave her five twenty-dollar-bills. "I'm sure she will not take it from me, but perhaps she will from you."

"Are you on something?" Standing with her hands on her hips, Pam looked at him as if he was loco. "She's too prideful to take charity. Besides, why would you want to give her money? Are you smitten with my friend? Because if you are, you are chasing up the wrong tree. My friend *ain't* like that!"

"I'm not like that," Andrew strongly opposed. "I am a Christian and that's the Christianly thing to do—give to those in need."

"Whatever!" Pam didn't buy it. *Perhaps Ash was right. He is a pervert.*

"Please, give it to her." Andrew attempted to put the money in her hands. "Please!"

"Would you do the same for me if I needed help?"

"In a heartbeat."

Pam stared at him, trying to see if she saw even a hint of malice in his peculiar eyes. Usually, Andrew wore glasses, so Pam had never paid attention to his eyes before. At the moment, his glasses were off. Andrew's eyes flashed like a bright neon sign. Something was strangely different, yet, familiar at the same time.

Andrew has crystal clear eyes like Ashley! What are the odds of that? Puzzled, Pam walked away.

"You have tomorrow off." Pam came from behind and slipped money in her pocket.

"What?" Ashley faced her friend. "I already told you…"

"Ms. Melrose says you look like you're going to fall flat on your face. Therefore, she is giving you tomorrow off." Prior, Pam had gone to Ms. Melrose to discuss her friend's current crisis, hoping she would concur to Ashley being off a day or two. She did.

"But I can't afford it," Ashley rebuffed.

"Look in your pocket."

Tears spilled over as Ashley held the money in her hands. Not only had Andrew given her a hundred, Pam added fifty of her own. "You can't afford it." Ashely assumed it was all from Pam.

"Oh, yes I can."

"But how?"

"It doesn't matter." Pam put her arm around her friend. "Let's just say that you have angels all around you and you don't even know it."

"You are an angel," Ashley hugged her tight. "I will repay you as soon as I can."

"And if you do, I will never speak to you again." Pam stepped back. "Ash, you are my best friend and I will do anything for you. I've got your back."

"Thanks. I love you." Ashley sniffed, still holding onto her friend.

"Ah girl," Pam wasn't good with expressing her feelings.

"You know I love you, too."

Later, Ashley was too tired to argue with Pam about riding home with Andrew. Besides, she didn't feel like riding the bus home tonight. Andrew had barely driven off before Ashley's head rested on her friend's shoulder and she slept.

"She's exhausted." Andrew peered through his rearview mirror. "I feel sorry for her."

"Ash is a fighter," Pam whispered. "She will be fine after a day of rest. That's all she really needs."

"Sure hope so."

About thirty minutes later, Pam gently shoved her friend. "Wake up sleepy head," she muttered. "It's time to get out of the car and go straight to bed."

"Oh, my," Ashley stirred. "I can't believe I fell asleep."

"Believe it, darling. You were snoring and everything."

"I don't snore," Ashley contended.

"How would you know?"

"Thanks for the ride," politely she replied, still wary of Andrew.

"My pleasure," he couldn't shake the peculiar feeling he had every time he looked into her eyes. Eyes that were identical to his own.

Friday morning after seeing everybody off to school, Ashley went straight to the hospital to visit with her mother. It was a luxury having the entire day off. The library was closed for Veteran's Day. She wished she could just stay next to her mother all day; but visits were limited for twenty minutes, every two hours.

"Mother, you have to pull through this," she whispered in

Sandra's ear. "Lacey, Danny, Donny and Thomas miss you so very much. I miss you," a teardrop slid from her eyelid. "I miss combing your hair, helping you get dress, reading the Bible to you and just talking to you."

Ashley gazed at the lifeless body. At one time, her mother was so beautiful. Her father commonly boasted of Sandra's beauty in their early years of marriage. She used to have an hourglass figure before taking all the pills, which expanded her waistline and hips. Subsequently, Tom mentioned his disapproval for plump women. Sandra's long, thick hair, which was now thinning, was pulled back in a ponytail. The mother had lost her appeal long before Tom Finley's death. At present, Sandra appeared older than her age. Still, Ashely saw her beauty.

People often compared Ashley to her mother. The only difference was that her mother had dark brown eyes and Ashley had crystalline eyes, '*pure as crystal*', people would say. Oftentimes, Ashley wondered who in her family tree did she inherit such rare eyes? Her mother revealed that no one on her father or mother's side had crystalline eyes. "You are special that's all," Sandra would faithfully reply.

Out of all Sandra's children, Ashley didn't look like any of her siblings. Her only link to her family was Ashley's resemblance to Sandra. Thomas, Danny, Donny and Lacey all looked like their father—dark skinned, whereas Ashely had a light, honey complexion like her mother. Many of their characteristics flowed from Tom's genes. Ashley had nothing in common with her father. They were totally opposite and she never felt connected to him. Regularly, Ashley mused over their father/daughter relationship—or the lack of it.

"I'm going to read to you a little while," Ashley took out

her pocket Bible.

"Surely, He has borne our grief and carried our sorrows; yet we esteemed Him stricken, smitten by God, and afflicted. But He was wounded for our transgressions, He was bruised for our iniquities; the chastisement for our peace was upon Him and by His stripes, we are healed."

She closed her Bible.

"By Jesus' stripes, mother, you are healed. I know you can hear me. You are healed. You have rested long enough, Momma. Now, wake up and live. *'You shall live and not die, and declare the works of the Lord.'*

"I love you, Momma." Ashley kissed her on her thin cheek and embraced her frail body with tender care. "I will be back at two o'clock. I have the day off at the Library and *The Palace*. I am going to go home briefly. I will be back with bells on my toes." She repeated her mother's platitude when she used to wake up the children for school.

Ashley could practically hear her mother saying, "I'm coming with bells on my toes. The bells should have wakened you long before I did." Those were the joyous days. The days when life did not seem so harsh. Oh, how Ashley longed to hear those bells again. Albeit, everything back then wasn't a bed of roses, but they had each other and Sandra Finley was overall healthier.

On the way home, Ashley stopped by the phone company to pay the overdue phone bill and have the service reconnected. Upon returning home, Ashley went straight to her mother's bedroom and undress down to her full-length slip. Then she set the alarm clock for 12:30, hibernated under the covers and dozed off into a restful slumber. It had been a long time since she had slept in a bed.

Instead of another horrifying dream about her mother's sickness, Ashley's subconscious freewheeled to something unexpected. The dream took her to a place she had never been before. She was lying on hammock with the breeze gently blowing. In view, there was a lake stretching out for miles and miles. Suddenly there appeared a man. He was tall and muscular built, wearing jeans and a blue polo short-sleeve shirt. The man's face was blurred. However, his eyes were familiar, drawing her to him, hypnotizing her. He opened his mouth to speak and Ashley laughed. He picked her up as if she were light as a feather and carried her toward the lake.

In his arms, Ashley rested her head upon his chest and basked in the beauty of God's perfect scenery. She felt so at home in his arms. Still holding her, he tilted his head lightly and brushed a soft kiss over her lips. Their eyes locked momentarily. Then he kissed her again, this time with more passion and desire. She could hardly breathe. Her heart exploded, like fireworks on the fourth of July. She had never felt like this before. Out of the blue, the mystery man was no longer a mystery. Ashley knew him. Gregg Jefferson had invaded her dreams.

The blasting of the alarm clock abruptly disrupted Ashley's subliminal rendezvous. Still resting, Ashley replayed the scene of the lake in her mind. The thoughts were pleasant, bringing a smile to her lips. A pounding at the door swiftly brought Ashley back to reality. Wiping eyes, Ashley threw the covers off and slipped on her mother's large robe.

Peeking out of the peephole, there stood a grinning Harvey with two bags in his hands.

"Harvey!" Ashley opened the door, not concerned about her disheveled look. It was just Harvey. He had seen her at her worse and at her best and it did not seem to move him one way or the other.

"I bring tidings of joy." Harvey entered, heading straight for the kitchen, feeling right at home. "And a feast for dinner."

"Harvey," Ashley pouted, "you really shouldn't have."

"I wanted to," he placed the bags on the table. "I have a twelve-piece family meal from Shady's Chicken Shack. I know how you love their wings. There are mash potatoes and green beans for side dishes." He drew closer to her, so close Ashley could feel his breath upon her. "Now you won't have to cook."

Harvey gazed at her penetratingly, making Ashley slightly uncomfortable. Harvey debated if he should kiss her or not. He wanted nothing more than to do so. Slightly leaning forward, Harvey closed his eyes, ready to give into his desires.

Without a word, Ashley took one-step backward. Harvey opened his eyes and watched her ardently. His resolve flopped like a pancake.

Ashley fixed her eyes on him, taking inventory of just how handsome Harvey appeared to her at that very moment. Looking beyond Harvey's big-rimmed glasses, which were too big for his face, old fashion hair parted on the right side, and his chubby cheeks, Harvey by no means was unattractive. He was a handsome man. *But still...*

Feeling rejected, Harvey turned and looked at the sink piled with the morning dishes. "I'll wash the dishes, while you go get dressed. I will take you to the hospital so you do not have to ride the bus."

"Thank you, Harvey."

"You're most welcome, Ashley. Now go!" Harvey shook off the rejection and put his best *face* forward.

While quickly freshening up in the bathroom, Ashley evaluated her feelings for Harvey. He was so kind and thoughtful. Always going out of his way to please her. He was a good Christian man. Hard worker. Considerate. Kind. Homeowner. Still, something potent was missing to convert a brotherly friendship into a betrothal.

He's no Gregg Jefferson. Ashley blushed thinking of her dream.

Oh, stop that! It was just a dream!

Yet, it seemed so real. I could never think of him as a brotherly anything!

Returning to the kitchen, Ashley beheld two bowls of chicken noodle soup, crackers and two large chocolate chip cookies awaiting her.

"Oh, Harvey," she covered her mouth, "it's too much."

"Nothing is too much for you," he held out her chair. "Sit and eat before I take you to the hospital."

She humbly obeyed.

"I was thinking," he began, "I can stay at the hospital with you, to keep you company and then come back here and stay for…uh…dinner…and then take you all back to the hospital to see your mother."

"That's sweet of you. I really don't want the children to see mother like this. It's hard enough for me seeing her."

"That's understandable. I can keep you company."

"That won't be necessary, Harvey," she noticed the hurt look in his eyes. "You've already helped me so much today. I really want to be alone with her and stay until the next visit."

"That's two hours. I don't mind keeping you company." Harvey reached over the table and gently touched Ashley's hand. "It would be my pleasure."

She felt pressured. "You're so kind, Harvey. I am going to use that time to journal and read my devotions. I know you understand. I need time to feed my soul."

"Yes, of course. I understand," his voice cracked. "Can I pick you up then? We both have the day off and it won't be any trouble at all."

"I'll call you," Ashley compromised.

For some time, Harvey's eyes held hers. She was the loveliest woman Harvey had ever seen. For years, he had pined after her. He knew she only cared for him as a friend, but he had hoped that one day her feelings would grow into a deeper affection.

"You haven't forgotten my…." Harvey knew he said he would not pressure her, but the young man was desperate for any kind of reciprocation of those feelings.

"No," she interrupted. "Surely, I cannot think about that right now."

"Of course not," he smiled. "Of course not."

CHAPTER 18

Finding Comfort

Following her short visit with her mother, Ashley sat in the waiting area and began to journal in her diary. As always, releasing her buried feelings brought about a peaceful relief. It was the only time Ashley wholly allowed herself to be free—to be real. Absorbed in putting her diverse thoughts on paper, Ashley noticed no one around her, including the bewildered man who took the vacant seat next to her.

Running his fingers through his hair, Gregg didn't even look to his right to see Ashley sitting next to him. All he could envision was the deathly look of his father after his operation.

Gregory Jefferson appeared lifeless and frail. The doctor conveyed to Gregg that he had barely survived the operation. Apparently, his father had lost a lot of blood and his heart had stopped beating two times during the operation. Gregg was floored by the horrifying news.

There were so many things left undone and unsaid between father and son. Gregg could find no peace, no quietness, and no rest. Only turmoil occupied his hollow soul. Unable to sit still, he fidgeted in his seat, brushing against the neighboring chair.

"Ah, please ex-c-u-s-e me," Gregg stammered, peering over at his neighbor.

Ashley gasped as she beheld Thomas' principal.

"Dr. Jefferson," she was surprised.

"Gregg," he tweaked out a smile.

"Gregg," she amended.

"What a surprise seeing you here," he spoke, relieved to see a familiar face. "What are you doing here?"

"My mother is in ICC."

"My father, as well. He's not doing good."

"Oh, I'm so sorry to hear that." Ashley felt more than pity for him. She felt deep-rooted compassion. The surefooted man she recalled, now appeared fainthearted.

"The surgeon said his heart stopped beating twice. He's going to need a pacemaker, but he's too weak to survive another operation."

"From what I remember," Ashley closed her journal, reached over and touched his hand gently. "Your father is a fighter. He is not going to buckle under. He will pull through this."

Gregg wanted desperately to believe her. "I appreciate that."

She was about to pull her hand away, when he gripped it tighter, needing the touch to comfort him. Continuing to gaze at her, Gregg concluded that Ashley was a gentle woman with a kind spirit. Perusing her face, her crystalline eyes drew him in, capturing his lonely soul.

Nervously, she looked away.

"I'm so glad you're here with me," he said sincerely. "How is your mother?" "She's in a coma."

"I'm sorry to hear that."

"She will pull through this, too," her tone wasn't so convincing.

"Yes." He sensed her uncertainty and squeezed her hand. "How long has she been in the hospital?"

"Since Monday," she sighed.

He hurt because she was hurting.

"It's my fault," Ashley confessed without thinking. Promptly, she withdrew her hand and covered her mouthed. She could not believe she had blurted out her guilt in front of him.

"It's okay. You can talk to me."

"I…uh…" Ashley bolted upward, feeling silly and giddy at the same time. With her journal in hand, she sprinted toward the door.

"Wait!" Gregg followed her. Catching up to her, he grabbed her hand. "Ashley," he said her name so softly, it reminded her of bells chiming, which reminded her of her mother's words. *I'm coming with bells on my toes.*

She crumbled in his arms and wept.

"It's all right." Gregg held her tightly. "Just let it all out." It felt so right to comfort her. He could feel her body shaking in his arms. For such a time as this, Ashley found comfort in Gregg's embrace. Tenderly, Gregg caressed her back with his hands, soothing her with gentleness. He hurt because she hurt.

"I'm sorry." Ashley tried to pull away, but he held onto her. "I didn't mean to breakdown like this. Seems like I'm always bawling around you."

"I think you put everyone above yourself." Reaching upward, Gregg caressed her tears away. "It is okay to be human. To release your repressed feelings. My mother used to say, 'Nothing like a good cry to cleanse the soul.'"

"It's all my fault." A ragged sigh tore from her lips, as Ashley lowered her head, again guilt consuming her.

"It's not your fault." Gregg tilted her chin upward, forcing her to look at him. "Let's go for a walk."

"I don't know," she felt confused.

"We have another hour before we can visit with our parents," he reasoned. "Let's just walk outside and get some fresh air."

Reluctantly, she agreed.

Walking in silence at first, the two found solace in the other's company.

"Why do you blame yourself?" Gregg finally asked.

"I pushed her too far," Ashley admitted. "I told her that Thomas needed her and that she was going to have to do her part so that he could play ball again. I shouldn't have pushed her. She is sick. She can't help it."

"Perhaps, she needed to be reminded of her worth and value to the family." Gregg verbalized a different perspective. "Perhaps, she needed the push."

"But look what happened. She's in the hospital, fighting for her life."

"Maybe it's the first time in a longtime that she has actually fought for anything."

Ashley halted her steps and turned to him. His words struck chords of truth and reality.

"I understand what you're feeling." Earnestly, he did. His dad never fought for him. Instead, he sent him away.

"I just want her to get better," she sniffed. "To be her old self. She used to be such a wonderful mother. She gave her all for our family."

"The apple doesn't fall far from the tree. You mother did a great job in raising you."

His words touched Ashley profoundly as they walked

again in sync.

"My father used to laugh a lot. He'd leave work and rush home to play with me," Gregg spoke so softly Ashley could barely hear him. "My mother brought out the best in him. Back then, he was a dad and I wanted to be just like him. After my mother died, he tossed me aside and sent me to boarding school. He didn't want to be near me."

"Maybe, your dad was crippled by grief, which had a crippling effect on his relationship with you. I read some article about perpetual grief hindering the heart from loving. When grief takes over it consumes everything that it comes in contact…like a forest fire. There is no room in the heart for both grief and joy at the same time."

"Maybe," Gregg shrugged, "but I needed a dad, not just someone who financially supported me." Gregg resented his father for many years. "I grew up without a mother and a father. I was an orphan as far as I was concerned. In my younger years, I couldn't stand the man."

"And today…"

"Today, I feel guilty for hating him," Gregg admitted.

"Hate is such a strong word," Ashley shivered at the thought. *It's a sin!*

"He earned it. Years of treating me like a stepchild instead of his own, biological son. I was only ten when my mother died. He wasn't even there when she died. I held my mother's hand when she breathed her last breath," his voice cracked at the remembrance. "Within a month of her death, he shipped me off to school and abandoned me."

She heard the pain of a boy, still hurting many years later. Gregg's heart was hardened.

"One night I went to bed, confused, hurting, longing for my

mother, then the next month I was in a strange room, sleeping in a cold, hard bed wanting to go home to my father who didn't want me. I feel nothing for him but hatred," Gregg confessed, a callous, vehement heart of a man who knew no other way, but to behave in the same manner of his earthly father.

"You're just angry," Ashley cushioned his words, "and rightly so."

"I hate him," Gregg faced her. "Before he was wheeled into surgery he said he loved me. I couldn't say it back to him. How could he utter those words to me and expect me to believe him? He deserted me for years. They were mere words with no substance."

"He loves you, Gregg. He just didn't know how to show it anymore. He got lost in his grief."

"We both were grieving," Gregg couldn't easily accept the excuse. "I needed him."

"And now he needs you." Ashley hoped to crack Gregg's hard shell.

Gregg shook off her words and put one foot in front of the other trying to run from its meaning. Years of anger had built up inside. He wasn't ready to release its hold upon his life. His father's abandonment was devastating to his childhood, spilling over into his adulthood. He had needed a stable parent to hold him, to give him security when he was younger. Now he didn't need or want anything from his father. Gregg was dutifully playing the role of a son, by being by his father's side for surgery, nothing more—nothing less.

"Enough about me, tell me something about yourself that I don't know," Gregg suggested.

"I used to dance when I was in college with this lyrical dance team." Ashley had never told her family about it. "I loved it. I was clumsy at first, but Faye, my roommate, insisted that I keep trying. I did and it was so rewarding."

"You look like a dancer."

"Not me," she chuckled. "I have two left feet for sure. But with a persistent coach, like Faye, I couldn't help but learn how to dance."

"You are too hard on yourself," Gregg said. "Why don't you dance anymore?"

"Who has the time?" she shucked it off.

"I can tell that you liked dancing by the way you talk. You should make the time."

"That was my old life."

"If you could dance again…right now…this very moment… with me would you?"

Gregg made her feel so alive and special. Before she knew it, her heart responded, "Yes."

Hmmm.

"Tell me something about yourself that I don't know," Ashley turned the tables.

"I scored the winning basketball shot during my junior year in college at a championship game. It was the biggest game ever. The Hornets against the Falcons. The Falcons sure felt the sting of the hornets that night. We won at the buzzer with my three-pointer. The score was 67 to 65."

"Wow!" she was impressed. "Do you still play ball?"

"Who has the time?" Gregg borrowed her line.

"You need to make the time," she replied. "I can see you playing ball. You have the athletic build."

"Oh, do I?" he coaxed, enjoyed watching Ashley blush.

"You do," bashfully she admitted. "Thanks for taking me away from the hospital. This has been so refreshing. I needed it."

"We both did." Gregg turned to her, reached up and tenderly caressed her flaming cheeks. Gregg yearned desperately to kiss Ashley. For a moment, nothing else mattered as their eyes locked.

"Uh…it's almost visiting time." Ashley nervously broke the trance. "We better head back."

"Time flew by," Gregg admitted awkwardly. Peculiar feelings emerged in the base of his stomach. Ashley had shaken his calmed world. Gregg hadn't known another woman like her, other than his mother and Naomi Rivas. She wasn't like the superficial girls he had known and dated. Women, Gregg could sweep of their feet with honey words of flattery. Ashley had substance. No doubt about it. Behind her *covered up* attire was a heart of gold. He knew it. There was definitely more to this humdrum lady. She intrigued him. He wanted to peel her like an onion to unearth the depths of her inward beauty that shone so brightly outwardly. The notion frightened and brighten his world.

Gregg stretched out his arm toward her, "Shall we?"

Gladly, Ashley put her arm in the crook of his. The fit was perfect. *Too perfect.* They had made it back just in time for visitation and parted ways in the ICU.

With mixed feelings, Ashley eyed her mother. A radiant smile and warm hug from her mother were all she longed for. Her heart ached to be held by her mother again. There was so much Ashley wanted to tell her. So much she needed to say. Yet, silenced filled the space. Lonesomeness filled her heart.

Meanwhile, Gregg watched his father with pity. Mr. Jefferson was hooked up to a breathing machine, tubes everywhere it seemed. No matter how hard he tried to push back the soft spot hidden in the crevices of his heart, Gregg languished over his paternal father's unknown fate.

I should have at least told him I love him. I should have…
Could've —should've —would've thoughts gnawed at his conscious. Time and distance had erased the bond between father and son, replacing it with un-forgiveness, bitterness, and loneliness. Receiving only scanty portions of affection from his father while growing up, Gregg could only dish out what was given to him—nothing. Tormented within, Gregg touched his father's cheek. Surprised by its softness, his fingers lingered, relishing the feeling. It was a small connection, but it was something.

If only…

Momentarily, Gregg walked out of the room, meeting Ashley in the hallway.

Immediately, he observed her wet eyes, fresh with tears. Gregg wanted to reach out, pull her to him and comfort her. Yet, he resisted the urge. "Are you okay?" he asked instead.

Ashley nodded.

In silence, they exited the ICU area.

"Ashley!" she turned toward the sound.

"Harvey!" she suppressed her disappointment. "What are you doing here?"

"Well, after you didn't call," he eyed the tall man next to Ashley. "I figured I'd come and check on you and your mother."

"I'm fine," Ashley replied stiffly, inwardly agitated that Harvey was there. She had Gregg…for now.

"How is your mother?" Harvey immediately felt Ashley's reproof.

"The same."

"Are you ready to go home?" he pushed further.

She looked over at Gregg who seemed out of place. "Oh,

Gregg, this is Harvey, a friend of mine."

Friend! Harvey was insulted.

"Very close friends," Harvey firmly shook Gregg's hand. "As a matter of fact…"

"We've been friends a long time." Ashley interrupted, detecting where Harvey was going.

"Any friend of Ashley's is a friend of mine."

"Are you ready?" Harvey asked again. "The children should be getting home soon.

"Quite chummy with the family," Gregg whispered for Ashley's ears only. He would never admit it, but he was feeling a wee-bit jealous.

"I guess so," she mumbled back. "Are you going to be alright?" she looked to Gregg again. He was distressed by his short visit with his father, just as much as she was by her mother.

"Of course," Gregg played it off. "What about you?"

"She'll be fine," Harvey wrapped his arm protectively around Ashley. "She has me to look after her."

"Harvey," Ashley withdrew from his embrace. To say that she was a bit perturbed was putting it mildly. "Can you give us a moment?"

"Sure." Reluctantly, Harvey walked a few feet away.

"Boyfriend?" Gregg couldn't help but ask.

"Friend."

"Seems a bit more to me than that."

"He's just a friend," she assured. "You look pale coming out of your father's room. Are you sure you okay?"

"He's on life support," Gregg sighed. "The fact that he is not breathing on his own is kind of surreal for me. If they took away the machine, he'd…be…gone…just like that." The truth hurt.

"I know it must be hard on you," instinctively Ashley grabbed his hand. "Your dad is a fighter, remember that. Hold onto it with all your might."

"I will." Gregg choked, swallowing the lump lodged securely in his throat.

"Do you have a piece of paper to write my number on?" she asked. "I want you to call me if you need anything or if you just want someone to talk to." Ashley sensed that he didn't need to be alone right now. He needed a friend and for some reason, she wanted to be that friend.

"Better yet," he reached into his pocket and retrieved his business card from his wallet. "Why don't you call me tonight?"

"Oh," she lowered her head. "All right."

"Thanks for everything Ashley," Gregg said. "I'm glad you were here even under terrible circumstances."

"Me too."

"You better go before your FRIEND pierces a hole into me from gawking so hard," Gregg chuckled.

Ashley looked over her shoulder and saw Harvey staring back. "See you later. Take care."

"You, too." With sadness, Gregg watched her walk away to leave with another man. He wasn't a wee-bit jealous. He was hugely jealous! The realization stupefied him.

CHAPTER 19

Harvey and the Finely Clan

"**H**ow do you know that guy?" Harvey asked on the way to Ashley's home.

"He is Thomas' principal."

"The Terminator?" Harvey was slightly thrown off guard. Albeit, he was a tall giant of a man, the principal didn't match Thomas' vivid description. He appeared more timid than frigid.

"He's no Terminator," Ashley dismissed. "True, he is a very firm man, but he's also fair. He doesn't allow the students to get away with wrongdoings—including Thomas."

"Do the crime, pay the time," Harvey deduced. "Thomas says he's a big bully."

"Well, that big bully sure is sticking his neck out, making it possible for Thomas to play basketball again. I'm sure Thomas is seeing him in a different light now."

Harvey looked over and glimpsed her eyes sparkling, something he hadn't seen in a long time. *She likes him!*

"Mother had a little more color today," she chatted. "She wasn't as pale as she was yesterday. Thomas says we have to have faith that she will pull through. Seems peculiar coming from Thomas."

"Spiritual training prevails every time."

"I know." Ashley peered out the window, thinking of how quickly life changes. Nothing stays the same. Bad things happen to good people. *Ultimately, the bad will work out for our good. It always does!*

"Thomas seems to be on the right track."

"He is," she stated. "Thanks to Dr. Jefferson."

The comment unnerved Harvey. Harvey gazed at her with wonderment. He envied the man who could make Ashley's eyes light up, even in his absence. His heart sank. Hope became a dim flicker in the midst of uncertainty.

Later, Harvey enjoyed dinner with the Finleys. He was glad that he had bought the dinner earlier. Attempting to forget about Dr. Jefferson, Harvey made the best of the evening.

Afterwards, the family gathered in the small den and watched a movie. The comedy birthed laughter in the room, even though their hearts were occupied with thoughts of Sandra Finley.

Enjoying the night off, Ashley couldn't remember the last time she had enjoyed a Friday night movie with her family, which included Harvey. Several times, she caught Harvey staring at her, which was disconcerting.

"I better be going." Harvey stood up after the movie ended. He didn't want to go, but he knew it was the proper thing to do.

"I'll walk you to the door," Ashley rose to her feet. "Danny it's your night to take a bath first, then Donny, and Lacey. Thomas, you're last tonight."

"No hot water for me," Thomas grunted.

"You probably could use a cold shower," Harvey winked. "I find that a cold shower clears the head. I'll probably take me a cold shower as soon as I get home, too." Harvey gazed at

Ashley with a look that caused her concern.

"Whatever! See you later, Harvey."

"Maybe we can shoot some hoops tomorrow."

"I didn't know you play basketball."

"How hard can it be?"

Thomas laughed. "I think I'll pass. Goodnight."

"I wouldn't mind taking him to the gym." Harvey felt snubbed by the sixteen-year-old.

"He's really good, Harvey. He doesn't want to play basketball with an amateur," she said tenderly. "Don't take it personally."

"I had a good time tonight."

"Me too."

"Good enough to have lunch with me tomorrow."

"I can't," she answered quickly. "I plan on going to the hospital at ten and stay for the next visit at noon."

"Can we go out for a late lunch?"

"I have so much cleaning to do before I go to work at night."

"At least let me take you in the morning and pick you up. It'll save time on the bus."

Ashley gazed at him for a minute. Not wanting to hurt his feelings, she agreed.

"Good. I will pick you up at 9:30." Harvey leaned over and pecked Ashley on the lips. "Goodnight!" He trotted away, rather satisfied.

Ashley stood outside long after Harvey's car had pulled away. She sat on the steps and allowed her mind to wander away.

Why can't I feel for Harvey what he feels for me? It would be so much easier if I did.

"Hey, Sis!" Thomas interrupted her thoughts. "Lacey is about ready for her bath."

"The twins must have jumped in and out of the tub." Ashley shook her head, leaping up.

"You know Danny and Donny."

"Yeah, they probably didn't even get in the tub."

"Harvey's got the *hots* for you really bad," Thomas, teased.

"He does not!"

"He does so." Thomas liked badgering his sister. "The question is do you have the hots for him?"

"We're friends."

"Harvey wants more."

"How do you know?"

"'*Cuz* he told me at the game. He says he wants to marry you and with me being the man of the house he asked me how I felt about it."

Ashley froze. "What? How dare he ask you!"

"I am the man of the house." Thomas stood taller, sticking out his chest.

"You are," Ashley didn't want to burst his bubble.

"I think you should marry him. He has a nice house. You wouldn't have to work two jobs."

"And leave my family? I don't think so."

"He said we all could live with him," Thomas went on. "It's in a better neighborhood. Danny and Donny don't need to be around this rough life. They could go to their old school. It's hard enough on me. I don't want them to end up making the same mistakes I made."

"Oh, Thomas," Ashley reached up and pressed her hand gently upon his cheek. "We all make mistakes. You can live in the best house, in the best neighborhood, with the best schools and make terrible mistakes. The key is to learn from your mistakes, which I believe you are learning."

"I am." Thomas wanted so desperately to win back his sister's trust. "So, are you going to say yes to Harvey?"

"I think Harvey is a great man and wonderful friend, but I am not in love with him."

"You can learn to love him."

"Wow!" Ashley earnestly looked at him. "Where did that come from?"

"I think love is overrated. Look at what it did to mother. She loved father to death—literally. Even after he treated her like crap. I think that what you and Harvey have is more stable than what our parents shared."

She hated that Thomas saw love in such a deplorable way. "Settling for less than God's best blocks us from experiencing life in its fullness. I want…"

"Ash!" Lacey yelled. "My hair is all wet."

"Oh, no!" Ashley rushed inside.

Lying in her mother's bed, Ashley held Dr. Jefferson's business card in her hand. She struggled with her emotions. She battled the strange feelings concerning the principal who had a swaggered strut that held one's attention. When he opened his mouth, people stopped just to hear what he had to say. Gregg's eyes, hazelnut and somewhat doleful, kept an audience captive. Tall, dark and handsome was his mantle. Though he appeared rough and mean, Ashley had glimpsed Gregg's mellow side, which intrigued her even the more.

I should call him. She fought not to. Lastly, losing the battle, Ashley dialed the number, anyway.

He answered on the third ring.

"I hope I didn't wake you."

"No, you didn't." Gregg looked at the clock and sat upward. It was almost midnight. "I can't sleep."

"Me either."

"I'm glad you called."

"Me, too. How is your dad?"

"He is still the same. The doctor's wanted me to think about if his condition worsens, whether or not I want to keep him on a life support."

"Don't give up," Ashley urged. "Your dad is a fighter, just like my mother."

"My dad stopped fighting a long time ago. The only thing he cares about is his precious business. Other than that, nothing matters. I'm not sure if he even wants to live."

"I think he just needs a reason." Ashley hesitated to say more. "You're that reason."

"I don't think so."

"Grief can kill a soul. It drains the life out. Even though his life is not over, he feels that way. Your father is afraid to live again, just like my mother. Life dealt both of them hard blows. I think they need us to help them remember that life can be good. Maybe not like it was before, but different—even better with time."

Silence followed as Gregg pondered her nuggets of wisdom. "Are you going to the hospital tomorrow?"

"Yes. I plan on being their around ten o'clock."

"Do you need a ride?"

"No, Harvey is taking me."

Harvey!

Silence followed again.

This time, Ashley broke the silence barrier. "How are you really doing?"

"I'm fine. Just a little tired. Even though I didn't go into work today, I am mentally exhausted. I have been working a little at home. I have to rewrite our school's focused renewal plan. It's a tedious task."

"I've been reading that if Brookland doesn't come out of the negative report rating the State Department of Education is going to take over or shut it down."

"Both are possible."

"That's so sad."

"It is because Brookland is expected to come up with the same results as a school like Richview. It is ludicrous. Our students come from two different worlds. Poverty plagues us while wealth engulfs them. Our students are from either a one family home or practically raising themselves. Schools like Richview have both parents thoroughly invested in their children's education. Not to mention our special education students encompass 40% of the student population." The conversation about the school went on for another twenty minutes or so. Gregg was passionate about saving the school.

"I think the school district has the right man for the job in turning around the school," Ashley endorsed. "Your passion for the students and wealth of knowledge on how to get out of the cesspool of failure goes a long way in my book. It takes firm discipline, too. Without it, the school and students wouldn't stand a chance. Seems like you were put in the right place at the right time. And…" Ashley bit her lip. "I'm going on and on like I'm some expert. I must sound crazy, babbling like this."

"Nothing you say sounds crazy to me. Please go on," Gregg asserted.

"But, I'm sort of glad Thomas got into trouble. It gave me a chance to meet you and to know you...in a different way. I mean, Thomas had me thinking you were the Terminator," she laughed. "But you're just the opposite."

Her words touched him deeply. "Thank you. I feel the same way. It has been a pleasure meeting you and getting to know you a little better. I think Thomas has helped me to see that the students are all different and they simply need to know that people care about them, personally and academically. Yes, I need to be firm and fair, but I need to listen more, as well."

"Well, it's late and I need to get my beauty sleep," Ashley joshed.

"It's working every night, because Ashley Finley, you are one beautiful woman."

If only he could see her flaming red cheeks. "What a nice thing to say."

"It's the truth," Gregg cleared his throat. "I will see you tomorrow, hopefully."

"Okay. Well, goodnight."

"Good morning, Ashley," he amended.

"You're right," she chuckled.

"Sleep well."

"You, too."

"Thanks for calling. I was feeling kind of down...about my father."

"We will all get through this."

"I didn't think his sickness would have this kind of effect on me," Gregg swallowed the pain, wedged in his throat. "I mean he's been a father in name only." Suddenly, the conversation started up again.

"But he is still your father and at one time in your life, you did have a relationship with him."

"It's just hard to believe that he might not make it, you know."

"He'll make it."

Gregg held the phone to his ear, while his thoughts ran wild. "I was just thinking, if something did happen to him, I have no other close family alive. That's a saddening thought... to be alone...with no one who really knows me or cares about me." The realization brought anguish to the core of his soul.

Ashley felt crushed by his gloomy revelation. She weighed her words carefully before speaking. "I care about you," her voice was sweet and soothing to the receiver. "You are not alone. I am here."

"Really?" Gregg swallowed back his emotions as best he could.

"Really. Anytime you need to talk or you need a...friend, I'm available."

A sense of relief washed over him, leaving Gregg with a peace he had not felt in some time. "Ashley, you don't know how much that means to me."

"You would do the same for me, I'm sure."

He thought about it and concluded, "In a heartbeat."

"We can be there for each other. When I'm weak I can lean on you for strength and vice versa."

"Sounds great to me," Gregg felt better. "I appreciate it so much, Ashley."

"I appreciate you, Gregg."

"Well, I really must let you go now. I'm sorry for keeping you up with my troubles."

"I've enjoyed talking to you."

"See you soon, Ashley."

The way he said her name was sweeter than honeycomb. "See you soon, Gregg."

CHAPTER 20

The Other Woman— The Other Man

"**G**regg," Naomi Rivas gently shook him. "Ms. Tiffany is waiting in the foyer for you."

"Who?" Gregg stretched, still trying to get used to staying in his father's house.

"Ms. Tiffany, your friend…her parents live next door."

"Oh," he looked at his clock. "Tell her I'm sleeping." Gregg closed his eyes, attempting to find sleep again.

"She insisted that I wake you."

Wiping his eyes, Gregg slowly pulled himself up. "What does she want?"

"You!" Naomi's eyes twinkled in merriment.

"Senorita Rivas, it's too early to be naughty."

"Tell that to Ms. Tiffany." She marched to the door. "Hurry up. You don't want to keep the queen waiting."

Looking at the clock again, he grimaced. "What is she doing here at eight o'clock in the morning?"

Growing up with the spoiled girl next door, Gregg knew that Tiffany cared little about intruding on other people's time and plans. Over the years, she would often pop up for a one-night stand. Neither she nor Gregg wanted anything serious, just a good night of pleasure. This promiscuity drew them together, whenever convenient.

After quickly showering and slipping on khakis and a navy colored shirt, Gregg trotted downstairs to greet his guest.

"I was just about to leave." Tiffany pouted, kissing him on the cheek. "Don't you know it's not nice keeping a lady waiting?"

"What lady?"

"Oh, Gregg," she playfully nudged him. "Let's go play."

"You're thirty…"

"Years young," she finished his sentenced, "and ready to have some fun. I thought we could go to the lake, get some sun, and then have fun." Boldly, she kissed him on the lips.

"I…I can't," he pulled away a little frazzled. Generally, he looked forward to the quickie tryst with the blonde-haired, three-time married, still married woman. Born into wealth, married for wealth, Tiffany lived a jollifying lifestyle. She enjoyed partying, drinking, and socializing with the opposite sex, which was why none of her marriages lasted long—except maybe her current one—over two years.

"You must." Tiffany pouted again. "I came back home just for you."

"You're running from which man this time?" Gregg was only the wiser.

"You know me too, well."

"My father is in the hospital."

"I'm sorry to hear that," earnestly she responded. "I've always liked your father."

At least you did. "I'm visiting him at 10:00 o'clock and again at noon time."

"Let us just visit him at noon."

"Us?"

"Yes, I will go with you. Then, we'll go to the lake to lift up our spirits," she came closer. "Then we'll come back here and celebrate some more," she fluttered her long, fake eyelashes.

Her intentions were clear to Gregg, but they didn't appeal to him. Something was changing in him and he didn't understand it. Perhaps, it was the fact that his father was possibly dying. "I'm not sure that I'm up to..."

Passionately and turbulently, Tiffany thrust her lips upon him and wrapped her arm around him, using her body seductively to change his mind. It always worked in the past.

And it worked at present.

"Okay, we'll spend the day together."

"All of it?" Her eyebrows arched inquisitively.

"Most of it. I still have to visit my father."

"Good," she embraced him.

"Gregg," Ms. Rivas interrupted the cozy scene, "breakfast is ready."

"Thank you, Senorita Rivas. Ms. Tiffany will be joining us."

Ashley spoke briefly with Dr. Phelps, who informed her that he had expected her mother to awaken from the coma by now. He and the staff had done all they could for Ms. Finley, but the rest was up to her. She wasn't getting worst, but she wasn't getting any better either.

"I know I pushed you too hard, and I am sorry. Please, forgive me." Ashley gently rested her head upon her mother's bosom. "Don't you hear the bells, Momma? They are ringing just for you."

Ashley stayed there, nestling as close to her mother's bosom as possible. She needed her mother's comfort. She felt down. Perhaps because she was anticipating on seeing Gregg earlier, but didn't. She spent more time in the mirror fixing her hair, letting it hang loose and free. She even wore a pink lip-gloss, which Pam had given to her. Ashley hardly ever wore pants, but today she wore black slacks and a purple blouse, just for Gregg.

During the noon visit, Gregg was with his father. Mr. Jefferson's condition was declining. He was dependant on the machine keeping him alive. His prognosis was grim. The weight of his father's probable demise consumed Gregg with guilt and regrets.

While Gregg and Ashley visited their parents, in the waiting area two different people awaited their return. Impatiently, Tiffany perused several magazines, glancing at the pictures, uninteresting in the various articles. Tiffany wanted nothing more than to leave the grim place and paint the town with Gregg on her arm.

Next to her sat Harvey. His heart agonized over Ashley's family having endured so much, and yet, the family bond was still strong. The Finley's faith in God kept them above water, and not under. Harvey used the quiet time to pray for the family. They mattered a great deal to him. The *Finleys* somehow filled the shoes of his belated loved ones.

Simultaneously, Gregg and Ashley exited their parents' hospital rooms. Gregg was the first to notice Ashley. Tears stung her eyes. Stepping toward her, Gregg tenderly reached over and wiped away her tears with his hand.

The simple gesture soothed Ashley somehow. A sensation

of peace washed over her being. She needed his touch more than Gregg could have ever imagined at that moment. Words were not spoken as their eyes transmitted a deep understanding. For a brief moment, the world around them did not exist. The problems of their parents did not crush them. Fleetingly, pain succumbed to the tranquility of the moment. Time stood still. Quietness engulfed them, as the two hearts connected.

Gazing at Ashley, Gregg beheld his mother in a sense. Like his mother, Ashley displayed her gentle heart on her face. Often, his father would say his mother was an open book for the entire world to read, with nothing to hide, but with everything to rightfully showoff. Maybe that is why Gregg found himself strangely attracted to her.

"How is your dad?" she asked, finding her voice.

"Not so good. His chances for survival look pretty grim." he shoulders slumped. "How is your mother?"

"No change," she sighed.

"The doctor said it's just a matter of time..." Gregg couldn't go on.

Grabbing his hand, Ashley boldly asked, "Can I pray for your father?"

Gregg shrugged, feeling uncomfortable and yet, his soul unfolded to the hope which prayer offered.

Ashley closed her eyes and prayed. "Gracious and loving Father God, we come to you in the name of Jesus, asking that you touch Mr. Jefferson. In spite of what the doctors say, I know and believe that You have the final word. Heal him, touch him and deliver him from death. He shall live and not die. Save his soul and make him whole again. Strengthen his human heart and his spiritual soul. Work a miracle for him and through him. And God, touch Gregg," she squeezed his hand, sending electricity throughout his body. "Strengthen his body, mind, soul, and spirit. Let him know that You are a God who heals and restores. Let him know that You are a Heavenly Father who will never turn Your back on him because You care about him and love him. Heal his father and restore their relationship, healing every hurt in their lives. This we ask in Jesus' name, touching and agreeing that You have heard and You have answered...."

Sensing the prayer was ending, from out of nowhere Gregg added, "And heal Ashley's mother and bless her family with peace, love, strength and joy. Meet every need in their lives. Amen."

"Amen," fresh tears flowed, but her face was radiant. His prayer touched Ashley deeply. The fact that he prayed was a miracle, for sure. Awkwardly, Ashley released his hands, which made Gregg suddenly feel cold and empty. "We'll get through this. God has allowed me to be here for you and vice versa, for such a time as this."

For such a time as this! Gregg thought of his mother's song. He stood, unsure and unsettled. Did God really send Ashley into his life? Was it providence that they both were visiting parents in ICU? Was it all just a coincidence?

"We better go before they kick us out," his smile was warm.

"You're right."

Immediately, their guests stood as the two came through the ICU double doors.

"Ash!" Harvey came forward. Once more, he felt threatened by the tall man who stood beside her.

Likewise, Gregg was disheartened by Harvey's presence. *I should have known he would wait for her.* The green-eyed monster showed his color again.

"It's about time," Tiffany joined them. "How is your father?"

Wow! She is gorgeous! Ashley felt under-dress, under-beautified, and under-privileged standing near the blonde bombshell attaching herself to Gregg.

"Ashley," Gregg cleared his throat to do the formal introductions, "this is my friend, Tiffany. Tiffany this is Ashley and her friend uh…" He played dumb. Rest assured Gregg knew the man's name.

"Harvey!" Harvey stated, shaking Tiffany's hand, all the while eyeing Gregg with a look of distrust.

"Nice to meet you," Tiffany replied, tossing her long blonde hair back. Glancing over at Ashley, Tiffany didn't feel the least bit envious. She didn't view Ashley as competition. Her dress attire was evidence that she was second-rate in Tiffany's book. There was nothing special about her, except for her eyes. They were magnetic. Oh, and she had the loveliest, thick hair Tiffany had ever seen. *Maybe she is a tad bit nice-looking,* Tiffany had to acknowledge.

"We better go." Harvey grabbed Ashley's arm. "We promised the children a picnic at the park." Harvey made sure Gregg heard their plans. He didn't like the way he was looking at *HIS* girl.

"Do you have to work tonight?" Gregg asked, delaying their departure. He wanted to knock the possession chip off Harvey's puny shoulders. *He thinks he is a part of their family. Maybe he will be.* The thought sickened him.

"Unfortunately, yes," Ashley kept her eyes on him.

"We're going to the lake," Tiffany spouted giddily. "I bought this awesome bikini just for you." Unashamedly, she faced Gregg with devilment, holding him tighter.

Ugh! How brazen of her! The green-eyed-monster piggybacked off Gregg onto Ashley.

"Have a good day." Gregg nodded to them both, and then escorted Tiffany down the hall. He felt ill, knowing that Ashley probably was thinking badly of him being with this seductive woman. Surely, Ashley thought the relationship to be more than friendship the way Tiffany was clinging to him.

Allowing Harvey to walk her down the long hallway to the elevators, Ashley just wanted to go home and have a good cry… then she saw Gregg and Tiffany at the elevators. Awkwardly, both couples rode the elevator down in silence. Gregg couldn't help but glance over at Ashley who was looking back at him.

Once again, their eyes spoke what their hearts felt. For a fleeting second, Gregg smiled and Ashley returned the gesture. Harvey witnessed the warm moment, which sickened him. Tiffany, looking in her mirror, was too absorbed in herself to notice anything happening around her.

Unable to contain himself, Gregg winked at Ashley.

Her cheeks brightened red just before Ashley lowered her head. She felt like a teenager, giddy and foolish.

Observant Harvey didn't miss the gesture as he looked at his opponent *right dead* in the eyes.

Gregg took the bait and stared back at him, not batting an eyelid. He did not feel guilty, even though he had a woman literally hanging on his arm.

On the ride back, Tiffany boldly spoke her feelings. "That woman looks like an old-maid. Did you see those threadbare black pants? And what woman goes out the house barefaced with no makeup on? She didn't even have on lipstick."

"Ashley is not an old-maid," Gregg defended. "Her mother is sick. She could care less about things like that. Her mind is on her mother."

"Someone needs to tell her that she's not fifty."

Gregg looked at her with disdain. How had he tolerated Tiffany all these years? How? Because he was just like her. Selfish. Narcissistic. Materialistic. More concerned about the outer appearance than what was on the inside. They both enjoyed having fun, even at the expense of hurting others. Neither wanted a serious relationship with the other, just a good time. Nothing more and nothing less.

"How in the world do you know her? You don't travel in the same circle?"

"Her brother goes to my school."

"Isn't it a bad school? Nothing like our private schools."

"It's not a bad school!" Gregg snapped, frustrated by her judgmental attitude.

"Touchy," she looked at him. "Don't tell me you like the girl. She is poor for goodness sake! Not one of us."

"She's...." he didn't feel like discussing her with Tiffany. She would never understand. "Let's drop it."

"Sure, Honey," Tiffany felt chided. "I'm ready to go to the lake. Do you think your housekeeper will prepare us a lunch for our outing?"

"Senorita Rivas," he righted, "will be happy to."

About an hour later, Gregg and Tiffany sat by the lake, enjoying the sun. The weather was perfect for Tiffany's tanning, but Gregg felt like the sun was cooking him from head to toe.

"I'm going to be two shades darker," Gregg replied. "The sun is okay for you. You can stand a tan," he teased. "But I'm a black man, already suntanned from birth."

"Yeah," she eased over, "and a perfect tan it is." Tiffany massaged her fingers through his curly locks. "I've always been attracted to you. I don't know why we never married."

"Probably because you have always had another man in your life."

"But I keep coming back to you."

"Only because you know I'm not looking for anything serious."

"Why not be serious?" she eyed him. "I think that all the other guys were just a tease. You're the real thing."

"All the other guys had huge bank accounts."

"So do you."

"No," he stated flatly. "My dad has a huge bank account. I'm a principal, living off a principal's salary."

"You don't have to."

"I want to."

"Life could be so much fun if you'd just spend your daddy's money."

"My life is fun."

"Really?" Tiffany pulled back. "I don't think so. You don't appear happy to me."

"My father is very ill," he reasoned. "It's kind of hard being happy when he just might die on me."

"You have never been close to your father."

"It doesn't matter." Gregg refuted, quickly leaping onto his feet. "He is still my father!"

"I'm sorry," Tiffany stood close to him. "I wish nothing but the best for your father…and you." She wanted to make things better, for selfish reasons. "I was thinking I might just stick around for a while. Maybe a week or two."

"You're really running this time," Gregg turned to her, knowing there was more to Tiffany's story. She didn't just show up on his doorstop for no reason. "What's up? Do not play games with me. I know you, Tiff."

"Trevor is seeing someone else," she began. "And he thinks I don't know about it. So if he thinks he can just treat me like that, I'll make him regret the day he ever cheated on me."

"He doesn't know where you are?"

"He probably thinks I went running to my parents."

"Well, didn't you?"

"Not yet. I was thinking I could just stay with you."

You got to be kidding! He was floored by her unexpected invitation. "Uh...um...I don't know if...if that's a good idea."

"I promise not to get in your way. I just need time to think."

"Right now, I'm staying with dad...to help take care of him."

"Even better! I can visit my parents, and Trevor won't know I'm practically next door...if and when he looks for me."

"We're friends and friends help each other out," Gregg said from the heart. "But, there will be no visiting each other's room. I'm serious, Tiffany."

"You mean we can't sleep together," she pouted. "That's always been a part of our friendship."

"This time I think you need to concentrate on your marriage. I think you really love Trevor. He's different from the others."

"He hurt me, Gregg. Usually, I can just shake it off, but he hurt me to the core. I don't think I can forgive him or trust him."

"What if you're wrong?"

"What if I'm not?"

"Time will tell," he replied. "Either way, we're friends, Tiffany...with no fringe benefits this time. Got it?"

She sulked. "Got it."

CHAPTER 21

Crystalline Eyes

Spending the day with Harvey proved to be more of a chore than recreational. Constantly, Ashley had to force a smile, fake a laugh, tolerate unwanted affections and pretend that everything was just dandy. She used to enjoy Harvey's presence and his friendship. Now, everything had changed. Although Harvey wasn't talking about marriage and a baby carriage, his actions shouted it all the same.

Watching her siblings enjoy a rare treat of fun was worth any discomfort Ashley was feeling. Danny and Donny played tag football against Thomas and Harvey, while Lacey cheered for them all. Ashley was supposedly keeping score. *Poor* Harvey, he did not have a lick of athleticism in him. He couldn't catch a ball. Plainly, Harvey feared being tackled even by the scrawny twins. After playing a simple game of volleyball, Harvey appeared dog-tired. Yet, Ashley had to give him credit because Harvey persevered and continue to play even though he bombed at sports.

The weather was perfect. The simple lunch, which Harvey provided was perfect. The enjoyment of her siblings was perfect. Harvey was perfect. *Too perfect.* Danny and Donny liked him. Thomas liked him. Lacey adored him. Still, Ashley could not bridge the gap of friendship to something more intimate.

I wish with all my heart that I could love Harvey. He's a Christian. He has good morals and integrity. The children think highly of him. Momma loves him. Why can't I feel more for him than friendship? He's like a brother to me. Why doesn't my heart quicken when he's near me, like with Gregg? I feel so alive with Gregg even though we're practically strangers. But...I'm nothing like that beautiful blonde at the hospital...

"What are you writing?" Harvey sat down beside Ashley.

"Private thoughts."

"Anything about me?"

"Maybe."

"Anything good?"

"Maybe." Ashley closed her journal.

"Anything bad?"

"Maybe."

"Anything hopeful?" Harvey subtly cracked the door to his proposal.

She didn't answer.

"Today feels so right. We're all one big family." Harvey openly shared his feelings, even though he felt Ashley tensed up when he wrapped his arm around her. "I love your family. I thank God for you all...especially you."

Ashley looked away. *He loves my family, but does Harvey really love me? Romantically?*

"When Mother Sandra gets better, hopefully, we can all be together."

"You're pushing Harvey," Ashley finally spoke. "You promised."

"I know," Harvey stared at her with longing. "It's just that I care for you so much, and I want us to be one big happy family. I know we can be."

"Harvey…"

"I'm not pushing. I am just expressing my feelings." He titled slightly to his right and kissed her on the cheek.

"They're kissing." Lacey pointed giggling, wholly amused by the simple scene.

"Hush!" Ashley said, a mixture of emotions going through her. "Are you all ready to eat?"

"I'm hungry," Lacey answered.

"Me too!" The others chimed in harmoniously.

"Let's eat then." Ashley busied herself fixing plates for everyone as they sat at the wooden picnic table.

"Harvey, will you bless the food?" Ashley turned to him. He was sitting so close Ashley could feel his body touching her, which irritated her more than anything.

After praying, Harvey grabbed Ashley's hand for a moment, squeezed it and let it go.

Ashley glanced at him, involuntarily forcing her lips upward.

Harvey's heart soared.

Ashley's heart fell.

For truly, Ashley cared and even loved Harvey. She just wasn't in love with him. It pained her to think that she could lose Harvey's friendship by not accepting his proposal. Now that would be a *hard pill to swallow*.

After the family returned home from the picnic, Harvey stayed until it was time to take Ashley to work. While she readied herself, Thomas and Harvey chatted.

"You really want to marry my sister, don't you?"

"I do," Harvey answered straightway.

"She's been through a lot," Thomas eyed him, "and I don't want to see her hurt."

"Do you honestly think I would hurt Ashley? I care a lot about hurt."

"Do you love her?"

Harvey hesitated a little too long for Thomas' liking.

"Of course. I have known Ashley for a long time and we're good together. We are best friends. There is no better way than to start a marriage with a foundation of friendship."

"But people hurt the ones they love all the time." Thomas thoughts went to his father, who professed his love for his mother time and time again, and yet he had so many women on the side.

"I'm not your father." Harvey put his hand on Thomas' shoulder sensing his concerns. "I love the Lord and I will not do anything to displease Him. I will take care of Ashley and her family. As I said to you before, I want you all to live with us."

"Maybe Ashley is not looking for a caretaker," wisely the young man spoke. "Maybe she just wants someone to love her."

"We've been friends for a long time…I've always loved her."

Is it the friendship kind of love? Or is it the marrying type of love? Thomas kept silent, pondering it all in his heart.

"Hey, Ash. You look refreshed." Pam greeted.

"I feel refreshed."

"How is your mother?"

"The same," Ashley answered, "but thankfully she's not any worse."

"She'll pull through," Pam encouraged.

"So what's up with you?" Ashley noticed a difference in her friend. She looked more like her old self. "You're glowing."

"Got a date."

"A date," Ashley was dumbfounded. "With who?"

"His name is Willie. We were friends a long time ago, but he moved away. He came here last night. We talked after work and he asked me to go out tonight after work."

"That's kind of late, isn't it?" Removing the friendship hat, Ashley replaced it with her motherly hat. She was concerned about Pam's wellbeing. Her friend's traumatic experience was still fresh in her mind.

"It's fine. I trust Willie. He's good people."

"People change."

"Not Willie!"

"How can you be so sure?"

"He's a minister," Pam turned away.

"What?" Ashley went and stood in front of her friend. "You got to be kidding."

"I'm not." Pam laughed. "He's not a preacher, but a minister of music or something like that."

"And you're going out with him?"

"Yes. It is not like we are getting married. It's just two old friends getting together and talking."

"My goodness!" Ashley was blown out of the water. As much as Pam snubbed church folks and the entire church concept, it was a miracle that she would even consider going out with a minister. "Miracles happen every day."

"Don't go getting all spiritual on me," Pam cautioned. "I'm

still me. I still drink when I want to. I still party when I want to. No man is going to change that." Pam turned on her heels, sashaying away.

"Don't be so sure," Ashley had the last word.

"Good to see you," Andrew interrupted her cheerful thoughts. "You look better tonight."

"Thanks."

"How is your mother?"

"About the same."

"My church is praying for her, but I didn't know her name other than Finley to put on the prayer request list."

"Her name is Sandra Finley."

"S-a-n-d-r-a Finley," he repeated, the light clicking in his head. "I used to know a Sandra from here."

"Oh yeah," Ashley smiled.

"What's your mother's maiden name?"

"Gantt."

Oh, my goodness. It can't be. Not the same Sandra Gantt who stole my heart and never gave it back? I should have known. She looks just like her, except...the eyes...she has crystalline eyes like... He turned white as a ghost. *Could it be possible? She has to be in her early twenties. It was over twenty-three years ago when...*

"Are you okay, Andrew?" Ashley thought he was going to faint. "Do you know my mother?"

He couldn't speak. He nodded slowly.

"Really?" Ashley could not believe it. This strange man, who made her feel creepy, just might have a connection to her mother.

"I...uh..."

"You need to sit down." Ashley tried to help him. "I need

222

to go get some help. You look ill."

"Just get me some water." He sat in the chair, perspiring, dropping sweat through his pores like a leaky faucet.

Quickly, Ashley complied. "Here," she handing him a cold glass of water. "What's wrong with you?"

"I'm fine," Andrew gulped down the water. His mind reeling a mile a minute. *Sandra Gantt! The love of my life. The one who got away. Oh my goodness. Lord, what kind of trick are you playing on me?*

"You're pale as can be," Ashley fretted.

"What's going on in here?" Pam rushed to her friend side, fearing that Andrew had come onto her too strongly and that Ashley had hit him or something.

"He's sick," Ashley stuttered.

"He was fine a minute ago," Pam was not convinced.

"I'm fine, "Andrew stood up, trying to gather his composure. "Excuse me, ladies. I'm going outside for some fresh air. I'll be right back.

"You better," Pam chastened. "We have a full crowd tonight."

"Just give me a minute," he looked at Ashley before walking outside. She was beautiful just like her mother. No wonder he felt protective of her. She was the daughter of the woman who meant the world to him, even after all these years.

"Are you sure you're going to be all right?" Ashley still fretted.

"Don't worry about me. I'm in good hands." Andrew pointed upward, smiled and then walked away.

"What's up with him?" Pam looked at her friend. "He sure is weird."

"I don't know what happened. I think he knows my mother.

They grew up together."

"Did you notice that you two have the same eyes—crystal clear?" Pam mentioned. "What are the odds of that?"

"I have never really noticed. He wears glasses most of the time."

"He had them off just now. You couldn't have missed his eyes," Pam would not let it go. "It's spooky. I have never seen anyone with your strange eyes before."

"My eyes aren't strange—just unique." Ashley grinned. "What can I say? God made me unique."

"Whatever! Do you still think he is a pervert?"

"Not really. He's just strange."

"He could just be a strange pervert, then," Pam laughed.

"Hush!" Ashley shoved her friend. "He's a Christian."

"That is what he keeps telling us, but I'm not so convinced," Pam stated. "Shoot, what's up with all you Christian people? I am surrounded by them everywhere I go."

"Seems like God's trying to get your attention," Ashley grinned. "And I think its working."

"Whatever!"

CHAPTER 22

Back from the Dead

Lord, what kind of trick is this? You cannot be for real! Silently, Andrew talked to his Master. *Sandra Gantt has a daughter that looks like her, but she has eyes like mine. No one has those kinds of eyes but my mother's side of the family. Ashley has to be in her early twenties...twenty-two or twenty-three, which would be the same time I left for the army. Sandra promised me she would wait for me, but then we had that terrible argument. She accused me of cheating on her with her best friend Lena, which was a complete lie. I was so mad. We both said things we should not have, but it was all in the heat of anger.*

Oh, God, Sandra would have told me if she was carrying my child, wouldn't she? When I returned home on leave, I had heard she had married that Finley guy. He was a jerk from what I heard about him. There had to be something good about him for Sandra to marry him. I have to see her! I have to know if the girl with eyes like mine is my child. Lord, You know how badly I wanted a family, a child.

When my wife died after only three years of marriage, unable to have children of her own, I was left alone. Could it be Lord? Please talk to me. Please show me the truth.

Heal my Sandra. Make her whole. Touch her. After all these years, my heart still pines for her.

What now?

I have ordered your steps…follow Me.

I will follow.

Andrew found it difficult to concentrate on cooking the rest of the night. Every time he saw Ashley, it was like looking into the lens of the past seeing Sandra in her younger years. Sandra Gantt was so beautiful. She could have had any guy and she chose him. He always felt truly blessed to be with her. His love for Sandra was genuine and eternal. To this day, Andrew still felt something for her. If it were not for him joining the army, he was certain that they would have married and would have been together to this day.

Back then, Sandra couldn't understand why Andrew was joining the army during wartime. She said it was ridiculous and gave him an ultimatum. If he joined the army, their relationship was over because she wouldn't wait, not knowing if he would live through the war or not. It didn't help matters when her best friend Lena came over his house pretending she wanted to talk about Sandra, saying she would convince Sandra that he was only joining the army to make a better future for them. Lena was always jealous of their relationship. Secretly, she wanted Andrew for herself.

Later, Sandra told him that Lena said he had made a pass at her. It was crazy! Andrew was angry that Sandra took her word over his. They both said offensive things in the heat of the argument, which neither could take back. Two days later, Andrew had left for basic training. When he was permitted, he called Sandra, but she refused to talk to him.

By and by, after completing basic training Andrew returned only to find that Sandra had a quickie marriage to some guy she barely knew. Andrew was determined to see her, alone.

For three days, he trailed her, finally, catching her alone in her new home. His mind could still behold the scene as if he was watching a rerun of that unforgettable day.

"Andrew," Sandra opened the door, surprised to see him. "Lena said you were in town."

"How could you do this Sandra?" Andrew blurted, unable to contain himself. "How could you marry another man when you know that I love you?"

"You didn't love me enough to stay," Sandra rolled her eyes.

"I told you this was for us," his heart was breaking. "I wanted us to have a good life, better than the hard life we both had to endure in our younger years."

"It's too late. You made your choice and I made mine." Sandra said stiffly, but inside she was miserable. Still, Sandra loved Andrew, but she had to forget him. She had to let him go. "Tom is a good man."

"So just like that, you just stop loving me," his eyes misted.

Sandra did not answer.

"Just like that, you turn to another man. I could never do that to you. You have broken my heart, Sandra. I don't think I will ever recover."

"You will."

"That is all you have to say."

"There is nothing else to say, Andrew. I am married now. You chose the military when you knew how much I hated it. Then when you returned home, the first person you go see is Lena. That says a lot."

"Lena!" Andrew nearly yelled. "I couldn't find you, so I went to Lena in hopes of discovering your whereabouts. And you know what? Lena made another pass at me. She is the one who wants me, not the other way around. One day you will discover that and when you do…"

"It won't matter," Sandra said sorrowfully.

"I guess it won't," he lowered his head. Taking a deep breath, Andrew reached for her hand and said, "I wish you nothing but the best. I want you to be happy, Sandra. That is all I ever wanted. If this Tom fellow makes you happy, then I am happy. God bless you." One last time, Andrew leaned over and kissed her softly on the lips. Sandra didn't budge and for a brief moment, she kissed him back.

"Goodbye." Andrew glanced at her one last time, walked away and he never looked back.

Had he looked back, Andrew would have noticed Sandra's fortified wall tumbling down as she wept. She wept for the man whom her heart belonged to even though she was married to another.

Andrew thought his heart would never heal. Upon returning to military duty, he poured all of himself to *Uncle Sam*. He moved up the ranks with his superiors noticing him. It was while in the military he enrolled in a culinary of art school. He loved cooking; he always did. Shortly afterward, he married Belinda on a rebound. He treated her good and she did likewise. However, Belinda was sickly, suffering from leukemia. She passed away three years after their marriage. Andrew knew he would never marry again. His heart still yearned for his first love.

After serving twenty years, Andrew retired from active duty and followed his heart. He worked for well-known restaurants as their master chef. Soon his name was known in high places. He was even offered his own restaurant several times, but didn't want the hustle and bustle of entrepreneurship. All

Andrew wanted to do was create masterpieces in the kitchen and that is exactly what he did.

Lord, I'm overwhelmed. Andrew cut short his trip down memory lane. He needed to focus on tonight's menu.

I am with you.

"You okay?" Ashley interrupted later, noticing his misted eyes. Eyes that were identical to hers. For the first time, Ashley noticed because he was not wearing his glasses. *What a fluke! Pam's right. What are the odds of this stranger having eyes resembling mine?*

"Oh, uh…" Andrew wiped his eyes and began dicing the onions. "Just the onions."

"I thought onions didn't make you cry," she wasn't convinced.

"Sometimes," he shrugged.

Ashley placed the next order on the peg, glanced over at him one more time and walked away. *Lord, whatever is troubling Andrew, take care of it and take care of him.*

Andrew looked up just in time to see Ashley go through the double doors. *That is my daughter. I know it is. Sandra kept her from me. She married another man, knowing she was carrying my child. How could she?*

Sunday, while everyone was in church, Andrew went to the hospital. He knew that only family members could visit her in ICU, but somehow, someway he would see Sandra.

"I'm sorry Sir, but only immediate family members can go back," the woman at the desk advised.

"I am family," he lied.

"I haven't seen you around," the nurse assistant mentioned.

"I couldn't come before now."

"You do have eyes like her daughter." She assumed he had to be related based on their extraordinary eyes.

"Ashley," he smiled. "Yes, it's a family trait."

"Okay, then. I don't know if you know this, but Ms. Finley is in a coma."

"I know."

"You can visit for about twenty minutes, but then you'll have to leave."

"I understand." Andrew suddenly felt lightheaded and uncertain. He didn't know if he could handle seeing Sandra lying in the hospital bed ill, again. Mentally, he remembered the times when she suffered from her medical condition.

Typically, during the cold months her RA flared up the most. Back then, Andrew would have traded places with Sandra in a heartbeat, taking the bulk of her pain for himself. Today was no different. Gladly, Andrew would still trade places with Sandra.

Slowly, pushing the door open, Andrew tiptoed near the patient. Even though he knew she was unconscious, inwardly he feared that Sandra would wake up and his presence might shock her to death. He gasped at the sick patient. His heart was beating like a hammer, pounding vigorously.

My Sandra!

He ached for the twenty plus years they had been separated from each other. He moaned for the pain she had endured. He grieved for her being in a coma. His soul silently wept for the unfulfilled love he still felt for her. His heart was still breaking after all these years. It was like a crushing load of weight pressing upon his chest. Andrew could hardly breathe.

"Sandra," he bent over and whispered in her right ear, "it's me, Andrew. I'm here, Sandra, and I'll never leave you again."

Through the eyes of love, he saw her. Even with age, Sandra was still beautiful to him. Even more beautiful, although the aftereffects of illness had changed her outer appearance, somewhat.

"Oh, Sandra, you must wake up," Andrew touched her hand. It seemed to tremble in his. Squeezing it, he spoke again. "You must wake up. We have so much to say to each other. So much time we have both wasted. Sandra, I need you, still. I need you more. Please, open your eyes. Fight to live."

Andrew prayed silently the remainder of the visit. His soul longed for her to arise. He hurt because she was hurting. Though, she betrayed him by marrying another man, Andrew had forgiven her a long time ago. Now, understanding that Sandra had most likely kept a daughter from him, he still extended mercy toward her.

Andrew had always wanted a family, especially a child of his own. At his age, he deemed that the dream could never be a reality. No children. No grandchildren. He had accepted the painful truth ages ago. Now there was a glimmer of hope—in someone with crystalline eyes—just like his.

Transitorily, the nurse peeped in, reminding Andrew that visiting hours were over, for now.

"I'll be back," he said, bending over, tenderly brushing his lips upon hers. "I promise."

Her lips were warm and somewhat responding. Hopeful, again Andrew kissed her hoping it would stimulate her to remember. Unexpectedly...Sandra's eyes popped wide opened. She was startled speechless, in an unforeseen quandary.

Sandra thought she was dreaming. It had to be. This could not be real. It couldn't be that after all these years, Andrew had come back. No way, not after the way she treated him. *Not after...* she silent wept.

"Sandra!" Andrew was overcome with emotions. Tenderly, he wiped her tears, matching his own. "Oh my Sandra, I knew you would come back to me."

She just gazed at him with a mixture of emotions. *This cannot be real! Am I in heaven?*

"I know you're confused about me," he saw her fright, "but it's really me." Andrew caressed her face with his hand and then leaned closer. "It's really me."

"Sir," the nurse came in ready to usher him out. "She's awake!" the nurse rushed to her side. "Ms. Finley," the nurse leaned over the patient. "Welcome back!"

Sandra smiled, still shedding silent tears.

"I guess your visit was the one she was waiting on," the nurse looked at Andrew.

"I guess so," Andrew replied, not taking his eyes off Sandra.

"I'm going to call Dr. Phelps, right away," the nurse headed to the door. "I suppose you can stay a little longer."

"Thank you," Andrew uttered.

"How…" Sandra's voice was low and hoarse as she tried to speak.

"God ordered my steps here."

Confusion displayed upon her face.

"It's a long story, Sandra. All I know is that I met our daughter and she led me straight to you."

Her eyes bulged, as she gasped loudly. "You know Ashley?"

"We work together."

Sandra closed her eyelids, allowing the tears just to fall like raindrops. Her heart raced as she tried to absorb it all. Sandra never thought the day would come when she would let alone see Andrew again, but the day when she would have to tell him about their daughter.

"I'm not mad, Sandra," in a soothing tone Andrew talked. "I'm elated. I do not have any children. I have always wanted a daughter. When I saw her, there was something strangely familiar about her. She reminded me of you. But, her eyes…I just have never seen another soul with eyes like my family. It threw me for a loop, but I still did not put the pieces of the puzzle together until recently when she seemed so upset. She told me about you. I asked her your name and when she said Sandra Finley, maiden name, Sandra Gantt I thought I would faint. I had to escape the room and get some air."

Sandra's eyes opened again. Guilt clouded her vision. "I'm so sorry."

"No need to be," he sincerely replied.

"I wanted to tell you before you left, but I didn't want you to marry me just because I was pregnant."

"Instead you gave me an ultimatum."

She shook her head. "That was wrong. I was scared I was going to lose you."

Saying nothing, Andrew's eyes searched her face.

"When you left, Tom asked me out."

"You don't have to tell me about this now," Andrew didn't want to upset her anymore. She had already been through a lot.

"I want to," she swallowed, gaining courage and strength as she spoke. "Tom took me out every night for a month. I was sick a lot, but I blamed it on my illness. Then Tom took me to the doctor. I knew what the doctor was going to say, but Tom didn't. He offered to marry me so my name would not be defamed. It seemed like the solution. In the beginning, Tom was a good person. He was there for me. So, we raised Ashley together. He signed the birth certificate and accepted her as his child."

"Ashley doesn't know she has another father?"

She shook her head.

Conflicting emotions steamrolled him, leaving him momentarily deflated. Andrew walked away briefly, trying to gather his composure. Sandra discerned that once again, she had hurt him deeply.

"I'm truly sorry, Andrew," Sandra spoke as loud as she could, but it was only above a whisper.

Turning to her, Andrew felt her anguish and beheld her remorse. "It's okay. I'm just glad that you have come back from the dead." He drew closer to her, intertwining her hand in his. "We have so much to talk about, but not right now. All I want for you to do is get better so that you can get out of this place."

She gave him a warm smile and closed her eyelids.

"Now you can sleep, but that's it. Do we have a deal?" Andrew was concerned that she would slip back into a coma. "You must wake back up."

Her eyelids flipped open again. "It's a deal."

CHAPTER 23

The Road to Damascus

Sandwiched between Thomas and Harvey in church, Ashley enjoyed the morning praise and worship service. Danny, Donny, and Lacey were in children's church. As the announcements were being read, Ashley headed to the restroom. She came to a complete halt when she noticed a familiar face.

"Pam!" she whispered, joining her on the backseat.

"I didn't know this was your church," Pam whispered back.

"What are you doing here?"

"Can't a girl go to church?" always the sharp tongue response.

"Of course." Ashley was still shocked. "But how come you're at this church?"

"Willie."

"Willie?" Ashley frowned, looking around to see if she knew a Willie at her home church. She did not.

"On the keyboards."

"William Moore?" Ashley couldn't believe it. William was Pam's Willie. She would have never guessed. Willie and Pam were as opposite as night and day. Willie was for sure the nerd type. Nerdier than Harvey. Of all their adulthood years of attending this church, William never brought a girl to church.

"I told you, we were just friends."

"But William? He's…he's so…not you."

"Hush!" Pam playfully popped her hand. "The kids always picked on Willie and I stood up for him. He was like my little brother…still is."

"You're such a softy," Ashley replied, full of pride. "William was blessed to have you stand up for him."

"Whatever!" Pam spouted her famous word, whenever uncomfortable about the conversation.

Ashley and Pam stopped talking when Pastor Smallwood started preaching.

"Today church, I am going to share my conversion with you. I have never shared my testimony of salvation with you before. It is a *doosey*. So get prepared. Put your seatbelts on, we're going for a wild ride."

You could hear the congregation sigh in wonder. Both Pam and Ashley sat straight, anticipating a stirring story.

"You see, I wasn't always saved like most of you. I did not live a squeaky-clean life. My parents did not raise me in the church. As a matter of fact, I didn't step foot in a church until I was twenty-six."

The church was a quiet as a mouse as Pastor Smallwood continued. They were eager to know the story of the kind man who practiced what he preached.

Ashley was so engrossed in his testimony she did not notice Thomas, who had slipped beside her.

"Is everything all right, Sis?"

"Oh, yes," she touched his hand. "My friend Pam came. I'm going to sit with her."

"Hi," Thomas greeted in a whisper. "Okay, just wanted to make sure that you were okay." Thomas went back to his seat.

236

"You know the story of Paul – he persecuted the church. He was zealous for his gang, the Pharisees. His job was to torture the Christians, and he did it with zealous. Well, church," he paused, scanning the entire congregation, "I was like Paul."

The revelation nearly shocked the church. Not Pastor Smallwood! He was too kind for that. He would never hurt a soul. He exemplified Christ-like behavior, giving of himself to anyone who needed help.

Surprisingly, Pam was fascinated by the pastor's narrative of his story. She sat still, waiting to hear more. Ashley glanced over and felt relieved that Pam was listening. *God speak to her heart through Pastor Smallwood's testimony.*

"While Paul persecuted the church, I persecuted my neighbors, my schoolmates, my friends and even my family," he confessed gravely. "I was arrested for drug possession when I was sixteen."

Several members of the church gasped simultaneously, almost in harmony.

"At seventeen, I had beaten a neighborhood boy nearly to death. I went to the detention center for a year. After serving my time, I lived the street life. I was never really in a gang, but I had my partners in crime. Three of us did everything you could think of that was illegal. My parents disowned me. They could not handle my lifestyle. They wanted no part of it and they wanted no part of me.

"Anyhow, one night, I remember me and the guys were planning to rob a store. There was such uneasiness as I parked the car in the back. My two friends jumped out of the car, but I stayed behind. One of my friends asked was I coming. I sat there for a minute or two and I told him something just did not feel right. I think we should just forget this tonight.

"They thought I was chickening out and tried to persuade me otherwise. I told them I was not going in. For some reason, I just could not. I practically begged them not to go, but they wouldn't listen.

"As I sat in the car, I heard a gunshot, and then another and another. I waited, for what seemed like hours, but only seconds, to see if the guys would run out. They didn't come. Panicky, I drove off like a madman. I drove for hours until I had to pull over for gas.

"I pulled into a gas station and just wept. I didn't know what had happened to my two friends, but I knew that my life had been spared. At that moment, I knew I didn't want to go back to jail. I didn't want to live a life of crime anymore. I looked around expecting to see some police car pulling up behind me. With darkness all around me and silence drowning me, I felt so alone."

The congregation was so quiet you could hear a pin drop.

"My mother and father had left me. My friends were probably locked up right now or dead. I felt so alone. There was a hole in my heart. It was getting bigger by the minute. All of a sudden, I heard this pounding on my window. I jumped, scared witless."

"'*You alright?*'" this older man asked.

"I couldn't move. The man was glowing. I mean it was pitch-dark and the man standing before me was shining like the sun.

"'*Samuel, it is time you stop running,*' he spoke again in a very deep voice. It was so deep, yet so tender at the same time.

I rolled down my window and asked the man how did he know my name?

"'*God knows you,*' the man smiled. '*You see, I had this*

dream two nights ago and in this dream, I saw you and this white Chevy. You were parked at this gas station and you were crying, just like you are right now. In my dream I had to come to you and tell you to stop running and to tell you God has chosen you to preach His Gospel.'

"I laughed at him.

"You got the wrong one Mister. God don't want a no-good person like me to preach His Gospel.

"'*You are the best kind,*' the man smiled again. '*God will clean you up and make you brand new.*'

"I thought the man was crazy, church." Pastor Smallwood glanced over the congregation, knowing he had their undivided attention. Some were staring in amazement, others eyes were misted, and some were being convicted by his never-told-before testimony. He didn't know why God wanted him to come clean before his members today; but the pastor trusted God with his life and knew God had a purpose in mind.

"Something in me that night was hungry for change. I was tired of living the life I was living. I was tired of hurting on the inside and hurting people on the outside. I wanted the bottomless pit in my heart to be filled with something.

"The man held out his arms to me. I looked around to see if anyone else was around. There was no one, but me and this strange man. I opened the door and fell into this nameless man's arms. When he hugged me, I felt cloaked in the garment of love. I cannot explain it, but all I knew was at that moment I did not feel alone. The next moment, I gave my heart to Jesus. Fully, I surrendered myself for His use and His glory.

"I have never been the same again," his eyes were glassy. "Later I found out that both of my friends were shot and killed by the owner. No one ever knew that I was outside waiting for my friends. For sure, God had arrested me on the road to Destruction. Where I was blinded by anger and sin, He opened my eyes to see Truth and to walk in love and not hate. Later, I felt convicted to turn myself in for possibly being an accessory to robbery. The cops laughed at me and told me to go…there was nothing tying me to the crime.

"Isn't that like God? He asked the woman that was caught in adultery, where are your accusers? Has no one condemned you? She replied there are none. Jesus simply replied, 'Neither do I condemn you; go and sin no more.'

"Like Paul, we all come to a *Road to Damascus* Crossroad. Maybe not as dramatic as Paul. Maybe, your conversion was not as treacherous as mine. However, whenever God whispers your name and speaks to your heart that it is time to stop running, stop doing wrong, stop stealing, stop mistreating others, stop being promiscuous, stop cheating, stop sinning— you had better listen. He is trying to get your attention for a reason.

"He is trying to stop you from ending up in jail. Stop you from ending up dead. Stop you before you destroy your life or the life of others. Stop you before you break up your marriage or someone else's. Stop you before you damage your children, permanently. Stop you before you spend eternity in Hell.

"God desires for not any of us to perish, but for all of us to come into the knowledge of Truth. For me, there was a second chance, but not for my friends. God tried to warn them through me, but they did not listen. Today, I believe God is trying to warn some of you."

Pam squirmed in her seat, her eyes glossy. Ashley reached over and held her hand. She sensed her friend's heart being pricked by God's loving needle. He was definitely trying to get her attention.

"Stop running, I beg of you, my sister, my brother," Pastor Smallwood's voice cracked. "Give your heart to Jesus. Let him fill that empty hole with His amazing love. Let the blood of Jesus cleanse you from all sin. Today, some twenty-five years later, I stand before you a changed man. I'm happier now with the Lord in my fifties than I was in my early twenties. God changed my heart and changed my life," he paused. "The altar is open now for those of you who need Jesus to come into your heart. If you do not know Jesus, please come to the altar. If you have backslidden and want restoration, please come to the altar. If you are struggling with sin, please come to the altar. Though your sins are as scarlet, Jesus will make you white as snow. He will wash away your sins, through His blood, and will remember your sins no more. That is what kind of God He is. A forgiving God who loves you–unconditionally.

"Salvation is simple. You don't have to roll on the floor, foam at the mouth, scream or shout. All you have to do is confess with your mouth the Lord Jesus and believe in your heart that God raised Him from the dead and you will be saved. For all who call on the name of the Lord shall be saved. That's found in the Bible, in the Book of Romans, chapter 10, verses, 9-10, and 13."

The altar began to fill.

Ashley silently prayed for her friend.

"Will you go with me?" Pam leaned over and whispered.

"Of course." Ashley extended her hand to her friend and escorted Pam to the altar.

William was playing softly when he noticed his longtime friend walking toward the altar. Tears of joy trickled down his face. He knew that Pam was hard on the outside because of her rough upbringing. In high school rumors spread about an uncle, who had repeatedly molested Pam. Her own mother didn't believe her, nor did she do anything to help her own daughter out. Consequently, Pam became promiscuous. She ran away at sixteen and never went back. She stayed at everybody's house. Gratefully, Pam continued going to school and graduated with her high school diploma.

Thank you, Lord! William praised as he played the old familiar song…*At the Cross*.

With a bowed head and on bended knees, Pam gave her heart to Jesus Christ with her friend standing behind her. Pastor Smallwood came around the altar and prayed individually with every soul. When he came to Pam, he whispered in her ear, "It's not your fault. What man did to you is not your fault. Forgive yourself. God has forgiven you. Go and sin no more."

With a tearstained face, Pam opened her eyes and looked at the pastor. She could not believe he knew what she was feeling. Did he know her story? Pastor Smallwood laid his hand lightly on Pam's head, instantly she felt the power of God engulf her being.

Pam would never be the same again.

After church service, Harvey drove Ashley and her family to his house for dinner. William and Pam followed behind them. Pam was still overwhelmed by her encounter with Christ Jesus. She had never believed in a thousand years that she would be a child of God. She mocked the very idea every time Ashley said something about Jesus to her.

Never say never!

She looked over at William, her dear friend, and felt nothing but gratitude. "Thank you."

"For what?"

"For introducing me to Jesus. You did it in the ninth grade, but I wouldn't listen."

"You remembered?"

"Of course," she said. "I often thought about it, but always pushed it in the back of my mind. Today, I understood what you were saying through your pastor. It was as if the pastor was telling my story. Oh, I didn't steal, beat up or kill people, but I sure hurt people, especially guys. I did to them what my uncle had done to me so many times." The truth was painful to admit such a truth.

"You were sexually abused," William acknowledged. "You couldn't help but act out."

"Recently, I was almost raped..."

"Pam," his heart ached for her. "I'm so sorry. Was the man arrested?"

She shook her head, unable to speak through the clog in her throat. The memory still caused her deep pain. Fresh tears streamed down her face.

"I didn't want to relive the past, so I just kept it to myself. The only person that knows is Ashley. Besides, the seed that I sowed by mistreating men came back to haunt me. I guess you do reap what you sow."

"God is merciful," William countered.

"Obviously, He saved a wretch like me," Pam grinned. "I know Ashley is probably doing some holy dance right about now."

"I can't believe you two know each other. Ashley is a sweetheart. Everybody loves her at church."

"Everyone loves her at work. She's my only friend," Pam stated, "besides you. I'm so glad I ran into you, Willie."

"Me too."

"Now we really are family," she said joyfully.

"We will always be family." William pulled in Harvey's driveway.

"Sure you can't stay?"

"No. I have to play for another church."

"See you later.

It was truly a family dinner at Harvey's home. Everyone enjoyed the food and the fellowship. During the meal, Ashley kept staring at her friend. She did not think she would ever stop smiling. Pam's salvation was miraculous! It meant a great deal to Ashley because she loved Pam wholeheartedly and wanted desperately for her friend to know peace in the depths of her soul.

Now Pam had peace, which surpassed all understanding.

Pam and Harvey got along great. Ashley noticed Harvey glancing Pam's way quite a few times. Likewise, Pam appeared at ease with Harvey. Pam was *cutting up* with her crazy sense of humor, making everyone around the table laugh.

They would make an unusual couple. Wouldn't that be great if the two friends who I care about most in the world end up together...romantically? Oh, my! It is too wonderful for my mind to contain!

Suddenly, Ashley found herself on a new mission...

CHAPTER 24

Friendship

Dropping Ashley and Thomas off at the hospital, Harvey and the other siblings went to the nearby park.

"Thomas, everything is okay," Ashley perceived his apprehension.

"It's been a long time since I've seen her."

"She's still momma."

Thomas shrugged, unsure of he was ready to feasibly look death in the face…again.

"Oh!" The nurse spotted Ashley. "I have been calling you all morning."

"Is something wrong?" Ashley freaked out, thinking the worse.

Thomas quaked in his shoes, literally.

"Oh, no!" the nurse beamed. "Your mother is out of her coma."

"What!" Ashley gasped. "Really?"

"Really."

The sister and brother embraced each other, doing a "happy dance", celebrating their good news.

"God is a Miracle-Worker!" Ashley praised. "Thank, You Lord!"

The siblings hastened their footsteps to Sandra's room.

"I'm coming with bells on my toes, Momma. The bells should have awakened you before I did." Ashley quoted her mother's truism. "Momma," Ashley called her name.

"I heard the bells," Sandra spoke.

"Praise You Jesus!" Ashley shouted.

"Oh, Momma!" Thomas came unglued, his strong exterior crumbling as he boohooed in his mother's arms.

"My babies," she whispered, "my precious babies."

For some time, they all cried and held one another. It seemed too good to be true.

"I knew you would come back to us." Ashley rejoiced.

Two Miracles! Pam's salvation! Mom's recovery. Lord, You are so good!

Later, when Harvey had returned for them, Thomas went downstairs and gathered the children so they could visit with their mother for a short while. Harvey joined them. None of the Finley clan wanted to leave when the nurse told them visiting hours were over for the day. The little ones pouted and cried, but Sandra reminded them she would be home soon. Thomas and Ashley stayed a few minutes more while Harvey waited with the children in the lobby.

Exiting her mother's room later, Ashley saw Gregg standing outside his father's room. He appeared distraught, his hand covering his eyes. He was trying to conceal his emotions.

"Thomas, go before Harvey comes in looking for us. Tell him to give me a few moments." Ashley urged her brother.

"What's wrong?" Thomas looked over and saw his principal. "Is that Dr. Jefferson?"

"It is. His father is not doing well."

"Oh," Thomas empathized with Dr. Gregg's pain, walking

in those same shoes just minutes before. The strong, Rock of Gibraltar Principal, appeared weak…human. "I'll pray for him."

"You do that. I will be there as soon as I can."

"Gregg," she walked over to him.

Instantly, Gregg recognized her voice before looking into her lovely face. "Hi, Ashley."

"How is your dad?" She already knew the answer by his countenance. The pain on his face was raw.

"My father has taken a turn for the worst. The doctors don't expect for him to live through the night," his voice squeaked. He was trying his *darnest* to be strong, but Ashley saw right through him.

"I'm so sorry, Gregg. Is there anything I can do?"

"Pray."

"Of course," she ached for him. "My heart is with you, Gregg."

"Thanks. It's rather hard right now."

"Where there is life, there is hope, Gregg," she hesitated to speak. "I know what the doctor says, but I also know that God is a healer and a deliverer."

"He's at the end of his rope, Ashley." Gregg was upset. "And I didn't even get to tell him that I love him. I really…." he sniffed several times, "I really do love him."

"He knows." Ashley reached for his hand, squeezing it slightly.

"I just wish I could speak to him one more time…"

"Gregg," she called his name sweetly, "do you believe that God answers prayers?"

"I used to."

"Right now, God is the only One who can help your father.

So, why not believe in God to do what no other human can do? To heal your father."

Gregg watched Ashley, saying not a word. He felt like the same frightened child who had just lost his mother all over again.

"My mother has come back from the dead, Gregg. It is a miracle! Doctors did their part, and God did His. She is living, breathing, and talking as if nothing ever happened. Truly, my mother is a miracle."

"I want to believe." Gregg uttered in a smooth hush tone.

"Mark 9:23 says, *'All things are possible to him who believes.'* All things are possible, Gregg, but it is up to you to believe."

"But what if…what if he still dies."

Ashley swallowed back her emotions and silently prayed for the right words to come. "God is the Author of life and death. Only He knows when it is our time to go. But even if we shed this earthly body, there awaits a heavenly body that will never suffer again—never no pain again—never die again," she paused. "Even so, God still heals…whether here…or in eternity."

He pondered her words of faith, trying to grab hold of the lifeline Ashley was trying to throw his way. "I believe."

"Good." Ashley felt relieved. "The Bible declares that if two people touch and agree on earth concerning anything, He will do it for them. Let's go pray with your father and agree for God's healing power to flow within him." She led him back into his father's room.

"Almighty God," Ashley held Gregg's hand while he was holding his father's hand, "we come before you knowing that You have all power in Your hands. Power to heal the sick. Power to raise the dead. Power to save our souls. Mr. Jefferson needs Your touch. He needs Your healing power to flow through him and cleanse his physical sick heart and to heal every part of his body, right now in the name of Jesus.

"The doctor says there is no hope, but God there is always hope in You. Now faith is the substance of things hoped for and the evidence of things not seen. We have the now faith and hope that Mr. Jefferson is already healed. For your promises are Yes and Amen. By Jesus' stripes, Mr. Jefferson is healed, whole and delivered from sickness and disease. Give him a second chance, like you gave Pastor Smallwood, and like you gave Pam…"

Gregg opened his eyes, not knowing of whom she was speaking of, but the sincerity of prayer convicted him to believe God had given them second chances. Closing his eyes again, Gregg continued to pray silently with Ashley.

"…like you gave my mother and me and countless others. Do not let him leave this world without knowing You. All things are possible if we believe, I believe and Gregg believes," she pressed his hand. "Therefore, we expect You to move because of our faith. We thank You in advance for Mr. Jefferson's turnaround. We give You all the glory for it in advance, in Jesus' name we pray, amen."

"Amen." Gregg looked at the woman who had touched his heart in many ways. Slowly, he gathered her into his arms and held her close to his chest. Gregg could feel her heart beat and she could feel his.

Ashley smiled and lifted her hand to his face. "All is well, Gregg."

Gregg believed it because Ashley spoke it, and he believed it because he felt the power of something stronger than man in the room. He reached up, placing his hand gently over hers.

"I needed you today." Gregg found it difficult to speak, "more than you know."

God knew. "I'm glad I could be here."

He pressed a soft kiss to her temple. "I felt so alone."

"You're not." His simple kiss made her feel disoriented as her pulse rate increase. Electrifying heat went throughout her body. Ashley couldn't define the foreign emotions. It felt so right being in his embrace. If only she could stay there.

"My ride is waiting on me." Ashley stepped back. She felt so empty and so uncovered with his arms no longer around her.

"Oh, I was hoping you'd stay with me."

"If you want me to." Ashley didn't want to leave him, not now. "I can go tell Harvey to take the children home."

Harvey! "No that's okay," he stood straighter. "I'll be fine."

"I don't mind."

"You've already done more than enough. I am going to be here for a while, so you really should go. You have to work tomorrow."

"Will you please call me later? Anytime."

"Sure," he agreed.

"Okay, then. I'll talk to you later," she gazed at him a few minutes more. Walking to the door, Ashley turned to him, staring at him with his heart in her eyes. "Promise me you will call me."

"I promise."

Ashley rode home in silence. Harvey cast several side-glances her way, but Ashley didn't notice. Her mind lingered on the man she had left behind. She wanted desperately to be with Gregg. He needed her and she needed him.

Harvey envied the man who could capture Ashley's heart.

For years, he had tried, but still she didn't reciprocate the feelings. Perhaps, his love for Ashley was not the marrying type of love after all. Maybe, like Ashley, he was lonely and he just wanted anxiously to fill his home with a ready-made family. He loved Ashley, no doubt about it. He knew that Ashley loved him, just not in the way two people considering marriage should love each other.

Harvey also had a lot to think about. Something about Ashley's friend Pam sparked something different inwardly. She was exciting and made him laugh. Pam was so unlike Ashley but her heart was just as big.

Maybe Ashley is right. We should stay friends!

Making sure that the Finley clan was safely inside their home, Harvey and Ashley shared quiet time together on the porch.

"It sure has been an amazing day," Ashley glowed. "Mom is better. Pam is saved. I feel as if I am going to burst wide open from pure joy!" *Yet…my heart is saddened by Gregg's hurt.*

"I know." Harvey looked at Ashley relishing her happiness. "It shows. I haven't seen you this happy in a long time."

"I feel guilty, somehow," she suddenly replied. "I mean, my mother is better, but…but, according to the doctors Gregg's father's health is declining. They do not expect him to live through the night, Harvey. That's so sad."

Harvey watched her long and hard before speaking, "I think you like this Gregg."

"He is just a friend. I hardly know him," she began to babble. "After all, he's Thomas' principal. It's just that he is hurting. He has no one, no family." Ashley looked at Harvey again. "You know how that feels."

"I sure do. It's awful. I didn't want to be alone, Ashley. I wanted a family…your family," he admitted. "That's why I asked you to marry me," out came the truth of his heart. "Plus, I wanted to take care of you."

"I know, Harvey." Ashley respected him more now than ever before. "You're my best friend, Harvey and I love you. Nothing and no one will ever come between our friendship."

"You're right," he held her hand. "I guess you won't need this," he pulled out the engagement ring.

"You keep it for the right woman."

"I carried it every day in hopes that you would say yes."

"Oh, Harvey, don't you see that what we have is rare and special just as it is. We are like David and Jonathan in the Bible. They shared a love so rare that it says David's love for Jonathan was wonderful, surpassing the love of women."

"You're right. It's just going to take some time getting used to the idea that we can only be friends. I love you, Ashley. I always have and I always will."

Ashley hugged him. The twosome stayed that way for a moment. They had endured a lot together. Their friendship had stood the tests of time.

CHAPTER 25

Another Miracle

While Ashley was writing in her journal, Greg called.

"I hope it's not too late," he stated worriedly.

"No," she answered. "I was just writing in my journal."

"Anything interesting?"

"As a matter of fact, yes. My friend, Pam, gave her life to Jesus today. I don't know if you remember her, but she's a waitress at *The Palace*."

"The loud lady with the bright red lipstick," he remembered.

Ashley laughed at his recollection of Pam. "She's the one. It was so incredible. First, I didn't expect that she would ever come to my church. I have invited her a *gazillion* times. Anyhow, she ran into her old friend and he invited her. William, the keyboard player, whom she calls Willie," she hardly took a breath as she rattled on. "It's such a small world."

"It is," her exhilaration was contagious. "Then the news with your mother only made it better."

"Most definitely. I just wish you could be this happy, Gregg."

"Me too," he sounded so melancholy.

"Any news on your dad?"

"He's holding on. It's midnight and he's still here."

"That's a good sign."

"Seems that way."

"Have you eaten anything today?"

"I had breakfast, but nothing since then."

"You have to eat," she chided. "Your dad is going to need you when he awakes. You can't afford to get sick now."

"Yes, mother," he chuckled.

"Funny."

"Let's talk about something else."

"Like what?"

"Like, how are things with Thomas at home?"

"He's so much better."

"His grades have greatly improved," Gregg replied. "The teachers are amazed at his turnaround. Coach Koon says he still *got game*."

"I'm so glad he's playing again. It is like having the old Thomas back at home. He is cheerful and playful. Danny and Donny adore him. Lacey cannot get enough of him. I can never thank you enough for giving him another chance."

"He deserves it."

"I think so," Ashley felt bias. "Thomas is a good young man. He just couldn't deal with our new life. He missed his old life...we all do."

Her tone changed. Gregg knew that Thomas was not the only one who had suffered. She had given up so much for her family but never complained. He admired her for that.

"Ashley..."

She loved hearing him call her name. "Yes."

"Are you happy?"

His question caught her off guard. "Right now, yes."

"What about most days?"

"I have learned to be content," she answered truthfully.

"Contentment isn't happiness," Gregg surmised. "I think I have settled with being content for so long that I forgot what it truly means to be happy."

"Happiness is just a feeling. It comes and goes depending on the circumstances. However, joy comes from a Source not dependent upon our circumstances. I'm joyful, Gregg, most of the time."

"Did you have a happy childhood?"

"My childhood was okay. I mean, we had laughter in our home. My father was gone most of the time. He was a good provider, but an absent father. He loved my siblings, that's for sure."

"Did he love your mother?"

"I don't know how he could truly love my mother and have so many affairs. He died in a car accident with another woman in the car. My mother never got over that."

"That's sad."

"Yes, it is," Ashley couldn't believe she was telling all of her private business to Gregg. It was just so easy to talk to him.

"You mentioned that he loved your siblings. What about you? Didn't you feel that he loved you?"

"Honestly, no," Ashley admitted. "I have always felt like the unwanted stepchild around him. Maybe it was because I was the oldest. Perhaps, because everyone was always saying how the other children looked just like him, but not me. I look like my mother. I would try to get close to him, but he would push me away."

"It was truly his lost," Gregg stated quickly. "Whoever could push you away has got to be a fool!"

She beamed.

"Ashley, when all of this is over, I would be honored if you would let me take you out."

"You're asking me out on a date?" her heart fluttered.

"Yes, I am."

I don't know! He is not a Christian. However, he is a friend. It is okay to go out with her friend. Her mind raced with indecisiveness.

"Are you still there?"

"Yes," she finally answered.

"Is that a yes to still being there or yes to going out with me?"

"Both." *One date won't hurt.*

"Good!"

They talked a little bit more before Gregg thought it best to let Ashley sleep.

"Call me tomorrow," Ashley said before hanging up. "I want to know about your father."

"I will," he replied. "Sweet dreams, Ashley."

"Thanks. The same to you. Are you staying at the hospital?"

"I'm stretching out next to my dad's bedside. They gave me a cot to sleep on."

"That can't be too comfortable."

"It's not, but I'm next to my dad."

She noticed he called him dad and not father. That was a big step for him. "I'll be praying for you and your dad."

"Thanks. Good morning."

"Good morning," she laughed.

"I like being the first to say that to you," Gregg philandered.

Again, she blushed. "Good morning, Gregg. Talk to you later."

Ashley felt warm inside just thinking about the tall, svelte, masculine, dark, handsome man who made her heart pitter-patter at just the sound of his voice. Gregg was like no other man she had ever known. No one had ever made moved her inside, not even Keith, her college boyfriend. Gregg touched her in the core of her being. His words were soothing like butter. Yet, he frightened Ashley.

How could she feel something so special for a man who did not know her Savior? They were on opposite sides of the fence. She was on the Lord's side and he was on the enemy's side. That truth sickened her. Ashley knew she could never lose her heart to a man who belonged to the devil.

Meanwhile, Gregg was tired of living in an unseen prison, caged and cramped behind bars with no way out, nowhere to run, seemingly sentenced to a life of loneliness. He wondered if someone like Ashley, pure and chaste could ever love someone like him. He was broken pottery. Surely, she wouldn't want someone so marred and flawed like him. He was messed up. There was nothing pure about him. He had lived a reckless life with women. Loving them one minute and leaving them the next. *If Ashley knew this, would she ever consent to go out with me?*

Gregg fell asleep with Ashley on his mind. Therefore, peace covered him like a warm, cozy blanket. Though the cot was uncomfortable, Gregg slept as if he were sleeping in his comfortable king-size bed at home.

"Dr. Jefferson," the nurse nudged him hours later. "Dr. Jefferson," she called again.

"Hmm…" Gregg leaped up, frightened that his father had passed away. "What is it? Is he…"

"He's asking for you?"

Gregg blinked his eyes, wondering if he were dreaming.

"Son," his voice was weak.

"Dad!" Gregg felt joy, like he never felt more. Ashley was right. It wasn't happiness, based on his circumstances. It was something deeper. Something that came from within.

Mr. Jefferson couldn't believe he heard his son right. "You called me Dad."

"That's who you are." Gregg chortled, pulling back a loose strand of hair on the side of his dad's face.

The weak man blubbered as his frail body trembled. The same son, whom he had abandoned all those years, showed him mercy and not judgment.

"It's so good to hear your voice again," Gregg choked. "I'm so glad you're back."

Mr. Jefferson only nodded, still too overcome with emotions.

"I love you, Dad," Gregg said proudly. "No matter what, I love you."

"Son, I love you, too," the father finally said, "with all my heart."

Father and son reunited their hearts, sealing their fate of unity with a loving embrace.

Sandra Finley and Gregory Jefferson were brought back from the brink of death. Their purposes on earth yet to be fulfilled. God is a Miracle Worker—still today—and forevermore.

"Hello," Ashley groggily answered the phone. Looking at the clock, somehow, she knew it was Gregg. It was four o'clock in the morning. In a few hours, she would get up.

"My dad survived. He's awake and doing good."

"Praise the Lord!"

"I just wanted to tell you," he said. "I'm headed home to take a shower. Then, I have to meet with the administration team."

"Gregg, you realize that we have had back to back miracles."

"We sure have," he sighed happily. "Back to back miracles!"

"One has to believe in God after such amazing miracles," Ashley went on. "Only God could do such amazing things. He's a healer for sure," she paused. "Do you see His handprint in all of this, Gregg? You have to believe He's God?"

He waited, cautiously finding the courage to speak. "I believe."

Praise God!

Another miracle!

CHAPTER 26

I smell a rat

Rushing, Gregg almost collided with Tiffany in the hallway.

"You're still here?" Gregg assumed she had left earlier today.

"Yes." Tiffany continued drying her hair with the towel. "I think I'll stay through the week, if you don't mind."

"I'm not sure." Gregg wasn't so certain his father would approve of her being there. Even though he and Tiffany were not *sleeping around*, Gregg felt slightly uncomfortable around her. She was still married to Trevor and Gregg didn't want to be in the middle of their relationship. Especially, since Tiffany kissed him on the lips the other night. Her excuse was that she had a little too much to drink. Gregg wasn't convinced.

"Hey, what's got into you?" Tiffany shoved him, nearly yanking off the towel covering his body. "Oops," she chuckled.

"I don't have time for this conversation right now," Gregg looked at her one last time and hurried to his room. Tiffany followed him.

"You're not going to work, are you?" she pouted. "I was hoping we could do something."

"I have to work. I have a morning meeting with my administrators." Gregg grabbed his white collared shirt, navy slacks and undergarments.

"What about after work?"

"I'm going straight to the hospital after work," he brushed past her. "Oh, by the way, my dad is out of the woods. He's doing much better!"

"Great! Then you and I can go out to dinner tonight."

Gregg stopped in his tracks and turned with an appalling look on her face. *She is one selfish broad, so unlike Ashley.* "I don't think so!" Gregg walked away shaking his head.

"You're no fun anymore," Tiffany shouted outside the bathroom door. "We used to have so much fun!"

"You're married!" Gregg turned on the shower.

"That never stopped you before."

"You are right! Let's just say, I want more. You should want more, too. Like making your third marriage work."

Quietly, Tiffany turned the knob, hoping Gregg had not locked it. *He locked it!* Disappointed, she went back to her room, slamming the door.

Shortly afterward, running downstairs, Gregg found himself annoyed once again by Tiffany's presence.

"I'm not taking no for an answer." Tiffany, dressed in a red sundress, clinging to her body, showing her every curb, stood at the bottom of the stairs. I've already made reservations for two at *The Palace* at eight o'clock sharp. I love the place! Do they have live entertainment tonight?"

"The Palace always has a live band." Gregg didn't want to go with her, especially since Ashley worked there and she might get the wrong idea about them.

"Will you pick me up from here or should I get the chauffeur to take me?" confidently she asked. "Does your dad still have the slow chauffeur…uh…Mr. Brown?"

"Yes," Gregg walked pass her. "Yes, I will speak to Mr.

Brown on the way out. See you at eight o'clock."

"Looking forward to it." Tiffany caught up to him and pecked him on the lips. "We're going to have a good time."

"We're going to have a good talk." Gregg rebuffed firmly.

"Don't be such a bore," she stood daringly before him. "I want the old Gregg back."

"See you at eight." On that note, Gregg exited the room.

"Now, I'm going to be late!" He cranked his Mercedes Benz and backed out of the driveway. "I have to get Tiffany out of my father's house!"

"Good morning!" Gregg greeted his secretary. "Is the Administration team already in the conference room?"

"Yes," she quickly fixed a cup of coffee for her boss. "Dr. Epson called. He wanted to know what happened with Ms. Myers. The position has to be filled immediately."

"Oh, I forgot." Almost inconceivable that he could forget about getting rid of the thorn in his flesh. "I'll call him after the meeting. Thanks for the coffee. You're the best," he smiled and hotfooted to the conference room.

She stood amazed. *He must be on something!*

"Sorry everyone." Gregg sat at the head of the table. "Let's get right to it. Ms. Neal, the Test Pep Rally was a huge success. The students enjoyed it. Is the next one still scheduled for the end of the month?"

"Yes," she replied excitedly. "I'm going to need some additional incentive awards. So many students got involved, meeting their goals and passing the practice exams."

"That's wonderful. I will see what I can do. Just email me what you want to get and the cost." Gregg scribbled on his notes.

"Daniel West and Ernest Weaver how many fights have we had in the past two weeks?"

"Only one," Ernest Weaver answered first. "Two ninth grade girls."

"Let me guess," Gregg intervened, "over some boy, right?"

"Yes," Mr. Weaver chuckled.

"It's still good. One fight in two weeks. I expect none for this month."

"I'm with you on that, Sir," Daniel West spoke up. "Since we are enforcing the rules consistently, the students seem to understand that if they fight, they will be arrested. They talk a good game, but when they see their friends handcuffed it's a different story."

"That's the plan," Gregg nodded. "We don't want anyone interfering with the education of others. If they do not want to learn, fine! However, they will not stop others from learning. In the long run, we hope the offenders will learn from their wrong behavior and want to do better. Plus, having an intervention plan in place, to help the offenders seems to be working as well.

"Coach Koon, are we squared away for the first basketball game next week? I want it to be big." Gregg found himself excited about the game. Secretly, he wanted to see Thomas play. He had worked hard with the young man and wanted to see if all the hard work would pay off.

"We're ready. JROTC will present. The cheerleaders will sing the national anthem. Mr. Weaver will do the announcing and I have a DJ to take care of the game music. The yearbook club is in charge of the canteen."

"Sounds good." Gregg felt confident. After discussing a few more important items, Gregg dismissed everyone except Ms. Myers.

"Ms. Myers," Gregg put down his pen and looked directly at her. "I noticed that you didn't have anything to say during the meeting."

"There was no need for me to say something," she eyed him back. "You addressed everyone in the room except me."

"And do you think I did that on purpose?"

"I do."

"Perhaps, you are right," he paused. "Your transfer to J.T. Moore has been approved. You can start working there next week."

Privately, Irene Myers' ego was deflated. It irked her that the principal took pleasure in hurting her. "And if I don't want to go?"

Gregg was taken back by her response. He expected Ms. Myers to be doing cartwheels to get out Brookland and to get away from him.

"You'd have to change. You can no longer work alone, but get on board and become a team player. You cannot undermine me, or talk about me in a derogatory manner to other staff or parents. Ms. Myers, you may not agree with what I do, but you cannot sabotage the strides we are making in turning around Brookland."

"I'll try." Ms. Myers lowered her head.

"Ms. Myers, I'm curious. Why do you want to stay here?"

"I love Brookland, Sir. I believe I can make a difference." With strong resolved, she meant every word.

"Okay then," Gregg stood up. "I would like a copy of the practice District Standardized Test scores. Can you and Ms. Neal pull the names of the students we need to target for getting extra help in passing?"

"Yes, Sir."

"Thanks," Gregg found the humbling Ms. Myers more pleasant to be around. He didn't know what sparked the change in her, but possibly things would work out with her after all.

"Principal Jefferson!" Thomas charged through the main office door.

"Excuse me, Ms. Myers," Gregg swiftly changed gears.

"Certainly Dr. Jefferson," she exited the conference room.

"What's up, Thomas?" Gregg answered.

"I really need to tell you something," Thomas looked worried.

"Come on back," Gregg walked ahead of him to his office. "Sit down. Now tell me what's wrong? It's not your mother is it?"

"No. She's doing much better. There's going to be a fight after school."

"What?" Gregg stood up. "Who?"

"I can't tell you." Thomas' palms were sweaty. "I probably shouldn't be telling you this now…but…I knew you could stop it."

"You have to be straight with me." Gregg sat next to him. "Tell me who it is."

"Some guys are going to jump Shane because he broke up with this girl, whose brother is Drake, a high ranking gangbanger. It's going to happen behind the gym before Shane comes to basketball practice."

"Are you sure?"

Thomas nodded. "I *gotta* go. Please keep my name out of this."

"Of course." Gregg walked him to the door. "Good-looking out, Thomas. I'm proud of you."

Thomas smiled and left.

Shane! Gregg remembered the sweet Aunt, who made a lasting impression upon him. *Lord, please help me to help Shane—and his Aunt.*

"This is unit 1. I need 2, 4, and 5 and all monitors in my office now!" Gregg uttered on the Walkie-talkie.

Within a few moments, Officer Anderson, Mr. Weaver, Mr. West and the monitors were standing in the principal's office.

"We have to head this off," Gregg finished up. "I will not stand for any kind of lynching at Brookland. I want to stop it before it starts, and then I want the offenders dealt with harshly. We have to send a strong message that this will not be tolerated. Gang violence will not be accepted here any longer!"

"May I ask, who tipped you off?" Officer Anderson inquired.

"It was an anonymous tip."

"It could be a prank," Officer Anderson tossed out. "You can never be too sure."

"You're right. That is why I want us to act as if it is the real thing. Everyone understands my expectations?"

"Yes." They replied in unison.

"Keep your eyes and ears open for anything unusual today." Gregg dismissed everyone.

A few minutes later, he called Dr. Epson.

"Hi Gregg," Dr. Epson answered. "I haven't heard from you in a while."

"My dad was pretty bad off," Gregg replied.

"Yes, I heard. How is he now?"

"Much better. He was at death's doors, but he pulled through."

"Mr. Jefferson is a fighter. It is in his blood to pull through. Now on a professional note, will Ms. Myers be transferring to

J.T. Moore next week?"

"No, Roy," Gregg sat comfortably in his chair. "She doesn't want to go. She says she loves Brookland and wants to stay."

"I thought you wanted her out of your hair."

"I did, but I think I'll give her another chance. Now she seems receptive to change."

"I hope you know what you're doing."

"Me too," Gregg laughed.

Before the last bell rang, Dr. Jefferson had all his security team in place, near the gym, ready to stop the plans of Drake and his gang from *jumping* Shane.

In the interim, Shane hurried toward the gym, not wanting to be late for practice again. Coach Koon didn't tolerate lateness or breaking any team rules. This was his senior year. Having made some bad mistakes recently, being locked up for three days behind bars, awakened Shane to wanting more—desiring better—and ultimately finding his way back to God. Thanks to his friend, Thomas, for sharing Jesus with him. Shane was finding joy again, not just in basketball, but also in life.

"Hi Shane," Tatiana, his ex-girlfriend approached him.

"Hi Tatiana," he was surprised to see her. "What's up?

She hadn't talked to him since he broke up with her. Tatiana was too clingy, pressuring Shane to do wrong things— cutting class, skipping school altogether, sneaking out of the house and stuff like that. She was putting the pressure on him to hang out with her brother and his friends. Shane had never met Drake, but his reputation spoke for itself. Shane could not afford getting involved with the wrong people, again.

He had plans of obtaining a scholarship for basketball.

Too much was at stake. Tatiana was a beautiful girl, but she was also dangerous. Shane knew it was a mistake dating her a month into their relationship. Tatiana didn't take the breakup well.

"I miss you," Tatiana reached for his hand.

Shane slipped his hands in his pockets and kept walking ahead. He didn't know what to say to the girl who was so topsy-turvy. All week she rolled her eyes at him and now she acted as if nothing happened. Like they didn't even breakup.

"Don't you miss me?" Tatiana pushed on.

"Let's not do this." Shane stopped, turned and looked at her. "We're not right for each other."

"Yes, we are." Tatiana wrapped her arms around him. "Give us another chance."

"I can't." He peeled her arms off him and hurried off.

"You'll be sorry!" she yelled after him.

I already am. He kept walking.

"Hey Shane," someone shouted from the side.

Shane turned, not recognizing the guy. "Do I know you?" Suddenly six other guys appeared. *This is not good!*

"The hotshot basketball player," he mocked. "Thinks he going pro."

"In his dreams," one of the guys said.

"Listen," Shane wanted to hall tail and run for his life, but knew they would be on him like bees on a honeycomb. "I don't want any trouble."

"Too late for that," someone came from behind him.

Shane turned and saw Tatiana with a heavyset guy, who he assumed to be her brother, Drake.

"Should have thought about that before you hurt my little sister."

"Yeah," she smacked her bubblegum. "Sure you don't want to reconsider my proposition?"

Shane felt chickenhearted. *Lord, help me!*

"He's a punk! I don't know what you see in this wimp!" Drake turned to his sister and then he snapped his fingers. And just like that, all the guys surrounded Shane. He couldn't run if he tried.

"No one hurts my sister." Drake stood nose to nose with Shane.

"I didn't mean to," Shane trembled. "We…"

Whop! Drake punched Shane in his midsection. Shane dropped to his knees. He was a baller, not a fighter.

"Stop!" Officer Anderson yelled with several other cops joining him. "Don't move!"

All the guys stood still, automatically putting their hands up.

Dr. Jefferson, Mr. Weaver, and Mr. West joined the scene. "I want all of these guys arrested for trespassing and attempted lynching on school property."

"I smell a rat!" Drake mouthed to one of the guys. "I'm going to find out who ratted and handle it as soon as we get out of this mess."

CHAPTER 27

Troublemaker Tiffany

"I know that I have been like an ogre," Mr. Jefferson turned to his son. "Losing your mother was like losing my will to live. We were one. How does one become half of one?" Gregg empathized with his father talking about his mother. "She was my everything," his voice trembled. "I still miss her very much."

"Me too, Dad."

"I missed hearing you call me dad," Mr. Jefferson appeared so frail. "You used to call me that all the time. Then you started calling me father like I was some stranger."

"You were," Gregg was honest.

"I know," one teardrop escaped his eyes. "You know before I went into surgery, I prayed."

The admission shocked Gregg.

"I asked God for a second chance with you. I messed up pretty badly. I hope it's not too late."

"It is not too late, Dad."

"Good. When I get out of this hospital, the first thing I want to do is go to church."

Again, Gregg thought he would fall out of his chair. His mother made her husband go to church. True, in time Mr.

Jefferson stopped fussing about it and accepted their Sunday church service routine. Now, he wanted to go to church of his own freewill.

"I think your mother would be pleased if we both attended church," Mr. Jefferson eyeballed his son. "Don't you think?"

Gregg nodded. He wasn't sure if he would go to church or not, but he wanted to make his father happy.

"Good!"

"Tiffany's at the house," Gregg said. "She's overstaying her welcome and I want her to leave."

"You used to like Tiffany."

"We were friends."

"I thought you two dated," Mr. Jefferson knew better.

"We would go out whenever she came to town. That's it," Gregg amended. "She and her third husband are having problems."

"Seems like every time she breaks up with her husband she comes running back to you."

"Sure seems that way."

"Perhaps, it is time you closed that chapter of your life for good," wisely the father suggested.

"I think you are right."

Rushing to get to *The Palace*, Gregg impatiently drove through the crowded streets. He wanted desperately to beat Tiffany there so he could talk to Ashley. He didn't want her to get the wrong impression about his nonexistent relationship with Tiffany.

Parking his car, Gregg quickly went inside. Thankfully, Tiffany hadn't arrived.

"Is Miss Finley here?" Gregg asked the woman at the reservation desk.

"Yes, she is."

"Would it be possible for me to speak with her for a moment?"

"Sure," the greeter went to the back area.

Shortly, Gregg saw Ashley walking in his direction. He could never get enough of seeing her. Tonight, she wore her hair pulled back in a fashionable ponytail, not the usual tight bun. Dress in a black dress, which fitted her well, she seemed to glow as she came closer to him. He studied her profile with pleasure. Gregg felt like a kid again—alive and happy!

"Gregg," Ashley greeted, pleased to see him. "Is everything all right? Is your dad okay?"

"Oh yes! Dad is better than I could have hoped for."

"That's so wonderful."

"How is your mother?"

"She's great, Gregg. I think she'll be home sometime next week."

"That's wonderful."

She has such dreamy eyes! I'm hooked on them! I'm hooked on her!

He looks so handsome in the navy suit with the bold red tie.

"Ashley," Gregg softly called her name, "you are so beautiful."

"Thank you," bashfully, she lowered her head.

Gregg tilted her face upward. With no thought of where he was or what he was doing, tenderly Gregg caressed Ashley's cheeks. Spontaneously, he kissed her forehead. Their eyes locked.

Ashley thought she would melt if he didn't remove his

hand from her face.

"I...wanted to tell..." Gregg began.

"Oh, darling," Tiffany barged in. "I'm sorry I'm late." She practically threw herself on him and kissed him boldly on the lips. "Oh, you wearing my lipstick," she teased, swiftly wiping his lips with her fingers.

Ashley's jaw dropped.

"Oh, you," Tiffany looked at Ashley with a self-satisfying grin. "You're the lady at the hospital."

"What do you think you're doing?" Gregg pulled away from Tiffany's embrace.

"Good to see you again," Ashley found her voice. "Please excuse me. I must get back to work."

"Ashley!" Gregg grabbed her hand.

She turned to him. Her face was so stiff it looked as if it would crack. "Enjoy your evening." Ashley walked away.

"We need to talk!" Gregg nearly snatched Tiffany's arm, pulling her forward.

After being seated by the waiter, Gregg let Tiffany have it.

"I don't know what games you think you are playing with me Tiffany, but I'm not having it! You and I are just friends! Nothing more! No more one-night-stands! You got it!"

"What's wrong with you?" she scowled. "You don't like me anymore?"

Gregg was frustrated. How would he ever get through to this self-centered woman?

"Listen, I'm getting too old for this...and so are you," he calmed down. "Don't you want a better life, Tiffany? You're on your third husband. Something is wrong with that. It is time we both grew up. Stop messing with people's lives and behaving like irresponsible swingers. Do you want to end up

274

old and alone, with nobody?" he paused waiting for her to answer. "Well, I don't. Not anymore."

"I'll be just fine." Tiffany endeavored to shake his comments off, but it wasn't so easy.

"Why don't you call Trevor? Maybe you two can go to counseling. Isn't your marriage worth fighting for?"

"Trevor hurt me."

"Okay," Gregg sympathized, "but haven't your hurt Trevor before?"

Her eyes watered, as she nodded. "Too many times."

"It seems to me that you should forgive him."

Tiffany reached across the table and placed her hands over Gregg's hands.

Ashley noticed their hands touching as she took the orders of her customers a few tables over. At that moment, she wanted to give Gregg a piece of her mind. *He can date whoever he wants to! We are not committed to each other.* Quickly taking her customers' order, Ashley trotted back to the kitchen.

"Are you okay?" Pam asked.

Ashley nodded.

"You can't fool me."

"It's nothing," Ashley shrugged.

"Just say you don't want to talk about it, but don't stand there and lie to me.'

Ashley laughed. "I don't want to talk about it."

"Okay. But can we talk about it later?"

"Maybe."

"It's a full house out there," Pam mentioned. "Andrew has a new special with lobster. Everyone is ordering it."

Ashley turned to see Andrew smiling at her.

"How is your mother?"

"She's better." Ashley returned the smile. "You never told me just how you knew my mother. Were you two very close?"

"We were," Andrew cleared his throat. "She was a wonderful lady. Everyone loved her."

"Was she sick a lot when you knew her?"

"She was, but she never let it get her down. She could be in pain, but no one would know it. The only way I knew it was when her right leg would shake. Somehow, shaking her leg would take her mind off the pain."

"She still does that." Ashley was surprised he knew her secret. "You must have known my mother really well to know that."

"We were close."

"How close?" Ashley was overcurious.

"Pam, table six needs refills." Ms. Melrose barged in.

"Sure thing, Boss," Pam saluted her. "Refills coming right up."

"She's so weird," Ms. Melrose mumbled and left.

"I guess I better go check on my tables as well. Talk to you later," Ashley uttered to Andrew.

His heart swelled with pride at how lovely his daughter had turned out. She was every bit of her mother with a hint of himself gleaming through her crystalline eyes.

God, I just want to hold my daughter and tell her how much I love her. Give me the patience!

"How is Harvey?" Pam asked Ashley while riding home in the back of Andrew's car.

Ashley's eyebrows arched at the inquiry. "He's fine. Why are you asking?"

"Just asking," Pam looked away, sheepishly. "He just seemed like a nice guy. I don't know why you just don't up and marry him."

"Because we're good friends. I value his friendship. I think of Harvey like a big brother, that's all."

The revelation secretly pleased Pam.

"I think you and Harvey make a great couple," Ashley cajoled. "I think he likes you, but he is afraid that it will hurt my feelings."

"How do you know?" Pam's eyes widened. "Did he say something?"

"As a matter of fact, he did. Harvey asked how you were doing and he said that you were pretty. Also, he said he never met a lady with such a great sense of humor. You made him laugh."

Color crept up Pam's face, making it glow in the dark. "I like him," she admitted. "Are you sure that's alright, Ashley? I don't want anything to come between us."

"I love it." Ashley clasped her friend's hands. "I couldn't think of anything that would make me happier than the two people I love the most, falling in love."

"Hold up!" Pam cautioned. "I didn't say anything about falling in love. I said I like the guy."

"Like now, love later."

"Whatever!"

Meanwhile, Ashley's thoughts drifted to a certain handsome man. She was so riled by the beautiful blonde hanging onto Gregg.

She was all over him! The nerve of him trying to speak with me before leaving! He is a player! One minute he is caressing my cheeks and the next he is kissing another woman!

Thomas maybe right, he is a Terminator! Terminate a woman's heart, leaving it broken into tiny pieces. Well, not mine!

CHAPTER 28

Going Home

"**Y**ou have to tell her," Andrew urged, sitting by the bedside of the woman who still occupied his heart. Not wanting to risk running into Ashley, Andrew visited every day while Ashley worked at the library.

"I know." Sandra sat up, feeling stronger. Something about being near Andrew always strengthened her. "Ashley is going to be so upset. I lied to her for twenty-three years. How will she ever forgive me?"

"You have raised her right, Sandy." Andrew was the only one who ever called her that. "It may take some time for her to get over it, but she's a Believer. Ashley will forgive you."

"I hope so."

"There is so much I want to say to you, Sandy. My heart longs to know all about you. Did you have a good life? Was Tom Finley good to you?"

Sandra looked away, her eyes spilling over from the remembrance of her unhappy past. She had made so many mistakes in her life, and marrying Tom Finley was at the top of the list. Although she was grateful and thanked God for her beautiful four children, Sandra regretted what he had done to all of them.

"Look at me." Andrew pleaded, his hand softly caressing her hand. "We don't have to talk about it now."

"I married Tom because I was ashamed. I didn't want my parents to know the truth about me being pregnant. Then when you left, I was so mad at you. I couldn't believe you left me. You chose the army over me."

"I didn't choose the army over you, I chose it for us." After all, this time, Andrew still wanted her to understand. "You never understood that, Sandy. I wanted a better life for us. We both had been dirt poor all of our lives, even though our families did the best they could with what they had. I was coming back. I came back," he paused, still affected by the event that changed his life forever. "But it was too late. You had already married Tom."

"You didn't even write me," she sniffed.

"Yes, I did," he frowned. "I wrote every day, but you didn't respond to any of my letters."

"What? I didn't get any of your letters."

"Well, your mother never liked me," Andrew thought back. "Perhaps, she kept the letters from you."

"No way! She wouldn't do such a thing." Sandra didn't believe her own words.

Sandra's mother smothered her and wanted no one to take her daughter away from her. Being a sickly child, Ashley's mother doted on her and kept everyone at arms distance. She was so against Sandra's marriage to Tom that she feigned sickness and didn't even come to her daughter's wedding ceremony.

"I would never lie to you, Sandy. I never have and I never will."

"I believe you."

"Your mother never liked me. She spent every waking moment scheming to separate us," he paused, realizing the truth hurt Sandra. "I never understood why she hated me so much."

"It wasn't you, Andrew. She just didn't want to lose her only girl. I was my mother's whole life."

"Where do we go from here?" Andrew asked, squeezing her hand. "I still love you…more than ever."

"Andrew, we are different people now. A lot has happened in our lives. I am not the same person. My illness is worse than ever. I'm practically an invalid, living off of my children."

"I don't care. You can get better; but even if you don't, I still want to be there for you. I have never stopped loving you. Even after I married Belinda, I could never wholly give her my heart. After her death, I never married because my heart always belonged to you."

His confession touched her deeply. Sandra felt undeserving of such love, especially after what she had done to him. She took away his rights of being a father.

"I married Tom because I was afraid."

"You don't have to fear anymore. Was Tom good to you?" he asked again.

She pondered his question, quickly having flashbacks of her miserable life. She needed to be honest with Andrew. Most important, she finally needed to be honest with herself.

"Tom married me knowing I was carrying your child. He promised me a good life. Unfortunately, he gave me just the opposite. I did everything to make him love me and to treat me right. I always felt guilty about Ashley, and Tom made sure I kept feeling that way. He provided for us financially, but he was a lousy husband. His weakness was other women, which hurt us all. There was always someone else. Tom said that he was tired of taking care of a sick woman and he needed an outlet. It was my fault he was sleeping around. It was my fault that he wasn't happy. It was my fault that he had seven mouths to feed. I was blamed for everything."

"I'm so sorry, Sandra." Andrew uttered, trying to mask his anger. "I wish I would have known."

"There was nothing you could have done. I did it to myself. For years, I accepted his behavior, thinking I deserved nothing better because of the lie. Sadly, my children were not happy, especially Ashley. I know that now."

"God has given us a second chance. I came back home, hoping just to glimpse you. However, God made it possible for me to hold your hand, to bask in your beauty, and to share my love with you, all over again. We serve an awesome God, Sandy. He's so awesome that He brought us back together—for such a time as this!"

Friday turned out to be a big day for everyone. For starters, Sandra Finley and Gregory Jefferson were both being discharged. Miraculously, God had healed them both. While both were weak and needed extra care at home, in time Mr. Jefferson and Ms. Finley would be back to their normal selves, if not better.

"Hi, Ashley." Gregg greeted, practically colliding into her as he headed to his father's hospital room.

"Hi, Gregg."

"How have you been doing?"

"Fine."

"I tried calling you."

"Oh," was all Ashley could say. She knew when the phone rang at midnight it was Gregg calling. She resolved not to answer. She wanted to get him out of her mind and erase him out of her heart. Unfortunately, it wasn't that easy. Ashley thought about the handsome man all the time.

Something within Gregg just wanted to claim Ashley for his own. He had never felt that drawn to any woman before.

Ashley refused to look him in the eye, for fear she would helplessly surrender her heart to him. She had to be strong… stay true to herself and her convictions.

"It's good to see you," his pearly whites glistened.

"How is your lady friend?" Ashley could not help herself.

"There is nothing between me and Tiffany." The door was opened for him to explain. "She's an old friend. She came to visit because she and her husband are having marital problems."

"It doesn't matter," she shrugged her shoulders.

"I think it does."

"Gregg, circumstances put us together, but now our parents are better. You needed me and I needed you. We don't need each other anymore. I appreciate how you have helped my brother and my family, but that's the extent of our connection."

His stance became tense, for her words cut him deeply. Inwardly, Gregg's heart burned, like a fire, leaving him feeling seared, deaden in some way. "It's more than that…for me," timidly, he responded. "You have to admit that there is some kind of bond between us—a strong chemistry."

"There could never be an us if you do not have a relationship with God," she put it bluntly.

Gregg hadn't expected that. She could have said anything, but to reject him for not being like her, he didn't know if he should be mad or glad. She had literally slammed the door in his face, without even knowing it.

"I have to go," she finally said. "Harvey is waiting on me. We have to go pick up a few things for mother before taking her home." Ashley hesitated, seeing the painful look in his eyes. "I wish you the best, Gregg," she smiled and walked away.

Harvey is a lucky man!

Disoriented, Gregg went to his dad's hospital room. "Are you ready to get out of here?" Gregg faced his father, trying to put on a happy face.

"Sure am," he accepted the nurse's help into the wheelchair. "Is Senorita Rivas ready for me?"

"Been ready! She's got the place fit for a king."

"Then take me to my castle."

After taking Ashley and her mother home from the hospital, and making sure the Sandra Finley was okay, Harvey rushed to pick up Pam for a late lunch. Feeling excited and nervous, Harvey wondered if he was doing the right thing. Pam was Ashley's best friend. Although Ashley encouraged the luncheon, Harvey had doubts whether or not he was just going out with Pam on a rebound, trying to blot out the rejection he felt from Ashley.

"So, how long have you and Ashley been friends?" Pam asked later.

"Seems like forever. I have known her since kindergarten. We have always been close."

"Hmmm," Pam read more. "So close that you asked her to marry you."

Harvey nearly choked on his ice-tea, half of it spilling in his lap.

Pam giggled.

Harvey frowned.

"Ashley and I are close, too," Pam finally said, struggling to keep herself from laughing anymore.

"How do you feel about me proposing to Ashley?"

"Maybe I should be asking you that," she turned the tables.

He thought some time before finally answering. "My pride was wounded that she said no. It seemed like the next step in our relationship. I wanted to help Ashley. As you know, she is the caretaker for the family. It is too much of a load for her to bear alone. I figured if she would marry me, then I could support her in many ways."

"It's a noble gesture, but marriage is rough. It's hard enough when two people really love each other, but to marry for convenience is like signing your death warrant."

"I do love, Ashley," Harvey felt the need to say.

"So do I, but I wouldn't marry her," Pam said seriously. Harvey chuckled. "I'm serious," Pam pouted. "My parents hated each other. They fussed and fought like cats and dogs, on a regular basis. I couldn't wait to get out of their house."

"How old were you when you left?"

"I was sixteen."

"Wow!" Harvey couldn't imagine that.

"I lived with friends at school for a while. Then I got a job, moved into a tiny one-bedroom apartment and never looked back."

"I would have been too scared to do such a thing."

"It was either that or risk being...uh..." *Too much information!*

Harvey sensed her uneasiness. It didn't take a Rocket Scientist to know that Pam had been through a lot. His heart went out to her. Like Ashley, she needed someone, as well. It was high time that someone took care of Pam.

"Anyhow," Pam bounced back, "I have been taking care of myself ever since. I've done a pretty good job if I say so myself."

"You have," Harvey smiled, "and now you're a part of my family."

"Huh?" she smacked on french-fries.

"You're a believer, just like me and Ashley."

"I am. I do not feel different, though. I'm still crazy as ever."

"Yes," he chuckled. "Salvation doesn't change our personalities. It just incorporates it into the new us. Like Saul changing to Paul. He was radical for the world. Likewise, after his transformation, Paul became radical for Christ. Peter was a hothead before Christ and he turned out to be a hothead in spreading the Gospel of Jesus Christ. You were crazy before and now you're crazy for Christ."

"I like that." Pam nodded. "I still get to be me."

The two enjoyed the rest of their luncheon. Harvey laughed so hard his stomach hurt. Pam's sense of humor was *off the chart*. She could say something seriously, but it cracked Harvey up.

Though they were as different as any two people could be, their differences complimented each other. Set in his ways, uptight, reserved and faithfully walking a straight and narrow line, Harvey was used to a simple life.

On the other hand, Pam preferably walked the crooked path, living spontaneously, going with the flow and never planning for anything, just taking things one day at a time.

In both lives, a balance was needed. Perhaps, balance had

knocked on the doors of their hearts for such a time as this.

"Someone seems to be in a good mood," Ashley playfully baited her friend at work.

"No comment," Pam turned away.

"Oh, no you don't." Ashley practically spun Pam around. "You would never let me off that easy. Now the shoe is on the other foot. Out with it. How was your luncheon with Harvey?"

"Fine."

"Just fine."

"Okay, good."

"Just good," Ashley was enjoying herself.

"Don't push it!" Pam faced her. "Harvey is a good guy."

"He sure is. I love him dearly."

"But you're not in love with him, right?" Pam wanted to be sure.

"Absolutely not." Ashley crossed her heart, playfully. "I told you I am happy you two went out. Are you going out again?"

"He's picking me up Sunday for church and then we are going out to dinner."

"How sweet. I am so happy for you, Pam. Harvey deserves the best…and well, I guess that's why God saved you…for him. The best of the best!"

Pam, never one to wear her emotions on her sleeves, squeezed her friend while struggling to keep her tears at bay. Pam failed.

"You're crying," Ashley had never seen this before in her friend.

"I'm becoming a softy, like you." Pam wiped her eyes.

"Ever since I gave my heart to Christ I am becoming all mushy and wimpy…like you."

"That means your wall is coming down. You are free now. Free to live. Free to express yourself. And free to cry. Welcome to the Club!"

CHAPTER 29

Naomi

Sitting in the dining room, sharing breakfast with Tiffany, Gregg's mind was elsewhere on a certain beauty with crystalline eyes.

"Hey, you!" Tiffany tossed a napkin at him. "Did you hear me?"

"What?" Gregg was rather irritated that she was still there.

"What are we going to do today?"

"We aren't going to do anything."

"Let's go to the lake."

"I'm staying here." Gregg forced himself to tolerate her presence. "My dad is home. I want to spend the day with him."

"He'll be sleeping most of the day. We can just do a quick picnic, swim a little and come back."

Gregg was becoming more frustrated by the minute.

"More eggs and bacon," Senorita Rivas entered with a tray. She knew Gregg all too well.

"Of course," he smiled. "Do you have any more orange juice?"

"Sure do," she winked. "I'll be right back."

"I don't want to just sit around all day." Tiffany pouted like a kid. "Please, just a little while."

"Go home, Tiffany!" Gregg ordered. "Go home to your husband!"

"I…uh…you're not…" Tiffany stopped talking when Senorita Rivas entered again.

"Anything else, Gregg?" she asked after serving him.

"No, thank you. Everything was delicious as always."

"Thank you," her smile was precious to him. "Mr. Jefferson ate a small breakfast. He has more color this morning than yesterday."

"That's good," Gregg replied. "I think I'm going to see if he wants to sit on the terrace later. He used to like that when I was little."

"He sure did," the remembrance was pleasant. Senorita Rivas remembered the happier times in the Jefferson's home. The trio would enjoy eating on the terrace and sitting on the benches near the private large pond. There was a light in Mr. Jefferson's eyes. After his wife's death, the dark eyes were dim with sorrow. Father and son had both lost their spark, replacing it with work and things that did not matter.

God is working a miracle with the Jefferson men. I can see it.

"Excuse me," Tiffany felt left out. "Did you clean up my room, yet?"

"Of course not. I will clean the guest room as soon as I'm finished in the kitchen." Senorita Rivas eyed the brazenfaced, high-and-mighty, thorn in her flesh, over-staying guest. "I'll check again on Mr. Jefferson shortly."

"I'll do it," Gregg expressed. "As a matter of fact, Senorita Rivas, you have been overworking. Why don't you take the rest of the day off and I'll look after everything around here."

"Gregg!" Tiffany was about to argue, but Gregg held his

hand up, signaling this was not up for a discussion.

"That will be all Senorita Rivas. I appreciate everything you do for us."

Her eyes nearly spilled over. Truly, Senorita Rivas was exhausted. Tiffany was calling her every five minutes. Plus, she had to get everything spick and span for the return of Mr. Jefferson. Further, now that Gregg was home, she had her hands full. She never complained because she enjoyed hard work. She enjoyed taking care of Gregg and his father. They were her extended family. But Tiffany was another story, alltogether.

Senorita Rivas was about to say something when the doorbell rang.

"You're off the clock!" Gregg skidded his chair back. "I'll get the door. Senorita Rivas, you just go and do whatever it is you want to do," he finished and went to answer the door.

"Wham!" Gregg was greeted at the door with a punch in his left eye!

"What the heck!" Gregg covered his eye.

"Where's my wife?"

"You must be Trevor." Gregg stood stunned. "I would say come on in, but considering that you punched me in the eye…"

"I ought to do more than that!" Trevor barked confidently.

"I wouldn't try that if I were you." Gregg stood tall, ready to defend himself. "Now, if you want to act like a civilized man and not a silly boy, perhaps we can talk."

"I don't want to talk to you! I want my wife!" Trevor stood nose to nose with Gregg. "Are you sleeping with her?"

"You should ask your wife that," Gregg purposely annoyed the guy.

"I'm asking you!"

"Tiffany!" Gregg hollered.

In a hot-second, she came.

"Trevor, what are you doing here?"

"I came to take you home!"

"Who says I want to go home?" Tiffany played the victim part.

"You do!" Gregg intervened, ready to get rid of the overbearing houseguest. She had overstayed her welcome and it was time for her to get out.

"Gregg!" Tiffany turned to him in disbelief. "Your eye," she noticed it was slightly swelling.

"It looks worse than it feels." Gregg tried to make light of it.

"You shouldn't have done that Trevor!" Tiffany chastised. "Gregg has done nothing wrong."

"So, you haven't slept with him?" Trevor just had to know.

"No!" Tiffany said self-righteously, knowing deep down it wasn't by choice she hadn't slept with Gregg.

"Good!" Trevor took her in his arms. "I have missed you terribly. I have been such a fool. I cannot live without you, Tiff. I need you."

"You cheated on me."

"I was a fool," he said softly. "I was a real fool. I promise never to cheat on you again. Please come home, Tiff. We can go to marriage counseling. Whatever you want me to do, I will do it. Anything to win you back."

"I'll think about it," her eyes brightened. She had Trevor just where she wanted him.

"What happened to your eye?" Mr. Jefferson asked while

sitting on the terrace with his son.

"Oh, it's nothing."

"A black-eye is something. What happened?"

"Tiffany's husband stopped by."

"Oh," Mr. Jefferson chuckled. "The jealous husband wanted to protect his turf."

"Something like that. I am sure glad he came, though. Tiffany was driving me crazy. And poor Senorita Rivas. Tiffany had run her ragged. I had to give her the day off."

"Naomi has been with us a long time," Mr. Jefferson called the housekeeper by her first name. Something he never did.

Gregg couldn't quite put his name on it, but something about that made him feel aflutter.

"This morning I woke up to her praying over me," Mr. Jefferson continued. "It was the sweetest prayer. She said something about, '*Make his latter days better than his former days. Restore to him all that he has lost, like Job, so that he will know You for himself. Rekindle the fire in him for life, for his son and mostly Lord for You.*'" Mr. Jefferson paused, reflecting for a moment.

"Your mother used to pray like that."

Gregg noticed his father's eyes brightened. He seemed almost a different man. *Perhaps facing death truly changes a man.*

"Why do you suppose that Naomi has stuck with us all these years?" he asked of his son, already knowing the truth. "I mean there is hardly anything to do. She does not have any family here. She never married and she's still young."

"She is fifty-three."

"Like I said," Mr. Jefferson turned to his son, "she is still young."

"You're not *crushing* on her?" It sounded ridiculous even as he said it, but when his father didn't deny it, Gregg was silenced stiff.

"I'm a lonely man." his father closed his eyes and reclined back in the lounge chair. "I have been for some time. Coming this close," he snapped his frail fingers, "to meeting your Maker is an eye-opener. Your mother would not want me to spend the rest of my life alone. She loved Naomi. They were more like best friends than an employer relationship. You know that."

Gregg nodded, still shocked by his dad's openness. "But… uh…she is the housekeeper."

"She's more than that." Mr. Jefferson's eyes popped open. "You've always said so."

"Uh huh," Gregg bobbed his head like a doll, "but you have always opposed fraternization with subordinates."

"Like I said, I've been an old fool. I see things differently now."

"I see." Gregg cleared his throat, not sure how he felt about the new idea of his father liking the woman who had nurtured him and cared for him like a mother. Did his father even deserve such a kindhearted woman like Naomi?

"So I take it that you disapprove?" Mr. Jefferson spoke, his eyes closed again.

"I don't know what I feel," Gregg answered truthfully. "Senorita Rivas means the world to me. I love her like…like a mother. I…uh, just don't know how she would feel about it."

"She'll think I am crazy!" Mr. Jefferson smiled. "She'll probably be right. Can you imagine what the neighbors and my friends would say?"

"The same thing you would have said before going into the hospital."

"Exactly!" his eyes flicked opened. "But it only matters to me what you think. If you're against it, I will not pursue Naomi."

"I'm not against it, Dad. It's just new to me. I want you to be happy and if Naomi can make you happy then I am all for it. But, you must know that Naomi may be totally offended by this."

"Let me tell you a little secret," the father's eyes twinkled. "Your mother asked Naomi to take us into her heart if something ever happened to her – to love both of us."

"How do you know this?"

"Naomi told me this about six months after your mother died. She gave me a note from your mother. It's in my Bible on the nightstand. Please get it and read it aloud."

After retrieving the letter, Gregg returned and read it aloud.

"*Naomi,*

I love you deeply. You are my best friend and my sister. If something ever happens to me, I want you to promise to love my son as your own and to love my Gregory. The Jefferson men are strong outwardly, but they need a strong woman to keep them grounded in what matters the most – God and family. Don't feel guilty for loving them. I'll be smiling from heaven knowing that they have you. It makes it easier going to my heavenly home. Please don't give up on them, especially my sweet Gregory. He acts all tough on the outside, but he has a heart of gold. Remind, Gregg that he was created for such a time as this…to do something amazing for God. I will never leave any of you. I'm in your hearts…always.

Love, Sophia

"How could mom have known she was going to die in a car accident?" Gregg was bewildered.

"You mother knew a lot of things. She might not have known how and when she would die," Gregory swallowed hard, pain lodged momentarily in his throat, before continuing, "but she had that kind of relationship with God—a discerning spirit to know her time was near."

Mr. Jefferson hesitated before speaking again. "Naomi promised she would never leave us, no matter what. She said, she cared about you and would love you as if you were her own son. Then she said to me that she would always be there for me...always. When she said always, Son, I turned cold as ice. I could not look at another woman without feeling I was cheating on my Sophia. Naomi didn't mean anything by it, I am sure. Nevertheless, I felt over the years, she was becoming protective of us, as if we were her only family. Therefore, I sent you away, so she wouldn't get too attached. However, it didn't work. She was even more attached to you. I treated her so cold and harsh at times, hoping she would leave, but she wouldn't."

"Wow!" Greg was blown over. It was just too much to take in.

"The truth be known, over the years, I started feeling something for Naomi," Greggory confessed. "But, she was my subordinate. I could never cross the boundaries that separated our worlds. Noble blood didn't mix with the lower class."

Gregg shook his hand, still floored by his father's confession. "Well Dad, you sure have made this an interesting day."

"I aim to please."

"Are you tired?"

"I could use a nap."

"You want to go inside?"

"No. I enjoy being out here…with you."

Warmed by his dad's sentiment, Gregg reclined back in the chair and closed his eyes. Father and son were slowly rebuilding a relationship of oneness and truthfulness.

Never in a million years, did Gregg think it was possible for him to enjoy being at the mausoleum again.

"Oh, by the way, I want to go to Naomi's church tomorrow," the father spoke.

Gregg's eyes popped opened as he turned and looked at his father. Mr. Jefferson remained resting with his eyes shut.

"You're just full of surprises, aren't you?"

"I told you that I wanted to go to church when I got out of the hospital. I have to mend fences with the Master."

"You're really serious?"

"I sure am. You should be thinking about mending those same fences. Your mother would want nothing more," Mr. Jefferson spoke with finality.

CHAPTER 30

Mending Fences

"**G**od is orchestrating the right opportunities, the right people to come across our paths, and even the right afflictions and inconveniences to propel us do what He wants us to do," Pastor Manuel began his sermon. "Remember, all things are working together for our good because we love God and have been called according to HIS PURPOSE, not our purpose. We have it all backwards. It is not about what we want with our lives, but what God wants us to do with our lives.

"Mordecai reminded Esther that she had come to this royal position for such a time as this. She was presented with the opportunity of a lifetime to become a queen. Success comes with responsibility. Even in the midst of success, God has expectations of each one of us. Esther was expected to help her people. You are where you are to help someone else. You must look beyond yourself and see others.

"Selfish people never reach their full potential in Christ. God blesses us so that we can be a blessing to others. Our success should open up new doors for others. You cannot mistreat people when you are the head boss in charge. Don't' forget those who helped you get to where you are today. Mordecai had to remind Esther where she came from in order to get her focused on where God was leading her.

"Some may say that I am well off, financially, and no one helped me get to where I am." The pastor recognized that his membership was a mixture of race, color, wealth, poverty, nationality. He purposely touched every home and every life with this message. "But think about your housekeeper, who keeps the house clean, some even take care of your children..."

Mr. Jefferson looked across the aisle at Naomi, who was looking back at him, before bashfully turning away. He smiled when he saw her cheeks turned a flaming red. Truly, he would have never survived without Naomi. She had watched over him and his son for years. He felt somewhat ashamed that he had taken her for granted.Gregg looked over at his father's awe-struck faced, as he soaked up every word of the minister. He wondered about the peace that covered his dad like a soft cloud.

"Many of you have the responsibility of supervising people." Gregg listened carefully as the pastor went on. "God has given you the awesome responsibility of making sure that you help your employees become better people. You should work diligently to make your work environment a pleasant environment and not a hostile, dogmatic environment.

"Don't always have the whip out, but instead give praise where praise is due. And if someone needs help, help them. Be an Esther or a Mordecai on your job. Look for opportunities to make someone's life better. To make a difference. Helping one person can have a domino effect on a family, a community, and ultimately the world."

Gregg pondered the words in his heart. *Am I making a difference? The students face so many challenges. Perhaps there is something more I can do for them, besides ensuring that they get an education, which is important. Look at Thomas. He and so many like him need extra incomes to help at home. Every time I try to find a solution, I encounter another roadblock. At least I could get Shane a part time job. But what about the countless others, like Shane?*

"Today is the day for you to search your hearts. You were created to make an impact on the world. Some in big ways, and others in small, yet, significant ways. God knew that each one of you would be here today. It is not a coincidence that you are here. It's a divine appointment. You were created for such a time as this! You were sent here for such a time as this!"

Instantaneously, Gregg's mother song chimed in his heart. He could almost hear her whispering the melody in the depths of his soul.

When you entered this world
It was as if the sun, the moon & stars had kissed
You were born to bring joy into our home
For such a time as this
Your life has a purpose
And only God knows what it is
You were created to help others find their way
For such a time as this

Following, Pastor Manuel made an altar call for salvation and prayer. Mr. Jefferson stood up, ready to make the needed walk to the altar.

"Do you need help?" Gregg whispered.

"Only if you're going for the same reason," Mr. Jefferson hoped.

Gregg shook his head.

"Then I must do this alone." Mr. Jefferson smiled and walked the aisle with a little more pep in his step.

Senorita Rivas gasped with delight as she beheld the man she had looked after for many years surrendering to a Higher Power than himself. Silently, she prayed for him, her eyes spilling over, reflecting her heart, which overflowed with unspeakable joy!

Feeling uncomfortable after service, Gregg rushed outside. The service had affected him strangely. He felt hot and fidgety. Gregg tried to convince himself that he just needed some fresh air. But, it was more to it than that and Gregg knew it.

"Mr. Jefferson," Naomi approached him in the aisle. "I'm so happy for you."

"I know you understand this," Mr. Jefferson eyed her, "but I feel like a new man."

"I do," she beamed. "It's an incredible feeling. Indescribable!"

"I'm still the same on the outside. Old. Ornery. Overly proud, but I feel different."

"First of all, there is nothing old about you," Naomi lowered her eyes. "And secondly, the Bible says you are a new creature. Old things have passed away, all things have become new." Naomi thought she was sure to burst. She had been praying for the Jefferson men's salvation since the death of her dear friend.

"I don't feel like going home," Mr. Jefferson stated. "I feel like going out for dinner to celebrate. Will you please join Gregg and I for Sunday dinner?"

"I've already prepared dinner," Naomi was touched by the invite all the same.

"It can wait till tomorrow."

"You don't eat leftovers."

"I will tomorrow," Mr. Jefferson grinned. "So, you don't have any excuse."

"I...uh, Mr. Jefferson..."

"Call me Gregory," he smiled like a young schoolboy with a crush on his longtime playmate. Only Naomi wasn't his playmate...she was his housekeeper.

"Gregory," Naomi humbly complied, "let me...uh... go tell Mr. Brown." Naomi always rode to church with the butler.

"Gregg and I will be outside waiting for you." He held her eyes for a moment longer. "Tell Mr. Brown after he takes the car home, he can have the next two days off."

"Okay," she stuttered. Either it was her imagination or Naomi had detected something more in Gregory's eyes and it alarmed her.

There was a time when Naomi had hoped that her employer would notice her. Oh, it was silly of course, the promise she had made Sophia—to be there for Gregg and Gregory. Insisting that Naomi had so much love in her to give. Sophia wanted her friend to fully be there for Gregory and Greg, as mother and wife.

What was Sophia thinking? I'm just a housekeeper! Gregory is a sophisticated, wealthy businessman. He used to look down on people like me.

Get yourself together. You are too old for this silly game. He is your employer. He is just excited about his salvation. That's all! Don't you read anything in it!

It's too late...

In due season, you will reap a harvest if you faint not.

Dinner was quite entertaining. To behold his dad appearing healthier and happier after one service was mindboggling for Gregg. He only related religion to his mother. While his mother was alive, Gregg counted himself among the Christian family. However, now there was a major disconnect between him and God.

"How does it feel?" Gregg asked his father.

"What?" Mr. Jefferson put down his fork. "You mean salvation?"

Gregg nodded.

"It feels liberating. For so long I have been in charge, and well now, I'm not. It is going to take some getting used to, but I must say I'm looking forward to following His lead and seeing where I end up."

"You mean you can just hand over the reins just like that?" Gregg just didn't buy it. It seemed too easy.

"Yes. I tell you, Son, it's liberating. This is what your mother felt."

Gregg eyed his dad keenly. It appeared as if he had erased ten years from his face. It was not so stiff and stern, creased with wrinkles of stress and agitation. Something was different. His earthly father was a different man.

"I wish I would have done this a long time ago," Mr. Jefferson turned to Naomi. "I have wasted so many years."

"He will redeem the time," warmth was in her tone as Naomi spoke.

"I sure hope so," his look was tender sweet.

Naomi smiled.

"Gregg and I," Mr. Jefferson glanced at his son for a moment and then turned his attention back to Naomi. "We never would have made it all these years without you, Naomi. I'm sure you wore the carpet out praying for this old geezer and young whippersnapper."

"You are both like my family," she said honestly. "It was an honor to pray for you, both."

"You are family," Mr. Jefferson extended his hand to Gregg first and then to Naomi. Nervously, she accepted the extended hand.

All the while Gregg, endowed with emotions, relished having the new-improved-dad back and the woman who nourished him with motherly-love by his side.

Later that night as Gregg was saying goodnight to his father, Naomi knocked on the door.

"Come in," Gregg answered.

Immediately the father and son knew something was wrong.

"I have to leave," Naomi spoke hurriedly. "My sister is very ill."

"I'm sorry to hear that." Mr. Jefferson struggled to sit upward. It had been a long day for him and his body was worn-out.

"I have to go to New York."

"Sure," Gregg came near her. "Is there anything I can do?"

"I need to get a flight out of here, but I'm not good with stuff like that. Can you help me?"

"Sure. I'll contact a friend of mine and see if I can get you a flight tonight."

"Thank you, Gregg," she forced a smile. "Just let me know how much it's going to cost. I'm sure it is going to be a lot, at this last minute," Naomi sounded worried.

"Gregg, handle this for me. Take care of all expenses." Mr. Jefferson ordered.

"No!" Naomi's prideful heart protested.

"I won't hear of it." Mr. Jefferson spoke sharply. "This is the least I can do for you, Naomi. Gregg, take care of it."

"Yes, Sir," Gregg exited to the room.

"I'll pay you back," Naomi felt obligated.

"You will do no such thing."

"But…"

"No buts," he interrupted. "You're family Naomi."

"Thank you, Mr. Jefferson."

"Gregory," he amended.

"It doesn't feel right calling you by your first name," she shook her head. "It's not proper."

"Forget proper! We're family, right?"

She stared, feeling uncomfortable. *It is a good thing I am leaving!*

"I hate that you have to leave us, but it certainly is understandable. What's wrong with your sister?"

"She has cancer."

"Is she a believer?" Now that he was a Believer, he wanted everyone to be, including his stiff-necked son. *Like father like son!*

"She is."

"Well, she's in good hands."

"Yes, she is." His assurance soothed her. "Are you okay? You look peaked."

"I'm tired, but in a good way. It has been a good day. I just hate for it to end this way."

Naomi gazed at him. She could surely see what other women saw in him. He was handsome, in a different way from his son, but still handsome. His confident air drew others to him. Although, there had been no significant other in his life since his wife's death, women, young and old alike, were throwing themselves at his feet.

"I'm not sure how long I'll be, but I asked Ms. Frierson to fill in for me. Do you remember her? She usually comes twice a year when I go home to visit my family."

"Yes, I remember. She's a bit crabby, but we will survive."

Naomi laughed softly.

"Promise me something," Mr. Jefferson spoke seriously.

"Anything."

"Promise me that you will come back."

His requested moved her deeply.

"I promise."

CHAPTER 31

Angels all around

Monday morning Gregg met with his administration team directly after work. He wanted to implement a plan for all athletes to earn money on Saturdays.

"I was thinking we could all pool our resources and make some contacts with business owners about hiring our athletes on the weekends. If they can work on the weekends, then they would be free to practice and for the games. Still, they would bring in some income to help their families," Gregg was brainstorming as he spoke. "For instance, I usually pay $75 for someone to keep my lawn up. He comes by every other week to rake, trim the hedges, and cut the front and back lawn as needed. He also does both of my neighbors' homes. I've already spoken to my neighbors and they agreed to give an athlete a try just for a worthy cause. "Any more ideas?" Gregg opened the discussion.

"My best friend owns a clothing store." All heads turned when Ms. Myers spoke up. Usually, the one to disagree and turn her nose up, they were all surprised that Ms. Myers was even interested in helping. After Gregg broached her about the subject of going to J.T. Moore High School, Ms. Myers made a complete U-turn.

"Go on." Gregg's ears perked up.

"She is always saying how she could use some extra help on the weekends. I know she will be interested. She supports education in every way she can."

"Good." Gregg smiled at Ms. Myers. "You talk to her and get back with me."

"Coach Koon, can you give me a list of athletes who you know need to work in order to support their families?"

"Sure can." Coach Koon was pleased. "I think this is an excellent idea. The students and families are going to appreciate our help greatly."

"We are providing a safe and learning environment for the student body. However, we can do more. We have to go beyond the realms of an educator. We have to show them that we care about them, individually. Yes, we want them to have a quality education, but we also want them to have the tools they need to survive outside of these walls." The team could feel his passion.

"Also, we could probably help out the families with food or with any fixer-upper projects to their homes. We could call it Brookland Handy Projects or Brookland Missions... we'll work on it," enthusiasm seeped through his mouth. "We need to extend our services beyond the school if we want the students to be productive graduates of Brookland."

Something had changed about Principal Jefferson and the change was good. The administrative team liked the new principal, buying into his vision to move the school beyond its prior failing rate. Further, under his leadership, everyone was on board, including Ms. Myers, to giving the students the tools needed to succeed in all areas of their lives.

By the end of the day, all of the administration team had

affirmed their efforts of finding vendors to hire the athletes. Thirty-three jobs were available, starting next Saturday for the athletes. Just like that, Gregg's plan had worked. *For such a time as this*, he was born to influence the lives of his students, not just in the classroom, but also outside of the classroom.

Later after school, Gregg watched Shane and Thomas practicing free throws in the gym.

Shane missed more than he shot. It was obvious the young man wasn't concentrating. Thomas hadn't missed one free throw. He was a natural. Gregg was so proud of Thomas. He had done an all-out turnaround in academics and his behavior.

"Hey Shane," Gregg called to him. "Can I talk to you a minute?"

Shane rushed to the sideline. "What's up Principal Jefferson?"

"Are you okay?"

"Yeah."

"Are you sure?"

"I found a threatening note in my locker," Shane admitted.

"Do you have the note with you?"

Shane retrieved it from his pocket and handed it to him.

Gregg read it aloud. "It's not over. You better watch your back. No one hurts my sister."

"Drake and the guys are out of jail," Shane sounded worried. "I don't know what to do. Drake is one crazy dude."

"I'll give this note to Officer Anderson. I am sure he can do something. In the meantime, you cannot show fear. Just like a dog senses a human's fear and pounces on him, those guys can sense yours. Even if you are scared, *faith* it to you can make it! That is what my mom used to tell me. Around here, *we* got your back. Nothing is going to happen to you here."

"I know," Shane felt assured of this. "I'm worried about my family. I know I shouldn't worry. It is just me, my aunt and my four cousins at home. I don't want anything to happen to them."

"It won't. I will talk to Officer Anderson about it."

"God knows how to encourage us. He sent you to me, Principal Jefferson. I feel a lot better!"

"Then go shoot some free throws."

Shane's declaration of God using him to encourage him seemed farfetched to Gregg. *Why would God use me? I am not even a Christian.* Gregg sat on the bleachers and continued to watch the boys. Shane was shooting better. Thomas glanced over at him and gave him the thumbs up.

"Your talk with Shane really worked," Thomas mentioned later. The two were heading toward the lounge where Danny, Donny, and Lacey were doing homework. "He really needed it."

"No need to thank me," Gregg said. "It's all about teamwork, Thomas. There is no 'I' in team. In order for the Tigers to win a game, all of the team members have to play well. If one team member is off, it can have a domino effect on everyone. Shane was off. He needed help in getting back on. That's what we do."

"Sure glad they didn't hurt him the other day."

"Thanks to you," Gregg admonished. "Your tip saved his life."

"He would've done the same for me," Thomas replied humbly. "We're brothers."

Gregg looked at him.

"Brothers in Christ," Thomas said plainly. "Shane is worried about his family. Those guys aren't going to let him off so easily."

"I know."

"But prayer changes things," Thomas asserted. "I believe prayer will change things for Shane."

Gregg stopped walking. "Do you really believe that, Thomas?"

"I sure do. God is able to do just what He says He will do. It may not look like it, but faith sees differently."

"I admire your faith," Gregg said honestly.

"Without faith, we are all a sinking ship without an Anchor. Ashley says that all the time. Are you a Believer?"

"I used to be when I was ten," Gregg admitted timidly. "But things happened that shook my faith...for good."

"Prayer can change that, too," Thomas counseled. "After we had to leave our good home and good neighborhood to go and live in a dump, my faith was tested. I had lost my way, briefly. I was so mad at God for turning His back on us. It seemed that He had taken everything from us. Ashley kept praying for me. She didn't give up on me, even when I gave up on myself. Her love for me was an example of God's love for me. Even when I was acting unlovable, she loved me anyway. She says love is not just something you say; it is something you do.

"Same way with God. Things are not always the way we want them to be. For whatever reason God has allowed the trial, it is not for our bad, but ultimately for our good or for the good of others. For example, Shane wasn't a Believer, but now he is. Being locked up for three days induced Shane to change. God made it possible for me to get back on the team, restoring our friendship. I was here, at the right place and the right time to tell Shane about Jesus. Plus, if I were at the other school, I would not have met Shane and he may not be saved today."

Gregg pondered Thomas' strong words of faith. Like his sister, he was a wise young man. Thomas had deposited something in the principal's spirit that he could withdraw from later.

"I'll be praying for you," Thomas said before he got into Coach Koon's van.

"Thanks," Gregg waved. As the van drove away, he felt so empty inside. The change in Thomas was incredible. The change in his father was amazing. Perhaps, he needed what they had – change.

Meanwhile, Gregg and Thomas had no idea they were being watched. One of Drake's boys followed them while they were walking near the staff's lounge and eavesdropped on their conversation. He couldn't hear everything, but he heard just enough to know Thomas was the snitch!

Gregg loosened the knot in his tie. He drew a breath and reclined against the couch. He was tired, physically and mentally. A war within was raging. Why couldn't he find contentment? Was he capable of finding peace of mind?

He was trying to make a difference with the students at Brookland. Wasn't that enough?

But it wasn't.

Gregg was disheartened, troubled like the raging sea. His heart was restless, beating against the captive bars of loneliness.

Like his father used to be, Gregg felt lonely. Not just for companionship, but for Ashley. However, it was even deeper than that. He needed to fill the hole inside of him. He had money, a good career, and women by the dozen if he wanted them—still, something was missing.

I will pray for you! He remembered Thomas' promise.

There could never be an us if you have no relationship with God. Ashley's declaration came to mind.

You should think about mending those same fences. Gregg recalled his dad's urgency. *Your mother would want nothing more.*

Everyone around him had discovered the secret of real peace, except him. Gregg had angels all around him, it seemed.

What is holding me back? Why can't I go forward?

He wanted what his mother, father, Thomas, Shane, Naomi, Pam, and Ashley had. He wanted it so much so that his soul ached.

"What's troubling you?" Mr. Jefferson entered the family room.

"Oh, nothing," Gregg sat straight. "I thought you were sleeping."

"I was."

"I just got home. It's been a long day."

"I can tell. Something happened at work?" Mr. Jefferson sat next to him.

His dad's concern for his welfare was refreshing. It would take some getting used to this new man sitting next to him.

"Thirty-three athletes are going to have weekend jobs." Gregg explained to his father about the poverty that most students faced and why getting jobs for them was so important.

"The message yesterday really struck a nerve for me. I pooled together resources to help the students…to make a difference in and outside of the school. The administration team strategized and came up with a plan. Now the students can work and play sports. They can do what they love."

"I'm proud of you, Son," Mr. Jefferson put his hand on

Gregg's lap. "Your mother would be proud of you. You were created for such a time as this."

"Do you remember her singing that to me?"

"I will never forget it. Sophia had such a beautiful voice. She said on the day you were born God gave her that song, just for you. That's why she framed it."

Gregg meditated on that for a moment.

"With such good news, why do you seem so down?"

"There are some gang members after Shane; he's on the basketball team. Shane is a good boy. He wants nothing to do with the gang, but they are after him because he broke up with the sister of the leader in the gang."

"Why was he dating his sister if he's such a good guy?"

"Stupid. He was making bad choices and really didn't know who she was related to. To his credit, when Shane found out who she was and the things she was involved in, he immediately broke it off."

"Oh, I see. Now he's in hot water," Mr. Jefferson surmised. "I'll pray for him."

"Everybody is praying for him."

"Are you?" Mr. Jefferson asked pointblank.

"God doesn't hear my prayers," Gregg mouthed. "He shouldn't. I'm a sinner."

"God hears a sinner's prayer," Mr. Jefferson stated. "He heard mine. I'm a changed man because of it."

"You truly have changed, Dad. Salvation looks good on you."

"It can on you, too." The father said with such longing. "Right now, you're troubled because you're running from the One who can change you, too. It's time to stop blaming God for taking your mother."

One teardrop escaped Gregg's eyelid and then another and another. "It wasn't just my mother He took," he sobbed, "He took you!"

"Oh, Son," Mr. Jefferson drew him into his arms and allowed him just to weep. "God didn't take me from you. I did that. But, I am here now and I will never leave you again. I love you, Gregg. You mean the world to me."

"I love you, too, Dad."

"It's time to mend those fences. Don't you think?"

Gregg nodded.

"I'm new at leading someone to Christ, but the preacher said all we have to do is confess the Lord Jesus with our mouth and believe in our heart that God raised Him from the dead and we would be saved."

Both Father and son dropped to their knees in submission as Gregg poured his lonely heart out to God.

"Dear God, I am a sinner in need of a Savior. Forgive me for my sins. Lord Jesus come into my heart. I confess with my mouth the Lord Jesus and I do believe in my heart that God raised You from the dead. I do not want to be alone, anymore. I want You to lead and guide my every footstep. I am Yours, Lord. Do whatever You want to do with me, in Jesus' name, amen."

"Amen," the father repeated with tears in his eyes. "Your mother is dancing with the angels in heaven."

"I'm sure she is." Gregg felt calm and at peace. "Senorita Rivas is going to be so pleased." He never took his second-mother for granted. He turned out as well as he did because she smothered him with her unending love.

"This is a great reason to call her tonight," the father turned to his son.

"You don't need a reason," Gregg smiled, "but please tell her I'm truly a part of the family, now."

"She'll be happy." The father wrapped his arms around him.

Gregg sang as his father joined him.

"When you entered this world
It was as if the sun, the moon, and the stars had kissed
Your birth brought joy into our home
For such a time as this
Your life has a purpose
And only God knows what it is
You were created to help others find their way
For such a time as this."

That night Gregg wanted to call Ashley. He wanted her to know that he, too, was now a part of the family of God.

She is involved with Harvey. I shouldn't be calling her at this time of night.

"Dear Lord, I thank you for accepting me," Gregg prayed as he lay in his bed. It felt so natural to pray again. "I sure would like to have a Christian woman like Ashley in my life. I know she is with Harvey and he is a good man. Help me to accept this and to move on with my life. It's just that...I can't get her out of my mind or out of my heart."

You both were created for such a time as this!

A peace stole over his heart. It was something new and strange. He finally had what everyone he cared about had—Peace that surpasses all understanding.

CHAPTER 32

Winning the Game and Winning Souls

Gregg stood on the wall with his arms crossed over his chest and watched the game as Shane and the opponent's basketball player leaped for the tossed ball. Shane hit it toward Thomas and off Thomas went to score the first three-pointer of the game.

Yeah! Gregg tried hard to maintain his composure.

"That's my brother!" Danny shouted, walking in with his family just in time to catch the shot.

Gregg turned and noticed them, his eyes lingering on Ashley. He wanted to walk over to them, but feared the rejection. He waved instead.

Ashley smiled and walked away with her siblings to sit in the middle bleachers. Watching Thomas shinning as a star on the court was riveting! He was awesome! He was definitely playing his best. No question about it, Thomas was born to play basketball!

Every time Thomas scored, Gregg's eyes found hers. He felt like a proud father, watching his son excel! It was an incredible feeling. The varsity boys' basketball team played their best, defensively and offensively. They worked together to set the ball up for each shot. Although their opponents were swift and quite the contender, it was hard to shatter the Tiger's appetite for their first win.

Ashley's eyes frequently roamed in Gregg's direction. She couldn't read his face, but he seemed less stress.

Dressed down, Gregg sure looks handsome with the school's shirt on and black slacks.

Their eyes spoke an understanding of how proud they were of Thomas. By the time the buzzer went off at the end of the second quarter, Thomas had scored eighteen points, leading the team in a 13-point advantage at halftime.

"I need to go to the bathroom." Lacey chimed after the cheerleaders did their first routine during halftime.

"Okay," Ashley stood up. "Are you guys going to stay here?" she looked to Danny and Donny.

"Coach Koon gave us some money to get something from the canteen tonight. Is it okay for us to spend it?"

"Sure. We can all go down together. I think I will get me a hotdog. You want one, Lacey?"

"Yeah!" she clapped her hands together. "But we better hurry to the bathroom."

Ashley picked her sister up and rushed down the bleachers."

"Everything okay?" Gregg noticed Ashley practically running out the gym's doors.

"Lacey has to go to the bathroom," she spurted out. "Which way?"

"Down the hall, to the left," he answered, following them.

Instead of letting the twins use their money to buy hotdogs, Gregg treated them, also purchasing hotdogs for Lacy and Ashley, with drinks and chips. This was a real feast for the

Finley clan. Just as Ashley was returning with Lacy, Gregg was interrupted.

"Principal Jefferson," Officer Anderson approached them. "I see trouble."

Gregg looked toward where Officer Anderson pointed.

"How did he get in?" Gregg recognized Drake and a few of his partners in crime.

"I don't know." Officer Anderson answered. "I showed Drake's photo to the security officers at the door and told them not to allow him inside."

"Excuse me," Gregg turned to Ashley. "I have a situation I must handle, but I really would like to talk to you later. Can I take you and the family home tonight?" Gregg reached over and gently touched her hand.

Ashley's pulse raced and heart pounded at his touch. "I don't know," her voice seemed so soft and faraway, even though she was near him.

"It's important," he pleaded.

"Well, okay."

"See you after the game," Gregg sprinted away.

"I want him and his gang out of here! Now!" Gregg barked at the other officer.

"Do you want to give them their money back?"

"I don't care! It's dirty anyway! And I want to know how he got in here in the first place!"

While Gregg and Officer Anderson were working on getting Drake and his crew out in a hurry, Thomas led his team back into the gym. Shane ran behind Thomas.

"You're mine!" Drake shouted to Thomas.

Thomas looked at him as if he was crazy and then turned to Shane. "What is he after me for?"

"I don't know," Shane shrugged. "He probably meant it for me."

"He was looking directly at me."

"We better pray," Shane replied. "I don't have a good feeling about this."

Something is wrong. Ashley watched her brother as he ran on the court. *Lord, help him. Whatever it is, You know all about it. Cover him, Lord Jesus.*

Following, Officer Anderson and several other officers escorted an angry Drake and his gang out of the gym. Drake was cursing like a sailor. Astutely, Drake stopped making a scene when he realized that he was about to be arrested. He had no plans of sitting in a jail cell tonight. Drake had other plans. "This ain't over," Drake shouted before leaving.

"They're gone." Officer Anderson whispered to Gregg inside the gym.

"Are you sure?"

"Yes. Drake doesn't want to go to jail. It'll be three strikes, which means he'll be behind bars for a long time."

Feeling relieved, Gregg focused his attention equally on the game and Ashley. He was looking forward to sharing his life-changing experience with her later.

All the way home, the Finleys were upbeat about the game. Thomas had scored thirty-seven points, assisting his team in a 66 to 61 victory. In the eyes of his siblings, Thomas was their hero. As they talked about the game, the children couldn't help but mentioned the mishap of their mascot.

"I couldn't believe how hard he hit the floor!" Danny laughed.

"Did you see how high he jumped, trying to do a flip?" Donny followed.

"He fell on his booboo!" Lacey laughed. Everybody laughed.

Ashley's laughter was infectious. Gregg wanted to bottle it for safekeeping. Gregg enjoyed being with the Finley bunch. They were such a loving family. Gregg considered it an honor to be among them all—especially Ashely. Despite his checkered pass with women, Gregg desired a woman like Ashley in his life—on a permanent basis.

Ashley couldn't quite put her finger on it, but there was definitely something different about Gregg tonight. Truth be known, she was so glad Gregg had offered to take them home. Her heart missed him—very much.

"Momma is going to be ecstatic about the game!" Ashley quickly turned to her brother. "You must break it down for her, so she'll feel like she was at the game."

"I can't wait." Thomas uttered. "She sure looks better. When we left this morning, she was in a chipper mood. She's like a new person."

"I know what you mean," Ashley felt the same way. "She's…." she stopped speaking as she noticed a familiar car pulling away from their driveway.

Is that Andrew? What in the world is he be doing at my house?

"Is something wrong?" Gregg asked after turning off his engine.

"No," she fibbed. "Thanks for bringing us home. Everybody thank Dr. Jefferson."

"He ain't *no* doctor!" Lacey blurted. "He's the *brincibal!*" Lacy had a hard time pronouncing her "*ps*".

Everybody laughed.

"Would you like to come in for some ice-tea?" Ashley asked.

"That would be nice."

"Hey doc," Thomas respectfully nicknamed him, "did you notice Drake at the game?"

Gregg nodded, as the two stayed outside, while everyone went inside.

"He was looking me straight in the eye when he said, 'You're mine!'" Thomas couldn't shake off the threat.

"He must have meant it for Shane," Gregg naturally assumed.

"I don't think so," Thomas shook his head. "He was looking me right dead in the eye. Perhaps he knows I was the snitch."

"I don't think so unless you told someone."

"Not even Shane knows I told you."

"Don't worry about it, Thomas. You know what to do."

Thomas looked at him in confusion. "Huh?"

"Prayer changes things," Gregg smiled.

"I knew something was different about you!" Thomas embraced him. "You're a Believer, too!"

"Yes, I am!" Gregg said proudly.

"Doc, that's wonderful! More important than winning a game! Another soul won into the Kingdom of God. Does Ashley know?"

"Not yet." Gregg was eager to share his life-changing, life-saving news with Ashley.

Right on key, Ashley opened the door. "Mom wants to know everything about the game."

"I'm coming!" Thomas hugged Gregg once again and whispered in his ear, "Now you're worthy to be my brother-in-law." Thomas winked and ran inside.

"What was that all about?" Ashley sensed she had interrupted a special moment between the two.

"Oh, nothing," Gregg smiled, staring at how lovely she looked under the porch light. Dressed in a pair of jeans and a pale blue short-sleeve shirt, she was so appealing. Ashley had such a youthful, fresh look.

"If you say so," she giggled nervously. "Come on inside. Have a seat while I go get the ice-tea."

Satisfying his curiosity, Gregg looked around the humbled room, awed by the homey atmosphere, which was so unlike the mausoleum he grew up in. The family was poverty-stricken, and yet there was an aura of wealth. This was a home filled with love.

Shortly, Ashley returned with the glasses of ice-tea.

"Do you mind if we sit out on the porch? The night air is refreshing." Gregg suggested. Not to mention, the house was rather warm.

"Sure."

They sat side by side on the front porch, hardly any space between them. "It is so peaceful out here." There was no other place Gregg would rather be.

"It's so peaceful out here."

"Not usually," Ashley chuckled. "Usually, we hear all kinds of sirens—from the police, fire trucks, and ambulances. We have our own live symphony, especially on the weekends."

"I'm glad it's not so tonight." Gregg eyed her intensely, his heart drawn to hers like a magnet. He felt out of control, and it felt good. "I'm surprised Harvey wasn't at the game tonight," Gregg indirectly probed.

"He had other plans. But, he is coming to the game Friday."

"That's good. I know Thomas will like that."

"How is your friend Tiffany?" Ashley had to ask.

"I don't know. You will have to ask her husband, Trevor. He came and took her home."

"That's good," Ashley beamed. "I think."

"Those two are made for each other." Gregg chuckled.

"How long have you and Harvey been dating?" He just had to know.

"We're not dating. Harvey and I have been friends, forever. As a matter of fact, as we speak, he is out on a date with Pam, my friend, at *The Palace*."

"The wild one!"

"Yeah, that's Pam," Ashley grinned, "but she's a lot calmer now."

"It's hard picturing Harvey with her," Gregg admitted. "But opposites do attract."

"That's what they say."

"Do you think we're opposites?"

His body was too close and his cologne triggered a sensation that caused Ashley's heart to soar. A winsome smile curved her lips.

Stop this! You cannot feel this way about this man!

"What was it that you wanted to talk to me about?" Ashley shifted the direction of the conversation. She practically gulped down the tea, trying to cool her insides.

"You said there could never be an *us* if I didn't have a relationship with God." Gregg's statement caused her to face him. "What if things have changed?"

I knew there was something different about him, she hoped with all hope. Ashley took a deep, deep breath before finding her voice. "Do you have a relationship with God?"

"I do!" Gregg answered without hesitation. "I'm just a baby—born again just yesterday."

"Oh, Gregg!" Ashley swung her arms around his neck. "I'm so happy for you!"

"Me too," he held onto her. "My dad, too."

"Your dad?" Ashley pulled away, tears trickling down her face.

"Sunday, he went to church and accepted Jesus as his Lord and Savior. Dad boldly did it." The son was so proud of his dad.

"This is great!" Ashley was overcome with emotions. "But, you can't be saved for me. It has to be for yourself."

"Oh, it is," Gregg assured. "I was so empty inside, Ashley. For years, I have been trying to fill this void in my heart with so many things and with women, but nothing worked." Gregg reached for her hand. Ashley willingly gave it to him. "I'm not alone, anymore," his eyes became glossy. "My dad said it's liberating. I have to agree with him."

"It's good to be free," Ashley understood.

"So, you didn't answer my question. You said there could never be an *us* without me having a relationship with God. Now that I do, is there a possibility?"

His eyes never left hers. Something in his look changed as he focused on her even more. It was intoxicating. For the longest, they stared at one another. Then, fear seized Ashley's heart and squeezed it pulseless.

"I need you, Ashley," Gregg spoke before she answered. Gregg was falling head over heels for Ashley, falling hard and fast.

Ashley felt goose bumps all over.

"Oh, Gregg," she reached up and caressed the side of his

face with the palm of her hands. "We're so different."

There was a quickening in Gregg's chest as she touched him. It was electrifying. "Our differences will balance us."

"You really think so?"

"I know so." Unable to control himself any longer, Gregg leaned over, his lips grazed her cheekbone and then their lips touched. The kiss was soft like a feather.

It was a mesmerizing connection for Ashley. It felt so right being in his arms. It was comforting, like a second skin, so close and so connected—and so right.

Love had found a place in his and her hearts.

Ashley scribbled in her journal that night...

Gregg is saved! Thank you, Lord! My heart is filled to capacity with thanksgiving. There may be an 'us' after all!

CHAPTER 33

Overcoming the Past

Pictorial visions of Gregg danced through Ashley's dreams, stimulating such a restful sleep. Thus, Ashley overslept the next morning.

Everyone had already dressed for school when she felt a tap on her shoulder.

"Huh?" groggily she awakened to a grinning Thomas standing over her.

"You're dressed!" she jumped up. "I'm late! Are the kids up?"

"Calm down. The children are dressed and eating breakfast."

Ashley stopped, turned and looked at her brother. "You cooked?"

"No," he smiled. "Mom did."

Her eyes bulged. "You're kidding."

"She says to hurry and get dressed so you can eat something before going to work."

Ashley was stupefied. *Mom, cooking!*

"Close your mouth before a fly gets in." Thomas chuckled. "Mom's back!"

Before going to the bathroom, Ashley peeped into the small

kitchen. The entire family was enjoying a simple breakfast with Sandra sitting at the head of the table. Ashley's eyes stung with joyous tears beholding the family scene. It seemed like an eternity since the family enjoyed breakfast together. Sandra sat in a chair and not a wheelchair. If she was in pain, Ashley could not tell. Her mother's face seemed so content, so alive!

I guess Thomas is right. Momma is back!

After showering and dressing for work, Ashley returned to the kitchen to see the kids hurrying to get their book bags.

"Momma looks pretty," Lacey said happily. "She fixed us breakfast *cuz* you were sleeping."

"I know." Ashley kissed her on the cheek.

"Good morning sleepy head." Sandra greeted. "I guess you didn't hear the bells this morning."

Too choked up, Ashley shook her head.

"I heard them," Danny spoke.

"Me too," Donny followed.

"You boys better hurry," Thomas intervened, noticing his sister's emotional state. "We're going to be late."

"Here," Thomas handed Ashley a glass of orange juice. "You better hurry or you'll be late too," he winked and touched her shoulder.

Ashley and her mother were left in the kitchen alone.

"Oh, mother!" Ashley put the glass down and went to her. In a loving embrace, she just held onto her mother, allowing the tears to flow.

"You need to eat something." Sandra gently pulled away.

"I'll just take the toast. I'm really not hungry."

"You're a beautiful, young lady," Sandra complimented. "I'm so proud of you. You have kept this family together for so long. Now it is my time to take over the parenting role again.

330

It's time for you to go back to college." Sandra held her hand up to keep Ashley from talking. "I don't know how we'll come up with the money, but God will make a way. You must finish college. You must start living your life again. I want that more than anything."

"Are you sure you feel better? You just went through a major ordeal with your body. You cannot overdue it."

"I'm feeling better than ever. It was like you said before...I gave up after Tom died. I stop fighting the disease. Well, I am fighting the disease with all my strength and with God's strength. It will not get me down again."

"That's good," Ashley felt her mother's determination in the depth of her soul. "What about the knee replacement surgery?"

"I'm going to do it."

Now that was a shock. For years, her mother insisted she would endure no more surgeries.

Ashley hugged her mother again.

"I better get out of here before I miss my bus." Ashley gulped down the orange juice and snatched the toast.

"Have a great day, mother, and don't overdue it."

"I won't. Have a good day at work."

Turning on heels, Ashley remembered something. "Mom, was Andrew visiting you last night? I thought I saw his car when Gregg brought us home."

Sandra's countenance became ashen.

"Are you all right?" Ashley rushed to her.

"Oh...of course," Sandra tried to play it off, turning to the sink for a moment. Taking a few breaths, she turned back to face her daughter.

"Yes, Andrew was visiting. He has been visiting me at the

hospital, too. We're old friends."

"I know," Ashley sensed more. "He told me that. I still can't believe you two know each other."

"It's a small world."

"You must have been really close friends," Ashley probed further.

"We'll talk about this later," the conversation was unnerving for the mother. "You're going to be late for work."

"Okay," Ashley shrugged. "Love you!"

"Love you, too," Sandra smiled.

Hearing the door shut, Sandra flopped to the chair, laid her head on the table, and cried.

How am I going to tell her the truth?

The Truth will set your free!

To no avail could Ashley channel her confused emotions elsewhere. Physically, her body was at *The Palace*, but Ashley's mind travelled all over the place. Her world had come full circle—from her mother, Thomas, to Gregg, to Pam, to Andrew and back to Gregg.

"You okay?" Pam asked again. "Is your mother okay? Did Thomas get into trouble again?"

"Everything is fine," Ashley forced a smile. "That's just it. Everything has been so crazy and now everything is normal. Mom cooked breakfast this morning. She's doing great. *And* Thomas, he is back on the right track. You should have seen him last night at the game. He scored thirty-seven points, leading the team to a 66 to 61 victory," Ashley's eyes sparkled with pride.

"That's good! Harvey wanted to go, but he wasn't sure if

that was such a good idea."

"Huh?" Ashley frowned. "Harvey is a part of our family. Nothing is ever going to change that. Thomas expected him to come and was disappointed that he didn't show up."

"This is crazy, Ash. Harvey asked Thomas for your hand in marriage. Now, he is going out with me. I think we're all loco!"

Ashley chuckled. "Harvey only asked me because he was settling. He figured we were like family so we ought to be family, in a legal sense. No one should settle," Ashley went on, "especially not Harvey. He's a great man with a lot of love to give to someone."

Pam stared at her friend. There was no one closer to her heart than Ashley. "We're taking it slow."

"Yeah right! If I know Harvey, he'll be proposing to you in a month."

"He better not," Pam scoffed. "Maybe in two months I'll consider it." The two friends laughed.

"Seriously," Pam gathered her composure, "what's troubling you?"

"I don't know," Ashley felt perplexed. "I had a good time last night, talking with Gregg on the porch."

"That's good," Pam didn't understand her confusion. "He's good-looking and rich." Some things just did not overnight. Pam was a work in progress, still on the Potter's wheel.

"Yes, but it's more than that. He's a Christian now."

"That's the most important thing."

"But we're different. What can he possibly see in me? I am nothing like the women he has dated. They have money, good careers…they're educated and…and beautiful."

"Are you kidding me?" Pam nearly shouted. "Money can't

buy what you have. I do not know of anyone who is one-hundred percent loving, kindhearted, honest, and genuinely caring. You're educated, knowledgeable through experience and books. And as far as beauty goes, girl, you are gorgeous! No, you are probably not like the *chick*s he dated before. You're the full package. Ashley, you're the real deal!"

Ashley adored her friend. "Thanks."

"It's the truth. Gregg should consider it an honor to have you by his side."

"So should Harvey," Ashley uttered, and then changed the subject. "Andrew has been visiting my mother."

"What?"

"At the hospital and I saw him leaving our house last night."

"Do you think he has the *hots* for your mother?"

"Wouldn't that be crazy?" Ashley shrugged. "He said they knew each other pretty well. It's hard to picture my mother with anyone other than Tom."

"Tom was a jerk. It's not hard for me to picture those two together. Andrew is a Christian, and he's handsome. Not to mention, you two have the most amazing eyes in the world."

Ashley frowned.

"I'm sorry," Pam sensed her friend's annoyance. "I'm just stating the truth. I don't understand why you're so touchy about him."

"Me either," Ashley admitted.

"Hey ladies," Andrew entered the cooking area. "You both doing all right tonight?"

They both nodded, their hands caught in the cookie jar.

"I must have walked in on a juicy conversation. Your faces are both red." he cackled and walked away.

Ashley and Pam burst with laughter.

"Better go serve our customers before Ms. Melrose *comes a calling!"* Pam jeered as the two grabbed their pads and went to wait on their early customers. The place was already crowded.

"It's going to be a lo…" Pam froze in place.

"What's wrong?" Ashley nearly collided with her friend.

"It's him…"

Ashley looked in the direction of her friend's gaze. *It can't be!* Ashley thought she recognized the man sitting with a few friends, gawking back at them. *It is! The nerve of him!*

Ashley seized her friend's arm, pulling Pam back into the kitchen.

"What happened?" Andrew hurried to assist Ashley as she held onto a limp Pam.

Pam was totally out of it. She was in a semiconscious state, for sure.

"What happened?" Andrew asked again, literally picking Pam up and carrying her to the backroom, placing her on a sofa.

"She saw someone," Ashley stated flatly.

"And…"

"And that's it." Ashley wouldn't break her promise to her friend.

"That's not it!" Andrew spoke harshly. "She's going into shock! Out with it!"

"She saw the guy that…tried to rape her and beat her up pretty badly," Ashley blurted, feeling coerced.

Pam moaned.

Ashley groaned.

Andrew roared. "Who? Show me the guy!"

"I can't," Ashley shook her head. "Pam wouldn't want me to."

"Pam!" Andrew bent over and eyed her. "I want Ashley to show me the guy. You have nothing to fear. I will not let that guy harm you ever again. Do you understand me?"

Breaking down, Pam nodded, tears rushing down the sides of her face.

"I don't know about this," Ashley headed toward the dining area. "What are you going to do?"

"I'm going to talk to the guy."

Ashley stopped. "Talk?"

"Talk!" he repeated. "Show me the guy."

Ashley pointed to the table. "He's the one with the purple tie."

Squaring his shoulders, Andrew headed toward the *creep!*

"Chef Watts," Ms. Melrose spotted Andrew. "We have a full house. What are you doing out here?"

"Everything is fine Ms. Melrose. I just need to speak with someone."

"But…"

"Please excuse me," he walked passed her.

"Excuse me," Andrew interrupted the group of five men. "I would like to have a word with you," he fixed his eyes on Randall.

"Do I know you?" Randall seemed amused.

"No, but you do know my friend Pam." Andrew didn't blink an eye, as Randall seemed to squirm in his chair.

"Pam," he faked amnesia. "I'm afraid I don't know anyone by the name of Pam."

"Should I go get her?"

"What's going on?" one of the men asked.

"Oh, nothing!" Randall chuckled, sliding his chair back. He knew the guy wasn't just going to go away. Fearing he would say something incriminating to his colleagues, Randall got up. "Excuse me, guys, I'll be right back."

"Hey, I don't know you, but there must be a misunderstanding here," Randall began as soon as they were outside.

"There is no misunderstanding. You're the scumbag who hurt my friend, Pam!"

"You're crazy!" Randall wanted to dismiss the man.

Andrew stepped closer to the man, so close their noses were almost touching. "You prey on innocent women, taking from them what doesn't belong to you. And, you have the nerve to hit a lady!"

"I didn't take anything!" he shouted back. "And she is not a lady!"

"You violated her!"

"I didn't." Randall cowardly stepped back. "It's her word against mine. And trust me, the law will take my word over hers any day!"

"Maybe," Andrew growled, literally. "But I don't!"

"What are you going to do?"

Forgive me, Lord! Wallop! Andrew punched him in the stomach, knocking the wind out of him. Randall fell to the ground, clinching his stomach.

"I'll have you arrested!"

"Do that!" Andrew took the bluff. "They may not believe me, but they sure will hear what I have to say about what you did to Pam."

Slowly, getting to his feet. "Pam was easy. She went to my home on the first date. She knew why we were there. She teased me, turned me on and then…"

"Said no," Andrew finished. "It was her right!"

"She's nothing!"

"She's something special." Andrew corrected. "You're nothing! You and your friends are not welcome here. You better leave and never return. Stay away from Pam!" Andrew walked away before doing something he would forever regret.

"You don't own *The Palace*."

"No I don't," Andrew swirled around and faced him. "I think I will have a little heart-to-heart with your friends." Andrew threatened, pivoted and headed back inside.

"Wait!" Randall caught up to him. "We'll leave."

"And never come back?"

Randall nodded and went inside. Within a matter of seconds, he and his friends were exiting *The Palace* doors with Andrew watching.

"What did you do?" Ashley leaped off the couch the moment Andrew returned.

"I got rid of the trash!" he answered.

Pam giggled. "It's about time!"

CHAPTER 34

Losing Naomi

As routine, the Finleys left the house together to walk to school, except for Ashley catching the bus to the library. Thomas tarried with Ashley until her bus came.

"Tonight is a big game," Ashley commented. "Are you ready?"

"I was born ready," confidence flowed through his lips.

"Okay, don't get too cocky!"

"I'm not cocky, just confident in the gift that God has given me. As long as I remember Who it came from, I won't get the big-head. All glory goes to Him!"

Respectfully, Ashley looked at her brother, appreciating the transformation in him. It was quite amazing.

"You're your mother's child."

With his chin up and back arched to make a point, he replied, "I certainly am!"

"Sure wish I could be at the game tonight."

"Me too. It's our rival game. Their guard can dish out some three-pointers!"

"So can you," Ashley quickly countered. "You're the best guard in the region, capable of playing all positions phenomenally."

"Hey, I'm not threatened. I like a challenge."

"Well, there's my bus. *You better* run along before you're late for school. Wouldn't want Dr. Jefferson putting you in detention."

"Doc wouldn't do that," he gibed. "We *got* it like that."

"Okay*, got* it like that…don't push your luck!"

"I won't!" Thomas trotted along, blowing a kiss to his sister.

Pretending she caught it, Ashley rested the palm of her hand on her cheekbone, cherishing the make-believe kiss.

Running ahead, not too far in distance from the school, in the corner of his eye Thomas glimpsed Drake and a few of his guys.

What the heck!

Drake stared him down, making it known that he had a beef with him.

But why?

Making good time, Thomas marched through the schools' doors before the bell was to ring.

Gregg deliberately looked at his watch. "Five minutes more you would have been late."

"But I'm not, Doc." Thomas grinned.

"Ready for the game tonight?"

"Born ready," he replied again.

"Good. Stop by my office at the end of the day. I have something I need for you to give your sister."

"Alright. By the way, Ash's birthday is tomorrow."

Gregg had no idea. *I spoke with her last night, and she didn't even mention it. She wouldn't.*

"Thanks for the information." Gregg's mind was already racing, mulling over what to do to make Ashley's birthday special.

"Oh, I almost forgot," Thomas drew near the principal and whispered for his ears only. "I saw Drake and his boys on the way to school. They were eyeing me down."

"Did they say anything?"

"Nope!"

"I'll have Officer Anderson to ride around the school to ensure they don't come on campus. Thanks for the tip."

"No problem."

"You have a phone call," his secretary informed as he entered the main office.

"Who is it?"

"Naomi Rivas," she answered.

Gregg was surprised. "Please put her through." He hastened his footsteps to his office.

Sitting down, he picked up the phone. "Senorita Rivas, what a pleasant surprise."

"Hi, Gregg!"

"How is your sister?"

"She's still recovering. That is why I am calling. My sister needs my help. I'm going to have to stay on."

"I understand. So, you're staying another week or two," he assumed.

"No, it's going to be longer than that."

Gregg sat straight. "Oh, I see. How much longer, do you think?"

"I'm not coming back," she replied.

"Senorita Rivas," he was breathless. "You have to come back! We need you. My dad needs you and I need you."

Naomi was near tears. She had cried all night and then all this morning after speaking with Mr. Jefferson.

"I have to stay here."

"Is it something else going on?" Gregg wasn't fooled. "Please, don't leave us," the boy in him sprang up. "You're the only mother I have now."

His words touched her deeply. "You will see me again. We can stay in touch," she sniffed.

"Is it because of my dad?"

"Gregg, you take care of your dad. He needs you more than ever." She avoided answering his question. "Please promise me that you will stay close to his side and look after him. He's still a weak man and his heart is not fully strong."

"I promise," Gregg felt deflated. "Senorita Rivas please pray about this."

"I have prayed, Gregg. It is for the best. I must go. It is about time for my sister to take her medicine. You take care of yourself and know that I love you. I always will, my *nino*."

"I love you, too," Gregg answered. Holding onto the phone even after she hung up, Gregg felt sick.

I wonder how my dad is taking this. He was developing feelings for her. Lord, help him through this. Help us all through this tremendous loss. It is almost like losing my mother all over again.

Later, at the ringing of the last school bell, Thomas ran to Gregg's office.

"Hey, Doc! I'm going home before the game. Coach Koon is going to pick me up in about an hour."

"That's good," Gregg looked up from his paperwork. Usually, he would be in the hallways when the bell rang to see the students off campus.

Thomas could tell that something was troubling him. "You wanted me to stop by to get something for Ash," he reminded Gregg.

"Oh, yes," Gregg pulled a wrapped box from his bottom drawer with an envelope attached. "Make sure she gets this tonight."

"She'll probably be home before I leave. I'll give it to her," he hesitated. "Are you okay, Doc?"

"I'm fine."

"If you say so," Thomas shrugged, not convinced. "I'll pray for you anyhow. Are you coming to the game, tonight?"

"Wouldn't miss it." Gregg tried to sound cheery. "It's going to be a tough win."

"Yes, but those are the fun ones! See you later."

"Bye!" Gregg turned off his computer, preparing to leave. Typically, he stayed at school on game days, but he needed to go check on his dad.

"Are you leaving?" his secretary asked.

"I'll be back before the game. Have a good day!"

"You, too."

"Are you alright, Dad?" Gregg found his dad sitting in his favorite chair on the back patio.

As his father turned to him, his pinkish-red eyes were evident of Mr. Jefferson's fresh pang of the heart.

"God won't put on us more than we can bear," the father quoted somberly.

"No, He won't." Gregg sat beside him and covered his frail hand with his own. "Senorita Rivas called me."

"I figured she would," he shoulders slumped. "It's hard to believe that she will never walk through this house again. We won't hear the sweet sound of her singing in the kitchen. She took special care in making sure we were cared for. Now it is all gone. We take so much for granted, Son—so much."

343

Gregg's heart ached for his dad. They both were aching for Naomi.

"I think I scared her away," Mr. Jefferson continued. "She sensed my feelings for her had changed. I think I have felt something for her a long time, but my own superiority blinded me. I could not see what was right there in front of me all the time. Naomi cared about me, Son," Gregory sighed. "There were times when I saw it in her eyes, but I rejected her with inferior words of my own. I treated her like the help and oftentimes reminded her of her place in the home. No wonder she ran scared. Who wouldn't?"

"Don't be so hard on yourself. You're a changed man."

"I guess the change came a little too late as far as Naomi is concerned. But don't worry, I will bounce back. Just give me some time."

"You take all the time you need, Dad," Gregg stated sincerely. "We have each other."

"Yes, we do. That is what matters most."

"A present for me," Ashley was elated. Thomas gave it to her shortly after he came home with his siblings. Ashley was sitting on the couch, resting before going to her second job. "My birthday isn't until tomorrow. But…Gregg doesn't know…." Ashley looked at her brother, "or does he?"

"He knows now," Thomas winked. "Doc bought it to for you before he even knew it was your birthday. I just told him today."

"You shouldn't have," Ashley frowned. "I didn't want him to feel obligated to buy me something. He hardly knows me."

"You deserve a thousand gifts," Thomas kissed her on the cheek.

"Thanks, Thomas," Ashley accepted his acclaim. "Harvey is coming to the game tonight."

"Great! I was hoping he was still going to be around."

"Always. Now, he may have Pam with him, but that's even better."

"Sure seems crazy, but whatever you say. I knew you didn't like Harvey like that anyway."

"I love him like a brother."

"Me too," Thomas sounded so mature for his age. "I'm going to see if I can help mom in the kitchen."

"You do that," Ashley touched his hand. "It's good having her back, isn't it?"

"The best!"

Impatiently, Ashley ripped opened the beautifully wrapped box. "Oh, a leather journal!" She had always wanted a leather one but could not afford it. "How lovely," she read aloud its inscription. "*May you always write words from the heart and may my name be found on many of the pages. Always, Gregg.* "Oh, how sweet."

Swiftly, Ashley opened the envelope and read the handwritten note.

Dear Ashley,

I would like to celebrate your birthday with you. May I have the honor of taking you out for lunch, tomorrow? If you have plans with your family, I understand, but if you can spend an hour or two with me, I really would like to enjoy sharing part of your birthday with you. Call me tonight when you get off to let me know. Enjoy your evening. I wish you could come to the game, but I know you have to work. I will be thinking of you. Until tomorrow...

Gregg

And I'll be thinking of you!

CHAPTER 35

Ashley's Birthday

"**H**appy Birthday!" The Finley clan shouted as Ashley entered the kitchen for breakfast.

"Thank you."

"How old are you?" Lacey naively asked.

"Twenty-four," Ashley covered her face. "I'm getting old!"

"Please!" her mother laughed. "You are young and beautiful. Sit down. I'll fix the birthday girl's breakfast."

"Thanks, Mom."

"Mom is making you a cake!" Lacey couldn't keep a secret.

"Lacey!" They all shouted.

"Ooops! It's a secret!"

Ashley smiled at her sister. "I don't know what kind, so it's still a secret."

"Pineapple," Lacey blabbed.

"Lacey!" In unison, they all shouted again.

Ashley laughed.

"I'm sorry," a fat droplet collided down Lacey's cheek.

"No problem," Ashley wiped her teardrop. "I don't like secrets anyway."

"Me either," Lacey mumbled.

"So how was the game?" Ashley turned to her brother.

Suddenly the conversation centered on Thomas and the amazing win they had last night. Once again, Thomas shot the winning three-pointer right at the buzzard, which tied the game; but it was the free-throw shot, he made after being filed that won the game.

Finally, the Finleys had a happy home, as they talked around the table. Sandra's reclaiming her life again filled the home with love and happiness. Albeit, she was in severe pain sometimes, Sandra's will to live and be a mother made her persevere through the aches and pains. Sandra wanted to live… for her children, for herself and for a certain secret someone.

"So what are your plans?" Sandra asked her daughter.

"I'm having lunch with Gregg." Ashley endeavored to sound nonchalant about her luncheon. She didn't want them reading more into it than it really was. Though deep down Ashley was exhilarated and anticipation.

Thomas grinned. His sister didn't fool him.

"The guy in the hospital, Thomas' principal?" Sandra inquired.

"Yes, Ma'am."

"That's good!"

"He's loaded, Mom," Thomas felt the need to say. "And he's a Christian, now."

"That's even better."

Ashley looked to her brother. *Always the protector!*

"Perhaps, you can be home by four, so that we can enjoy your cake together. It's been a long time."

"I'd like that."

"And invite Gregg to join us," her mother added.

Ashley nodded. *Life is good again!*

"What time is your date?" Thomas asked.

"My luncheon is at noon. Oh, did Harvey come to the

game?" She wanted to change the subject. This was a new thing for her. Endeavoring to remain levelheaded about dating Gregg, Ashley couldn't stifle the yearning in her heart. She liked Gregg a whole lot.

"Yes, Harvey brought us home," Thomas answered.

"That's good," Ashley commented.

"We're cool," Thomas went on. "He's bringing Pam to Tuesday's game."

"That's good."

"Pam's crazy!" Danny chimed in.

"Really crazy!" Donny added. "She makes me laugh, though."

"I like Miss Pam," Lacey wasn't going to be left out.

"Me too," Ashley winked at her little sister.

Later, while dressing for her special luncheon with Gregg her mother entered the bathroom.

"Oh my," her mother's hand covered her mouth. "You are so beautiful. Is that a new dress?"

Ashley turned to face her teary-eyed mother. She looked a vision of pure perfection wearing a soft yellow spaghetti strap dress with matching pumps.

"No, Pam gave it to me. She can't wear it anymore."

"It's lovely!" Sandra meticulously looked over her daughter from head to toe. With her lovely curly locks, flat ironed, hanging straight and long, down her back, a smidgen of makeup and lip-gloss, eyes framed with dark brown eyeliner and eyelashes popping with mascara, the mother's heart was full to the brim with joy for her selfless daughter. "You're gorgeous!"

"Thank you, Momma," Ashley kissed her on the cheek.

"You really like this guy, don't you?"

Ashley nodded. "But we're so different."

"That's usually how it is. God knows we need balance. So, he sends us a helpmate totally opposite from us."

"He's been so wonderful to Thomas and the children."

"I know. Thomas can't stop talking about him."

"Thomas used to call him the Terminator."

"Now he calls him Doc," Sandra laughed. "Things are really changing." *How will I ever tell her about Andrew? The truth is going to change a lot for her—and us!*

"Change is good," Ashley beamed.

"Your date is on time," Sandra stated at the sound of knocking at the front door.

"Oh goodness!" Ashley pivoted and looked in the mirror, brushing her hair one last time.

"You're perfect. I will let him in. "Have a wonderful lunch, Ashley. Be free and allow yourself the pleasure of being pampered for a change. You deserve it more than anyone I know."

"I love you, Momma."

"I love you more!" Sandra blew a kiss and left.

Gregg was feeling right at home with the Finley clan. Immediately, he noticed the resemblance of Ashley to her mother. *An older version of Ashley*, Gregg took a liking to her instantly. She was so sweet, also having the characteristics of his mother—kind, gentle, thoughtful, and doting over him.

When Ashley, at last, entered the room, his breath caught in his throat. She was the epitome of loveliness. Rising slowly to his feet, Gregg was overwhelmed. She was doing something strange to him without even trying.

"You're gorgeous," he whispered, an innocent smile lingered on his lips.

"Thanks," Ashley blushed with her heart going pitter-patter. Likewise, Ashley admired the man standing before her with his tailored fitted black slacks and baby-blue shirt. *He is so handsome! Be still my beating heart!*

"Look at these beautiful roses Gregg gave me," Sandra held out half-dozen red roses in her hand. "He said there for the mother who gave life to the loveliest woman 24 years ago, which he is so grateful for."

Ashley secretly pinched herself to validate that she wasn't dreaming. Never had a man made her heart soar to heights unknown. Never had anyone complimented her in such a way, that she could literally feel its truth. And never had anyone ever given her mother roses. To witness her mother's afterglow was all the birthday present Ashley needed. It was priceless.

"And these are for you," Gregg drew closer, handing Ashley a dozen of roses, mixed in an array of colors. The roses were a rainbow of perfection.

"Gregg, these are so lovely!"

"Not half as lovely as you are. Happy birthday, Ashley." He pecked her on the cheek.

This will be the best day ever! Thank God, I didn't settle for Harvey! Thank God, I didn't remain at college, dating... what's his name? God, You always know what's best for me! Praise You!

"We better be going," he squeezed Ashley's hand. It was so soft...just like her.

"See you all later." Ashley was glowing as she handed her mother her roses.

"Don't forget the cake," Sandra beckoned.

"We'll be here, mother." Ashley grinned and walked away with the man of her dreams holding her hand.

A knot twisted in Ashley's stomach as she sat across the

table from Gregg in an upscale restaurant. She was anxiously nervous, feeling woozy and scared all at once. Then Gregg gazed at her, as only he could, causing the tempo of her heart rate to accelerate. *I'm in love!*

After ordering, Gregg reached across the table for her hand. Freely she gave it to him.

"You're so beautiful, Ashley."

She smiled, her face turning two shades of red.

"You're blushing?" he adored her innocence. Gregg was content at staring at her–forever!

Lowering her eyes, Ashley sipped her glass of raspberry ice tea.

"Your mother looks well," Gregg commented still gazing into her hypnotic eyes

"Oh, she is. It's amazing how God has healed her. She is a different person. Something has happened to her. I know she still endures pain, but the pain is no longer controlling her. She is so lively. So…so…" she paused, trying to come up with the right word to describe her mother's transformation, "happy."

"Maybe she's just happy to be alive."

"It's more than that, Gregg. She was totally lifeless, before."

"Whatever it is, thank God for it."

Ashley nodded. "What about your father?"

"As far as health goes, he's improving. He's still weak. It's his emotional state that has me concerned." Gregg told her about Naomi, leaving no details out.

"That's incredible!" The story was enlightening and rather romantic. "After all these years, now he realizes he cares for her."

"Yes, but now she's gone and not coming back." Gregg's tone was subdued. "She means so much to us. I mean, she practically raised me. Even being away at school, she stayed in touch with me. Faithfully, she sent me fresh chocolate chip cookies, weekly letters and cards. I looked forward to her phone calls, which always cheered me up. I don't know how my dad is going to function in the home without her. She ran it."

"Maybe she's scared," Ashley surmised. "I mean, it is different being a housekeeper and then all of a sudden your employer has feelings for you."

"I don't think it's all of a sudden," Gregg replied. "I think they both had feelings for each other. Of course, Naomi would never admit to it and stayed in her role. Over the years, I witnessed strange looks passing between them. I often wondered if I was just wishing they would like each other."

Gregg released her hand when the waitress brought their food to them. Suddenly, Ashley felt empty without his touch and so did he. Not really hungry, the twosome ate little and stared much.

"Would you mind if we leave now? I want to take you to a special place."

Ashley nodded. Her heart was overflowing with a powerful feeling.

Ashley looked around the unfamiliar area. It appeared to be a park or some kind of forest area.

Gregg hurried out of the car, opened his back door and retrieved a gift bag. He felt extremely happy...like a kid! Two amazing things were happening to him. His new, exciting relationship with the Lord and now, hopefully, a new relationship with Ashley. He felt satisfied!

Holding hands the two walked the well-walked path with Gregg leading. Ashley was deliriously happy. This was a great birthday, for sure. The best yet!

"Ah," she gasped, observing a spectacular scenery. Among the forest, abided a crystal-clear aqua pond. Surrounded by magnolia trees, which were in full bloom, the secluded area produced a magnificent representation of tranquility. The air smelled of a mixture of magnolia aroma and honeysuckle. The wind was calling Ashley's name in the soft breeze. She felt to the bone invigorated. This was such a sweet, peaceful atmosphere, Ashley felt as if she was walking on the clouds of heaven.

"How did you ever find such a place?" she turned to him, bright-eyed.

"My mother brought me here a month before she passed. She loved this place. It was her piece of heaven, she said." Gregg replied, dazzled by how adorable she looked. "I know we're not dressed for it, but I just wanted this day to be special and because this place means so much to me, I wanted to share it with you."

"I'm honored," her heart was mush in his hands.

Moving closer to the pond, Greg wrapped his arm around her waistline. They fitted so well together.

"It's breathtaking! I've never seen such beauty," Ashley was awestruck.

Gregg tilted her chin toward him and said, "I'm looking at it."

Once again, her cheeks became rosy, enhancing her natural cuteness. *She's a knockout! I'm in love with you, Ashley Finley!*

His gaze intensified.

Her heart ignited with such passion, she felt she would

likely explode from pure joy.

Gregg wanted nothing more than to kiss Ashley like she had never been kissed before. Like fire kindling on a very cold night, warming his once frigid heart, Ashley was good for him and he knew it.

"This is for you." Gregg handed her the gift bag.

"You shouldn't have. You already gave me beautiful roses and a lovely journal."

"It's my pleasure to give you this and so much more. Please open it."

Opening the bag, Ashley retrieved the small, velvet box and nervously opened it. "Oh, my," she gasped. "It's beautiful." Ashley held a two-carat 12k yellow gold diamond tennis bracelet in her hand.

"It's too much, Gregg." She had no idea how much the expensive bracelet really cost Gregg.

"Nothing is too much for you," he replied softly, framing the bracelet around her petite wrist. He specially had the jeweler to size it down that morning, paying a hefty price for it.

"Thank you, Gregg," Ashley embraced him. He electrified her heart and soul.

Gregg enfolded her in his arms. He could hear and feel her heartbeat. The rhythm matched his own. As she looked up at him, a smile played on her perfectly, natural lined lips. Slowly, Gregg leaned over and his lips touched the corner of her mouth, softly, lingering. Then, he claimed her full waiting lips.

Ashley feared she would faint at that precise moment. The kiss was gentle, tender and full of passion. Her emotions went haywire. She had never been kissed like that before. Her heart was racing like wild horses trotting to the finish line with such vigor and passion. She moaned with pleasure.

Breaking away, Ashley gazed up at him with tears unashamedly running down her cheeks. She was awestricken by this handsome man.

"Why are you crying?" Gregg wiped at her eyes with such finesse she could hardly feel his touch. Helpless, Gregg ran his fingers through her long locks.

"I'm just so happy. I've never been happier," she honestly confessed.

"Me too," Gregg choked. "Ashley, I hope I don't scare you away when I say this, but I must tell you something."

"Say it."

"I have fallen in love with you," earnestly, he admitted the secrets of his heart. Gregg loved her and nothing would ever change that fact. Unknowingly, Ashley had deposited the most precious gift of all into his barren soul…the gift of love.

Ashley's heart flipped-flopped. Now her tears cascaded down even more. She felt overwhelmingly blessed. "I have fallen in love with you, too."

Gazing into her hypnotic eyes, Gregg lost sight of reality in her presence. Once again, he kissed her passionately and she kissed him back.

As a tree is planted deeply in the soil, roots not seen, but firmly there, so was their love…Planted, rooted and grounded.

Returning home a little after four, Sandra immediately noticed the glow upon the faces of both Ashley and Gregg as the couple held hands. Her heart soared at her daughter's newfound happiness.

"Andrew!" Ashley was surprised to see him.

"I hope you don't mind," Andrew drew closer to her.

"Sandy told me that your birthday was today and invited me over." Andrew did not want to miss his daughter's birthday ever again. Being here, watching joy radiate in eyes, literally, meant more to Andrew than she could ever imagine.

"Of course not," Ashley embraced him, giving her mother a look. *Sandy! He called my mother Sandy! There is more to this story than meets the eye! Maybe they are developing a relationship. Glory Hallelujah! God is so faithful!*

Like a child on Christmas day, Ashley showed her bracelet to her family. They were all delighted. Her mother's tears didn't escape Ashley. She understood them. She cherished them. She felt them, too. They were tears of indescribable, unspeakable, joy.

"This is for you," Andrew handed her a gift.

"Andrew, you shouldn't have."

"It was my pleasure," he handed her a small box.

Opening it, Ashley's eyes widened. "It's beautiful!" She held out a silver necklace with a diamond cross on it. "I've always wanted a necklace like this. Andrew, it's wonderful!" She hugged him.

He held her, fighting back tears of old and new. "I'm glad you like it."

"I love it," she gazed into his eyes…crystalline eyes that were so familiar and warm.

"I am so blessed," Ashley looked around at her family members, Andrew and lastly Gregg. "It's been a hard year, filled with many trials; but through it all, God has been with me…with us…and today…I feel Him through all of you. I love you all, so very much! Thank you for making this the best birthday ever."

That night Ashley wrote in her journal…

I am in love with Gregg and he is in love with me! This has been the greatest birthday ever! Mom is healthy and whole again! Thomas is excelling. Danny and Donny are dynamite! And Lacey is exceptional! Harvey is dating Pam. And I'm dating Gregg. And I think Andrew is dating my mom...who knows what is next with them! Thank you, Lord for everything! The struggle has been worth it.

CHAPTER 36

The Truth and nothing but the Truth

Gregg sat next to Ashley in church on Sunday, along with her mother, siblings, Harvey, and Pam. Thomas intentionally sat next to Gregg. He secretly revered the man, who once irritated him to no end.

Gregg and Ashely struggled to concentrate on the sermon. The newness of their love was thrilling and filling, their cups overflowed.

The pastor struck a few chords with the family in different ways.

"The Truth and Nothing but the Truth," Pastor Smallwood repeated. "There is no such thing as a white lie, a little lie, or a good lie. A lie is a lie. Most important, a lie is a sin. Liars are listed among those who will not enter into heaven's doors."

"Church, I want to talk to you today about the importance of being men and women of good character, integrity and trustworthy. You see, today so many Christians are compromising their characters and morals just to be accepted, just to fit in, just to please others. We are afraid that if we tell the whole truth, and nothing but the truth, that we will be rejected. We are terrified that if others knew our hidden secrets—if someone discovered that we have skeletons in our closets—or if someone realized that we aren't as perfect as we appear to be—then our lives would be ruined.

"Recently, I shared with you my testimony—my truth. It wasn't easy. It wasn't pretty. It was a rather ugly truth. Nevertheless, because of me telling the truth and nothing but the truth, forty plus souls were won into the kingdom of God that day. Glory to God! Knowing the Truth will set you free!

"Let me tell you, King David had a secret. David had some skeletons in his closets. He did some terrible things. Yet, God loved him and said that David was a man after His own heart. We read in Second Samuel, the 11th chapter David's indiscretion, one of his cover-ups, about his hidden skeletons...

"'Then it happened one evening that David arose from his bed and walked on the roof of the king's house. And from the roof he saw a woman bathing, and the woman was very beautiful to behold. So David sent and inquired about the woman.

"And someone said, "Is this not Bathsheba, the daughter of Eliam, the wife of Uriah the Hittite?" Then David sent messengers, and took her; and she came to him, and he lay with her, for she was cleansed from her impurity; and she returned to her house. And the woman conceived; so she sent and told David, and said, "I am with child."

"Instead of telling the truth and nothing but the truth, David tried to cover up his sin, his betrayal, his own lustful self. Verse 14 reads,

"In the morning it happened that David wrote a letter to Joab and sent it by the hand of Uriah. And he wrote in the letter, saying, "Set Uriah in the forefront of the hottest

battle, and retreat from him, that he may be struck down and die." So it was, while Joab besieged the city, that he assigned Uriah to a place where he knew there were valiant men. Then the men of the city came out and fought with Joab. And some of the people of the servants of David fell; and Uriah the Hittite died also.

"David didn't physically kill Uriah himself, but he ordered the hit…just as guilty! But God loved David and he wasn't going to let him stay in that sinful state. God gave him another chance. So, what did God do? He sent Nathan. Nathan told a parable, which convicted David. I encourage you to read about it later in Second Samuel the twelfth chapter. There were consequences to David's sin. He would lose a child, which he fathered by Bathsheba. His wives would be taken. Those in his household would be against one another and so forth. David repented. David admitted that he was a sinner. That he had messed up. That he had lied. That he wasn't perfect. The Truth set David free."

The message pricked Sandra's raw heart. She had a secret that only she, Andrew and God knew.

"Some of us our in bondage to our past lives of sin and shame." the pastor was drawing close to the end of his sermon. "The keyword is that it is in the past. Now you may say, why dig up dirt? Why should I unmask my past and cause hurt to others? Surely, some things are best left in the past. However, when the lives of others are hurt by it, we don't have the right to just think about ourselves.

"Tell the truth and nothing but the truth! It will set you free and perhaps set someone else free." Pastor Smallwood concluded his sermon.

Sandra fought the tears; but to no avail could she hold them back. Her heart was troubled.

Ashley reached over and put her arm around her mother. She didn't know what it was about the message that was causing her mother to cry, but obviously, it had affected her.

After the offering, the pastor stepped down and faced the congregation. "What a blessing it is to have Sister Sandra Finley back with the family. Please, Sister Finley, come forth," Pastor Smallwood said unexpectedly.

Sandra did not want to go up to the altar. She was convicted by the message and felt too guilty.

"Go ahead." Ashley mouthed.

With reluctance, Sandra walked the aisle. The church body stood and applauded.

"It's been a long time," Pastor Smallwood continued, "since our Sister has been here. What a miracle! God performed a miracle through the hands of doctors and by His omnipotent power!"

Reaching the altar, the pastor and first lady embraced Sandra in love. With blissful tears, she cried.

"Let's show how glad we are to have our sister home," the pastor beckoned the congregation. Without hesitation, one by one, the church family came forward and embraced Sandra. She was overcome with emotions. *How pleasant it is for brethren to come together in unity and fellowship.*

After church, Gregg treated all of them out to dinner, including Harvey and Pam. It was truly a family affair. The fellowship was good, with the exception that it seemed Sandra's mind was occupied elsewhere.

Leaving the restaurant, Sandra quietly pulled her daughter aside and said, "I need to talk to you about something very important."

"Sure," Ashley worried.

"Tonight." Sandra had to be truthful, even if it would cause pain to her daughter. In the end, the truth would set her free—she hoped.

Upon returning home, Ashley sat on the porch with Gregg, while everyone went inside.

"This has been a wonderful day," Gregg held her hand. "My father would have enjoyed it."

"Next time, if he feels better, he'll have to come."

"We'll see. He likes his new church a lot."

"Well, we'll go with him," Ashley compromised.

Gregg loved her so much. She made life so easy. "You would do that?"

She nodded.

"Can I kiss you?" Sensitive of her feelings, he inquired.

She nodded.

Gently his lips touched hers for a brief second, which felt like a lifetime.

"I love you," he could not say it enough.

"I love you," she could not hear it enough.

"We're going to be alright, Ashley."

"Yes, with God as the Head of our lives, we will be."

"Pray for me, Andrew," Sandra spoke in hush tones on the phone. "I'm going to tell her tonight."

"It'll be fine, Sandy," Andrew said confidently. "We've prayed about this and God will take care of all of us."

"What if she hates me?" she sniffed.

"Ashley doesn't have a hateful bone in her body. She may be upset. She may be hurt by the lie. She may even resent you for not telling her the truth. However, Ashely will never hate you. Ashley loves you and her love for you will override all the negative feelings."

The two talked a little more before ending their riveted conversation.

"Mother, is this a good time to talk now?" Ashley peeped her head in the doorway.

"Yes," her mother motioned for Ashley to come sit on the bed.

Sandra sat still, looking directly into the eyes of her daughter. The stain of guilt was horrendous. Tears were very near, but she needed to keep them at bay. It was her time to be strong for Ashley.

"What I am about to tell you…is going to…hurt. I want you to know that I never meant to hurt you. All I wanted to do was to protect you and make sure that you were loved."

"Momma, you're scaring me." Ashley was troubled. "Just be straight with me. What is it?"

"Tom was not your biological father," Sandra confessed, dropping her eyes in shame.

Ashley's hands came over her mouth, stifling a groan. She was bowled over by her mother's confession. *I knew I was different. I didn't even look like his child. Tom never treated me like the others. He was always so standoffish. Now I know why.* It all made sense. Yet, the truth hurt something awful.

"Who is my real father?" Tears collided down her cheeks, while a wedged clogged her throat as Ashley attempted to wrap her brain around the shocking news.

"Andrew Watts."

"A...n...d...r...e...w," his name lingered on her lips. "The same Andrew that works with me at *The Palace*?"

Sandra nodded.

"It can't be."

"It is, sweetheart."

"We have the same eyes."

"I know," Sandra smiled. "I have been haunted by those eyes for twenty-four years. Every time I looked at you, I saw him."

"I don't understand," Ashley sat down. "Did Tom know?" Tears came from a deeper well within. Years of feeling left out and unloved by the man who she thought brought her into the world. Now, only to discover that it was all a lie.

"Yes. He married me so my parents wouldn't know and my reputation wouldn't be tarnished. You see, Tom had some good in him. He gave you his name and treated you like his own."

"No, he didn't, Momma!" Ashley rebutted. "I have always felt like a stepchild around him. He was good to me when you were around. Other times, he completely ignored me. I was starving for his attention. He never freely gave it to me."

Sandra winced at her daughter's confession. All this time she thought she was giving Ashley and her siblings a happy home, when in truth, their family was anything but happy.

"Does Andrew know I am his daughter?"

"He does now. Actually, when you told him about me, he knew then. He was amazed that you had his eyes. It all made sense to him."

"Is he happy about it?" she fretted. *What if he doesn't want me either? What if it is too late for us to have a father-daughter relationship?*

"He was ecstatic," Sandra clapped her hands together. "He

has always wanted a child, ever since I could remember. He never had any children of his own. You are it and he wants to get to know you. He told me that you thought he was some kind of pervert for staring at you all the time."

"I did." Ashley laughed.

"How are you feeling?" Sandra asked, worried this was too much for Ashley.

"I'm shocked," Ashley looked at her mother, "but in a way, I'm relieved. I...uh...still have a father," one fat drop plummeted down her cheeks. "And perhaps, he will love me like Tom loved Thomas and my other siblings."

Oh!" Sandra held her arms out to her daughter and hugged her closely to her bosom. "I didn't know you felt that way. I am so sorry. Please forgive me."

Ashley's heart wrung with compassion for her mother. She now understood more why her mother had withdrawn from the world because she had lost her first love. She was living a lie trying to cloak the pain of the past. Sandra settled for less, endured Tom's two-timing, adulterous affairs because she felt as if she deserved it and that she owed it to him for marrying her.

"Mother, I completely forgive you," Ashley said in a calm, loving tone. "You did what you thought was best. I have no regrets. I have always had your love and that was enough."

Later, lying on the couch, Ashley wept. The truth had hurt and freed her all together. She was overcome with an array of emotions. She would never let her mother know just how much the truth had affected her.

How am I going to face Andrew? Will he really accept me

as his own, after all these years? What does the future have in store for us as father and daughter? Uncomfortable questions rose in her mind. *What if he rejects me like Tom? What if he wants nothing to do with me?*

The ringing of the telephone interrupted Ashley's train of thought. Looking at the clock, she knew it was Gregg. Trying to suck up her tears, Ashley answered calmly.

"I hope it's not too late," he began. "I just needed to hear your voice one more time before turning in."

"It's never too late for you."

"What's wrong?" Gregg knew right away that something was not right.

"Nothing," she endeavored to sound chipper.

"You can't fool me, Ashley."

Taking a few deep breaths, she revealed the shocking truth about her identity.

"Whew! That's heavy," he said. "Do you need me to come over?"

"Oh, no. I am fine. It's just a lot to take in," she uttered. "But I knew it all along, Gregg. Deep down I just didn't have any connection with Tom. He made me feel like an outcast— like a stepchild—I was a stepchild."

"Are you relieved?"

"I'm just overwhelmed right now. I'm not mad at mom, but I am hurt."

"That's understandable," he paused. "We'll get through this…together."

"Thanks, Gregg. I needed that."

"Seems like Pastor Smallwood's sermon was right on time."

"Yes. It convicted my mom to finally come clean with me.

I am glad she did. Now…I just have to move forward…and hopefully get to know my real father."

"He's blessed to have you as a daughter."

"Thanks for saying that Gregg."

"It's the truth, Ashley, and nothing but the truth."

CHAPTER 37

The Calm before the Storm

The sky was grey and overcast as Thomas headed to school on Monday morning. A storm was sure to come. Whistling the familiar hymn of Amazing Grace, Thomas felt gratitude for God's amazing grace and mercy toward him. He had made so many mistakes in the past, and yet, God was merciful enough to not only to forgive, but to forget.

Undeserving of such love, Thomas wanted now to please God by doing the right thing. By living his life in a way that incited others to want to know Him.

Remembering the light in Ashley's eyes this past weekend, and how she seemed happy for the first time in a long time, heightened his own happiness. He had put his sister through a lot. Still, Ashley never gave up on him.

Doc is good for her! And she is good for him. Thank You, Lord, for bringing them together.

So absorbed in his silent prayer, Thomas didn't realize that he was no longer walking alone.

"You're happy this morning," Shane discerned.

"This is the day that the Lord has made. I will rejoice and be glad in it."

"Amen, brother."

Thomas and Shane had a common bond of Christianity, which linked their hearts together. Further, they both loved basketball and were naturally good at it. Though they had been only friends for a short period of time, their hearts were united. Their bond was strong and solid. God had brought them together for such a time as this.

"Coach says scouts are going to be at the game tomorrow," Shane's tone elevated slightly. Hopes of obtaining a basketball scholarship ran through the athlete's mind often. It was his only way of being able to afford college and he knew it.

"I know," Thomas spoke. "No need to worry about it. We just need to play ball and show them the talent that God has given us. God's favor will surround us like a shield."

"You're right. My pastor's sermon yesterday talked about God's favor."

"We have favor with God and with men," Thomas added. "We serve an awesome God."

"I'm so glad I know Jesus, for myself," Shane admonished. "I couldn't make it without Him. No matter what happens, I know that I'll be all right because God is with me. When I leave this place called earth I will be with Him, forever!"

Thomas turned to his friend. Shane was glowing. "What an awesome promise!"

"It sure is!" Shane nearly shouted. "So many people are content with this world, but I'm not. I know God has prepared a better place for us and…"

"What the…" Thomas felt something sharp penetrate his left side.

"No one rats on me and gets away!" Drake snarled in Thomas' ear.

"No!" Shane shouted simultaneously at one of Drake boys.

To no avail could he prevent what had happened next. Two guys pounced on him, both having long blades in their hands. Repeatedly, Drake's boys knifed Shane in his chest area.

Both Thomas and Shane were left for dead on the sidewalk, as the attackers jumped into a getaway car and drove off.

"Shane," Thomas sputtered, looking over at his friend. Shane didn't flinch. He was prostrated, stock-still on the ground.

Thomas hadn't known how many times he had been knifed, but the overflow of blood coming through his tan shirt alarmed him. "Shane," Thomas tried again, feeling rather swoony himself. "Sha--------," he passed out.

"Gregg! How are you?" Harvey looked up from the computer in the library. Immediately, Harvey knew something was wrong.

"Where is Ashley?" Gregg loathed being the bearer of bad news.

"She is in the back," he stuttered. "What's wrong, Gregg?"

"Thomas is on his way to the hospital in an ambulance," he said with a straight face, though inside, he was quaking.

"What!" Harvey gasped. "What happened?"

"He was stabbed several times, but I don't have time to go into details. I need to get Ashley."

"Sure," his hands were shaking, identical to his voice. "Go through those doors on the right," Harvey pointed, "and…"

Gregg didn't hear another word as he sprinted to the doors.

"Gregg!" Ashley nearly collided with him. "What's wrong?" she read his tormented face.

"Thomas…"

"Thomas," she interrupted frantically. "What Gregg?"

"We have to hurry to the hospital and I'll explain on the way." Gregg grabbed Ashley's hand and hurried her outside.

"Hospital?" she was in a daze. "What happened? Is he alright?"

"Officer Anderson found Thomas and Shane lying on the sidewalk a block away from the school," he explained in the car. "They were both unconscious...only Shane," Gregg choked, swallowing hard before going on. "Shane didn't make it."

Ashley gasped loudly, sick with worry.

"They were both stabbed many times. Thomas lost a lot of blood and he's...he's..."

"He's what!" She nearly shouted. "Tell me, Gregg."

"He's in bad shape," Gregg fretted. Ashley looked like she was going to collaspe. Gregg caught Ashley just before her knees gave away. He had to carry her to the car.

Distraught, Ashley found it extremely difficult to catch her breath. This was unbelievable! In a blink of an eye, her world was turned upside down–again. A whirlwind of calamity was swirling down and she could do nothing about it—but pray.

Nothing could have prepared her for this. Everything was going so good. Life is a combination of cycles. Good cycles and bad cycles.

One minute good...and then the next, the rug is pulled out from under you. Lord, help us. I look to You for strength.

I am with you. I am with Thomas.

Thomas' life hung on the cliff of life and death.

"God is with Thomas," Gregg reached over and held her hand tightly, pulling into the emergency room parking lot.

"Thomas Finley," Gregg pronounced to the woman at the emergency room desk.

"Are you family?"

"I am," Ashley mumbled with knots in her stomach. "I am his sister."

Keying in his name, the woman peered at her with pity. "He is in surgery."

Ashley's hand cover he mouth. She could say nothing.

"Is there anyone we can talk to?" Gregg took charge, literally holding Ashley up with his arm.

"Someone will be out to talk with you, shortly," she answered.

"Thank you," Gregg said politely and guided Ashley to the waiting area.

She collapsed in his arms and bawled. He embraced her with a therapeutic hug. Resting her head on his broad chest, Ashley allowed the tears to flow freely. His strength was a much-needed infusion to her weary soul.

"I need to call, Momma," Ashley drew in a ragged breath.

"I'll call her," Gregg informed. "I'll be right back."

"She's going to be so worried. This could cause a setback for her, Gregg," Ashley fretted. "Maybe we should wait until we talk to someone."

"That's probably a good idea." Gregg sat, his arms around her. The perpetual hush of the atmosphere was treacherous. Tenderly, his hands went from caressing her hair, to her shoulders, and arms. The rhythmical, soft touch helped soothed her frayed feelings.

Momentarily, someone came out and talked with them.

"I'm Dr. Stroman," he introduced.

"I'm Dr. Jefferson and this is Thomas' sister, Ashley

Finley." Gregg greeted as they both stood anxiously.

"Your brother survived the surgery. He lost a lot of blood and we had to give him six transfusions. We had to remove part of his intestines, but other than that, he is going to be just fine. He was stabbed seven times, but luckily they didn't puncture any of his major organs."

"Praise God!" Ashley shouted.

"Thank you, Lord," Gregg praised.

"He's in recovery," the doctor went on. "Shortly, the nurse will take you see him."

"Thank you, doctor," Ashley grabbed his hand. "God bless you."

The doctor smiled.

"Oh, Gregg!"

With a gentle touch, he reached out and drew her into his arms. Looking down at her, his salty tears matching hers, his lips brushed her forehead. Bared-face, no makeup on, Ashley stood a vision of loveliness in the midst of the storm. Though the storm was raging, it did not touch her.

Then his thoughts reflected on his morning Bible reading. *Though you go through the fire, you will not be burned. Though you go through the waters, you will not drown.*

"I can't imagine the pain of Shane's mother," she whimpered.

"He lives with his aunt," Gregg stated. "Lord, be with her and comfort her. She needs You more than ever," Gregg prayed aloud.

"I'm so glad you are here with me," Ashley looked up at him.

"I will always be here for you," Gregg stroked her cheek.

"I better call, Momma."

"You want me to do it?"

"No," she smiled. "I can handle it."

"Use my cell phone," he gave it to her.

Surrounded by family, Thomas awakened in a daze about his whereabouts. "Where am I?"

"You're a Craft Memorial," Sandra replied, happy to hear her son's voice.

He grimaced.

"You're going to be just fine," Sandra stated.

"Drake stabbed me," his mind tardily replayed the tragic event.

"Yes," Ashley chimed in. "The police are looking for him and the others.

"You had to undergo surgery to stop the bleeding. Thankfully, none of your organs were touched," his mother informed, still rather emotional by it all. "God was with you."

"You'll be out of the hospital in no time," Ashley wiped her eyes, so elated that her brother would be okay. He may have a few battle scars, but Thomas would heal completely.

"Shane," he mouthed. "How is Shane?"

Sandra and Ashley looked to Gregg, who hadn't left their side. At once, Gregg drew closer to Thomas' bedside.

"Doc, please tell me the truth," his voice cracked. "How is Shane?"

"He is in a better place," he answered truthfully.

Silently, Thomas wept, understanding that the soul of his friend had shed his fleshly temple called a body. The words of his friend resounded in his heart.

I am so glad I know Jesus, for myself. I could not make

it without Him. No matter what happens, I will be all right because God is with me. When I leave this place called earth, I will be with Him, forever!

"He was prepared," Thomas finally spoke. "I will surely miss him."

"We all will," Gregg carefully hugged Thomas, sensing his need to be comforted.

"He was looking forward to tomorrow's game," Thomas breathlessly uttered. "College scouts are going to be there and neither of us will be playing."

"That's okay. There will be other games," Gregg replied.

"For me," Thomas said solemnly, "but not for Shane."

"You'll just have to play for the both of you," Gregg proposed. "Shane will be watching."

"He will," the thought caused a smile to adorn his shivering lips. "He will!"

Leaving the hospital about an hour later, Gregg was about to take Ashley out for a bite to eat when the couple ran into Andrew.

"How is your brother?" Andrew inquired in a genial tone.

"Much better."

"Hi," Gregg broke the awkward moment. "I'm Gregg Jefferson."

"Andrew Watts," he shook his hand. "It's a pleasure to meet you." Andrew looked the tall man over with fatherly eyes. On the surface, he approved.

"We are about to grab a bite to eat and bring back Ms. Finley something," Gregg enlightened. "Would you like for us to bring you something back, as well?"

"No, thank you," Andrew answered him, but his eyes were fixed on Ashley—his daughter. He knew that she knew the truth and wondered what was running through her mind.

"Can I have a moment with you…in private?" Andrew politely asked Ashley.

She looked up at Gregg nervously.

"Go ahead," he whispered.

"Okay." Ashley walked a few feet away from Gregg, glancing back once. He winked. She smiled.

"I didn't know," Andrew began. His voice was thick with emotions rising to the surface.

"I know."

"I have always wanted a daughter," he went on.

Ashley smiled.

"You look just like your mother. You're so beautiful."

"I have eyes like yours," timidly she responded.

"It's a Watts' trait," his eyes were misty. "I am so happy. There are no words that would do justice in describing my happiness. From the first day I met you, I felt connected to you. I wanted to protect you and to shield you from everything. You thought I was a pervert."

"I did." Ashley giggled.

"Ashley," he put his shaky hands on her shoulders, his eyes watering. "I want to know everything about you. I want to be a part of your life, in every way. We have so much to catch up on. From this day forward, if there is anything you need, I will be there for you. You may not think of me as your father, right now, but I truly do think of you as my only daughter. I love dearly."

Ashley's heart thundered at his kind words. With teary eyes, she gazed at him. The heaviness of her uncertain heart melted away. He opened his arms and she fell into his fatherly embrace. Finally, she had a father who freely loved her for who she was—his child.

CHAPTER 38

Thomas Scores for Shane

Soon as Thomas' name was called for the starting lineup, the crowd stood on its feet, giving him a standing ovation. It was his first game since the stabbing, five weeks ago – the final game of the year.

This is for you, Shane!

He ran through the cheerleaders, high-fiving his teammates. Looking around, pumped for the game, Thomas spotted his family in the bleachers and gave them the thumbs up.

"We need this win to make it to the playoffs," Gregg leaned over and whispered in Ashley's ear. "The team has been struggling without its two star players."

"Thomas couldn't sleep last night," she whispered back. "He's so excited."

"A couple of college scouts are here tonight, just to see Thomas. Of course, they have heard about his incident, so they don't expect him to be fully up to par."

"They don't know Thomas," Ashley said proudly.

"You're right."

"Hey, you guys," Pam greeted as she and Harvey joined them in the bleachers. Pam sitting next to Ashley and Harvey sitting next to Gregg. The men had developed a friendly relationship. Now that they were all attending the same church, Gregg was learning a lot through Sunday school, which Harvey taught. Once a week, Gregg and Harvey would share lunch together and talk about spiritual things and life in general.

"Glad you made it." Ashley beamed, happy that Pam and Harvey were hitting it off so well.

"Wouldn't miss it."

"You and Harvey look good together."

"So do you and Gregg. Who *woulda thunk* it? For you, yeah, I expected you to find your *Knight in Shining Armor*. But for me," Pam fanned her hand, "I thought I would end up like my momma, with a man who left me broke, busted and disgusted."

"God had other plans. He knew that you were special, so He sent you a special guy. You both deserve a special life of happiness, Pam."

"Thanks. Now, let's stop all this mushy stuff before I start crying again. I'm not used to being a water bucket like you."

They laughed.

"Thomas is going to be great tonight," Pam changed the subject. "I can feel it!"

"Me too," Ashley replied. "He's been through so much. Mom wanted to come but..." Ashley looked up and saw her mother, Andrew, and the children walking up the bleachers toward them.

"Mom!" Ashley stood up.

"I wanted to surprise you." Sandra had succeeded.

"Thomas is going to be ecstatic!" Ashley said, trying to make eye contact with her brother. Concurrently, Thomas looked up, a wide grin spreading across his face. Giving the family the thumbs up again, Thomas quickly focused his attention back to the game. He was on a mission–to play and win for Shane!

"Ashley," Andrew winked at her.

"Dad," she said easily, "I'm glad you're here."

"Me too. You're looking wonderful, tonight."

"I feel wonderful," she admitted. Being in the presence of all of her loved ones was truly wonderful. Only God could bring her family to full circle—complete—with no chains broken.

That night, Thomas scored his highest ever. He led the team to an 82-80 victory. When asked how he could shoot so well after sitting out for five weeks due to the stabbing, he simply replied, "I had help."

"Your team did do well, but you were playing exceptionally well, considering your recent stabbing ordeal," the television reporter stated.

His thoughts went to Shane. "I played this game for Shane. This win is in his honor."

"How do you feel about the police finally capturing Shane's killer?" the reporter asked.

"Let's not go there tonight," Gregg stepped in, putting on his protective hat. "As the principal of Brookland, we want to celebrate this victory and Shane's life. Shane's legacy will forever remain here at Brookland. We are excited about tonight's win. We have an awesome opportunity of being in the playoffs now. The odds were against us, but we have overcome them."

The interview continued with the principal about other events happening in the school.

"Great job," Ashley spoke privately to Thomas.

"I miss Shane," Thomas spoke truthfully, "but I felt his

presence. I know that sounds strange."

"No, it doesn't. He's watching, no doubt about it and smiling that crooked smile of his."

Thomas chuckled. "I believe it."

Ashley admired her brother. Although he was still grieving the loss of his dear friend, he was pressing forward with the right attitude.

"I hate that I have to testify in court next week," Thomas shrugged. Drake was being prosecuted for murder and Thomas was the prosecutor's star witness.

"You're not afraid, are you?" Ashley asked.

"Nah! I just don't like the idea of being in court. But, I'll gladly do it to put Drake behind bars, hopefully for life."

"Gregg told me that the police have been trying to get Drake for years. They suspected he has killed others or ordered his gang to do it for him. The prosecutors never had any solid evidence on him to convict him. Finally, he's off the streets and thanks to you it'll be for a long, long time."

"Sis, I could have been with Drake, you know? He me to hang out with him several times. I did once. Remember when you found out I had been smoking weed after shooting ball?"

She nodded. "Thomas, you have come a long way. God has always had His hand on you."

"Amen to that."

After dropping the family home after the game, Gregg and Ashley drove to his father's home. He wasn't feeling well earlier that day. Gregg just wanted to make sure he was okay.

Ashley waited in the den area, while Gregg went upstairs to his father's room.

Tiptoeing in, he went over to the bed. Mr. Jefferson stirred, and his eyes popped opened.

"What are you doing here?" he groggily asked. Gregg had moved back into his home.

"Just checking on you. Are you feeling any better?"

He nodded. "Stop worrying about me. You're hovering over me like Na..." he stopped, closing his eyes. Naomi's absence still pained him.

Gregg hurt for his dad. He figured that his dad's sudden illness had more to do with Naomi's leaving. He was suffering from a broken heart.

"Dad," Gregg whispered, "I love you."

With misty eyes, the father looked up at his son, whom he had almost lost forever, and said with tenderness, "I love you, more."

"You get your rest. I'm going to take Ashley home."

"She's a sweet girl. She reminds me of Sophia."

"I think so too."

"I'm glad you have a good woman. I can tell she really loves you. Your mother would be so proud," he caught his breath and went on. "Handle her like china—carefully, delicately and lovingly."

"Thanks, Dad. I will come back and stay here tonight. We can have breakfast together in the morning."

"Sounds good."

Ashley walked toward Gregg when he entered the den. His glossy eyes concerned her. "Is everything okay?"

He nodded.

Reaching up, she tenderly caressed the sides of his cheeks. Gregg relished her touch. It comforted him.

"My Dad misses Naomi," he paused. "I miss Naomi. Still,

I can't believe she's not coming back."

"She'll be back," Ashley hoped. "Her family needs her right now."

"It's more than that, Ashley. I think she is afraid like you said. Dad *kinda* made known his feelings for her and I think she couldn't handle it."

"Well, remembering your dad before, I think it would have frightened me, too. He seemed so....so..."

"Blue-blooded!" Gregg chuckled, sensing her desire to speak delicately about his father. "He was the most self-centered, arrogant, high-minded man I've ever known. Short of not addressing him as Your Highness, he sure wore the royal hat.

"I remember at the restaurant when he suspected for a second that I knew way too much about you, a sister of a boy who went to my school."

"Oh, really," Ashley was surprised. "What did he say?"

"Something about, I'm of royal blood, coming from a family of noblemen and women," Gregg mimicked his father by sticking his chest out and laughed. "He was a real piece of work!"

"Maybe he's right," timidly, Ashley spoke. Perhaps, they were too different to make this relationship work.

"He was wrong," Gregg lifted her chin upward, "and now he knows it. We are the same, Ashley. We both belong to the same God. That's all that really matters."

She agreed.

"The blood of Jesus has cleansed my dad's heart. He doesn't feel the same way anymore. He sees you through the eyes of Christ. He's so glad that we are together. He said so just a moment ago."

"He did?

"Yes, and he also said that you were a sweet girl and reminded him of mother. He said that mother would be so proud that I have found you. Oh, and then he said to handle you like china— carefully, delicately and lovingly."

"Oh!" Ashley was touched.

"I plan on doing just that," he leaned over and kissed her forehead. "I'm going to handle you carefully," he pecked her cheek, "delicately," he pecked her other cheek, "and adoringly," lastly his lips claimed hers.

EPILOGUE

Happily Ever After

"**H**i, Dad!" Gregg greeted, looking up from the seating chart he and Ashley were working on at the dining room table. They had papers spread all around. Now engaged, and their wedding two months away, Gregg and Ashley were tediously working on the reception seating chart.

"Hi Son," Mr. Jefferson took off his jacket.

"Hi Daughter," Mr. Jefferson lovingly addressed his son's future bride.

"Hello, Dad." At Mr. Jefferson's request, Ashley preferred addressing him by that title. Now, she had two dads, who cherished her and treated her as if she was the most precious daughter in the world.

"You look tired," Gregg worried. "You're not overdoing it at work, are you?"

"Not anymore," the father answered.

"What do you mean by that?"

"I've sold Jefferson Realtors."

"What?" Gregg was dumbfounded by the unforeseen news. Pushing back his chair, Gregg forgot all about the seating chart.

"We'll talk about this later, Son. I want to go take a shower and change clothes."

"But Dad," Gregg watched his father walk away.

"Later," Mr. Jefferson went upstairs. The conversation was abruptly put on hold.

"Can you believe that?" Gregg sat back down with his mouth wide opened.

"He looks happy." Ashley mouthed.

Gregg looked at her as if she were crazy. "Jefferson Realtors meant everything to dad. It was his life. He has satellite offices all over," he shook his head in a daze. "It's unbelievable."

"Your dad has changed," Ashley got up and stood over her man. Gently, massaging Gregg's tensed shoulders, she prayed for guidance. "You've said it yourself, after his salvation, he didn't seem interested in working. His mind is elsewhere."

"He's thinking about Naomi," Gregg uttered hopelessly. "He still calls her number every other week, but Naomi is never home, or can never come to the phone. I don't understand how she can just forget about us like that."

"She hasn't forgotten either of you," Ashley refuted. "How could she ever forget the two handsome men, who were a part of her life for so many years? It is impossible. I am sure she's suffering just like your dad—and you."

Gregg remained silent on the matter.

"I think it's a good thing that your dad sold the business. His health isn't fully up to par and he looks tired when he comes home."

"You're right," he pondered. "He hasn't been happy. I thought it was because of Naomi. It might be a combination of being burnout at work and missing Naomi."

"I think so," she continued massaging his shoulders.

"That feels good." Gregg covered his hands over hers and glanced up at her. "I love you so much, Ashley. I hope you don't get tired of hearing me say that."

"I could never get tired of hearing that."

"We make a good team?"

"We sure do."

"Okay, well as a team, we better get back to this unending seating chart."

"I love you," she chuckled and smacked him playfully on the lips.

"Oh, no you don't." Gregg grabbed Ashley and pulled her into his lap. "You can't go teasing a man and think you can get away with it."

She laughed.

He stifled her laugh with a passionate, enduring kiss.

"Okay, Dad, let's talk about Jefferson Realtors," Gregg plopped down in the recliner across from his dad, who was sitting on the couch. He and the father were alone, now.

"It's not going to be a Jefferson Realtors, anymore." Mr. Jefferson stated. "I sold the business to Max Diamond, you know my Assistant Executive."

"You have been partners for a long time. It still doesn't make sense. Jefferson Realtors has been your life, Dad. To just up and sell it like that, without even mentioning it to me, doesn't make sense."

"You made it perfectly clear that you never wanted anything to do with Jefferson Realtors," the dad eyed his son. "Has that changed?"

"Of course not."

"Well, since I can't pass it down, I sold it to someone who loves the business more than I do. Listen, Son, I'm tired. The bottom line is that I do not have the passion for real estate anymore. I want something different in my life. I've paid my dues. Now, I want to see the world. I want to travel and experience things I was too busy to experience before. Besides, I am no fool. I know that my heart cannot physically take the pressure cooker work that I've been doing for over thirty years. I want to live, son, and not die."

"Die!" Gregg shuddered. "Do you feel ill, Dad? Is there something you're not telling me?"

"My doctor advised me to quit working before I got out of the hospital," the older Jefferson finally admitted to his son.

"Dad!" Gregg shot upward. "Why didn't you tell me?"

"Because I knew you wouldn't let me leave on my own terms." Mr. Jefferson joined his son, resting his hand on Gregg's shoulder. "I've prayed about this and I have peace. I'm leaving on my terms."

Gregg eyed his father. His dad was a proud man, for sure. "Okay. So now what?"

"Son, I'm just going to enjoy life. I sold the business for a hefty sum. I'll probably never have to touch the money for my own personal needs. Nevertheless, I will give a large sum to the church to help build the new school and some to Brookland to put in a fund for scholarships and such."

"That's a great idea." Gregg put his arm around his dad's shoulder.

"I'll call Pastor first thing in the morning."

"I'm proud of you, Dad."

"That matters a great deal to me."

"Dad, there is something really bothering me," Gregg sat back down.

"What is it?"

"My wedding is a special day and I want everyone that I love dearly to be there."

"Of course, Son."

"But something is not right. As we were making the seating chart for the wedding reception I realized that a key person is missing."

Mr. Jefferson understood perfectly well.

"Naomi is missing, Dad," Gregg replied earnestly. "She's been like a mother to me. I love her so much. I cannot imagine her not being at my wedding."

"Me either."

"What are we going to do about it?"

Mr. Jefferson stared at his son for some time, before saying something. "We are going to go get her…that's what!" Mr. Jefferson leaped up with a new agenda—to get Naomi back!

"What?"

"You heard me! I am going to get Naomi and bring her back here! She has to be at the wedding!" Mr. Jefferson marched forward.

"But Dad…."

"Don't but dad me! I'm going to bring her back here where she belongs!"

The next day.

Standing at the unfamiliar door, nine hundred miles away from his home, Mr. Jefferson felt something he had not felt since he was a little boy. Scared. What if he had come all this way for nothing? What if Naomi didn't even live here? What if she rejected him and refused to talk to him like she did over the phone?

God, strengthen me! I need Your help.

It seemed like an eternity that he stood at the door, trying to muster up the courage just to knock.

I have come too far now, to turn back now!

Gregory knocked several times, but no answer. He knocked a little harder, still no answer.

His courage was wavering, but he knocked one last time.

At last, the door swung opened. Panic gripped him as he beheld Naomi's sunken eyes, disheveled hair, ashen face and a gaunt look. She was ill, no doubt about it. He drew closer to her just in time before Naomi collapsed in his arms.

Carrying her inside, Gregory gently laid her on the couch.

"Naomi," he repeatedly called her name.

"Who are you?" A little boy entered the room.

"I'm a friend of Naomi's."

"Momma!" the boy called. "Somebody is in our house!"

A few seconds later, a stocky looking woman entered the room. "Who are you?" agitation boomed in her voice.

"I'm a friend of Naomi," he stood up. "She's ill."

"She's fine," the woman brushed it off.

"Naomi!" The woman shouted. "Naomi, get up!"

Like a frightened child, Naomi's eyes opened.

"What are you doing here?" Naomi forced her body upward, her eyes fixed on Gregory.

"See, I told you she's fine!" The woman snarled and turned away. "Come on Brandon!"

"I came to see you," Gregory sat next to her. Fear consumed him. In all his years of knowing Naomi, she was never sick.

"You shouldn't have come." Naomi looked away, self-consciously, smoothing her hair down. "You shouldn't have come," she mumbled again, choked up with emotions.

392

"Gregg is marrying Ashley," he threw out his ace card.

"Oh!" her hand covered her mouth. "That's wonderful!"

"They are very much in love and they make such a perfect couple."

"I'm so happy for him," tears of joy collided down her cheeks. "Sophia would be so proud of him."

"She would be," Gregory nodded. "But, Gregg can't marry the love of his life without the woman, who helped raised him, at the wedding."

Naomi remained silent.

"He wants you to be there," Gregory went on. "You've been a mother to him. He said it wouldn't feel right without you."

"I can't," Naomi's voice was low.

"Please, don't do this to Gregg?" he pleaded. *Please don't do this to me!*

Naomi closed her eyes for a long moment before responding. "I'll send him a gift," she slowly arose. "You have to go now. I have much work to do."

"I thought you came to take care of your sister? She doesn't look ill."

"It was my other sister and she is doing better. Marla needs me now. She has five little ones, and one on the way. Her husband works all the time," she tried to explain. "I'm needed here."

"You're needed at home," Gregory said tenderly.

"This is my home now." Naomi fought the tears.

"Naomi, you're sick," he said frustratingly. "You need to see a doctor."

"I'm fine. Just a little tired."

"It's more than that," he worried. "Please let me take you to a doctor."

"No!" she snapped. "Please go home, Mr. Jefferson. You don't belong here."

"I'm not leaving without you." He had a stubborn streak, not accustomed to giving in to anything or anyone.

"Go home," she said again.

"I can't," he drew closer. "I'm dying without you, Naomi. These past seven months have been torture. I eat, sleep and think of you all the time. I was a fool to have waited so long to let you know how I feel about you. I need you, Naomi... desperately. Sophia knew it. She knew that Gregg needed you and that I needed you," his eyes glistened. "Please come home."

A bittersweet pang gnawed at her heart. She ached more than he could ever imagine. For over twenty years, she secretly loved him without repentance. Yet, he treated her like a maidservant. Oh, he had been good to her. She had lived in a small cottage on the estate, paying no rent. Her salary was more than anyone she knew in the same occupation. On a personal level, Mr. Jefferson kept his distance. Although sometimes, she caught him staring at her. Sometimes, she saw a look of longing in his eyes that matched her own.

For years, Naomi pined over him. She even felt guilty for romanticizing about her employer because of her friendship with Sophia. She never wanted to betray her memory. Yet, Sophia wanted them to be together—to be a family. Sophia entrusted Naomi with the ones she loved most. It was Sophia's last wish to keep the family together and Naomi was a part of their family.

"You're used to having everything handed to you on a silver platter," Naomi said, finding her voice. "A platter I once brought to you. I am a maid and you are a Master. It would never work."

"I'm sorry if I treated you that way." Gregory's voice was raspy with melancholy. "I was a different man then. My heart was cold and rigid. I wouldn't even let Gregg in, remember? But I am a Believer, like you. I'm a new man."

"It doesn't matter," she turned away.

"It does." Gregory wanted to hold her but knew she would shun him. "Please look at me, Naomi. Please!"

Lingeringly, she obeyed, her eyes watery.

"You remember the night you told me that Sophia wanted you to look after us?"

She nodded.

"You promised her that you would always be there for us. You remember that?"

She nodded again. His gaze was penetrating her exterior wall of indifference.

"You made that promise to Sophia and to me," he inched his way closer to her. "You promised me when I was sick that you would come back. You promised, Naomi. I believed you."

"I'm sorry," she broke down and cried.

Gregory went to her, held her tenderly in his arms, and coddled her like a fragile baby. "No need to apologize," he whispered in her ear. "Just come home. Please come home."

"Naomi!" Her sister entered the room. "Donald will be home shortly. He'll be ready to eat before going to his night job. The kitchen is a mess and you know how he gets when it's messy."

She sick! Gregory wanted to shout. *You clean it up yourself!*

"I'm coming," dutifully, Naomi replied.

"Hurry!" the rude woman spun on her heels.

"I have to go," she said regretfully. "I'm so glad that you look better. I pray for you and Gregg all the time."

"I'll help you in the kitchen," he volunteered.

Naomi laughed. "You don't know a thing about cooking Mr. Jefferson."

"Gregory," he amended. "You'll be surprised by what I can do in the kitchen now. Ashely has been teaching me a lot. I wanted to learn so that we could make great dishes together in the kitchen when you returned. I know how you love cooking."

Naomi blushed, lowering her head, so Gregory wouldn't notice. He did and followed her into the kitchen.

It's a mess! Apparently, the morning dishes were waiting on her. No wonder she is sick! She is taking care of five little children and a rude, cantankerous sister, who has no pity on her.

"You sit down," Gregory kindly ordered. "I'll wash the dishes."

"Let's do it together," she compromised.

"Okay." The two quickly washed the dishes and then Gregory helped Naomi prepare a delicious meal of fried chicken, mash potatoes, corn, and biscuits. The meal was ready just in time when Donald barged through the door. All of the children, eight and under, greeted their father and quietly sat down at the table.

Perusing the family gathering. Gregg observed a selfish, ungrateful mother and overworked husband. *Why in the world would they keep having babies when it is obvious they are dirt poor and cannot handle it by themselves?* The atmosphere was tensed. The conversation between the family, lifeless, with no emotions. Gregory felt so out of place. Yet, this is how his home used to be.

He had assumed Naomi's family was close-knit, but they were not. She came to take care of her sister, but no one was taking care of Naomi. She was ill, but no one seemed to care. Naomi was pushing herself, working from sunrise to sundown, caring for her sister and her five little children. It was too much. Boiling mad, Gregory fought to stifle his emotions. He wanted to just take Naomi out of this unloving home and take her back to the place where she was truly loved.

Every time Naomi looked up, she caught Gregory openly staring at her. He looked at her with a look of empathy and longing. His gaze made her shrinking heart quiver under the intensity of his stare.

Fuming, Marla kept belittling Naomi at the table. "The chicken is overcooked. The mash potatoes are too salty. You just threw something together because of your guest," she accused.

"The meal is wonderful," Gregory couldn't be quiet. "Naomi has always been an excellent cook." He gave her the warmest, dearest big smile.

Naomi thanked him with her eyes.

"Marla," her husband interrupted. "You should have helped her, then," he angrily faced her. "The meal is absolutely delicious, Naomi."

"Thanks." Naomi lowered her head, ashamed at her sister's behavior in front of Gregory.

"We pay her to cook and take care of the family," Marla barked back. "She's hired help."

"She's family," her husband reminded.

Gritting his teeth, Gregory wanted to reach over the table and slap some common sense into the ungrateful woman. When he looked over at Naomi, he knew she was vulnerably near tears. It irked him that this sister could hurt his sweet Naomi. A woman who spent her life looking after others and caring for them with unconditional love.

"I know that," Marla looked at her sister and then their guest, who was obviously offended. "I'm sorry, Naomi."

That you are! Gregory kept his thought to himself.

"No problem," Naomi feigned a smile.

"Kids leave the table," Donald ordered the children and quickly they obeyed.

"What's wrong with you?" Marla was mad. "They haven't finished their meal."

"Excuse me, Sir," Donald looked sympathetically at their guest. "But Marla has to understand that Naomi came here to help us out. We pay her little for her services and yet, she gives all of herself and then some. Look at your sister, Marla. Look at her!" he demanded. "She's sick! Can't you tell? She is rundown. She is doing everything. She was supposed to help you, but you are doing nothing! You sit on your butt all day barking out orders to her as if she is a dog or something. Well, I am tired of it! I sick and tired of it! You don't treat family like that."

"She's not my family!" Marla lashed out, quickly covering her mouth in shame.

Naomi gasped, her eyes wet with tears. Sliding back her chair, she swiftly left the room. Gregory followed.

"What did she mean by that?"

"I was adopted when I was eight-years old," she sniffed. "My parents worked for her parents."

"Oh, Naomi," Gregory was about to hug her, but she stepped back.

"I had loving parents," she sniffed again. "They adored me. After they died, I had nowhere to go, so the Rivas' adopted me and gave me their last name. They were good to me, but Marla always—always treated me differently."

"She was jealous of you and she's still jealous of you." Gregory suspected.

Naomi shook her head, not agreeing. "She had everything growing up. She had the big room filled with toys and beautiful clothes…everything I wanted but couldn't have. I slept in a small room, like a closet. She had friends, I had no one. Now, she has a husband, children, and a lovely home," he throat was dry. "I have none of that."

"You have Gregg, me, and a home," he spoke softly. "Didn't you feel at home with us? Didn't you love Gregg as if he were your own child?"

She nodded, her face marred with tears.

"Naomi," he impatiently came closer and caressed her cheek with the palm of his hand. "I love you with all my heart. Please come home."

Her stomach turned. Openly she studied his face. At fifty-eight, he was still rather handsome.

She took a deep breath, trying to relax in his presence. "We're no spring chickens."

"We're no old roosters either," he chuckled.

"We are from two different worlds. What will your friends and colleagues think of us? It will never work."

"Horse feathers! I'm a free man!" he said happily. "I sold the business."

"You didn't!"

"I did," Gregory held her tighter. "I wanted to be free to experience life and free to love you."

Naomi couldn't believe this was happening to her. The man she carried a torch for in her heart forever was now holding her in his arms.

"Naomi," he said, his eyes crinkling with merriment, "I'm going to kiss you."

Her eyes widened.

"Right now," Gregory bent over and their lips united with electricity.

"Naomi," he whispered, slightly pulling away.

"Huh?"

"I'm taking you to the doctor…"

"Okay," she was bedazzled by the kiss.

"After I do this again," he kissed her again.

Wedding Day.

"You are so beautiful," Andrew said again to his daughter while walking her to meet her anxious groom.

"Thanks, Dad," her face was fluorescing, beaming with unspeakable joy.

"Who gives this bride to married?" Pastor Smallwood asked.

"Her mother and I do," Andrew said proudly, then sat next to his wife, Sandra. Being married only three months, they were still on their honeymoon.

Gregg felt overwhelmed as he took the hand of his bride. Ashley was breathtaking. She had unmatchable beauty. No words could describe just how lovely she appeared to him. He felt unworthy of such a blessing and yet, so grateful for God's generosity toward him.

Briefly looking over, he winked at his father and stepmother, Naomi. Soon as they returned, Gregory insisted on getting married. They had a small ceremony with just a few friends and family on the patio, a week after they returned. God had restored so much love into their lives and their home.

What a glorious wedding! Marrying at their special place, the small pond in the forest, Gregg and Ashley had a lovely outside wedding. The weather was perfect. The sun was shining, but not too hot. It was a perfect day for a perfect wedding!

Later, as the two danced their first dance, Gregg felt overwhelming blessed.

"A penny for your thoughts, Dr. Jefferson," Ashley said adoringly.

"I was just thinking, Mrs. Jefferson, how amazing God is. I mean, He strategically orchestrates our lives. Look at how he positioned me to work at Brookland, a school considered unsalvageable. Not only did we overcome the odds that were against us by advancing from a failing school to the most improved school, with a "B" rating. Now, I am working with the community businesses by continuously finding jobs for the youth so they can work on the weekends and still participate in extra-curricular activities.

"Also, now we have the mentoring program established with well-known athletics to mentor students heading down the wrong path. I was placed at Brookland to help the young boys become productive men in society and the young women to become young ladies who value themselves. I was so lost Ashley and I needed Jesus, but I couldn't see past my anger. Then God placed Thomas in my life, which brought you into my life."

Gregg gazed at Ashley with adoration. "Look at Thomas. Now, he's in college on a full-scholarship. Look at how God brought me and my father back together after a near life and death illness," he swallowed. "With his near death-experience, my father recognized his need for God in his life. Consequently, we now have a father/son relationship. In addition, God didn't just bring us together, but now he is happily married to Naomi. Saving the best for last, I'm married to the smartest, wisest, sweetest, loveliest, prettiest woman in the world. God has been good to me…Now, I am whole again. My life is complete. It's overwhelming."

"I know what you mean." Ashley felt the same way, abounding joy ringing in her heart. Her life was now complete with her father in it and her mother healthy again. "It was a tapestry of divine interventions, which led me to you. God created you for me and me for you. Doors of love and endless possibilities were opened for us, **For such a time as this!**

When you entered this world
It was as if the sun, the moon & stars had kissed
You were born to bring joy into our home
For such a time as this
Your life has a purpose
And only God knows what it is
You were created to help others find their way
For such a time as this.

Dear Reader,

What a journey! We all are familiar with the story of Esther and Mordecai. God had positioned them to be at the right place, at the right time to save an entire nation. Esther had to step out of her comfort zone, put her faith into action and trust God to grant her favor before the king.

Just as it was for Ashley. God had positioned her to be at the right place, at the right time to link up to Dr. Gregg Jefferson. This encounter revolutionized the entire high school and affected the lives of the young boys and young girls, who needed a Redeemer.

Ashley went from the pit of despair to a mountaintop experience of unspeakable joy. There were times she just wanted to give up, to throw in the towel. However, her faith sustained her. We have all been there. Times, when we only see one set of footprints in the sand, because we're unable to walk it ourselves. Those are the times God is carrying us to our promise Land. Remember nothing catches God by surprise. We were created to handle the storms in our lives. The good news is that we don't' have to weather the storms alone. God is with u. He never leaves us or forsakes us.

God used the bad situation of Thomas to soften the heart of the principal, causing him to step outside the box and get involved in the lives of his students. Gregg's purpose was more than saving a school. It was about saving lives and giving the students hope in hopeless circumstances.

Remember, God has a purpose for you being exactly where you are—right now. God wants to use you to influence somebody's life, which may affect countless others. You were created for such a time as this to help save lives—one life at a time. God has plans for you, of good and not of evil, to give you a future and a hope. I would love to hear from you, please email me at: rlwbooks@gmail.com or visit my website: RaiLindsayWallace@gmial.com

Love Always,
Rai

Finally Reader,

If you don't know Jesus as your personal, Lord and Savior, or if you have backslid, God is waiting on you with open arms to accept you into the family. He loves you and desires to take care of you, from now and into eternity. Accept His gift. Accept Jesus into your heart...today!

"If you confess with your mouth the Lord Jesus and believe in your heart that God has raised Him from the dead, you will be saved. For with the heart, one believes unto righteousness, and with the mouth, confession is made unto salvation. For whoever calls on the name of the Lord shall be saved."

Romans: 10:9,10

Prayer:

Father God, I am a sinner in need of a Savior. I confess with my mouth the Lord Jesus and believe in my heart that God raised Him from the dead. I accept your gift of salvation, by accepting Jesus Christ as my Lord and Savior. Fill me with Your Spirit so I may walk in the path you have for me to walk. I surrender my heart, my mind, my soul to you. I am Yours Lord. Thank You for making my heart Your home. In Jesus Name. Amen.

Discussion Questions

1. Thomas stole the teacher's blackberry, so he could sell it and have the electricity turned back on. Is there ever really any justifiable reason for stealing or breaking the law or even sinning? Should the judicial system and people be more lenient with those going through hard economic times? If so, explain.

2. Harvey seemed to care deeply care for Ashley, but Ashley only felt friendship. Marriage should have a firm foundation of friendship. However, is friendship enough for marriage? Should you marry your best friend, even if there is not a real, passionate love for him/her? Explain.

3. Sandra Finley has given up on life. She was alive, but not living life. What would you say to someone in a similar situation as Sandra to encourage him/her to get back in the game of life?

4. Pam just wanted to forget her violation and not talk about it. People think if I bury a problem, it will just go away. What are examples of ways that hidden secrets/problem can surface?

5. Dr. Jefferson was trying to make a difference in the lives of the football players. How can you make a difference in the life of just one person, which might

have a domino effect on others?

6. Dr. Jefferson had an estranged relationship with his father. It's hard building bridges with family members. Name some ways that one can go about slowly healing broken relationships.

7. Thomas wanted to fit in, like so many teenagers today. What kind of advice can you give to a teenager seeking the approval of others?

8. Everyone needs some type of outlet to deal with life. I love writing. It is therapeutic for me. Some like to knit or crochet. What is your outlet and why?

9. Ashley advised Gregg not to give his father power, by allowing him to control his emotions. The only way people can steal our joy, make us angry, or control our emotions, is by us allowing them to. Either we can give them power to control us or we can keep the power by remaining in control. Easier said than done. What are some ways we can deal with people who so easily push our buttons?

10. Gregg's mother believed that her son was born with a special purpose and plan in the mind of God. What about you? What is God's special purpose and plan for you?

11. Friendship is truly a special bond. The Bible says two are better than one. A friend loves at all times. List five qualities a true friend should possess.

12. Thomas shared Jesus with Shane. As a teenager that takes courage and boldness. Have you shared Jesus lately with someone? If so, explain. What happened? If not, explain why not and what's holding you back.

13. Discovering that your birth parents are not your

biological parents can be life-changing. How would it make you feel?

14. When young people like Shane die, people tend to blame God. They say, "God could have spared his life. If God is All-powerful and all-knowing, He could have let Shane live," and so forth. How do you respond to such pointing fingers at God?

15. Naomi's sister treated her badly and disrespectfully. Yet, Naomi remained humble and loving. The Bible requires us to love our enemies and to love our neighbors as we love ourselves. We have to love unlovable people…in our homes, on our jobs, in the community. Yet, God wouldn't ask us to do something that was impossible. Think about an unlovable person in your life. What are ways that you show or express love to that person. Remember, love covers a multitude of sin. Your love… can be the love that he/she is waiting for.

About The Author

Rai Lindsay-Wallace is from Columbia, South Carolina, where she lives with her devoted husband, Kent. Together, the Wallaces' have three amazing children and five grandchildren. Rai is retired and spends much of her time writing inspiration fiction, singing, writing music with her husband and ministering. She is also graduate of The Ministerial Seminary of America, LLC, as a licensed Christian Minister. She is a pastor at God's House of Healing. Her mission is to spread the message of love, hope and healing to the churched and un-churched through creative writings and ministering the Gospel of Jesus Christ. For more info, visit *RaiLindsayWallace.com or email her at rlwbooks@gmail.com.*

Additional Books by Rai:
- *No Longer Captive*
- *No Longer Brokenhearted*
- *No Longer Oppressed (July 2017)*
- *For Such a Time as This*
- *Sunset/Sunrise (Will be republished in 2017)*
- *Destiny*

www.ingramcontent.com/pod-product-compliance
Lightning Source LLC
Chambersburg PA
CBHW021424240626
47153CB00001B/18